WILD
BLUE
UNDER

JUDI FENNELL

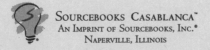

SOURCEBOOKS CASABLANCA™
AN IMPRINT OF SOURCEBOOKS, INC.®
NAPERVILLE, ILLINOIS

Published by Sourcebooks Casablanca, an imprint of Sourcebooks, Inc.
P.O. Box 4410, Naperville, Illinois 60567-4410
(630) 961-3900
FAX: (630) 961-2168
www.sourcebooks.com

Printed and bound in the United States of America
QW 10 9 8 7 6 5 4 3 2 1

As always, to my family, for supporting and encouraging me. You all are my real-life heroes.

To my grandmother, Fran. (Because I can.)

To the real Valerie, for friendship and Fudge Stripes.

To Beth Hill, for all of your time, generosity, and wonderful insights.

To Steven, because I always said I'd do this if I got the chance. You told me, "Jude, you have a story for everything." Bet you never saw this one coming!

And to Maynard, because he asked.

*"That which was lost must be found...
or that which is known will be lost."*

—Mer Prophecy

Chapter 1

"SO YOU'RE REALLY GOING TO GIVE UP YOUR TAIL AND LEAVE the sea? On purpose? First your brother, now you... What is *wrong* with this family?"

If Rod Tritone heard that question one more time, he was going to strangle Chumley Masticar's thin, white-striped neck. The fish didn't know when to quit.

It wasn't as if he *wanted* to do this, but when The Council decreed something, it had to be done. Gods knew, when he became the High Councilman, he'd demand the same obedience.

"Yes, Chum, I'm going. Right after I grab my bag." Rod kicked his tail for a burst of speed to outswim the fish and headed to his lair in the hills of Atlantis. The one thing he had to remember to pack was the gods' oil that would ensure his tail returned when he did.

"Lose it and lose the tail forever," his father, the current High Councilman, had said. As if that was an option.

"Do you want company?" The suckerless remora wriggled his long body for all it was worth to catch up, and Rod didn't have the heart not to let him. "Reel said he'd put in a saltwater tank so I could visit. Not that I'd be thrilled being in a cage, but still, it would be nice to see where he and his wife live. Check out the Human world without worrying about someone wanting to eat me or anything."

Humans ate remora? Rod couldn't imagine why. Unless it was to shut them up.

Rod swerved around the magma well whose emissions refracted through seawater and off the gold-covered walls of the cavern city, turning the darkness into light. He skimmed above the coral topiaries, nodding to the parrotfish who kept Atlantis so beautiful. He'd traveled the world's oceans from Bimini to the South Pacific, from the icy waters of the north to the crystal blue glacial waters of the south, but nothing compared to the beauty of the Mer capital.

"Sorry, Chum, but this is a solo mission. Simple recovery."

One that involved him getting legs, traveling to the middle of the landmass, and retrieving a Human. Of all things to pull him off his Trench Survey for.

"Oh. Right. Gotcha." Chum glided beneath a ray who had emerged from a sand pond inside a circle of stone-faced statues. Without a sucker on his head, the remora wouldn't have much luck sticking to the ray for a meal.

Poor guy. Always trying to relive his glory days.

"So," Chum said, returning to Rod's side, "tell me why The Council thinks this Human is the answer to The Prophecy. I mean, how old is she? I thought only the royal family lived forever. That Prophecy is almost two millennia old, and The Oracles haven't come up with an answer yet. I don't get it."

"Well, first of all, she's not Human. Not completely." Rod veered up to the top of the Commerce Building for one last look at the city before venturing into the shark's nest that was land.

One day, this would all be his. The rule of the seas, the unlimited wealth of the diamond Vault, the history of his people. All of it his to protect and serve. Just like his father. And his grandfather. And generations before him.

The responsibility settled on him like an anchor. Rod sucked in a pint of seawater, shook off the feeling, and headed toward home. "Before he died, Lance Dumere admitted to an affair with a Human that resulted in a child."

Chum puckered his lips and tried to whistle. He'd never been successful before, and this time wasn't any different.

"Once Lance came clean," Rod continued as they reached the ornamental gates to his neighborhood, "The Council started its own search. The Members didn't want to start a panic, but they couldn't leave a landed Mer out there for Humans to discover."

"So now they've found her and want you to go after her?"

"That's it in a conch shell." Rod swam over the marble-domed roof of his lair and opened the weathered oak door, grimacing as it shuddered on its hinges. Seawater had a corrosive effect on the hinges after a while, no matter what they were made of. He had hoped to be living in the High Councilman quarters before they needed to be replaced.

"So how's she supposed to fulfill The Prophecy? She's a Hybrid, for Apollo's sake." Chum swam in behind him, wending through a natural fissure in the lava statue in the foyer that Rod's sister, Mariana, had sculpted.

A flick of Rod's tail propelled him to the sofa, which a sea cucumber colony had overtaken, and where his sister, Angel, had dropped off a watertight package containing a duffel bag and clothing for his trip. Angel was the repository of all things Human these days. "Since she's Dumere's long-lost offspring, The Council feels she's the 'that which was lost' part of The Prophecy. By bringing her back, they're hoping to prevent the world— 'that which is known'—from being lost."

"Huh?"

Pretty much his reaction when his father, Fisher, had explained it. He'd figured it to be another of the many tests the gods had put to him throughout his life to prepare him for his title. Although as far as Rod was concerned, The Prophecy was more the drunken ramblings of one of the gods after too much ouzo and ambrosia than any great revelation. No test the gods devised would include sending The Heir onto land without a valid reason.

Saving the planet was a valid reason.

Rod flipped open a pirate's chest that held the diamond decanter containing the gods' oil, as well as the packet of paperwork The Council had included to convince Lance's daughter. "The polar regions are melting, Chum. The Council hopes to mitigate that damage by fulfilling The Prophecy."

"So what's she going to do? Give the ice caps the cold shoulder to keep them stable?" Chum laughed at his own joke.

The short seaquake that hit the Mer capital proved the gods didn't find it a laughing matter. The Humans on Bermuda—the island directly above Atlantis—probably didn't think so either.

Rod sure as Hades didn't. As soon as he finished this mission, he could get back to the business at fin by finally claiming the throne—the job he'd been born to do—and figuring out some way to work on his Trench Survey.

Cataloging the offshoot of the world's deepest ocean trench, one Humans had yet to discover, was his chance to be known as someone other than the lucky Son of a Mer who'd inherited the oldest throne on Earth simply by virtue of his birthright. A way to become the Mer he could be if he weren't The Heir.

And a way to erase the collective memory of that damn dare to Reel so long ago. Rod had broken the biggest rule of their world with it by risking Humans learning about Mers, thereby setting the pattern for the rest of his and Reel's lives.

"But what happens if something goes wrong? What if you don't get your tail back? Or fall in love with her and opt to stay on land like Reel did? Isn't Drake next in line? Do they really want that idiot running the show?" Chum helped himself to a piece of the calamari Rod's mother had sent over.

Opt to stay on land? Fall in love with her? As if that would happen. The High Councilman couldn't dilute the bloodline of future generations, and this woman was a Hybrid.

No, losing Reel from their world was more than enough of an incentive for him. Add in everything he'd had to do since the fallout from that dare—studying, learning, memorizing, following every rule, statute, dictate, edict, and proclamation the gods had set down—and he wasn't about to blow it now.

One failure in his life was enough.

Rod tucked the Human items inside the chest and latched it closed.

The last thing this family—and the Mer world—needed was another Mer hooking up with a Human.

Chapter 2

AFTER YEARS OF HOPPING FROM JOB TO JOB, OF MOVING FROM town to town, searching for that *one* thing to give her life meaning, trying to find her place in this world, Valerie Dumere had decided that, truly, there's no place like home.

And how ironic was that?

Val parked her battered old Nissan in the gravel lot behind Therese's Treasure Trove. She never would have thought that selling ocean *tchotchkes* in the middle of Kansas would be her life's work, but then, she'd thought a nine-to-five office job was. And driving a cab. Vet assistant. Pizza delivery person. Construction worker.

It was the fiasco of that last one that'd made her realize that the only place she'd ever felt she "fit" had been Mom's shop.

Val gathered her things, ready to spend the afternoon cataloging an inventory of sand globes, seashell jewelry, and delicate, glass wind chimes. And if that didn't make her heart go pitter-pat, at least she had the satisfaction of making Mom's dream come true and honoring her memory—and finally having her own life on a path.

Dashing from the car to the back door, Val kept an eye on one of the sparrows that had been following her around recently, laughing when she shut the door behind herself without so much as a single bird-dropping mishap.

Get a grip, Dumere. There are no such things as stalking birds.

Oh? Then what about the seagull attack?

Val shrugged and picked up the latest delivery slip on the metal desk beside the door. Seagulls were known for stealing food out of your hand. She shouldn't have tempted them—although, what had made them yank a hunk of hair from her head was anybody's guess.

Oh, well. The whole thing had happened three weeks ago, and she highly doubted a sparrow could do that kind of coiffure damage.

"Val!" Tricia, her best friend and co-worker, poked her head through the sheers that divided the front of the store from the workroom at the back. "There's someone out here I think you'll want to talk to."

"I will? Who?" Val dropped the packing slip and her bag onto the pile of boxes beside the door as Tricia swished through the curtains while practically hopping up and down.

"I have no idea who he is, but he asked for you, and, God, if I had someone like *that* asking about me, I'd be damn sure to get out there as quick as possible."

"Tricia, what are you babbling about? He's just a guy."

Tricia snorted. "That's like saying the David is just a statue. Val, this guy is *hot*."

"Every guy who comes in here is hot. It's summertime in Kansas, in case you've forgotten."

Huffing, Tricia crossed her arms and cocked a hip. "Fine. Don't believe me. But you are going to want to prepare yourself before going out there."

Jeez. You'd think a movie star had walked into the place the way Tricia, married mother of four, was acting.

Then Val peeled back the side of the curtain and saw why.

The guy *could* be a movie star. Cross Matthew McConaughey with Hugh Jackman, toss in some extra brawn, a few more inches in height, and, yeah, that's about what you'd get.

"Sooo?" Tricia leaned over her shoulder. "What d'ya think?"

Long legs encased in dark blue jeans that hugged a damn-near-delicious set of glutes, a yellow golf shirt stretched across flat abs and broad shoulders, square jaw, black, wavy hair that brushed just above his collar...

"Impressive." She got the David reference with one look. "But what's he doing here?"

The guy held a duffel bag in one hand and was picking through the coral sculptures—*faux* coral sculptures, as her mother had liked to call them—with the other, as if he was on a treasure hunt. He picked each one up, turned it upside down, sniffed it—sniffed it?—then went on to the next one.

When he was done there, he moved to the next table and peered into each of the sand globes as if he'd never seen one before. Sure, snow globes were more common, but sand wasn't off-the-charts odd. They were some of her best sellers.

"I think he needs help selecting the right one," Tricia, the self-appointed head—and only member—of the Valerie Dumere Matchmaking Initiative, whispered.

"Tricia, they're all the same. And that was lame, even for you."

"Well, you aren't marching out there on your own. Too bad you weren't the early bird today. You could have caught that big, juicy worm yourself, but, no, you had to sleep in. Just be thankful I'm happily married."

Val slid her eyes sideways to glare at Tricia.

"Oh. Right. Birds are a touchy subject. Sorry. I forgot."

"Don't worry about it." Besides, a hot guy was a good way to banish bad bird memories. "Oh, and for the record, I wasn't sleeping in. I was finishing packing. I had to be out of my rental today."

"Good. Now you can move in with him instead of the apartment upstairs." Tricia lifted one of the curtains.

Val rolled her eyes and adjusted the lay of the cute, pink, scooped-neck shirt she'd paired with her jean shorts, tucked a few short, blonde curls behind her ears, then straightened her shoulders and stepped into the front of the store.

"Hello? I'm Valerie Dumere. Can I help you?" Not the most auspicious of beginnings, but still, it got his attention.

The smile he gave her after a quick once-over with his deep green eyes got her attention, too. Kicked back to one side, a deep dimple slashing the back of it, making little crinkles appear around those eyes… Oh, yeah. That got her attention.

So did the nicely muscled bicep that flexed when he held up the sand globe. "Is this really supposed to be Atlantis?"

She walked over and picked up another one, and gave it a shake, sending sand and glitter shimmering around the spires of the castle and the not-to-scale seahorses twirling among open clamshells and treasure chests. She smiled at him. "What? You don't like marble castles? Or is this one going to be too drafty for you?"

"Drafty? Don't you mean wet? Atlantis is in the ocean, you know. You might want to read up on your history." He smiled that devastating smile again and set the globe down.

She set hers down next to it. "You mean my mythology."

"Oh. Right. Mythology." He switched the duffel bag to his left hand and held out his right one. "Hi. I guess I should introduce myself. I'm Rod Tritone. I'm here to take you away from all of this."

"That's a hell of an introduction." She couldn't help laughing as she took his hand. Big, enveloping, warm, just the right amount of roughness to let her know he was a man and she was a woman.

He laughed along with her, rich and deep and sending shivers down her spine, which also made her acutely aware of her femininity.

"Then how about this one? I'm here to make all your dreams come true."

Yeah, that worked. She could imagine some fairly wild dreams.

"Is your name Prince Charming, by any chance?" Tricia added, emerging from the back.

Geez. Could the woman give her a few minutes on her own?

Wait a minute.

Val held up a finger toward… Rod. Right. That was his name. "Can you excuse me for a sec?"

He inclined that gorgeous head of black waves with an almost royal nod, and she spun around to steer the grinning Tricia over to a wall draped in fishing nets and sea-themed, stained-glass pieces.

"What do you know about this, Tricia?" she whispered.

"I believe it's called a windfall, Val," Tricia stage-whispered back, waggling her eyebrows and doing a really bad surreptitious head nod toward Rod. As if the guy didn't already get that Tricia found him attractive.

A dead man would get that Tricia found him attractive.

"Seriously, Tricia, is this another of your set-ups?" Val tried to keep her voice down. No sense in embarrassing everyone.

Tricia had no such compunction. "Valerie Hope Dumere, I would never do that."

Val arched an eyebrow. Tricia had done it more than Val cared to think about since she'd been home. Matter of fact, she had a date tonight.

"Well, okay, I've set you up before, but I wouldn't do it with you in *that*."

Val rolled her eyes. So much for the cute top. Now she had to add burning cheeks to the equation. "So you don't know him?"

"Trust me. If I knew him, you wouldn't be going out with Glen." Tricia took Val by the shoulders and turned her back around. "'Take you away from all this'? 'Make all your dreams come true'? And you're standing here talking to *me*? I think you've been smelling the paint fumes in this place for too long. Go talk to him."

Good point.

Especially when he gave her that sexy grin again as she faced him.

Even though turnabout was fair play, she tried not to give him the once-over—but failed miserably. So instead, she plastered a smile on her face, rolled her shoulders back—Oh, wait. No need to draw attention to the girls...

She nibbled her upper lip and fiddled with the lay of her shirt again, then headed back over to him.

"Let's try this again, shall we?" She stuck out her hand. "Hi. I'm Valerie Dumere. Is there something I can do for you?"

She *really* hadn't stuck out her hand because she'd wanted to touch him again, but her nerve endings were still happy with the result when he took it.

"No, there isn't, but there is something I can do for you."

He certainly could…

Focus, Dumere.

She tugged her hand gently, almost disappointed when he let go, and stepped back. "Oh?"

"I'm here about your father."

And there went that moment.

"Her father?" Tricia squeaked, and Val knew why.

No one could have seen that coming—because no one had known her father. Herself included. The bastard had left before she was born. "My father? You know him?"

"No, I don't—didn't. Lance Dumere was… a friend of the family."

"Was?"

Rod nodded.

Ah, so Lance was dead. She'd never liked thinking her mother had lied to her all those years, even if she'd done it for a good reason. At least now, it was the truth.

And, no, that wasn't a hollow thud in the vicinity of her heart. The man had no claim on her heart whatsoever. He'd given up that right when he'd walked out.

Val nibbled her lip again and tucked her hair behind her ears. "So… what does he have to do with you being here?"

Rod set his duffel bag on the glass-topped register counter and unzipped it, removing a stack of papers bound in a blue cover. "I'm here to give you this."

"What is it?" Val took it, totally ignoring the sparks that zipped along her happy nerve endings where their skin touched. Well, trying to ignore them.

"Your father's legacy."

And there went any sparks.

Her father had a legacy?

"That's not something tangible one usually puts on paper," she said, flipping the cover open to find the obligatory lawyerly mumbo-jumbo.

Tricia leaned over her shoulder. "Hey, maybe he wrote a book. Or a song. A screenplay. Just think, Val, your dad actually left you something. And maybe... maybe it couldn't be delivered until you're—"

"Twenty-nine and three months? Right, Tricia. That's the usual stipulation on long-lost inheritances from dead fathers. You've been reading *Princess Diaries* again, haven't you?"

"Hey, the dad doesn't die in the book. Just the movie."

"It's a shame a grown woman knows that." Especially when Tricia knew the man had been a rat-bastard family-abandoner. Val had shared the comment she'd overheard her grandmother make the one and only time Mom and she had visited her mother's parents. But then, Tricia always was a sucker for happy endings. Val, on the other hand, wasn't. Dad was a case in point.

"Ladies, I assure you, I haven't been reading any royal diaries lately, but this is, indeed, an estate for Valerie."

One she didn't want.

And regardless that the messenger was a guy a woman could fantasize over, nothing changed the fact that Lance Dumere—the one man in the world she should have been able to count on but couldn't—was posthumously asking for forgiveness for something she couldn't forgive.

She was about to fling the papers back into the duffel bag when something behind Rod caught her eye.

A stuffed seagull. Standing on the shelf by the window.

She definitely hadn't ordered that. She wasn't into taxidermy, though seagulls were, now, appropriate subjects in her opinion.

Mom must have ordered it and Tricia must have unpacked it today because it definitely hadn't been there when she'd locked up last night. With the way her life had gone to the birds—and specifically seagulls— recently Val would have remembered finding *that*.

"Valerie?" Rod's fingers ignited another small fire under her skin when he touched her upper arm. "Is something wrong?"

"Wrong?" She looked up at the concern in his voice. If not for the seagull and Lance butting in where he was no longer wanted, she'd have said absolutely nothing was wrong at that moment with Rod's hand on her arm and his eyes staring intently into hers, concern etched into the vee of his brow…

But there was.

And it had a yellow beak, and gray and white feathers, and was standing in her shop.

"It's just that…" Hold on. She couldn't explain her recent bout of paranoia to Rod. He was going to think she was crazy enough when she told him what he could do with Lance's legacy.

"No. Nothing's wrong." She glanced back at the bird.

Wait a minute. Hadn't that thing been facing left? She could have sworn it'd been turned toward the register.

"Val? What's going on?" Tricia asked.

Val shook her head. She was seeing things.

"Valerie?" This from Rod.

She set the papers on the counter then put a finger to her lips and walked toward the thing. She had to be imagining this. The bird hadn't been on one leg before... Had it?

Taking a deep breath, Val stopped. What was wrong with her? Taxidermic birds didn't switch legs. They didn't move, and they didn't stalk people.

Just to prove it to herself, she picked up the bird...

And the freaking thing started squawking and flapping—and most definitely *moving*.

Which was a good thing because she dropped that sucker at the first squawk.

It fluttered around them like something from a Hitchcock movie, knocking items off the displays with its feet as it tried to gain speed, and she could have sworn it was screeching, "Help!" but that could have been her as she dodged the thing, wanting to keep what hair she still had on her head away from that beak.

Tricia ducked behind the counter, while Rod tried to avoid both of them and lunged for the bird.

Half a dozen sand globes hit the floor with a domino-like series of crashes, and a wooden lighthouse teetered off a shelf, smashing onto a pile of spoon rests below it.

How the hell had the thing gotten in here, and more importantly, *why*?

The bird swooped toward her, knocking a pile of shell necklaces onto the floor. Val headed left and ran *smack!* into Rod, who was heading right.

Her five-six, one-twenty self shouldn't have been able to knock over a guy like him, but apparently, when fueled by broken necklaces that acted like marbles beneath her feet, she became a roller-derby chick.

She tried to break her fall and ended up breaking a few faux coral pieces instead, landing on top of Rod with an "Oomph!"—and unsure which one of them said it.

"Sorry." She scrambled off him, thinking she was more bummed that she couldn't stay sprawled on top of him than she was at having knocked him over.

Then she really *was* sorry she'd scrambled off him because she tripped over his leg, slid on a necklace, and went sprawling—though not on top of him this time. No, this time she hit the carpet head on, with a nasty wrench of her ankle, and knocked over a carton of T-shirts that spilled over her like very large and very heavy confetti.

"I'll get it!" Tricia jumped up from behind the counter, waving a wreath covered in seashells above her head, and ran toward the bird, shooing it toward the back, while Rod dashed over to Val.

"Are you okay?" He dug her out from under the shirts.

"Okay is a subjective term," she mumbled as he helped her sit. Damn, her ankle hurt and she'd probably looked like a ditz falling all over the place. She really wasn't liking seagulls these days.

A squawk emanated from the back room, and Val looked behind her. Thank God Tricia had unlashed the curtains. At least the thing would stay back there, though Val could only imagine the mess it'd leave.

Seemed like she couldn't avoid bird droppings after all.

"I need to help Tricia," she said, struggling.

"You sit here. The bird's not going anywhere."

"That's what I'm afraid of."

"And he's not going to hurt you."

"Oh really? Did you see that beak? Trust me. I know exactly how painful that beak can be." She rubbed the back of her head where the stubble was just starting to grow back. "And I wouldn't exactly call this"—she lifted her sore appendage—"not hurting me."

God. Her life really *was* going to the birds. Talk about bad luck.

And then Rod lifted her leg in his hands. "Let me take a look."

Hmmm, maybe her luck was about to change...

Chapter 3

ROD RAN HIS FINGERS OVER VALERIE'S SMOOTH LEG, DOWN the curve of her calf, around the heel, and gently probed the indentation below the anklebone.

"I don't think it's broken." Zeus, there were so many little bones in there.

And if he focused on that, instead of the soft puffs of breath brushing his cheek and the scent of flowers clinging to her skin, he might be able to ignore the heat radiating from her like the volcanic rock that lit his world.

Then he touched another spot that made her flinch and she grabbed his arm. Electricity raced from her fingers straight to his groin.

There was no ignoring that.

But he had a job to do, not to mention a throne to inherit by doing it, and he'd focus on that, and not the fact that her shell-fillers—breasts, Reel said Humans called them—were mere inches from him.

He shifted another inch or two away from her just to ensure he stayed focused, which also ensured that she'd remove her fingers from his arm.

A High Councilman *did* have to make sacrifices for his people.

"Rod, I'll be fine." She tried to stand and nibbled her upper lip again, an action so insignificant it shouldn't have caught his attention—but did.

Especially when she did it again.

Chum's words about falling in love with her came back to taunt him.

But that was ridiculous. He wasn't falling in love with her because she was beautiful. He'd been around beautiful women before. Hades, all Mer women were beautiful.

It was just that Humans *weren't* beautiful, and he hadn't expected her to be.

Her Mer blood must be shining through. Just like her eyes, blue as the Tyrrhenian Sea, shone beneath the jumble of blonde curls that framed her face with those adorable sun-dots bridging her nose.

"Um... Rod?" She tapped his shoulder this time, and, clothing or not, it had the same effect as when she'd touched his bare skin.

Not a thought he needed at the moment.

"Yes?" He cleared his throat and willed his body to simmer down. This attraction was odd. Stronger than he'd had to anyone before. Must have something to do with the air...

"Could you help me up? The shirts... they're too soft to push off of."

Then she nibbled her lip again. *Good gods.*

But what could he say? No?

So instead, he prepared himself to touch her again, stood up, and held out his hand. "Uh, certainly."

Her fingers rested in his palm. Yeah, there was no preparation for *that*...

"Thanks. I'm sorry for knocking you down—"

"It was nothing, Valerie."

She arched an eyebrow at him, steadying herself with yet another touch to his shoulder. "Really? You have women bowling you over all the time, do you?"

None before her, and he didn't mean the incident on the floor.

Zeus. What was wrong with him? She was just another female. Half-Human at that, and he was the next High Councilman. He needed to back off.

But then she stumbled as she tried to take a step, and he instead swung her up in his arms. Big mistake. It was as big a gesture on land as his brother had said.

He deposited her on top of the counter. "You should stay off that leg." And out of his arms.

Valerie looked up at him with those beautiful blue eyes, startled wide now, and a blush tinged her cheeks before she quickly lowered her golden lashes. "Um, thanks, but I have work to do. This mess has got to go."

And she had to go, too; that was the thing.

That bird, whoever he was, had a lot of explaining to do, and Rod would put out a call to Air Security to follow up once he and Val were on their way to the ocean. But right now, Val had something more pressing to deal with.

"Don't worry about it, Valerie. You have your father's estate to concern yourself with now."

She licked her lips, moistening their soft pink sheen, then nibbled one again. He still found the action mesmerizing.

"Right. My father's estate. Um, listen. I appreciate you coming here to tell me about it, Rod, but I'm going to pass."

"What?" That statement got his eyes off those perfect lips. "You can't."

"Yes, I can. I don't want it. At all." She slid to the edge of the counter. "Thank you for stopping by, but as you can see, I've got my work cut out for me, so if you don't mind…"

She was refusing?

No. That wasn't possible. She *had* to accompany him.

"Valerie, you don't understand. You must accept this inheritance. And soon. Time's running out. Just come with me to New Jersey, and the estate will be all yours."

In Rod's experience, the words "legacy," "inheritance," and "dreams come true" brought people swimming—make that, running. The Council had fabricated this story for that very reason.

He'd hated the thought of lying to her. Oh, there *was* an estate. But it wasn't a cherished memento or a bag of currency he could hand over. No, Valerie stood to inherit the governorship of the Southern Ocean. They'd all agreed, however, that spouting off about Mers and Atlantis to an unsuspecting Human would damage Rod's credibility and risk her refusal. Not to mention break that rule again—and *that* was not an option.

Hades, they'd gone to the trouble of manufacturing those papers to make the story seem legitimate in Human terms. All he needed to do was get her to the ocean where one drop of seawater would begin her transformation so she could learn—and believe—the truth. A tail was very convincing. But if he couldn't even get her to come with him…

No. That was not even a consideration.

"Thanks, really, Rod, but I want nothing from that man. Just take the inheritance and… I don't know, donate it to a children's hospital or something."

"Donate it?" An entire ocean and the fact that she was the salvation of their world? Right.

The gods had to have gotten this wrong. She couldn't be the answer to The Prophecy.

He felt a rumble beneath the store. Ah, they'd followed him even here.

"Yes. Donate it. Let him do good for *somebody's* kids before it's too late, but he missed the boat with me."

Rod stared at her. No one had seen this coming. What person—Mer or Human—wouldn't want wealth?

Valerie, apparently, as she picked up the papers, rolled them, and tapped them against her lips.

"Seriously, Rod, pretend you didn't find me. Let it revert to the state, or whatever happens to unclaimed inheritances. Give it to the kids, a college… I don't care. I don't want to see any part of it. I'll stay here and run Mom's shop, and Lance can do with his inheritance what he's done for me my whole life." She slid off the counter, making him back up, and handed him the papers.

"Absolutely nothing."

Chapter 4

OF EVERY SCENARIO THEY'D RUN, REFUSAL WASN'T ONE ROD or The Council had anticipated—and one he had to find a way around because he couldn't fulfill The Prophecy and claim the throne without Valerie.

Bundling up the papers with his bag, Rod told her he'd be back tomorrow and walked out. This wasn't over just because she didn't want to go. No way. He had too much at stake for that.

Hades, the *planet* had too much at stake for that, which meant she did, too.

He'd convince her; he had to. Another failure was not an option. No, he'd filled that quota twenty-one *selinos* ago with that prank with Reel.

Prank.

Bullsharkshit.

It hadn't been a prank. More like his blatant disregard for the rules of their world, all because he'd known his brother wouldn't be able to resist. And now, Reel had turned down Immortality and chosen to live a mortal life on land, and it was all Rod's fault.

Rod shook his head and tried, as usual—and with the usual futility—to ignore the guilt, immersing himself in the steps needed to achieve his goal.

He headed toward the real estate office down the street, mentally thanking his brother for the forethought and insistence to rent the apartment above Valerie's shop. He'd hoped he wouldn't need it, but perhaps one more day would be all he'd need to convince her.

He purchased a few items from the grocery store, then walked back to Therese's Treasure Trove.

The lights were still on inside the beige stucco building, although a "Closed" sign hung on the sun-bleached red door. Rod didn't see Valerie through the bay window bracketed by Mediterranean-green shutters, where more glass spheres filled with sand and poor imitations of the Mer capital were on display. If only Humans knew that Atlantis really existed, this would be so much easier.

Rod climbed the outside staircase to the apartment, then dropped his shoes inside the small, stuffy living area. He opened a window for fresh air—an action he found as repugnant as being pulled from the Trench Study just so he could return a woman who didn't want to go to a world she didn't know.

Rod tossed his bag and the fake papers into one of the bedchambers then went toward the galley kitchen to put the food away and cook his meal, banging a toe on the low coffee table. Damn. Sometimes he misjudged the spatial relations of the new body parts. Would Valerie do any better with a tail?

Hades. They might never find out.

He wanted to know why. What Lance had done to Valerie that she obviously despised him. Why her mother hadn't told her anything about who and what she was.

Therese had seen Lance; the Mer had confirmed it. She'd known what he was. That was why The Council had agreed to the search for Valerie in the first place.

Humans couldn't know about Mers and her mother was a full-blooded Human.

The timer sounded on the electric appliance his sister-in-law had taught him to use to prepare his meals. He hadn't quite grasped the concept of "micro waves"—in his world they were called ripples—but they did the trick. Not that he enjoyed the meals nor their non-biodegradable packages, which ended up littering his world, but according to Reel, kelp wraps weren't easily obtainable and this town didn't have a sushi bar. Since he'd never needed to prepare food himself, he was stuck with these plastic-covered abominations.

Just one more reason he wanted to get back in the sea.

"How in Hades am I supposed to make her come with me?" he asked his reflection in the appliance's stainless-steel door.

"You could always kidnap her."

Rod stared at his reflection. Talking appliances? If Humans could design something that complex, surely they could fabricate something other than plastic to keep their food in.

Then he saw movement behind him and turned around.

A herring gull.

And if his hunch was right… "Livingston, I presume?"

The bird confirmed his identity by stretching his wings, revealing the legendary star tattoo on his breast, then inclined his head in the traditional acknowledgment of royalty.

Forget niceties. The Council's Chief of Air Security had only one reason to be here. The renowned aerial spy didn't "happen" to show up inland without a very good reason: like making sure Fisher's son was following orders.

Zeus. Could someone cut him some slack?

"What do you want, Livingston? And what were you doing in Valerie's store earlier?"

The herring gull ruffled his black-tipped wings before he hopped off the window ledge onto the dining table. "In her store? I have no idea what you're talking about."

"You expect me to believe that?"

Livingston shrugged, then worked his gray feathers back into place with his yellow beak. "Hey, what you believe is up to you."

The gull turned his head to the front, the red spot on his beak always a perfect way to distract someone.

But not Rod. He knew all the tactics—had studied each and every one. And if The Council would only remember that, he wouldn't have to deal with the Chief of the ASA.

Of course, that put the kibosh on the report of the rogue gull in the store.

"What were you doing there, Livingston? You scared her and made a mess of the place."

"Rod, I wasn't anywhere near her today. Haven't been for a few weeks."

"Oh, really? Then you want to explain who decided imitating a stuffed seagull would be funny? She ended up getting hurt."

"Imitating a stuffed seagull?" Livingston rolled his eyes. "I'm going to kill Ace. It's his newest hobby."

Ace? Hardly. That gull had been a menace at flying, not an ace. "Not if I get to him first."

"Is she going to be okay?"

"I believe so."

"Oh. Good. So, you got anything to eat around here? I just flew in from Bermuda and, boy, are my wings tired. Cod? Herring? Toasted cheese sandwich?" The bird kicked one webbed foot over the other and brushed his forehead with his wing. "Trifle warm here, isn't it?"

Rod opened a cabinet and grabbed the tin of sardines he'd planned to save for a snack, offering them instead to Livingston. Bribery might work. "Yes, it is. Much warmer than we're used to, especially without sea breezes. Which, again, brings up the reason you're here. And how long are you planning to stay?"

The bird slurped one of the sardines down with a satisfied gulp. "Those are good. Nicely salted." He helped himself to another then settled down next to the tin. "So, how's it going?"

Rod exhaled. The bird was a well-known inter-rogator, and if he didn't want to squeal—or squawk, nothing could make him. "It's… going. Not with quite the results I had anticipated, but I'll get her to come. Even if I have to toss her over my shoulder."

"That well, huh?" Livingston grabbed another fish. "Caveman tactics don't go over so well these days, I hear. You could always tell her the truth."

"Sure, Livingston. Water-breathing people with tails who live in Atlantis go over *so* well with Humans. Especially without proof."

"Hey, you don't have to get snippy with me. It was only a suggestion. I do work in an advisory capacity to the High Councilman, you know." The gull snorted then coughed out the sardine. "Ugh. That's not pretty." He fluffed it off the table with his wing. It landed on the floor with a *splat*.

Both of them looked at the gelatinous mess, then at each other.

"You want to get that?" Rod asked.

"Ummm." The gull spread his wings, turning the black tips upward. "Do *you* see opposable thumbs?"

Rod sighed and shook his head, grabbing a paper towel from beside the sink. The gull had climbed the ranks of the Sky Service faster than anyone in the agency's history. His ego was legendary; cleaning up a mess was obviously beneath him.

Not that Rod was in line to be the ruler of all the seas or anything.

"So, here's how I see it, Rod." Livingston grabbed another sardine. "The Hybrid—"

"Can you please not call her that? She's a Mer."

"Half."

"The better half, so let's stick with that."

Livingston shrugged. "Oh, I don't know. Humans certainly have better tasting food than your kind. Say, you wouldn't happen to have any cheesecake around here, would you? I think that's probably one of their best. The cherries can get a bit gummy, but still... *What*?"

Rod held up the sardine tin he'd yanked out from under the gull's bill. "I didn't come here to sample their food. I came here to," Rod cleared his throat, "bring her back. So, you want to explain exactly why *you're* here, Livingston? I'm too old to need a nanny and you're certainly not bodyguard material."

The last brought Livingston to his webbed feet. "I'll have you know that I've dive-bombed with the best of them. We've turned breaching whales around, thrown off dolphins' running rhythm, even kept a hunting party from a harp seal nursery. I can be quite effective when I want to be."

"So you're here to protect me from orcas in the middle of the landmass?"

"Uh, well... no." The bird sighed and dropped onto his belly. "If you must know the truth, The Council sent me."

Rod snorted. Not surprising. "How much are they paying you?"

Livingston fanned himself. "Not enough clams to hang out in this Zeus-forsaken place. How are you going to stand this for long?"

Not so long. Rod patted the front left pocket of the shorts for the bottle of oil he needed to apply to avoid the two-sunset limitation on legs. If he was out of the water any longer without the oil, his tail wouldn't return.

It was not an unending supply. He had a certain time-table to get back, and with Valerie's refusal, the deadline loomed even larger.

Rod slid the tin back onto the table, then walked over to the cabinets and leaned against the countertop, crossing one ankle over the other. "I don't plan to be here long, Livingston. Tomorrow, hopefully. The next day at the very latest. These legs are all right for a few days, but why anyone would be willing to give up a tail and the freedom of the seas for them and this world is beyond me." Especially his brother, who'd finally earned the tail he'd always wanted—only to give it up.

Rod still blamed himself for that, no matter what absolution Reel gave him, or how many of the gods' tests he passed.

And with this latest wrinkle in the assignment, the gods didn't appear to have forgiven him either.

"Oh, I don't know." Livingston rifled through the remaining sardines before inching a fat one into his beak. "You've seen Reel's wife. Erica isn't hard on the eyes. Neither is Valerie."

"Don't even go there."

Livingston stopped eating, a tail dangling from the side of his bill. "Go where?"

"Tossing Valerie in my face. Yes, she's beautiful, but it doesn't matter. I'm here to bring her home and that's it. Nothing else."

"Uh oh."

"What?"

"Could it be that you want something more with the Hybrid?" He polished off the fish.

"What? I—No. Knock it off, Livingston. This mission has nothing to do with what she looks like and everything to do with me gaining the throne."

"Pity. The boys back on the roost were taking bets."

"Taking bets? On what she looked like?" Unbelievable. His first official duty would be to increase training missions if the "boys" had enough time to concern themselves with a Human and fly around her shop instead of performing their duties.

Rod removed his dinner from the microwave oven, the aroma of chicken nowhere near as appetizing as the sardines, nor the idea of eating it as pleasant. Hmmm, maybe he'd find another use for those "boys."

Allowing himself a grin, Rod knew he'd never follow through on that threat, but he still probably shouldn't let Livingston have any idea he was having fowl for dinner.

"Don't you want to know the odds?" Livingston tossed another sardine down his gullet.

"No. I don't." Rod pulled the liner—damned plastic— from the container and set the food behind him on the counter, then reached into the refrigerator for a beer. He popped the bottle top off against the countertop.

"Why?"

He took a swig. Different taste than kelp wine, but not bad. One thing Humans had to commend themselves. "Livingston, is there a point to this?"

Livingston scratched the top of his head with a webbed foot. "Odds are flying high in favor of you being down on bended knee inside a week."

"I hope you didn't take those odds since I don't plan to have knees inside a week."

"Uh huh. Then I guess you'll have to get cracking. Nardo said her hoo-hahs would do it, while Deuce was certain you'd see beyond them and take the time to get to know her. Ace, on the other hand, was still wondering what hoo-hahs were when I left."

Rod poured a good portion of the beer down his throat in one long swallow. Zeus. He didn't need this. "I am not discussing her hoo—her shell-fillers with you or anyone else. They—it doesn't matter. She's the answer to The Prophecy and I have to return her to The Council. Anything else is just a figment of your collective bird-brained imaginations."

Livingston clacked his bill shut, the corners of it turning up, and he whistled an off-key sea shanty.

"What?"

"Oh, toss around a few 'methinks' and 'protests,' a 'doth' or two, and I'm sure you can come up with it."

Rod glared at the bird. He knew what he wanted to toss around. And it didn't have a 'methink' in it, though the 'protest' part was a definite possibility.

Instead, he took one last swig of the beer and set it and his dinner on the countertop, then strode to the door and worked the shoes back onto his feet.

He hoped Valerie was still in the store below, because he was going to enjoy proving the bird wrong.

Chapter 5

WHEN THE FRONT WINDOW RATTLED, THE FIRST THING VAL noticed was his eyes.

The second was his smile.

And the third, well… the third was all the rest.

Rod was back.

Val reached for the edge of a display table to keep from falling over the pile of T-shirts she still had to clean up. Not because he made her weak in the knees, as some would argue—namely Tricia, if she hadn't left to feed her family—and headed to the door.

She opened it, trying to tuck a few wayward curls back behind her ear again. "What are you doing here?"

"I couldn't leave you to clean this up by yourself. It's late. Have you even eaten yet?"

"Really, I'll be fine." She did a good job of hiding the limp as she shut the door behind him, if she did say so herself.

"Valerie, you're injured."

Okay, so maybe not as good a job as she would have liked.

His arm brushed hers as he walked past her. "I can do it for you."

He certainly could, and she didn't mean clean up.

God, what was wrong with her? She'd vowed when she'd returned home this last time that she was going to stand on her own two feet—

Okay, so that wasn't the best analogy at the moment.

But she'd come back with every intention of making this work. Of making Mom's dream come true. The last thing she needed was to change her focus just because a guy who had a killer smile wanted her to up-and-leave. She was not about to be swayed by a pretty face.

But when Rod bent down to grab the pile of shirts, she did start to sway.

And it didn't have anything to do with the nice butt she got a glimpse of.

Really.

"You want to help in *those* clothes?" She had to get her mind off that butt.

He stood up and looked at his clothes. "What's wrong with them?"

Not a blessed thing. "Well, they're not exactly clean-up quality."

"Oh. That's easily remedied." And before she could react, Rod had whipped the shirt over his head from the back of his neck the way guys did, and she almost swallowed her tongue.

"Is this better?"

So much it was sinful.

"So where do you want to start?"

The countertop would be a good place. Followed by a bed in the apartment upstairs, then maybe a nice, long, erotic soak in the claw-foot tub...

Luckily she was saved from answering when Mr. Hill, her mother's accountant, knocked on the door then pushed it open. He stopped short at the sight of Rod—and Val could totally relate.

"Come in, Mr. Hill. This is Rod, um…" She looked at him. She knew she knew his last name. It was on the tip of her tongue.

Okay, not a thought to be having when she was staring at a chest to rival the best Olympic swimmer's.

"Tritone," Rod offered, one corner of his mouth kicking back into a sexy grin.

"Uh, right. Rod Tritone. He was just leaving."

"No, I wasn't. I offered to help and I mean to."

So much for getting out of here quickly tonight.

"What can I do for you, Mr. Hill? Did my mother order something for you?" Simon Hill had been a mess at Mom's funeral, leaving Val to wonder if more had been going on there than Mom had let on. She hoped so. Mom had deserved someone special.

"Is there somewhere we can speak privately?" Mr. Hill slid his glasses up the bridge of his nose then jammed his hands in the front pockets of his faded navy polyester pants, jostling his change. "It's a business matter, Valerie."

Val gestured around the shop. "This is as good as it gets, Mr. Hill. The back isn't any better." Especially since the arrival of her seagull visitor.

"Oh. Fine. Well, then…" He looked at Rod.

Rod looked back.

Val looked at Rod. "Rod, if you wouldn't mind?"

"No. I don't mind at all." He crossed one foot over the other and his arms across his chest, and leaned against the shelves. "Carry on."

Both she and Mr. Hill did a double take, but Rod didn't seem to notice.

Okay. Whatever. She didn't have time for this. She had a date. One she wasn't looking forward to anymore for some reason. "What's this about, Mr. Hill? Is there something you need?"

"Actually, Valerie, there is." Mr. Hill cleared his throat and fiddled with his gray-and-navy striped tie, the brass tie tack popping off as he pulled it too far from his white shirt, revealing a coffee stain beneath.

"There's, um…" He brushed back the comb-over that had fallen over his glasses after he picked up his tie tack. "There's an issue. With the taxes. For the building. It's why I'm here."

"Taxes? Issue?" Those two words ranked right up there with "fired" and "IRS." Her knees buckled and it felt as if the air had been sucked from the room. "What issue?"

She didn't protest when Rod helped her onto the counter, posting himself at her side.

Mr. Hill's hands switched from his front pockets to the back ones then back again. His shoulders rose and fell in a sigh that was bigger than he was.

"I'm sorry, Valerie. I didn't want to have to do this. You understand? I wanted to give you time, but there just isn't any anymore. It's all coming due and I can't think of a way to stop it and she'd be so upset that she'd cry and I couldn't stand to see her cry, she'd been through so much and if I could only make it easier for her, so I did. In the only way I knew, but now there's nothing more I can do and she'll be so sad that I've failed her—"

The man looked like *he* was going to cry and it cut through Val's haze. "Mr. Hill? What are you talking about? Who's going to be sad? What did you do?"

Rod gripped the man's arm, steadying him. "Take a breath and compose your thoughts. Then tell us clearly and concisely."

Val wasn't so sure about the collective "us," but since Rod had managed to calm the man down, she couldn't exactly complain.

"Your mother," Mr. Hill said, swallowing hard.

Val nodded. She'd figured as much.

"The taxes are overdue and, well, the county wants them, and that developer is willing to pay them and, well… the law's the law. I tried to find some way around this, but there just isn't any, we've exhausted every avenue and—"

"Taxes? Mr. Hill, what are you talking about? Mom loved this place. She wouldn't risk losing it."

"You're right. She was very responsible. But, well, you see… This place… it, well, it wasn't earning enough, but she wouldn't sell it and she wouldn't consider another type of merchandise."

That's right. She wouldn't. Mom had said the ocean theme was to remind her of Val's father. She'd said they were so in love, and Val had found it so romantic…

But it was a lie Mom had created for her, to give her a happy history of her father, while, all along, the man had left them—

"Don't worry." Val straightened her shoulders. "I'll get that money, Mr. Hill. This shop is staying in my family and no developer is going to tear it down to make another strip mall. How long do I have?"

"Two weeks," Mr. Hill whispered as if he were afraid that saying it would make the situation worse than it already was. "That's the longest I could get. After that, the building and all its contents go up for auction. I'm so sorry, Valerie." He blinked against the tears.

But Val didn't have any tears. Oh, no. She knew just where and how she was going to get that money, and it made perfect sense in the cosmic scheme of the universe.

Lance was finally going to make Mom's dream come true.

She slid off the counter, babying the injured ankle, and looked at Rod. "So, is tomorrow soon enough to go collect my inheritance?"

Chapter 6

AFTER AN EVENING SPENT DOING RECONNAISSANCE ON A certain seagull who'd been *a little too* interested in Therese's Treasure Trove lately, Maybelle Merriweather, the sparrow of 215 Main, second eave on the right, went for the swoop-and-flutter landing onto her friend Adele's perch on the Parkers' garage in the alley kitty-corner to the shop.

Not a bad landing at all. She was getting better.

It might have something to do with that cute new flight instructor…

Maybelle ruffled her feathers and glanced at the gift shop. Hmmm, from this angle, she couldn't see through those annoying blinds Therese had used to cover the windows.

"Adele, forget about nest-keeping. Let's go see what's going on over there." She'd been keeping an eye on Valerie ever since the girl had returned home. *Especially* with all the gulls who'd been making quick flybys over the shop recently. With the added news of the Mer Heir's visit, well, she hadn't been hatched yesterday. Something big was going on.

And she had the proverbial bird's-eye view.

"What are you chirping about, Maybelle?" Adele rearranged the same twig in her nest for the third time. Poor Adele really needed a mate. Ever since Seymour's passing, she wasn't handling the empty-nest syndrome very well at all.

Maybelle, on the other hand, was loving it.

"The Mer Heir's in there."

"No he's not." Adele fluttered her wings to keep from falling off her narrow ledge.

Narrow ledges were what you got when you chose to live over a garage. And in an alley, of all places. Maybelle had never understood that. It was all about location, location, location. Why, from her own eave above Archer's Bakery next door to the gift shop, she could see a good three-fourths of the town, whereas Adele, poor dear, only saw part of a road and the back half of the alley.

"Yes, he is. And he's *de-lish*. For a Biped, I mean," Maybelle clarified.

Adele adjusted the twig again. "No, he isn't in there. They all left a little while ago. Valerie drove off; Mr. Hill chatted with Mrs. Archer; and The Heir went back upstairs to the apartment." She pointed to the shop with the twig in her beak. "See? The lights are off."

"She left, huh? Then why is she heading up the apartment stairs with an overnight bag?"

"What?" Adele craned her neck over the ledge, almost dropping the twig in the process. "But Rod's staying at the apartment."

Maybelle took the twig and stuffed it into place. "Ahhh. This could get interesting."

"I fail to see how you think Valerie will find it interesting, Maybelle. She's injured. She's not going to want to climb back down those stairs on that leg."

"Exactly."

"Maybelle, what are you tittering about?"

Maybelle arched the feathers above one eye. "Oh, come now, Adele. It can't have been *that* long." She turned around as Valerie made it to the uppermost stair. "I just hope they don't close the door."

An hour after Valerie's sudden capitulation and subsequent departure to prepare for their trip the following day, Rod turned when the door to the apartment opened. Valerie stood there, teetering on the threshold on one leg, looking as surprised as he was.

"Rod? What are you doing here? We aren't leaving until the morning." She looked even more surprised when her momentum carried her forward. Her fingers slipped off the doorframe and she fell. Before she could hit the floor, he swept her up in his arms. Again.

He could get used to this.

"What *is* it about you that has me falling all over myself?" Her bag landed on the floor with a *clunk* while her fingers splayed below his heart. Rod had a momentary vision of her wrapping her arms—and, yes, those legs—around him.

At least one part of him was greeting that image with a salute.

He tried to form a coherent reply as he pulled her close to his chest. This rescuing thing was becoming a habit. A rather nice one, he had to admit. "Perhaps it's my charm?"

Her lips twitched.

He knew because he was watching them. Closely.

"Okay. If you say so."

"Then I say so."

"All right then, Prince Charming." She chuckled, and her breasts brushed his arm. "Is there any chance you want to put me down?"

None whatsoever.

"There's a problem with that." And he didn't mean the one in his shorts.

Or maybe he did.

"Oh?"

"If I put you down, you'll find another part of your anatomy in as much pain as your ankle." He lifted her away from his body to show her they were in the middle of the room where the only thing cushioning her fall would be a thin carpet.

Of course, he also pulled her back against him when he realized that clothing didn't hide as much as he'd thought.

"Ah, good point." She wiggled her feet and, when she shifted, he hefted her back into the cradle of his arms, which had the added bonus of placing his fingers against the side of her soft breast. "How about putting me on the sofa instead?"

"I think I can manage that." He *hoped* he could manage it.

Then he once again smashed his toe into the coffee table, which was far too low to drink from in the first place (not to mention *see* with her in his arms), almost pitching them both to the floor.

"Hades!" Rod tucked Valerie tighter against his chest and regained his balance, while she threw her arms around his neck. He knew she'd done it every bit as instinctively as he'd held on to her, but he couldn't deny the reaction her embrace sparked—as if he'd landed in a bed of fire coral…

Only this didn't sting.

It burned.

Long, slow and hot. From the point of contact through the rest of his body.

For the space of a heartbeat or two, their eyes held. He saw a flicker of the burn in her eyes, felt the slight shift in her breath before she unwound her arms from his neck, her fingertips barely touching his chest as they returned to her lap.

Barely, but he felt them. Every single one.

She looked up at him, those blue eyes soft and warm and swirling, and she said softly, "You want to let me down?"

Not really.

Especially once the word "bed" had made an appearance in his thoughts. In relation to fire coral or not, with her in his arms, it created a force unlike anything he'd ever experienced.

And thinking those thoughts, with her fingers *just* grazing his skin... her in his arms, well, the next thing he knew, her lips were so close he could taste them.

So he did.

The kiss was everything he'd thought it'd be and nothing he'd ever imagined. A short gasp of breath, and he was swimming in a whirlpool of feeling, every curve of her body pressing against him, all the soft hollows beneath his fingertips urging him to explore further. Her lips opened under his, the warmth of her breath stealing his, and Rod found himself mesmerized by the tiny sound she made as his tongue found hers.

Her fingers slid upward again, tentative, and those minute touches were enough to make his knees weak, electricity spiraling from that one touch to every part of him.

He released her legs, sliding his arm around her, up over her tail end, slipping around her slim waist, to bring her face level with his so he could fully explore the delicious warmth of her mouth. Her breasts flattened against his bare chest, her nipples pointed and hard against him, her legs cradling his erection as his tongue traced the sweet outline of her lips... her cheek... her eyelids.

Valerie's fingers tangled in his hair, pulling his head down to hers or herself up to him. Rod didn't know which. Didn't care either, because her movement ignited new threads of electricity, new sensations, new awareness of how their bodies matched. How they were different in the most elemental and fantastic ways possible, and he didn't mean race.

His shin hit the sofa and Rod laid her down on the cushions, covering her with his body, sinking into the softness of her and the furniture without breaking the kiss. Hades, he didn't think he could break it—not that he had any intention of doing so. There was a whole new world to experience here, the feel of her legs as they parted around his, the rise of her mound against him, the soft gasp as he traced the cord in her neck, the soft hollow beneath her ear—

"Hey! Uh... Oh. Hello." Livingston flew in the window and crash-landed onto the table beside the sofa, breaking both the lamp and the mood.

Valerie dragged her lips from Rod's, her eyes wide, the blue irises almost as dark as her pupils.

It took her a few seconds to find the words... and Rod enjoyed the moment. He was not about to apologize. He didn't know if he could anyway, and he sure as Hades didn't want to.

Tension hung heavy between them, then Rod felt embarrassment crawl up her body. He knew the moment she registered they had an audience—*and* that she'd been as engaged in that kiss as he had.

She started struggling, worming her way out from beneath him, eyes downcast, and her breathing still as shallow as it'd been when he'd nibbled on her earlobe.

"Rod... what did we... what happened... a bird..." She inched upward, her knee coming dangerously close to a part of him that wouldn't enjoy making its acquaintance.

He lowered one of his knees to the floor, lifting himself from her. "Here. Let me help you—"

"That's okay. I can do it." She swatted his hands away then righted herself with another example of the grace he'd witnessed earlier.

"There's—" She gulped. " A bird. In your living room. My living room. Whatever."

Rod sighed. Talk about bad timing. "Yes."

"It's a seagull."

"Yes."

"Why?"

"Why?" That was a new one. "Because his parents are seagulls?"

Livingston snorted.

Valerie did a double take, then her eyes narrowed. "Did that thing just snort at me?"

Thing. Oh, Zeus.

"Hold on." Rod jumped to his feet as fast as he could. He swooped Livingston off the table and into the kitchen before the bird could come up with one of his scathing retorts, as he was known to do.

"Rod, we've got to talk," Livingston said, getting over her insult quicker than Rod would have imagined—which didn't bode well for whatever Livingston wanted to tell him.

Rod clamped his hand around Livingston's beak, a huge breach in etiquette, but he didn't care. "Not now."

The gull shook his bill free. "Look, you can play kissy-face later. Right now—"

Rod glanced around the corner at the sofa and repeated his clam-up job on the bird. "I said, 'Not now,' Livingston. She doesn't know you can talk."

The bird used his wings to pry himself out of Rod's grasp and dropped onto the tiny kitchen table. "Well she's going to find out at some point. Especially with what I have to tell you. Might as well do it sooner rather than later." He ruffled his feathers, then settled his wings on his back while twisting his neck, opening and closing his beak as if he had a cramp. "Oh, and by the way? You've used up your two allotted beak-grabs. Don't do it again. I don't care who your father is or what you're in line to become. My bill is off-limits."

"Knock it off, Livingston. We can't tell her yet. It's a little complicated."

"A little complicated? Rod, you have no idea. Talking seagulls are nothing." Livingston shook his head and clacked his bill shut. "Not when we're talking about—"

"Not *now*," Rod whispered harshly. "Let me get rid of her."

"You might not want to do that." Livingston mimicked in an equally harsh whisper—one of his lesser-known talents.

"Oh?" Rod leaned back to peer at the sofa. If she were to overhear this conversation… "Why?"

"Because what I have to say concerns her, too. I'll show you complicated, and it's not what you'd call little. That's why we need to tell her now."

"It's not part of the plan, Livingston. Or didn't The Council clue you in?"

"What I just found out wasn't part of the plan either, Rod, but that doesn't seem to have stopped anyone from putting events in motion."

Rod took a deep breath. "You can't tell her, Livingston. She's too freaked out by the sight of you. You can thank your friend Ace for that. I've just gotten her to agree to go with me. That'll change if a talking seagull shows up. Give me a few minutes to tell her something."

"Fine, but we need to have this conversation sooner rather than later. So, while I'm waiting for you to bring her onboard, is there anything else to eat around here? The pickings in this town aren't what I'm used to." Livingston glanced around the kitchen, his bill pointing at the cabinets.

"Here." Rod grabbed a packet of crackers and tossed them onto the table. "Make do with these while I try to come up with something. Then we'll talk."

Val shook off the creeps that bird had given her. Well, she tried to. If she hadn't canceled her date, this wouldn't be happening. But after meeting Rod, well, she just hadn't been up for meeting Glen.

Now, however, she was reconsidering.

There was a *seagull*. Here. Now. That was beyond weird and entirely too coincidental to be a coincidence.

First seagulls, then Rod. Then seagulls again. In her store and in her living room—both Rod *and* the gulls.

Wait a minute.

What *was* Rod doing here? Those had been her first words to him before he'd sidetracked her with that kiss and he still hadn't answered her.

And, no, she was not going to think about that kiss. Just because it was the best one she'd ever received and the man had the sweeping-her-up-in-his-arms thing down pat and he certainly knew what to do with his tongue, not to mention those little puffs against her skin, a moist kiss in that spot beneath her ear—

Val shook her head. *Focus.* What was he doing here—and looking way too comfortable doing it? Shirtless and barefoot—a very good look on him. One that screamed of domesticity and squatters' rights. In her apartment.

She was going to find out right now. She stood up and started for the kitchen, only to almost lose her balance again. And, once again, it had nothing to do with her sore ankle and everything to do with the fact that he was rounding the corner from the kitchen, still shirtless, still barefoot. And still incredibly hot, as Tricia had so correctly pointed out.

She was not going to think about that kiss.

Of course, that made her look at his lips, and she remembered exactly what they'd felt like on hers, and that not-thinking-about-it thing wasn't working so well.

So she just wouldn't look at him.

Again, not working.

Then he spoke, all velvety, rub-all-over-her-nerve-endings

delicious, and her one supporting knee trembled. So she wrapped her arms around her midsection and tried to retain both her composure and her balance.

Again, not working so well.

"Valerie, I—"

"Don't say it."

"It?"

"Whatever it is you're going to say."

"You know what I'm going to say?"

"Yes. No. Well, not exactly. But I have a pretty good idea." She rubbed her arms, and it certainly wasn't because she was cold, though some might think differently if they saw the goose bumps. But she knew better. "That—" She nodded at the sofa. "Is not going to happen."

"In case you've forgotten, it already did."

She hadn't. She *definitely* hadn't. "I mean, it's not going to happen again."

"Oh?"

"No."

"May I ask why?"

"Because I don't even know you." And couldn't think straight when he did that, as evidenced by the fact that it'd taken a *seagull* to get her attention.

"That's easily remedied."

She arched an eyebrow at him and tucked her hands into the back pockets of her shorts, wobbling once to steady herself. "Rod, what's going on? Why are you here? Why is there a seagull in my kitchen?"

Rod nodded. "Ah, yes." He swept a hand toward the sofa. "Let's sit."

"Why?"

"Because it's comfortable?"

Good point. She sat. "Okay, so now are you going to answer my questions?"

"Yes. I'm here because I rented the apartment. I presume that's the way one usually gets a key?"

Great. Now she was homeless.

Homeless, soon to be storeless, *and* an heiress—which would take care of the first two "-esses," once she spent a few days with a guy who could kiss her so senseless she didn't notice a seagull flying into the room.

"You rented it? No one told me."

"Ah. A dilemma, to be sure. But I did tender my currency, so you'll have to take that up with your agent. As to the seagull—"

"Wait a minute. *Why* did you rent the apartment and not a room at a motel? Most people I know don't usually rent an apartment for one night." She was going to have to have a chat with her real estate agent. Great that he rented the place, but he could have told her, especially since she'd been planning to move in...

"Ah. Well." Rod cleared his throat and leaned back, draping an arm across the back of the sofa and an ankle over a knee, none of which should have had anything to do with the fact that he still didn't have a shirt on, but... *did*. "Consider me unlike most people you know."

Another good point. She *didn't* know anyone like him... except maybe her. He attracted seagulls as much as she did.

Right. That.

She sat up straighter and pressed her knees together, linking her hands around them to keep any body parts with wandering tendencies where she could monitor them. "What's with the bird?"

As if on cue, the thing flew into the room again, perching, thank God, on the back of the chair on the opposite side of the room.

Val braced herself on the edge of the sofa, fingers ready to push off if need be. She wasn't frightened exactly, but that whole adage about it being good luck if seagull poo landed on you… well, there'd been no poo yet, but she figured with the way things were going, that'd be next.

Then it said, "Rod"—which was wrong for so many reasons.

"It talks? *And* knows your name?"

Oh yes, the proverbial poo had just met the proverbial fan.

Oh Hades.

Rod glanced at the gull and saw a crease above Livingston's brows, his beak working in small movements that made Rod thankful the bird didn't have lips.

"Yes, he talks." Rod pressed on his thighs to stand up, his brain working rapidly for a way to find out what Livingston wanted to tell him without letting Valerie know who and what the gull was. "And he can be, ah, persistent when he gets hungry, so let me feed him. Then we can finish our discussion. Why don't you put that leg up, and I'll be right back."

He strode from the room, not giving her the chance to answer because she'd just taken a big breath, and he knew from experience what that meant. Conversations following big intakes of air—or water—by any female were best avoided.

Luckily, Livingston could take a hint.

"Rod, we need to talk. Or we need to leave. Or, preferably, talk while we're leaving," the gull whispered from Rod's shoulder the minute they were back in the kitchen.

"I get that, Livingston." Rod held out his palm for Livingston to alight on; he hated having a conversation with his shoulder.

"No, you don't. I mean now."

"Why, Livingston? The Prophecy isn't going anywhere." Valerie, neither, if he couldn't get her to accept her father's legacy, which, with her dislike of seagulls, was a good possibility if Livingston kept hanging around.

"It's not The Prophecy. My network says there's going to be trouble."

"Your network? Here? I thought you only operated on the coasts."

"Then you think wrong. Don't worry about it; I'm sure they were going to tell you once you took office. But, yes, we've got a bicoastal network, and my sources tell me something's fishy about this operation. You need to get to the water ASAP."

"I know, Livingston, and I had her convinced until you showed up. In case you haven't figured it out, she's not all that keen on your species these days. And I can't say I blame her."

"I don't give a flying hoot if she likes me or not. She'll thank me when we get her to the coast in one piece." Livingston punctuated his words with a flapping of wings, which moved him to the countertop amid the food—not a surprise. "And that's why I'm here. One of my operatives reported seeing an albatross in the area."

"An albatross? Albatrosses don't travel this far inland."

"I know. You see the problem."

"You think it's JR?"

"In all probability. My network here wasn't aware of him. There was no need to brief them on a seabird who's never been known to venture this far inland. Obviously, times change, and since we don't know what he's up to but do know what he's capable of," —Livingston nudged one of the cans toward the edge of the counter— "my instinct says we need to get you and the Hybrid out of here now."

Rod picked up the can. Calamari. The bird had an excellent *instinct* for food. "*My* instinct says you're here to do more than ensure I keep up my part of the plan, Livingston." He pulled the tab, rolling the lid back but holding the can in his palm.

Livingston shifted between his webbed feet, his head cocking to the side. "Come on, Rod, I've got my orders."

Just as he suspected. The Council wouldn't send the Chief of ASA here on a babysitting mission. Livingston was too valuable. "You'll soon be taking those orders from me, so talk."

Livingston eyed him, turning his head so both eyes could study Rod. Or maybe the seagull was trying to distract him with that red spot, but, again, Rod wasn't going to be deterred.

"There are rumors of a coup."

"A *coup*? You're kidding."

Livingston puffed out his chest, that octopi-ink tattoo glaring against the white of his feathers. "I do *not* kid about possible takeover attempts." He'd forgotten to lower his voice.

Rod shushed him, leaning back to peer around the corner. Damn, Valerie was hopping their way.

"Right," Livingston continued, his voice back to a whisper. "Listen. My department takes all threats seriously. And we consider ignition lines in a trench The Heir was to survey very serious."

"She's coming. You'd better explain this and the ignition lines later."

"You'd better get rid of her so I *can* explain it later. Or better yet, get both of you out of town so no explanations are necessary."

"Rod?" Valerie hopped around the corner. "What's going on? How long does it take to feed a seagull? And why does it *talk*?"

"Hey, you should be off that ankle." Rod set the tin on the counter then slung his arm around her waist and turned her back toward the living room. "I'll get you something to put on that leg, then we'll talk, okay?"

"We can talk about everything tomorrow. Since you rented the apartment, I'll get out of your hair so you can finish feeding... *that*." She wobbled on the last word.

"We have something to talk about right now, Valerie—namely, how dangerous it is for you to attempt the stairs with your injured leg." He handed her a pillow for her ankle when she was back on the sofa. "Wait here. I'll get him some food and you some ice."

Rod returned to the kitchen and opened the freezer for the ice, still marveling that what took thousands of *selinos* to create at the poles could be so readily available in one appliance. No wonder Humans weren't doing enough about global warming.

"Use the gods' oil," Livingston said with a ring of calamari around his beak. "We need her in perfect shape."

Oh, he could tell Livingston all about her perfect shape, but that was for his own edification. Still, it was a good suggestion.

Rod put the ice in a paper towel then went to the bedroom for the bottle. He tilted one drop of the oil into his palm, replaced the stopper, and then returned to the living room.

"Here." He knelt before her, lifting her ankle into the palm with the oil.

"I can do it."

"So can I. Relax. You'll enjoy it."

She exhaled, but didn't argue with him, thank the gods. He removed her shoe, tracing those small bones in her ankle again. She was so slight. He'd never noticed how fragile a female Human's bones were, how little kept them upright. Legs were more complex than he'd realized.

And hers were sexier than he'd ever imagined.

He slid his fingers over her instep, around and up the back of her leg, her groan covering one he couldn't suppress. She felt so good, so smooth. He kneaded the muscles, trying to focus on what he was supposed to be doing, but gods—he wanted to keep going. To trail his fingers up her leg. Circle behind her knee, graze the sleek line of her thigh, up... to the apex.

Valerie's voice was low and husky. "Mmmm, that feels good."

Didn't he know it.

Taking a ragged breath, Rod concentrated on bringing his hands back to her ankle. His first and foremost reason for touching her was to heal her.

That little contented moan she gave when his fingers resumed the massage would be the second.

And with a black-tipped wing waving from the kitchen, the third reason would be to keep her out here while he discovered what Livingston knew about a coup.

He picked up the ice and put it over her sprain, which was now healed—not that he could explain that to her yet.

She yelped when the cold registered. "What'd you do that for?"

"Ice will help it heal."

She sat straight up and pushed her hair off her face, the soft relaxed look replaced with the shock to her system the cold had done. "You could've warned me."

"And have you tense up? No, this way the ankle got the full effect of the cold." Now two wings waved at him from the kitchen. Rod stood, drawing the coffee table close enough to rest her foot on. "Are you hungry?"

A flash of something crossed her face and Rod could bet it was the same flash that went through his mind.

Hunger… Oh yeah.

"No, thank you. I'm fine. I'm perfectly capable of fending for myself."

He nodded at her ankle. "I can see that."

The corners of her mouth tilted up with a hint of dimple high in her cheek. "Current situation excluded."

"Duly noted. Now, sit here and relax. You don't want to let all my hard work go to waste, do you?"

He handed her the remote control—a brilliant invention—and headed back into the kitchen to finish the conversation with Livingston—and *not* think about anything "hard" that had to do with Valerie.

Chapter 7

BESIDES THE USE OF MICROWAVES, ROD HAD LEARNED HOW to prepare basic Human food from Erica, and he'd become quite enamored of tuna melts. Since the earlier meal had turned to rubber, he resumed the discussion with Livingston while toasting the muffins and draining the tuna. "So, about the rumors?"

Livingston tossed another circle of calamari into the air, ringing it on his beak. "Two points," he squawked from the sides of his beak before sliding it off and gulping it down. He wiped a dribble of liquid with his foot then reached for another piece.

Rod slid the can out of reach. "Hey, LeBron? The coup?"

"Been studying Human culture, have you?" Livingston sighed then shook his head. "It was only a rumor before we found your Trench Survey wired to blow. That's why you got pulled off the study. Someone's not happy your dad's retiring. Or that you're coming into power."

Wired to blow. Rod cursed. They'd told him the Survey had been put on hold for a special project, which he'd assumed had been Valerie. Not a bomb. "What happened?"

"Initially, one of the guards reported seeing the ignition wires, but he never checked with the royal construction crew. He'd assumed they were for the preliminary blast for your soon-to-be-built Pacific palace. It was only after his supervisor read the report that The Council was alerted. I just got notification."

Livingston edged closer to the calamari. "Add in a recent shortage of diamonds in one of the older kimberlite pipes, and that compounds a coup scenario. Now that JR, who'd gone to ground a few months back, has been spotted, and with the large amount of unaccounted-for currency, well, it doesn't take a marine biologist to figure out something's fishy. You need to be settled on the throne — with Immortality — before everyone will be at ease. And word's out about Valerie being found, so don't take your eyes off her, either."

Rod glanced back at her, catching the way her tongue darted out to wet her lips, and he remembered how incredible those lips had felt beneath his.

Don't take his eyes off her? That wasn't going to be a problem.

"So now she's in danger."

Livingston cocked his head, looking over his bill with both eyes. "Considering we don't know who's behind this, I'd say it's better to be cautious than not. This trip couldn't have come at a worse time."

This couldn't be the gods' doing. They might devise a test for him, but they wouldn't include her. Especially if she was the answer to The Prophecy. No, something was going on that put not only him *and* Valerie in danger, but also the fate of the planet.

He needed to get her to the water as soon as possible.

Val flipped the channels, limited though they were since she'd turned off the dish service after the last tenant's departure.

She didn't have to wonder what she'd have to turn off after Rod's departure.

Tricia had definitely called it. He was hot. But it was more than his looks. He was charming and funny and chivalrous and caring and compassionate and helpful and yeah, sexy. She had to include that because he just... was. He also came bearing gifts that any normal woman would probably swoon over.

And even though she hadn't swooned, she had to admit that, as messenger service went, he was perfect. Yes, his overnight accommodations might be off the beaten path, and he did have a talking seagull, but those problems could be overcome.

Well, no. That seagull thing couldn't. And since the feathered friend was presumably staying here, she'd better head over to Tricia's family's motel. Tomorrow she'd have a few words with that real estate agent.

Oh, and have this place fumigated after the seagull left.

Val removed the ice from her ankle, amazed that it felt so much better. There was something to be said for the healing power of massage—not to mention what else massage was good for.

Okay then.

She was halfway to standing when Rod came back with something heavenly smelling on the plates in his hands, two beers under his arm, and his shorts riding low on his hips.

Her knees buckled. Good thing there was a sofa behind her.

"Here you go," he said, handing her a plate and setting the beers on the coffee table. "You really should keep that foot up."

So she did. It was either that or risk putting it in her mouth.

Val opted for the tuna melt instead.

And it did. Melt. In her mouth. As it was supposed to do, she guessed.

Or maybe the melting had something to do with the incredible muscle contractions his abdomen did as he sat in the chair kitty-corner from her.

No, actually, those dried her mouth out.

She slugged back a good swallow of the beer and choked on the fizz.

Rod leaned over to pat her on the back and set her plate down. "Are you okay?"

Moisture pooled at the corners of her eyes, yet she managed to nod. He couldn't be blamed for stealing her breath just because he was half-dressed.

Well, okay, maybe he could. She should probably ask him to put on a shirt.

Then he leaned back and the six-pack contracted and flexed and did all sorts of wonderful, nether-region-quivering things.

What was she supposed to ask him again?

The seagull chose that moment to swoop back into the room, landing on the coffee table. Surprisingly, she was glad for the interruption, but she hoped the health inspector wasn't planning to stop by any time soon or she'd end up having issues with two local government agencies.

The bird ruffled its feathers, doing a wing-over-wing thing on its back, then settled down on its belly—a little too close to her plate. At least it hadn't stolen anything. Yet.

But just in case, she put the beer down and slid the plate sideways, then tucked her hair behind her ears. That was more to be ready in the event this one decided it needed her hair for a nest than because of any wayward curls obstructing her view. "Does it have a name?"

Rod swallowed the bite he'd just taken. "He."

"Sorry?"

"He's a he. Not an it."

Okay… "Oh. Does *he* have a name?"

"Livingston."

She laughed. "That's original."

The bird hopped to its feet, one wing stretching toward her.

"It's a famous name. I figured he'd do it proud," Rod said, tossing a piece of English muffin at the bird.

"You really shouldn't do that. It only encourages them."

The gull took his time with the muffin, and Val could have sworn the thing, er, *Livingston*, was giving her the Evil Eye. She lifted her tuna melt to take a bite. "So how'd you end up with a pet seagull?"

The bird turned its bill toward Rod who sighed, then tossed another piece of muffin. "Oh, he's not a pet. He just sort of showed up."

"Well, at least you don't have to worry about what to feed him." She nodded at the muffin. "Seagulls are like trash dumps. They'll eat anything." Including someone's lunch.

The bird proved her correct as he took off from the table right then and grabbed half her tuna melt in his beak.

Okay, so that was her dinner, but dammit! He could have taken off a finger.

Rod plucked the foul fowl from the air in mid-flight, stormed over to the window, and tossed the bird out with a, "Good night, Livingston. We'll see you tomorrow," before he slammed the glass shut with a rattle loud enough to make her wait for the crash. Luckily, it didn't come.

"Sorry about that," Rod said, reaching behind his neck to massage the muscles there as he headed back to the seating area.

The apology had the added bonus of stretching every taut inch of skin; that sexy line above his hip looking incredible as his shorts sank lower.

The temperature spiked in the room. She'd like to attribute it to the fact that he'd stopped any airflow when he'd shut the window, but, honestly, who was she kidding?

"How about some air-conditioning?" She took another swig of beer, needing something to cool her off. Although, short of flying in an iceberg, the A/C was probably the better bet.

Or dressing him in a parka—and he'd probably look good in that, too.

"Air-conditioning?" Rod stopped a foot from the sofa, drew his hand from his neck and shoved it onto his hip. Which only highlighted that hipline even more.

"Yes. You know, that unit in the window in the bedroom? Turn it on. It should do the trick."

Rod turned so precisely that he could have been military, then strode to the bedroom. A few moments—or sixteen perspiration droplets falling from her lip—later, the low hum of the ancient unit emanated from his bedroom.

No, she *wasn't* going to think about low hums and his bedroom in the same thought.

Again with the not-working thing.

She elected not to finish her beer. It was time to find someplace else to lay her head for the night, or she just might end up begging to use his left pectoral. Or his right. Really, she wasn't picky.

She was on her feet, halfway around the table, when Rod walked out of the bedroom, his shorts still low, no line of boxers anywhere to be found. So, either they'd headed south, too, or he didn't wear any…

"What are you doing?"

Lusting after you? "What do you mean?" was the answer she elected to verbalize instead, thank God.

"Your leg. You need to stay off it."

Oh. Her leg. Right. Injured.

Val shook her head. For crying out loud, her ankle was fine and he was just a guy. She'd worked with construction workers, some of whom had taken great pride in their physiques. It wasn't as if she'd never seen a naked chest before.

"It's much better. I should be going." A long time ago, actually. "It's getting late and I need to find a place to stay." Val skirted the rest of the table and limped toward the door, grabbing her bags from the floor where she'd dropped them, thankful (she guessed) that he didn't stop her.

"You don't have any place to go?"

After the conversation with Mr. Hill, that wasn't a question she wanted to answer right now. "Sure. The motel always has rooms."

Rod ran his fingers through his rumpled hair, then put his hands on his hips. The waistband gapped just enough to be inviting.

"There are two sleeping quarters here, Valerie. You can use one of them."

Oh she did so want one of them. Preferably the one he was sleeping in.

Bad idea, Dumere.

"That's okay. I'll head over to the motel and—"

"Valerie, that's ridiculous. Contrary to what you might think, I'm not in the habit of kissing every woman I meet. You're more than welcome to stay here. We're going to be traveling together. Our fathers knew each other. It's not as if we're strangers."

"Rod, you've already come to my rescue once today. I'll be fine."

Fine being a relative concept. She was wiped out. Finding out her deadbeat dad had left her an inheritance, followed by the possibility of losing Mom's store… it'd been one emotional punch after the other. Throw in lust for good measure, and, well, frankly, she was beat.

"Then let me make up for tossing you out of your home."

"But you didn't."

"Where would you be staying tonight if not for me?"

"Well, here, but—"

"Never mind." Rod strode to the door and picked up a pair of running shoes. "*I'll* go to the motel. This is your home. You should sleep here." He took a step toward the door, but Val put a hand on his arm.

"Now who's being ridiculous? You paid for the apartment."

He looked at her hand on his arm then back into her eyes. "It seems we're at an impasse. You know what that means, don't you?"

Val dropped her arm. "Rock, paper, scissors?"

He leaned back against the doorframe, away from her, but not enough that she wasn't aware of every inch of him being only inches from her. Especially when the corner of his mouth pulled up in a half-smile that was way too sexy for her own good.

He might not be in the habit of kissing every woman he met, but since she was the only one around, she might not mind if he took up that practice.

"No. It's called compromise." He slid his hands into his pockets and crossed one foot over the other. "You stay in that bedroom." He nodded to the smaller one closest to the door. "And I'll stay in mine. Fair enough?"

When he cocked his eyebrow like that, he definitely made her forget why she shouldn't agree to this...

"Or are you worried I might be too much of a temptation?"

And when he smiled like that, he made her remember every reason she should.

Or maybe that was why she shouldn't.

See? She was exhausted. And the bedroom door had a lock. "Like I'm going to answer that. But I will take you up on your offer—only, no more funny stuff."

"Funny?" Rod reached over her head to close the door and turned the deadbolt with a loud *click*. "Trust me, Valerie. Funny is the last word I'd use to describe any 'stuff' you might want to revisit."

No way was she touching *that* invitation. Val left him standing there and headed into the bedroom, locking the door behind her.

Revisit? He should be so lucky.

She climbed into the twin bed and clicked off the light on the bedside table.

Or maybe she should be...

Chapter 8

DRAKE CABOT, SECOND IN LINE FOR THE MER THRONE NOW that that Reel had left the sea, sat at his parents' table in the temperate, volcano-warmed waters of Atlantis for the weekly command-performance family dinner. Gently waving sea fans, brilliantly colored corals, and hundreds of sea creatures surrounded them—all were his father's toadies.

That was the thing with this place. No privacy. Someone was always watching. Wrasses, gobies, angelfish. Hades. Gary, the moray, had claimed the giant sea-snail shell on the mantel Drake's first day of school—and hadn't budged since. And, Milli or Melli, or whatever her name was, had draped her eight tentacles around the stalactite over the table for the last five moons and hung there like a chandelier, always listening.

Why anyone would want to listen to the nonsensical chatter of his sisters, Drake couldn't imagine. He'd much rather be back in his home waters of the Caribbean.

Kept clear of nosey angelfish and stupid chubs by the hagfish he'd persuaded to work their slimy magic, his home was his refuge. If not for the magical Travel Chambers that turned the three-hundred leagues between Atlantis and home into just a flip, swim, and a tail-flick, he'd have an excuse to miss these time-wasting family dinners.

"So even if Rod brings The Hybrid home, one of us could still marry him, right, Daddy?" Doria picked up her tuna fillet with her fingers. Uncouth. *As if* she'd make a decent queen.

"Honestly, Doria, do you really think he'd pick you?" Andrea threw back a swallow of kelp wine with all the finesse of a grouper. "At least I've had a conversation with the man."

Doria and Andrea had to be the two biggest water-heads in the sea. It was stunning that he was related to them. Stunning and disappointing. He could see why his father, one of the six members of The Council, had pinned his hopes of dynastic brilliance on him. His sisters couldn't pronounce the word 'dynastic,' let alone understand what it meant.

He picked at his seagrass salad while Doria tossed a snail shell at their sister. "Asking him which road The Coliseum is on isn't having a conversation, Andrea. It's acting like a blind whale shark. Everyone knows where The Coliseum is. All you have to do is look up and swim in a circle. You can't miss it."

His sisters bandied insults back and forth while his father, Nigel, systematically cut his meal, one bite at a time, followed by exactly six chews, then a sip of wine.

Drake had to give his dad credit; were these two his daughters, he'd be guzzling wine by the cask.

Of course, that's what happened when you weren't careful when doing "the deed." Doria had been that little surprise.

Drake looked at his mom. Hair in a bun, a pair of coconut shells lashed together with seaweed for a shirt, the purple-tentacled sea anemone his father had given her for their engagement now snoring quietly above her ear, Mom had retreated into her shell in the *selinos* since he'd left home. He felt bad for her, in a way. From the stories he'd heard, all she'd had going for her was being the daughter of a somewhere-in-the-line-of-succession heir to the throne.

His father had been caught in the oldest net known to Merkind, yet knowing Dad's social aspirations, Drake had to wonder how much of it had been an accident.

Once Rod and Reel had been born to the High Councilman, however, his father's hopes of a succession to the throne had been relegated to hoping one of his grandchildren would rule—effectively ending any hopes dear ol' Dad had of power.

But Drake hadn't given up. Reel was out of the running since he'd abdicated any claim to the throne by marrying a Human and living as one, and Kraken—an heir only his mother had known existed—was no longer a threat. That left only Rod in his way.

The throne was within his grasp.

Drake sloshed a slice of sea cucumber in the guava sauce. He was sick of coming in third—and hearing about it his entire life. The Tritone brothers had always finished ahead of him. Better grades, better athletes— how *had* a two-legged Mer beaten him in water polo anyway? Drake didn't even want to think about that tournament. The biggest embarrassment of his life.

And his father hadn't let him forget it.

"So, Drake." His father actually looked at him. "Have you heard from Ceto recently?"

Ceto? The mother of all sea monsters? The denizen of the Bermuda Triangle? The two-tailed Mer—both literally and figuratively—who hated The Council and lived near him?

Actually, he had.

He'd advised her to stay away from the stupid booze cruise off one of the islands. Pickled Humans could not taste good and were hazardous to her health.

"Um... no, Dad. Why would you think that?" As a rule, everyone tried to stay away from Ceto.

Which was why his plan was working so well.

"It's said she's been in better spirits recently, and I just wondered if you'd heard why." Nigel waved over their Serving Cuttlefish for the tray of oysters—complete with gleaming pearls. Dad did like to remind himself of his wealth and power—most of which would disappear when that Hybrid returned to her "rightful" place as governor of the ocean that the Cabots had cared for since Lance Dumere had admitted to the utter idiocy of cavorting with a Human and leaving "evidence" of Mers behind.

And The Council considered *her* more worthy than him to rule the Southern Ocean? Let's see how they'd do when he was ruling all of them.

"The Council gave Ceto that Human to keep her busy after turning Kraken loose last year. Didn't that do it for her?"

"Did it?" The oyster shell paused halfway to Nigel's mouth, his eyes widening in innocence.

But Drake knew better.

The old man thought he'd pulled one over on him. The Council had hired Ceto to watch him the minute Reel went aground. Talk about the crab pot calling the steamer kettle black...

Members of The Council might be old—and one of them his own father—but they weren't stupid. Drake was next in line. It only made sense they'd be concerned he'd try something.

With very good reason.

"Beats me, Dad. I try not to get in her way, you know what I mean?"

Actually, he'd gone out of his way to get *in* her way—with exactly the results he'd wanted.

Ceto had been known to hold a grudge for... well, a lot longer than recorded history. So when The Council had stripped her of her propagating abilities and given her the token Human to amuse herself with, Drake had seen an opening.

He'd promised her her freedom if his plan worked, in return for her lying to The Council about his actions. So far, it had been a bargain made in... well, if not Olympus, not Hades either. It worked for both of them.

"I've heard she doesn't like the Human," said Doria, slurping a snail from its shell with noises unworthy even of a catfish. "Supposedly he talks too much."

"Then he ought to be perfect for you," chimed Andrea. "Maybe you ought to go see Ceto."

"No way. I like to keep my tail."

Nigel cut another piece of fillet, his eyes never leaving Drake.

"So what are you doing to keep yourself occupied these days, Drake?"

Again, an answer Drake had prepared—with just enough nonchalance that Dad would assume it was real. After all, dear ol' Dad thought he was incompetent; he didn't want to ruin the image.

Especially now.

Drake waved off the squid who propelled over to him with a plate of shrimp in his tentacles. "I'm working on an underwater writing utensil that will make tablets, urchin spines, and octopi ink obsolete."

"Hmmph." Nigel bit into another slice. "If it works, we'll have to look into getting you a patent."

If.

Dad *had* to preface the statement with "if."

"*If* it works," "*if* you pass," "*if* you finish…"

Never "when."

But now… *When* this plan worked, he'd be out from under Nigel's thumb and finally get the respect the Mer should have shown him his entire life.

Drake met his father's gaze across the table through the anemone centerpiece, looking for some sign of approval.

And just like always, there was none.

Ha. The old man didn't know what he'd planned. Didn't have a clue what he was up to.

Not yet.

Because the thing was, Nigel would probably try to stop him. Oh, the old salt would love to have him on the throne, but not the way Drake was planning to do it. No, apparently getting someone knocked up was an acceptable way to insinuate yourself into the succession lineup, but murder wasn't. Dad was a real stickler for the rules.

Heh. *Whatever worked*. As long as it did. Then the method wouldn't matter.

He couldn't wait to show Dad the results. Have him accompany him to the crowning ceremony, then watch Fisher's daughters line up to marry him.

Watch his father bow before him.

Drake helped himself to more of the scallops scallopini they had, *ad nauseum,* every week. Things never changed around here—

But they were about to.

Because, come Hades or high tide, there was no way Rod was going to make it back to claim the throne.

Drake had hired JR to ensure it.

Chapter 9

TAP, TAP, TAP.

"Should we tell him, Maybelle?" The two sparrows shared their breakfast, huddled beneath Adele's weather vane in hopes of both avoiding the nasty weather that was rolling in with the clouds *and* finding out why that herring gull was back, this time tapping the outside of Valerie's window.

"No. I don't think so."

"But it's *her* window."

"I know."

"But then she'll find out we can talk."

Maybelle closed her eyes as a particularly blustery wind kicked up. "No—she'll find out *he* can talk."

"I don't understand you, Maybelle."

Tap, tap, tap.

"Do you remember Foghorn, Adele? My third mate?"

"The one with the big—"

"Uh huh." Maybelle's shudder had nothing to do with the weather. "Don't remind me. The day he lost that tail feather was the happiest day of my life."

"But what does that have to do with Valerie?"

"Well, Foggy always thought he knew what was best. The best place for bread crumbs, the right park bench for Fiddle Faddle…" The sparrows paused a moment to remember the lovely, buttery taste of their favorite treat. "The fastest way to cross Grove Street, where to get the plumpest sunflower seeds… everything. That male was an authority on everything."

"I still don't see—"

"Pay attention, Adele! Foggy thought he knew what was best and would never consider anything else, least of all what a female had to say or what she ought to know."

Tap, tap, tap.

"Those two males over there aren't planning to tell her the truth."

Adele gasped. "That sunflowers don't really grow in your stomach if you eat the seeds in their shells?"

Maybelle rolled her eyes. "No. Not that. They're not going to tell her she's a Mer."

"How do you know? You can't possibly hear anything. The air cooler is on, and they've shut all the windows."

"Oh… well… I might have overheard—"

"Maybelle Merriweather!" Adele's high-pitched chirp soared an octave. "You did *not* go over there and eavesdrop!"

"No, actually, I eave-sat. And a good thing, too, or we'd be telling Mr. Flying High there that he's beaking up the wrong window, and she won't learn the truth."

"This wouldn't have anything to do with that gull telling you to mind your own business when you followed him yesterday, would it?"

Maybelle fluffed her feathers, then set to preening them. Honestly, it was so blustery today, what with the wind tossing up all sorts of particles. And she'd just groomed herself.

"Of course not, Adele. And he didn't tell me to mind my own business. He said it wasn't any of my business.

Which, of course, is wrong since this is my street and we don't want any riffraff moving in."

She glared at the big, hulking gull. "Males! They think they're the gods' gift to females. And now he's got The Heir treating Valerie as if she were a featherhead..." Maybelle tsk-tsked. "No. We girls need to stick together, and she deserves to know what she's getting into."

Tap, tap, tap.

Val pulled the pillow over her head. Dingy-gray morning light was barely making its way through the vinyl blinds.

Tap, tap, tap.

She slammed her arms on top of the pillow, anchoring it to both sides of her head and wishing she had an A/C unit in her room to block out sound.

TAP, TAP, TAP.

Something was bound and determined to wake her up.

She fumbled with the blinds next to the head of her bed, feeling for the string to draw them.

"Hurry up, already, will you? We have to get out of here!"

She sat up and yanked the cord and found herself staring at that seagull, with its eyes and beak in a decidedly grumpy configuration, its wings half-spread, and the feathers on its back fluttering in the wind.

She looked behind it, expecting someone (okay, Rod—and she wasn't *hoping to*, just *expecting to* see him, and, no, she hadn't been dreaming about that kiss) to be there. But then she remembered she was on the second floor above the store, and the fire escape was off the other bedroom, the one where the guy who'd kissed her slept...

So who was doing the talking?

"Livingston?"

"Oh, Hades." The bird shook its head and resettled its wings on its back.

The bird had cursed. At her.

The bird could curse?

He did a two-step on the window ledge. "It's getting windy out here. Could you let me in, please?"

Let him in? A talking, *cognizant* seagull? Was he crazy?

No, actually, she thought she might be the crazy one.

The bird sighed and focused his eyes on her. "I can explain, Valerie."

The bird *was having a conversation with her.*

Even if she wasn't crazy for thinking that, her next action cemented the tenuous state of her sanity. She unlocked the window, allowing a gust of damp air laden with the perfect blend of strong coffee and banana-nut muffins from the bakery next door to waft in with the bird.

"I thought you were Rod," the bird said, hopping onto the bedside table.

"And I thought you were a trained mimic." She sat back on the mattress, a little too stunned to do more than stare at him. How could a seagull talk? She'd heard of talking parrots, macaws, canaries, but seagulls?

"Where is he? I've got news for him." Livingston hopped onto the dresser, leaving little wet webbed footprints on the veneer.

For some reason, the sight of those footprints released her from her stupor, and she glanced at her bedroom door. It was still closed. And locked. "I've got news for *you*, Livingston. You're not going anywhere until you tell me how you can talk."

"Air vibrating through nasal tubes is what the scientists have come up with." He flapped his wings once, gliding over to her door and cocking his head when he landed. "Can you let me out so I can speak with Rod? We don't have much time."

"Much time for what?"

"You'll find out if I don't talk to him. Open this door, already. We'll explain later." The gull hammered his beak against the luan door as if he were a woodpecker, chips of the thin veneer pinging off with each bill-strike.

"Hold on." She jumped out of bed, momentarily registering the fact that her ankle was back to one hundred percent—one of two odd things about the morning and she'd only just woken up—and turned the knob.

Livingston reached Rod's door faster than she'd thought possible, a mixture of half-flight and half-run. He barreled into the room, beak leading the way. "Rod! Get up! We've got trouble and we need to get moving!"

Still trying to process coherency and verbalizations in waterfowl, Val hadn't given a thought to the idea that maybe she shouldn't follow the bird in.

Rod slept in the nude.

And seemed very comfortable with that fact.

"Good morning, Valerie," he said, rising from his side to sitting, all appropriate muscles doing all appropriate actions which just seemed, well, so appropriate…

"Uh… well… uh…" Babbling, too, seemed appropriate.

"We don't have time for formalities!" Livingston zoomed around the room, grabbing Rod's discarded shorts—no boxers, she'd been right, followed by his shirt, dropping them on Rod's shoulders. "Throw some clothes on, grab your bag, and let's get moving, people!"

Rod scratched his head, rumpling the bed head he sported, which didn't do as much for her coherency as those flexing stomach muscles, and, er, other areas did for her libido.

"What are you squawking about, Livingston? And—" Rod pointed the red shirt at Val—"in front of her?"

"The catfish is out of the net, Rod. She knows I speak. I thought her window was yours. Shows what happens when you don't have enough time for proper reconnaissance. Nothing to be done about it now. Just be thankful she's on our side, but JR, he's definitely not, and he's definitely on his way."

"JR?"

Rod jumped to his feet, flipping his shirt over his shoulder, and stepping, commando, into the shorts so fast Val almost missed the gluteus-maximus show. Almost, but to her eternal happiness, not quite. The man didn't have one ounce of fat on him and those legs were *toned,* one fluid line of muscle from hip to ankle. He must work out for hours every day to keep his body in such amazing shape.

Rod threw on the T-shirt, swiped something from the dresser and shoved it into his pocket, then grabbed his duffel bag from beneath the foot of the bed, and zipped it closed. "You're sure it's him?"

"Absolutely. And he's working fast. Crows, jays, cowbirds… We need to make waves right now."

Rod yanked the zipper the final few inches, then headed for the door, grabbing Val's hand as he passed her. "Livingston's right, Valerie. Let's go."

Val slammed her other hand against the doorframe before Rod could pull her through it. "What do you mean, 'Let's go'? Go where? Who's JR? Why are we worried about him? And what's with a *coherent*, talking seagull?"

Rod exhaled and tugged her arm. "We don't have time for explanations now. Let's get going and I'll explain on the way."

"But—"

Livingston flew into her back, the top of his head between her shoulder blades, the wind from his flapping wings puffing her hair into her face. "Not now, Human. This concerns you, too. Get in your vehicle and head east. We'll talk while we're moving."

Thanks to the two of them, she barely had the chance to grab her bag, and then only because she'd put her purse and keys in it the night before. Apparently they'd stop for keys, but not for her to change clothes. Thank God she hadn't unpacked.

She rammed her feet into her shoes and they were out the door before she realized she hadn't even brushed her teeth. Ick.

Rod preceded her down the metal stairs, Livingston not cutting her any slack from behind. She slid once on the mist-slick stairs, stopping herself with a hand to Rod's shoulder. They ran to the alley behind the building, Val's Sentra the only car there other than Mom's van.

Rod slammed to a stop in front of her so quickly that she ran into his back—all hard and sculpted against her breasts and tummy, said body parts hitching from the exertion.

Yeah, exertion. Right. That wasn't why she was breathing so fast and she knew it.

"*That's* your method of conveyance?" The disbelief in Rod's voice was matched only by the scorn—enough to bring her out of her hormone-induced fog.

"It'll get you where you need to go." Wherever that was. A swirl of damp air swept a handful of hair into her face and she shoved it out of the way.

The gull and the man shared a sigh. "Fine," Rod said, "let's go."

Val ran to the driver's side and tossed her bag behind her seat. Rod jerked the passenger door open, tossing his bag in the back as well. Livingston flew in and Rod folded his legs between the seat and dashboard, looking like a human pretzel.

"Sorry. I wasn't expecting you to have to fit into my car." She leaned over the stick shift and reached for the seat adjustor beneath his thigh, behind his calf—his really toned, tight thigh and calf, which still had the warmth of sleep emanating from them.

Val took a deep breath then catching herself, shook her head and released the lever. Rod slid back, taking his scent with him.

Well, not all of it.

Val straightened, tucked her hair behind her ears, jammed the key in the ignition, and threw the car into reverse.

"Buckle up," she said, doing just that, then glancing in the rearview mirror, not really sure what she was expecting to see. With the tension these two had exhibited in the last ten minutes, she'd expected a herd of buffalo heading for her car, or at least a phalanx of tanks.

Not the bird—Livingston—with his wings outstretched across the top of the backseat, his beak aimed at the gray sky.

"Livingston? Are you okay?" Good God; had she *really* just asked a *bird* if he was okay? At some point she would have to try to process this otherworldly series of events.

And figure out why she was going along with it.

The gull turned his white head her way. "Just drive. I'll let you know if you have to make any tactical maneuvers."

Like that made any sense. But then, none of this did. Which was why she changed gears and did as he asked.

She was really hoping this was some strange dream, and that if she just went along with the program, she'd wake up to find herself in the apartment bedroom.

However, if it were only a dream, no way would she have cut it short by having Rod step into those shorts, so now she needed an explanation of why her reality had shifted dimensions...

"Did you find out why JR's here? What can he possibly hope to accomplish this far inland?" Rod turned to look back at Livingston, his shoulders obliterating any view she had out the side window.

And why she'd want any view other than him was beyond her.

"Watch it!" The bird let go of his hold and fell to the seat when she swerved around a dumpster on the turn. "We can't afford any accidents."

"Sorry." She was being chastised by a bird. There had to be something funny in that somewhere, but at the moment, it eluded her. And solidified the realization that this was actually happening.

Didn't explain it, just solidified it.

She shifted into third.

Livingston fluttered back to his perch, for lack of a better term, hanging from the back of the seat by his feather-tips. "I don't know yet, Rod, but after those ignition wires, I'm not discounting anything. He's definitely a bird of interest in my mind. Having him show up here just confirms that."

Bird of interest, ignition wires... Val was having a hard time trying to keep the car on the road while glancing between Rod's worried expression and Livingston's balancing act, not to mention checking out the windows to see what Livingston was looking for. Oh, and trying to process the whole talking-seagull thing.

"Who's JR?" she managed to slide into the conversation as she slid into fourth.

"An albatross," Rod answered.

"An albatross? Here? In Kansas? I'd say he's a bit lost." Someone's morning newspaper fluttered across her windshield, obscuring her view long enough for Livingston to comment on it.

"Watch the road," he admonished, which was just as wrong as him speaking. "And, lost? Not JR. He doesn't get lost. That's the trouble. When JR shows up, it's because he has a reason and the only reason for him to head this far inland is a reconnaissance mission of his own. I know for a fact he's not on The Council's payroll."

With the road clear ahead, if not the sky, Val adjusted the rearview mirror to look at the talking bird. "Okay, you guys are starting to freak me out. What are you? Some specialized branch of the FBI? CIA? What?"

Livingston shook his head. "I'm Chief Special Agent, ASA."

"ASA? Never heard of it." She looked at Rod.

"As well you shouldn't," he said, his eyes hooded—but not in the same way as they'd been during that kiss last night. Those lips that had been so pliant and urgent against hers now thinned to an almost invisible line—

"But you will," Livingston said. "Air Security Agency."

"Don't you mean the FAA?" She pulled her mind back on the conversation—with a bird!—and off the kissability of Rod's lips.

"No. ASA. I don't work for your government."

"You're a foreign operative? A spy? Oh, hell, what have you two gotten me into?" One of the tires hit a pothole when she half-turned to gape at him.

"Eyes on the road, Valerie." Livingston turned his attention back to the sky. The clouds were growing darker. "Technically, yes, I am a foreign operative. But not to you. And that's all the explanation you're getting from me until I know what's what." Livingston readjusted his hold on the seat.

"We need to know who he's working for, Rod. I've been over the lists of known anarchists and I can't come up with one. We've got the top wrasse working on it. They've studied those wires, the method of ignition planned, the locations they were stolen from, patterns of known movement among those on the list, and no one fits. It's got to be someone else, someone new. Someone who doesn't want you to take the throne."

"What?" Val yanked the car to the right, almost hitting Mr. Morris's 1957 Chevy, his pride and joy.

Rod grabbed the wheel, avoiding an accident at the last second. "Valerie, please. You must retain your composure."

"Retain my composure? Are you insane? Yes. Yes, I think you are." Val shoved the car into fifth and zipped onto the highway. "Anarchists? Throne? What throne? Who are you? *What* are you?"

"He's a prince, Valerie."

"Really? Whose? England's? Monaco's?" The porcelain god's? She *had* to be dreaming this.

Rod glared at the bird then turned to her. "While England's throne once sought to rival the territory of mine, today they don't compare. As for Monaco, it has acceptable beaches, but the buildings, overabundance of Humans, and many conveyances have ruined the shoreline."

She gaped at him.

"Watch it, Valerie," the bird—the bird!—said from the backseat. "You don't want to catch any flies with that open mouth."

Wake up, wake up, wake up.

She pinched herself.

Ouch. Dammit. She was awake.

"So you're really a prince? And I'm going along with the program as if heading off into the wild blue yonder with talking seagulls and royal princes is *normal*?"

"Valerie, we'll explain everything later. Right now we need to find a way to go faster. We'll never outrun JR in this." Rod patted her arm, and, amazingly, that settled her rattled nerves.

Until she realized what he'd said.

"Are you saying that an albatross—and I can't believe I'm even asking this question—can fly faster than a car?"

"He doesn't need to keep up with us," Livingston said from his regained position on the backseat. "Besides the operatives he's been amassing, he's able to find a meal miles away on the open ocean, so I'm sure he boned up on Rod's scent before embarking on this mission. This damp air is only helping matters, though I'd be surprised if he did anything but report on our progress."

"Report to whom?"

"That, my dear, is the fifty-thousand clam question. And once we know the answer to that, we'll know the threat."

"What threat?" She slowed down to veer around cattle that had escaped from their pasture and had decided to amble down the highway. Mr. Stromer had better check his fence line.

"If we knew why this was happening, we'd stand a chance of figuring out who's behind it. Until last evening, I was under the impression this was a simple recovery mission." Rod's fist thumped the seat.

"Recovery mission? Okay, now I'm totally lost." Val swiped a trembling hand across her forehead, brushing the hair that had adhered to the sudden perspiration. "Why don't we just go to the nearest police station and let them handle this? Or the embassy if you really are a prince." Or the Funny Farm for her...

"Oh, he's a prince all right," said Livingston. "You can count on that. As well as the fact that a lot of M—er, *people* are going to be upset if anything happens to him. And you."

She pinched herself again—just to check.

Still awake.

The blare of a semi's horn as it passed confirmed it.

She looked in the mirror. Yep, that most definitely was her. Behind the wheel of her old Sentra, barreling

down a two-lane highway with Rod and a talking seagull
as her passengers, toothpaste and a cup of coffee only a
wish on the horizon.

Chapter 10

"OH MY, MAYBELLE. WHAT SHOULD WE DO?" ADELE DID A perfect pirouette on the ledge as Valerie and The Heir ran from the apartment.

With that *seagull* close behind.

"I'll tell you what we're going to do, Adele." Maybelle scanned the sky. "Do you see those cowbirds?"

"The ones over by the playground—"

"No." She swept a wing over Adele's head, just brushing the top feathers, then pointed her wing to the west. "Those. On the church steeple."

Adele followed the direction. "Oh. Thoooose." She twitched her head so her feathers would fall back into place. "What about them?"

"They work for that albatross. He's behind this."

"Maybelle, you have such an imagination. Cowbirds don't work for albatrosses. They're an entirely different class of avian."

"I'm telling you, Adele, those cowbirds are working for him. He's running this show and we need to do something about it. I don't know why an albatross is gunning for The Heir, but he is not going to succeed on my watch."

"So what are you going to do?"

"I'm going to stop those cowbirds." Maybelle girded herself for battle by tucking her wings tight against her sides and puffing out that plump breast she was so proud of. "And you're going to help me."

Adele looked a little green around the gullet. "Me?" Her chirp sounded more like a chickadee's than a sparrow's.

"Yes. You."

"How in the sky am I going to stop a cowbird?" That green color deepened.

Maybelle took pity on her friend and drew her under her wing. "Come now, Adele. Didn't we just have a discussion about males and their strutting? It's easy. Just turn on your charm."

Adele wasn't so sure about that. Ever since Seymour had flown to that Big Meadow In The Sky, her charm had gone into hibernation.

High-octane silence filled the car as Val pushed the pedal to the rusting metal floorboard and sped east. She'd had to turn off the air-conditioning to get the car up to speed, but luckily, the gray skies kept the temperature down. Now if only the approaching storm would hold off until they got to wherever they were heading, they'd be fine.

She hoped. She wanted to ask Rod and Livingston exactly where "east" they were headed, but between the open windows making conversation difficult and the fact that both of them were so intent on staring at the sky, with an occasional, "Do you see anything?" she wasn't sure she wanted to know what they were talking about.

It was all too much to process. Talking birds, claims of royalty, secret government agencies, reconnaissance missions, a throne... Throw in an inheritance, back taxes, a city developer, and it was as if her life had turned into a surrealistic version of *It's a Mad, Mad, Mad, Mad World*—minus the hilarity of Buddy Hackett and Ethel Merman.

But a person could only be expected to take so much on faith and Rod had gone beyond the limit of crazy she was comfortable with.

"Rod," she asked during a lull of "Do you see?"s. "Will you please tell me what's going on? Where we're headed? *Why* we're headed? Why I'm in a car with a prince?"

Rod swung his gaze from the window. He exhaled, his chest expanding in a way guaranteed to make her forget her own name, not to mention the questions she'd asked him.

But she wasn't going to allow herself to be distracted. Good looks and charm—and a crown—only got someone so far. Right now she needed to know she wasn't heading toward some hostage situation or international incident.

And *why*. Why her? All she wanted was to collect the inheritance so she could save her store.

"This won't be easy for you to understand, Valerie."

"Tell me something I don't know."

"He's got a lot to tell you that you don't know," said Livingston, with what she would swear was sarcasm, as he ran from one side of the backseat to the other, beak skyward, "but now's not exactly the right time for it. Albatross, remember? Just go east."

"I remember, Livingston. That doesn't necessarily mean I believe it. Besides, I have more important concerns on my mind."

"Nothing's more important than this right now, trust me."

A talking bird? She was supposed to trust a talking bird?

"Valerie," Rod, a voice of reason, answered. "There's a lot you need to know, but most of it you won't believe without proof. When we get to our destination, I promise to explain everything."

"Does this have anything to do with my inheritance, or was that all a story to get me to come on this mission for God-knows-whatever reason?" She should have taken a closer look at those papers.

"Indirectly, yes, it does have to do with the inheritance," Rod answered.

"Indirectly? How indirect are we talking?"

"Direct enough that if this albatross succeeds," quipped Livingston, "you won't be able to touch the inheritance. My guess is you won't be able to touch much of anything."

Words she did not find comforting.

"What if I don't want to go to this mysterious destination of yours?" she bluffed. She was going, but only to get her inheritance. She hadn't signed on for albatrosses, and surely she didn't need Rod with her to claim the inheritance. "You can just tell me the lawyer's name and I'll contact him myself. I'm perfectly capable of getting to New Jersey without you guys. Then you can take your albatross wherever it is you want to go and none of this will affect me."

"No can do, Valerie," the bird said through tight lips—er, beak. Which was an interesting ability.

"Sure I can—"

"Valerie, he's right." Rod touched her arm again. "Once we get to the beach, The Council will administer your inheritance. It's all been spelled out. So you're along for the ride."

As long as she wasn't being taken for one…

Wait a minute.

"The beach? You mean the beach town where they're going to meet us, right? Not the actual beach?"

"No, our rendezvous point is on the beach behind my brother's home. He has… facilities there for such a meeting. Is that a problem?"

For her? Yes. Big one. "Okay, what's going on? This isn't funny. I've got taxes to worry about and you guys are taking me on a wild-goose chase."

"Al-ba-tross, Valerie. Not a goose," Livingston said from the backseat. "Albatross are bigger. More cunning."

"*Someone's* trying to be cunning. What? Are you guys working for the developer? I've already told him I'm not selling. Is this the next tactic? Trying to make me late with the taxes by getting me out of town?"

"Valerie, I have no idea what you're talking about," Rod said, all insulted.

She was insulted. "Look, I don't like being made a fool of. I'll find some way to come up with the tax money. I'm not selling to him, especially after he's pulled this, and that's final. You and your trained bird can tell your boss to take a hike. I'm turning this car around right now so you two can go find some other patsy to play your prank on."

"Prank?" Rod almost growled the word as he grabbed the steering wheel. "I am not playing a prank on you, Valerie. I don't play pranks. I came here to tell you about your inheritance and bring you to it."

"On the beach."

"Yes."

"See? That's where this falls apart, Rod." She wrenched the wheel out of his grasp and turned them back the way they'd come, jamming the stick shift into the correct gear. "Even with the seagull, I was onboard with this whole thing, but next time, you should do your homework before you try something like this."

"Something like what? I have no idea what you're talking about."

"Fine. Here's the problem with this scenario." She jerked her head to face him. "I can't go to the beach."

"Why not? It's not that hard to get to."

The sarcasm came from the bird, so she threw it right back at him. "Because, Livingston, I'm allergic to the ocean. *Deathly* allergic."

Chapter 11

ALLERGIC?

Rod didn't think he'd heard correctly, but Livingston's gaping beak told him he had.

How was he supposed to fulfill The Prophecy and claim the throne if she was allergic to the ocean?

There had to be a mistake. If she was allergic, then she couldn't possibly be Lance's daughter and The Council would have been wrong.

He looked at Livingston. "The gods—they'd never allow a mistake of such proportions to continue."

"Oh no? Talk to a platypus about that," Livingston mumbled.

Yes, the ground shook. Rod doubted Humans felt that little wiggle, but he knew what it was. And since they'd "commented" on Livingston's platypus statement and not his, he had to be right. Which meant The Council was. Which meant she was Lance's daughter.

He waited.

No rumble.

"Valerie, you aren't allergic to the ocean."

"Yes, I am."

"No, you're not."

She brushed her hair off her forehead, but the curls fell back in place. "Rod, we could play this game all day, but it's not going to prove either of us right."

"Exactly. Which is why this conversation must wait until we're at the ocean. Then you'll see."

"You mean, then I'll puff up like a balloon, my airway will close, and I'll keel over at your feet."

"That won't happen." One reason being that he wouldn't have feet.

"And I should believe you, why?"

"Oh, for gods' sake," Livingston muttered. "Humans."

Rod echoed the sentiment, but couldn't say it or he'd lose her for good. "Valerie, you aren't allergic to the ocean. The farthest thing from it, actually."

"Which is still not proving you right."

"*Exactly*." Livingston shoved his beak between their seats, his head flopping from one to the other. "So how about we turn around and continue our journey, *then* you two can play truth-or-dare to your hearts' content. In case you've both forgotten, there's an albatross to worry about."

Rod hadn't forgotten. And that, more than anything else, determined what he was about to do. He had to convince her. She had to want to go with him, and he wasn't about to spend the next day or so arguing with her.

Rod pulled the diamond decanter from his pocket and stood it on the dashboard.

"Uh, Rod?" Livingston's beak dropped open again. "What… what do you think you're doing?"

Valerie looked between the two of them then glanced at the bottle.

The car slowed a little. Just a little, but enough to tell him he'd gotten her attention.

"What's that?" Her blue eyes rounded when she looked at him.

Livingston gulped. "Are you sure you want to do this?"

No, he wasn't sure. This hadn't been part of the plan, but a High Councilman did need to react to situations beyond his control and this, surely, had to qualify as one of them.

"It's a diamond."

"You had that in your pocket? What's in the other one, rubies?"

Rod pulled out a stack of currency. "Not rubies."

"Uh, Valerie?" Livingston had a chuckle in his voice. "You want to turn around now?"

"Hold on." She wasn't doing this while she was driving. The surprise alone could make her have an accident. She veered onto the shoulder of the road as a few raindrops bounced onto the windshield.

"Oh come on! Don't stop! Turn around! We need to get going!" Livingston screeched.

She really didn't like that sound.

"Livingston, I'm not risking my life for this." She reached out for the diamond. "May I?"

Rod swept his hand toward it. "Be my guest."

It was heavy, heavier than she would have thought, with perfectly formed facets colored by the amber liquid inside.

"Diamonds don't contain liquid." Which he'd have to know that she'd know, so where was he going with this?

"This diamond does, Valerie," the bird answered, replacing Sarcasm with Smug in his repertoire.

"It's rare," Rod said, *un*-smugly. Nicely. The bird should take lessons. "It's called The Pollux Diamond and was formed this way naturally. There's only ever been one other like it—"

"The Castor Diamond," Livingston interrupted, hopping up and down in the middle of the backseat. "Get it? Castor and Pollux? Twins who went on to become constellations?"

She glanced at him over her shoulder. "I know my Greek mythology, Livingston."

"Oh it's not mythology—"

"Livingston, let's stay on topic, shall we?"

If Rod weren't royalty, he was giving a darn good impression with that haughty tone and look-down-his-nose glare at the bird.

"This diamond is yours, Valerie, if you—"

"What?" Livingston screeched. Again. "That's not hers. It's not anywhere even close to being hers. It belongs in The Vault. It was only given to you—"

"Exactly. It was given to me. And when we return, I'll be in the position of doing with it what I want, so, yes, Valerie, consider this diamond yours if you come to the beach with us."

"What about my inheritance?"

"That's real, Valerie. I'm not lying to you, but even if you don't believe me, you'll have that diamond for your troubles. Is that enough incentive to come with us?"

Val didn't know what to think. *If* that thing was a diamond, then, yes, inheritance or not, she'd be able to save Mom's shop. And hell, *with* it, she wouldn't have to touch one red cent of "Dad's" money, which made it all the more attractive. "But people don't carry rare, bottle-like diamonds in their pockets."

"She needs more proof, Rod." Livingston stretched his wings across the back. "And make it snappy, if you would. That albatross is still on our tail."

"Right. Here you go, Valerie. Proof that this journey is not a waste of your time, nor am I playing a prank on you." Rod dragged the diamond along the top of the windshield. It screeched—though not as annoyingly as Livingston—and left a nasty gash in the glass.

Diamonds could cut glass.

Holy mackerel. "Whoa. It really is a diamond." She would have liked to keep the awed desperation from her voice, but here was the answer to her troubles and she wasn't blasé enough to pretend it wasn't.

"Told you." Livingston did an encore presentation of Smug. "Now can we please get back to outrunning JR?"

Okay, she was onboard for the rest of the trip. "Fine, but I need to make a phone call. I'm assuming you won't have any objections to that, Livingston?" She didn't wait for his acceptance but was subjected to him turning his beak to the side so that red dot "stared" at her and sighing so heavily that she could guess what he'd had for breakfast.

"I have to let Tricia know I'm gone so she can reschedule a few appointments and let the electrician in today." Not to mention, one didn't hop in a car with a virtual stranger—and his talking bird—and thousands, if not millions, of dollars worth of diamond, as well as a stack of hundreds, and head east without a word or a phone call to anyone.

"Yeah, sure. Whatever. Just let's get going already, will you?"

"Hold that thought and hand me my bag."

"Sure. Fine. Whatever. Let's just—oh, shit!" Livingston hopped through the seats and jumped onto the stick shift, his feathers hitting Val in the face.

"Incoming!" he screeched in all his seagull glory. "Turn us around! Get this thing moving! Now!"

The "oh shit" screech was effective. Val fumbled with the clutch after Rod plucked the bird out of the way. Jamming the stick shift into first, she tore back onto the road with a spray of gravel, grinding the gears as she forced the transmission into a quick shift to second.

Livingston flew back to the rear seat, leaving feathers scattered in her lap and one sticking to her bottom lip. Val overcompensated for the heavy wrench of the steering wheel to the left with a sudden swerve to the right, spitting the feather out as she tried to look out her window.

Incoming what?

A huge *splat!* on her windshield answered that question.

What looked to have once been a fish obscured her view and left a lovely spider vein across the glass to match the diamond's. Val rolled up her window, then groped for the windshield wiper while Livingston screeched from behind, giving a whole new meaning to the term "backseat driver."

"Go left!"

Rod twisted the wheel that way before Val had a chance to process the directive. Another fish ricocheted off her side mirror.

"Right!"

Rod turned the wheel right as Val finally switched the windshield wipers on. The next fish bounced off the fender, followed by the mess of the first one.

"What's going on?" Val hollered.

"He's trying to run us off the road." Rod's voice was tight. "We're too open. We need cover."

"No way," Livingston directed. "If we stop, we'll never get rid of him. You're going to have to do some fancy driving, Valerie."

"I'm trying," she muttered, zigzagging the car back and forth across the road. Thank God there was no oncoming traffic, a plus to living in the middle of nowhere that she'd never appreciated until right now, but she wouldn't mind a tunnel or two.

"How long can he keep this up?" she asked, dodging yet another fish bomb.

"JR can fly for hours, but I can't imagine he's got too many missiles left. There's a limit to how many he can carry." Livingston hopped from one side of the backseat to the other, his beak pointed northward, scanning the sky.

"You've done studies?" Rod asked while she veered farther right, dodging another pothole and a few dozen cornstalks that had probably been plowed into the road by teenagers on a late-night joyride.

Stupid kids… didn't they know she'd have to *dodge an angry albatross*?

"Not studies. Personal experience." Livingston glanced out the back window. "He's got two, maybe three left."

Number five hit the road ahead of them, jarring the car as the tire flattened it into the asphalt.

"Son of a Mer!" Rod said. "We're sitting ducks on this road."

"Son-of-a-what?" Val asked, her fingers wrapped so tightly around the steering wheel they were starting to ache. "What do you suggest I do? Drive through the corn?"

Rod opened his mouth, but Val cut him off. "No way. The shocks could never take it, plus I'm not about to plow through someone's livelihood. I'll see how fast I can get her to go. Maybe we can outrun him. At the very least, his aim should be off."

Wait. Had she *really* just said that?

She worked the car into fifth gear… and another fish bounced off the trunk.

"One left, if he had the energy," Livingston reported from the backseat.

Val maneuvered the car back and forth across the yellow lines in no discernible pattern, hoping to prevent her windshield from cracking. Well, any more than it had. That spider vein had meandered across her line of vision.

"I can't see him anymore." Livingston sounded out of breath. "Rod? You?"

Rod peered through the raindrops on the windshield, then out his side window. "No. Too many clouds, but that doesn't mean he's not there. We have to find some way to lose him until we get to the airport."

"Um… Rod." Livingston hopped up to resume his feather-tip hanging position beneath the back window. "About that. I'm not so sure we want to go that route."

"I thought the way a crow flies is the quickest way to the coast?"

"Crow, yes—especially if it's being chased by an albatross. But people…? JR's going to expect it, and with his state of mind these days, who knows what he'll do?"

"State of mind? What are you talking about?" Val interrupted. Could an albatross even *have* a state of mind? Another feathered ability she didn't want to contemplate.

Rod leaned toward her to look out the driver's side window. "JR hasn't been himself since he lost his mate in a trawling incident."

"Trawling incident?" She tried not to take her eyes off the road to look at him—and was proud of herself for *almost* succeeding.

The pothole she hit signified she hadn't *completely* succeeded. What did municipalities do with tax money anyway? Road repair didn't seem to be on that list. It burned her up that the money she was racing off to get wouldn't even benefit her.

"After that incident, JR snapped," Livingston said. "Like a sailboat mast in a hurricane. Now he does whatever he feels like doing and doesn't care who he hurts."

"He's a mercenary?" Val asked, dodging another pothole. And what was wrong with that question?

Rod, fully upright in his seat (damn), covered her hand on the stick shift (yay) and nodded. "Among other things, Valerie. He's smart, he's wily, and he's got nothing to live for. A dangerous combination."

"Which is why we can't put anything past him." Livingston huffed, dropping back onto the seat. "He set up an impressive network in a short time. I've got to come up with a way to outwit him." The bird started pacing across the backseat and muttering to himself.

Biologists, bird experts, Darwin… they'd all have a field day with what was happening in her backseat. Her? Not so much.

You know, she'd come home to escape the drama. To stop running from a situation the minute it wasn't to her liking. To settle down and get her life in order.

Some order. A talking seagull, an angry albatross, and a prince—of all things—who could kiss like nobody's business.

Somehow this settling down thing wasn't *quite* what she'd expected it to be.

Chapter 12

"HELLO, BOYS." MAYBELLE TRIED TO PUT AS MUCH TAIL action into her swagger as her sparrow's body would allow. At times like this, she wouldn't mind being as svelte as those doves who'd come in from out of town last year for a Human wedding.

The cowbirds stopped pacing along the church's verdigris roof. "Ma'am?"

She hated that. Made her feel like someone's doting old auntie.

"Oh, please," she twittered, affecting the same pose she'd seen that pristine (prissy, actually) dove do that had gotten all the males fluttering after her. "Do call me Maybelle." She added a little blinking action, going for the dumb and wide-eyed look—also courtesy of that dove.

Either she'd done it right, or these cowbirds hadn't seen a female in, like, forever. One of the cow-boys strutted past her, leaving the package he'd been guarding unattended.

Success.

"Hello there, Maybelle," said the avian, "you're looking quite pretty. Did you just moult?"

Maybelle restrained herself from laughing. Moult. Sheesh. No wonder this guy was ripe for her ploy—no way was he getting any action with that line.

But she played along, hoping the other would find her just as irresistible.

Oh, not for anything *remotely* physical. No, she needed the cowbirds distracted from the bags of metal tacks they were guarding so Adele could switch them out with the replacement washers and nuts they'd collected. She knew what sharp metal would do to car tires. Valerie and the Mer prince didn't deserve that and the albatross didn't deserve to win.

And wouldn't *she* be the heroine when the girls on the park bench heard about this? They'd be a-twitter for seasons to come.

Rod couldn't believe JR had tried to run them off the road. Oh, he understood the anger well enough. Two Mers had gotten caught in the net along with Margot, JR's mate, and The Council hadn't been able to save them either. He'd been there that day but hadn't done anything to merit the bird's revenge.

Fishing boats were a risk; every Mer knew that. Just as they knew what to do if the unthinkable happened and they were captured. They turned into dolphins.

Besides the obvious benefit of Humans never learning of Mers' existence, that mandate had curtailed Human fishing practices over the years, making fishing more dolphin-safe and waters more Mer-friendly. But, sadly, it hadn't enabled those Mers who'd been trapped in the net that day to free themselves. It also hadn't helped the Mers who'd only been able to tread water and watch in horrified silence.

JR hadn't been silent. He'd brayed until he'd gone hoarse, but The Council hadn't intervened. Humans could not learn of their existence, or the entire Mer world would be at risk.

Rod looked at Valerie. She was going to have a tough time believing him, which was why he couldn't tell her the truth until he had proof. She'd never believe anything about Atlantis or Mers. Even with the "carat" he'd dangled before her, he could see her abandoning them if he began spouting mythology as fact. With JR on their tails, he couldn't afford to lose her. Gods knew what that bird had planned.

Or, *did they*?

According to common theory, the gods knew all. Would they condone something like this?

Rod couldn't imagine why. Unless they didn't want him on the throne.

A tremor shook the road. Valerie compensated with a quick jerk of the steering wheel and a muttered curse.

Rod cursed, too, but for an entirely different reason. Was that it? Had he proved himself unworthy with that stupid dare so they'd decided to give Reel the throne?

No. Not Reel. Drake.

Drake?

He didn't believe it. *Couldn't* believe it. Sure as Hades didn't *want* to believe it. He'd spent every day— every damn day—making up for his lapse in judgment. Drake, on the other fin, made more bonefish-headed decisions in a single day than he had in his entire thirty-four *selinos*—even if none were as grave as the exposure Rod had risked. Still, would the gods punish him, and their world, for one stupid mistake?

And why did Valerie think she was allergic to the ocean?

"What's that truck doing?" Livingston dove from the back window to the dash, interrupting Rod's train of thought, thank the gods.

Rod looked out the window—and wasn't sure he should be thanking them.

A truck zigzagged haphazardly all over the road, the sound of squealing tires reaching them from twelve leagues away. "You might want to do something to catch his attention, Valerie."

"Right." She pressed the horn and the strident tone tore across his nerves. What he wouldn't give to be under the sea again where sounds were as soft against the waves' caress as her skin had been beneath his fingers.

Soon. This would all be over soon.

The truck fishtailed again, the back end swerving almost out of control. The tempo of the rain increased.

Shit! Maybe this would be over *too* soon. Matter of fact, it looked as if it was on course straight at them.

Valerie blasted the horn again, but the truck didn't change lanes. And then Rod saw why.

Birds—dozens of them—of every color and size covered the truck's windshield, their flapping wings obscuring the driver's view.

"JR." Rod knew the albatross had staged this as sure as he knew the tidal schedule. "Valerie, we have to get off the road."

"I know."

"Now."

"I know."

"So why aren't you?"

"There's a fence. You want me to go through it?"

"It's bound to be softer than the grill of that vehicle."

The truck was mere car-lengths away, and the noise from the flock drowned out hope of further conversation. Damn JR. That bird was too smart to be on the opposition's side.

Who was he working for? The stakes had to be high for him to go after The Heir.

Valerie shifted gears and the car slowed. She turned the wheel to the left, angling toward the far side of the road.

The truck's brakes peeled like a harpooned whale as the driver applied them harder, tires still squealing, the smell of burning rubber permeating the air. The monstrous piece of machinery swerved across the road, its front lights aiming right for them.

"Valerie—"

"I see it." She slowed the car even more. "Come on, come on…"

The truck filled the width of the road, from the cab to the swerving cargo load behind it. There was no way around it.

"Valerie, are you sure—"

"No, I'm not. Do you have any other ideas? I'm all ears."

Sweat glistened on her skin as she worked the pedals, keeping the car opposite the truck's path. No, he didn't have any other ideas. He had no ideas. He'd never driven one of these vehicles.

Livingston flew to the backseat and shoved his head beneath his wing.

Rod braced his arms between the dash and her seat. "You can do it," he murmured.

She *had* to do it. The consequences of defeat were too horrific to contemplate. Both from a personal standpoint and a dynastic one.

"Thanks," she muttered, but he didn't know if it was in appreciation or sarcasm.

Then, it didn't matter.

The roar of the birds crested, the truck's brakes screeching above the din as it came upon them. Dozens of bird eyes honed in on them behind pointed, sharp beaks.

Valerie slammed the stick shift into a new gear with a grunt, her feet stomping the pedals, and she wrenched the wheel so the car jerked to the side. The engine protested, and the smell of the burning rubber filled the interior, but Valerie held the turn as the truck thundered past them so close Rod could feel their little vehicle shudder, every part of it straining to cling to the road and avoid the draft of the truck's momentum.

The car fishtailed to the right, the back end skidding around with a squeal—or was that Livingston?—so they ended up facing the back end of the departing truck and Valerie brought it to a stop on the yellow lines. Gods, they'd almost...

No. He wouldn't go there.

"You did it!" Adrenaline surging, Rod ripped off his seat belt and, without thinking about it, kissed her, sliding his hands into that glorious tumble of blonde hair, pressing her face to his, crushing her lips, plastering himself against her as she opened her mouth beneath his. Their tongues clung, teeth *clink*ing, her fingers gripping his shoulders, and Rod angled her head to taste every corner of her mouth, to slant his lips over hers, taking her small cries inside.

He sank against her, sliding a hand down her slim back, his other hand seeking the release on her seat belt. He wanted her closer, needed to feel every inch of her against him, to know she was alive. That he was.

The belt clicked and Valerie slid in her seat, her lips not releasing his, her tongue still where he wanted it, where he could taste it, her, when a nasal cough came from the backseat.

Livingston.

Ah Zeus, they weren't alone.

Rod gentled the kiss, his hand stroking her cheek, his breath slowing just a little.

Valerie went slack at the gull's second cough. Her eyes opened—right there, before him, so turbulent and languorous. He would've sworn the two emotions could not possibly share the same space, but there they were.

"Um…"

He kissed her again quickly, then dropped a soft peck on her nose. "Don't say anything. You did a great job. You saved us."

"Yeah. Not bad for an amateur." Livingston cleared his throat before wriggling beneath them to hop onto the dashboard. "You gotta give the other guy credit for that maneuver, too. He was trying to stop."

Rod didn't want to stop staring at her. She hadn't looked away. Her tongue made a quick appearance to dart over her lips—swollen and moist from his kiss—and all he could think about was kissing her again.

"So? What are you waiting for?" Livingston gave up coughing to tap his beak on the dashboard. "Let's get moving, people!"

Right. Moving. They had an agenda.

Too bad it didn't match his personal one.

Valerie's cheeks turned pink. She fumbled with the belt and averted her eyes, but only to point at the windshield. "Oh no! The truck driver—he's going to crash!"

"Valerie, we've got more important problems to worry about." Livingston shrugged and hopped onto the stick shift, forcing Rod to resume his seat. "Let's go."

"'*Go*'? How can you say that?" She glared at Livingston. "It's not the driver's fault a flock of birds showed up. It could even be argued that it's ours." She put the car in gear and it lurched forward. "The least we can do is be on hand to pull him out of the wreck."

Compassion, spunk, and an ability to focus on the matter at hand; you had to love a woman like that.

Love a woman like that? Rod sat back in his seat and shook his head, staring at the raindrops that plunked rhythmically against the window. No. He couldn't. It was just a figure of speech.

Livingston hopped between them again and stretched his bill toward the window. "Uh, Valerie?"

"I see it."

So did Rod. About four leagues down the road, the truck was, surprisingly, still upright with the cloud of birds still hovering above it...

No, not above it.

In front of it.

The birds had moved away, in unison, from the truck.

One of the first things Rod had learned in Ornithology 101 was that different species had no instinctual compatibility to flock together. That's what made this maneuver a surprising and impressive event.

Until he realized the *reason* for the impressive event was even more surprising.

The flock was now zooming straight at them.

Chapter 13

"ROD MADE CONTACT." THE LOW-FLYING STORM PETREL gasped the words as it plowed onto the surface of the Caribbean with enough splash to alert the Humans strolling along the quay.

Drake had chosen this place because it wasn't overly populated with Humans, but, just like everything else with this mission, it wasn't working out as he'd planned.

Uttering a quick "Damn," Drake dove beneath the waves, dragging the bird by the foot through the ripples until they were under the pier.

Gods, he was sick of this. Bad enough he had to risk an approach to the shore in daytime, but to hear exactly what he'd told those incompetents he didn't want to hear was a huge pain in his tail.

Rod was with her. Had met her. Son of a Mer, that shouldn't have happened. JR was supposed to have arranged for her to be missing when Rod got there.

"What happened?" He shook the bird's foot, demanding an answer.

The thing looked at him with eyes like a flounder.

Oh, Hades, he was drowning him. That wouldn't do. He needed answers. Then perhaps he'd send a message to the albatross he'd hired to take care of his problem. JR was a little too sure of himself.

Drake released his grip on the bird's leg and followed as it rose to the surface, tucking his tail as close to vertical as possible. He didn't need some nosy Human to wonder what he was doing beneath the pier and come investigate. Luckily, the sun glinting through the crystal-clear water onto his scales made his tail almost invisible to the Human eye.

"What happened?"

The bird gulped in air, back-paddling so fast he was in danger of creating his own whirlpool and dragging himself under again.

Drake splashed water over the petrel's beak to calm him down. "Talk."

The bird, eyes wide, beak open and panting, ruffled his feathers while scanning the area under the pier. "The Heir arrived at the Hybrid's dwelling yesterday—"

"Yesterday! This happened yesterday? Why am I only finding out about it now?"

The bird's eyes narrowed and his chest puffed as he stilled his ruffling feathers, drifting in the small rise and fall of the waves' back draft when they hit the pier's pylons. "Sir, you hired the best air-messaging firm in the skies. Our orders were to report what we learned from your contact. The first communiqué was delivered only hours ago. No other firm could have relayed the information so many miles so quickly."

Drake swatted a young parrotfish that zoomed around the pylon, too inquisitive for his own good. Gods damn it. What was JR up to? Why hadn't he sent word immediately? What in Hades was going on inland?

He hated being this far away. Hated that it was all happening so far from the coastline—hated that it was happening at all.

He'd been *this* close to staging that "accidental" quake for Rod's trench survey. He'd swum around like a mad-Mer to hide the Human explosive devices he'd accumulated over the last *selino* since Reel had left, stooping to becoming a salvager for hire so he could pay a rogue mako to guard them.

It should have been so easy. The Heir and one tiny avalanche in a narrow trench.

But some plankton, wanting to be a big shot, told The Council about the bomb. Then they'd found *her,* and Rod had been summoned to Council Chambers. That had been the end of the survey, and Drake had had to come up with Plan B.

And now, Plan B looked to be in the throes of falling apart around him.

"JR said to tell you he has it under control and not to worry."

Not to worry? Easy for JR to say. The albatross didn't have a care in the world. Some wondered if anything got to him anymore, if he lived for anything other than the next job.

Drake didn't care. All he cared about was making sure JR didn't fuck up *this* job.

He wanted it over with. This was his one shot. If Rod returned with that Hybrid, Drake's chances of taking over the throne were gone.

He had to find some way to keep The Heir and The Hybrid from returning.

Chapter 14

THE FLOCK OF BIRDS WAS ALMOST UPON THEM.

"Retreat!" Livingston ordered.

"Haaaaaaaaaang ooooooooon!" Val slammed on the brakes.

Again.

She downshifted.

Again.

She wrenched the wheel.

Again.

And prayed—again—that the car wouldn't roll.

The car didn't, but Livingston unfortunately did— across the backseat, into the door, then onto the floor, landing with an "oomph," while Rod smashed against his door and the force of the turn threw her practically horizontal across his lap.

Any other time…

Rod pushed her upright, bracing himself against her seat and the dash, the car teetering on two tires, gears screaming, and she compensated by hauling the steering wheel back the other way.

Livingston took another tumble to the opposite side of the backseat, a nasty *thump* accompanying the moment when the car straightened out.

"They're coming," Rod said, looking out the rear window.

"So is another car," Val said, looking out the front one. She changed gears, and the car jumped forward.

Livingston landed with a *splat* and shook his head. "I knew I should have retired after that typhoon recovery mission," he muttered, settling back on the seat.

"You might want to buckle up, Livingston," she said, trying to get the car to maximum speed—in her own lane. That other car was approaching fast.

"With what?" Livingston griped. "If I put that lap thing across me, I'm going to end up looking like roadkill. No thank you. You just drive straight and I'm good."

"Better to look like roadkill than be it." Truer words were never spoken. Val took a deep breath and focused on preventing the roadkill as the other car drew closer. "How's our pack of bloodhounds, Rod?"

"Peregrine in the lead, godsdammit! We're not going to outrun him. Not in this."

"Hey, I just outmaneuvered a tractor trailer. I'll give that peregrine my best shot. I was a cab driver at one point." One job among many. "Trust me, I can outmaneuver a lot of things, and they can only keep that speed for so long."

A peregrine. *Now* she was dealing with peregrines—the odd, ironic part being that she'd accepted Rod's word at face value. Not one "you're kidding!" in sight.

"Here he comes." Livingston popped back onto his webbed feet, tap-dancing across the seat. "Son of a Sandpiper, there are two of them! Get ready for more fancy driving. I'm going to wedge myself under your seat and keep an eye out the back. You take the front, Rod."

"I'm on it." Rod leaned forward, resting his forearm on the dash. His shirt stretched tight across the vee of his back, slipping out of his waistband and distracting Val for way longer than she had, as the oncoming car blared its horn and whizzed past them.

The road. Right.

"One's approaching from the north at forty-five knots, the other from the northeast, thirty knots."

"Knots? What are knots?" Val leaned over the steering wheel, not seeing what Rod did in the cloudy sky. "Where are they?"

"Valerie, knots are a nautical term. Slightly slower than your miles per hour," Livingston piped up from somewhere under Rod's glorious gluteus—something she didn't need to think about right then. "Do you see anything, Rod?"

"Portside, coming low. They're packing." Rod's voice was low, almost a growl as his gaze slid across her.

Val glanced out the window then wished she hadn't. Packing. As in, carrying what looked to be something feathery and limp in their talons. This was not going to be pretty.

"Get ready to slam on the brakes." Rod sat back.

"Brakes?" At this speed, the car would spin out, and having already done its lifelong quotient of Indy driving today, that probably wasn't a good idea. She'd been a cabby, not a stunt driver.

Rod braced his hands on the dashboard. "You wedged in, Livingston?"

"As well as possible. How much longer?"

Rod leaned over as far as the belt would allow, which, in her small car, was pretty darn close. "Twenty seconds."

"Okay, Valerie." It felt weird to be taking directions from a voice beneath Rod's tush. Not that there was anything odd about this situation to begin with.

"… to let them fly past."

"What?" She shook her head. *Mind off his butt, Val*.

"Fish, woman, weren't you listening?"

"Livingston—" Rod's interjection was harsh.

"Right. My apologies. What we need you to do, Valerie, is slow down at the last possible second. Apply as much pressure to the brakes as you can without spinning us so the peregrines miscalculate. Their missiles tend to be other avians, which are more dangerous than JR's small fish. Got it?"

"Yeah." She exhaled. She so did not want to be doing this. But then, she wasn't exactly into cleaning roadkill—airkill?—off her roof either.

"Ten." Rod braced his palms against the dash.

Val scanned the road ahead. No more cars, thank God.

"Nine… eight…"

Val swiped her palm against her side, wrapping the fingers of her left hand around the steering wheel.

"Seven… six…"

She then dried her right hand on the other side of her shirt and curled her hand over the stick shift.

"Five… four…"

She inhaled.

"Three…two…"

"Now!" Livingston screeched.

Wanting to close her eyes, amazed she was going to do this yet again, and *still* hating that screech, Val took her foot off the gas, stepped on the clutch, swung the car out of gear, and slammed on the brakes.

Two slate-blue projectiles shot inches above the hood of the car, whatever it was they were carrying missing them by a hair's breadth.

"Go go go go go!" Livingston roared.

A seagull could roar? Val shook it off, reversed everything she'd just done and forced the protesting engine back to work.

But peregrines could turn on a dime and they weren't known as some of the best hunters for no reason.

"Guys, we can't keep doing this," she panted, a bead of perspiration trickling its way down her temple.

"They misfired. They'll have to reload. That'll give us some time."

"What if we just pull over and talk to them? Maybe offer them more than whoever-it-is is paying them?"

Rod looked at her as if she'd suggested a transgender operation, and even Livingston poked his yellow beak out from under the seat.

"What?" she asked the two testosterone-spouting males.

"We do not negotiate with terrorists." Rod said it so low that, by rights, she shouldn't have been able to hear it, but the timbre of his voice vibrated the words through her very bones.

That was silly. They were just birds. Okay, birds with dead things in their talons, but still… "Terrorists? Let's be real here, guys." Guy and bird… Whatever.

The bird popped out from under the seat. "Look, chicky—"

"Valerie." Rod gripped her arm. "I don't think you comprehend the seriousness of the situation. They are—"

"You're right." She yanked her arm away then had to straighten out the car because being manhandled did not gel with high-speed driving. "I don't comprehend it, because you won't explain it. I don't see how falcons can be terrorists. I don't see how any of this is even possible. Yesterday I'm minding my own business, worried about seagulls, and now I've got albatrosses and peregrines and God-knows-what-else dropping dead stuff on me! And you're acting like I'm supposed to think this is *normal*!"

"Enough chitchat, people!" Livingston was back to peering out the rear window. "We can discuss it later. Right now, I've got avians on the wing, starboard, coming in low. Two missiles each. I repeat, two missiles each."

"I heard you the first time," Val muttered under her breath. She took a deep one, re-gripped the steering wheel, and pushed the gas pedal down.

"No. Slow down." Rod's hand on her thigh was not sending "slow down" messages to her nerve endings by any stretch of the imagination.

"What?" She looked over at him, amazed to see him so composed. She felt—and had since Livingston had woken her up—as if she was one frazzle short of bedlam. The skin-to-skin contact was only making matters worse. Or better, depending on her take of the situation.

And she honestly couldn't say what that was at the moment.

"Stay at a slower speed. They expect us to stop again. They're overcompensating for it." Rod pointed to the black dots against the gray skies to the south. "See how they've changed their angle so they're behind us?"

Oh, yeah. "So we're not going to stop?"

"Hades, no!" Livingston almost sounded like he was enjoying this. "Their success in hunting is knowing prescribed reactions. Avians fly a certain way, at a certain speed, react in a certain way to attack. The peregrines can't compensate for Human independent thought. That's why we actually have a prayer of escaping."

"These two, maybe, but what about—"

"You're going to want to veer southeast, Valerie, so you won't be where they expect. Get ready." Rod squeezed her thigh. If he kept touching her like that, she was going to be ready all right, but she didn't think that was what he had in mind.

And even if he *did* have it in mind, there was this little matter of bird droppings—in the very essence of the term—to consider.

"Here they come," Livingston said in his best scary-movie-announcer voice. "Get ready to punch it…"

Rod's grip tightened.

"A little more…"

Val's breath caught in her throat, adrenaline spiking through her. It had nothing to do with Rod's large, muscular, masculine hand three inches from the top of her thigh.

"Get ready… almost… almost… and… NOW!"

Rod's hand pushed down on her leg, shoving the pedal back to the floor. Val remembered to turn the wheel to the right, enough to *aim* for the cornfields; she wasn't planning to go through them. Of course, should the unthinkable occur…

The peregrines tried to swerve at the last minute, screeches of despair and anger racing over the sound of squealing tires.

The abrupt silence didn't sound good. For the peregrines, that is.

Val hit the brakes and swung the car between the correct line markings on the road, trying to bring her heart rate back to normal. Which would be so much easier to do if the man next to her would kindly remove his hand from her thigh.

She thought about asking him; she really did. But thinking and doing were worlds apart.

Her gaze met his while Livingston resumed his favorite position, hanging off the back of the seat, *his* gaze on the road behind them.

"Well, ick," said the seagull. "*That's* not pretty."

Chapter 15

THEY'D DONE IT!

Maybelle looked at the tire-shredding metal she and Adele had hefted to the dumpster behind the gun shop. The tacks were a little lighter than what they'd replaced them with, but cowbirds weren't known for having a predilection toward *any* objects. Hades, they pawned their own eggs off on other avians; it wasn't as if they cared what they put where.

"Do you think they'll notice?" Adele shifted from foot to foot.

Poor dear had worried herself sick about getting caught. She almost hadn't been able to keep up with Maybelle when they'd flown the first bag here.

"Honestly, Adele, do you think any cowbirds who fell for that 'hey, boys' routine are smart enough to notice a difference? As long as there are shiny objects in their bags, they won't notice a thing."

"I guess not."

"Not that it matters anyway. They're off, headed north like we told them." Maybelle snorted. "Silly things thought the closest ocean was *north*. This is why it pays to pay attention in school like I'd always told Kenneth, my first hatchling."

"And now he's the director for the Fly South Program. Yes, Maybelle, I know."

"You don't have to get chirpy about it, Adele."

"I'm sorry. I didn't mean to. I guess I'm just tired. Let's go home."

Poor Adele. What tuckered her out only rejuvenated Maybelle.

Which was why Maybelle wanted to act on something the cowbird had said. Apparently, they'd tried to get into Valerie's store, but the hole they'd found was too small.

Sparrows were smaller than cowbirds. Doves, too. Maybelle had never been more thrilled with that fact.

"Hey, Adele. Let's do one more thing."

"Maybelle, please. It's been a long day."

"One more, Adele. This will be easy, and I guarantee you'll love it."

Adele fluttered her head, casting her top feathers in a style so *last season*. She wasn't the fashion plate Maybelle knew herself to be, but she was a dear.

And an accomplice.

"What is it, Maybelle?"

"Remember those gourmet seeds Therese used to put in that feeder in front of the store?"

"Of course I do. We were the most popular chicks around with them right outside our window."

"Exactly. So how would you like to get some?"

"Is it dangerous?"

"Of course not, Adele." Maybelle crossed her lower two wing feathers. "They're seeds. How much trouble can we get in?"

Tricia let herself in the back door of the shop, surprised that Val hadn't opened the place already. Oh, well, maybe she was taking care of something else.

Like Rod.

Tricia grinned as she lifted a box of Life's a Beach! T-shirts out from behind the door. She hoped Val *had* hooked up with Rod. The guy was hot—and seemed pretty nice, too. Delivering an inheritance didn't hurt, either.

Val needed someone in her life. For years, it'd been just her and her mother, and Tricia knew how strong their bond had been. Strong enough to survive the years Val had spent "finding herself," or whatever she wanted to call it.

It was somewhat ironic, and more than a little sad, that Val had chosen to come home after her mother died. But Val was bound and determined to turn this place into everything her mother had wanted it to be, and Tricia couldn't help but be excited to be a part of it.

She flicked on the lights to the front of the store and tied back the curtains that divided the two rooms. The electrician would be here soon, so she might as well get started on moving the inventory away from the circuit-breaker box.

She lifted the top carton—of heavy sand globes, it figured—from the chest-high stack, careful to get a good grip. She didn't want to drop these; Val couldn't afford to replace stuff at this point.

Although, with that inheritance…

Tricia carried the box to the stack in the corner, working her grip so she could slide it on top of the others when she stopped.

How had those sparrows gotten in here?

Maybe Val's recent paranoia about birds was justi-fied. It could certainly help explain yesterday's seagull visitor. Now sparrows?

Tricia backed up very slowly, but the birds seemed too interested in a few crumbs to pay her much attention.

She set the box down on the desk and, tucking her arms by her sides, tried to slide unobtrusively to the far side of the stack so she wouldn't scare the sparrows. Which boxes had the fishing nets in them? She didn't want to hurt the little things, but she also didn't want to spend time cleaning up anything she didn't have to, and she'd rather get them out of the shop before Val arrived.

Pecking away, they didn't even look up.

Tricia inched into a space near the back of the boxes. Aha. No wonder the birds were so busy.

An entire bag of birdseed had spilled. Tricia smiled. Therese had bought a special brand that had kept the front sidewalk filled with songbirds—and with customers. The birds had been a nice draw.

Tricia lifted the bag. That got the sparrows' attention. One fluttered behind the door where Tricia saw a sliver of rainy daylight. That's how they'd gotten in.

The other sparrow hadn't budged. Matter of fact, it furrowed its little brow, and Tricia could swear it stomped its foot.

Stubborn thing. Well, at least it wasn't flying off in fright. Made it easier to capture this way.

Tricia swept a handful of the spilled seed onto her palm, and wouldn't you know? The little foot-stomping sparrow hopped aboard and went right back to eating. The nervous one by the door peeped.

The brave sparrow lifted its head long enough to let out a pair of chirps, then went right back to eating. Tricia moved slowly toward the door, and the nervous one ruffled its feathers.

Tricia opened the door, spreading the seed on the pavement outside, and her hitchhiker hopped off to enjoy the feast. The nervous one flew down from the hole.

That'd been easy.

But she didn't want them to come back, so Tricia grabbed one of the T-shirts and stuffed it in the hole. Val wouldn't mind the lost income from one shirt if it meant keeping birds out of the shop.

Then she went back to clean up the spill. If Val wasn't interested in attracting the birds back to the store, her kids would love if they showed up at their house.

She brushed the spill back into the bag and was turning to leave when something caught her eye. Something wrapped in bright yellow paper.

Addressed to Valerie. From her mom.

Oh, no. It was a birthday present. Her mother's car accident had happened right before Val's birthday, and she'd never gotten the gift her mother had chosen for her.

Tricia lifted it, sniffing back tears. She'd give it to Val as soon as she saw her.

First Rod, then the inheritance, now this gift.

Aside from the birds, Val was having the best run of luck since, well, ever.

Chapter 16

VAL WAS HAVING THE WORST LUCK.

She couldn't believe it. Things just kept dropping from the sky in a shower of the bizarre—and she wasn't talking about the intermittent raindrops.

Pizza crusts, tin cans, an old shoe…

"Does he have every bird in the Midwest working for him?" she grumbled as she swerved to avoid a wad of soggy paper towels.

They landed on her wiper blade, pinning the thing against the windshield. Val upped the wiper speed, only to hear a painful *whir-whir* as the mechanism tried to respond and couldn't.

Great.

"Let's hope not," said Livingston. "Oh, and by the way, we prefer the descriptor *avian*. *Bird* is so mundane. Leave it to Bipeds to come up with such a harsh-sounding word for creatures who are grace on the wing. Able to soar through the stratosphere, ride currents like waves, dive from great heights, perform tactical maneuvers with elegance and speed and just the right amount of *chutzpah*—"

"Incoming," Rod said, looking out his window.

"Right!" Livingston squawked.

Val went right. A Frisbee bounced off the hood.

"Valerie! I said right!" the gull growled.

"I went right!"

"You were supposed to go left."

"But you said right."

"I meant it was *coming* from the right. Rod was looking out his window—what other direction could it have been coming from?"

Val shook her head. Bad enough she had to take directions from a seagull, but now she was supposed to add logistics into the equation?

"This is really annoying." She shifted gears, missing the next one and having to rattle the shift to find its niche.

Hmmm, the parallels to her own life in that maneuver weren't even worth contemplating.

"You're doing great, Valerie." The warmth in Rod's voice *was* worth contemplating.

For just a moment, it made everything right in her world.

And then a T-bone hit the side mirror.

Ya know? Rod certainly was taking all of this in stride. The seagull, objects falling from the sky, near-misses…

"Rod, what's going on? This isn't a normal inheritance, is it?"

The bird snorted from the backseat. "This I have to hear."

Rod looked over his shoulder, a black wave of hair falling just above his eye. She wanted to smooth it back—as she'd done when they'd kissed.

Uh oh. She shouldn't be thinking about that right now. Bad enough she'd turned the A/C off for power; thoughts like that only increased the heat in the car.

"Go left, Valerie."

But why banish thoughts when all Rod had to do was say her name like that and there'd be no outrunning that heat.

Since she wanted to outrun the falling soda bottle, however, she jerked the car to the left and hit the gas. Granted, a plastic bottle wouldn't normally do much damage, but that thin crack from the fish was spider-webbing upward. One wrong *ding* from another object, and the windshield could shatter.

A pacifier was next. A *pacifier*? What? Had the birds run out of trash to pick so they'd started stealing from babies?

"Rod, what's going on? Why is an albatross after us? *How* is an albatross after us? I'm having a hard enough time with the talking seagull. I mean, birds just don't talk to humans!"

"For a very good reason," Livingston muttered.

Rod massaged the back of his neck and exhaled. A fine glimmer of perspiration graced the strong column of his throat, the faint musk of man filling her car.

"I wish I knew what was going on, Valerie." He lowered the visor and peered in the mirror. "Livingston? What do your sources say? When did this come to light?"

The seagull clacked his beak. "We don't have much to go on, Rod. The manatees were the first to report the rumblings of a coup after the wires were found, but JR's name never came up until the diamonds went missing."

"I want someone down in the Keys to question the manatees further."

"Already on it."

"Hold on." The car swerved as Val adjusted the rearview mirror. "Manatees? You're telling me *manatees* alerted you to a coup? Who are you, Jacques Cousteau?"

Livingston snorted. "Hardly. That guy spoke French. And he's dead. If you'll notice, Rod isn't dead."

Oh she noticed.

"But manatees? I've seen documentaries. They can't talk."

"And you've seen documentaries of talking seagulls?"

Good point.

"Valerie," Rod put his hand on her arm in what she supposed was to be a comforting manner but was so not. Which didn't help. "There's a lot I can tell you that will seem impossible, which is why I can't until I have proof. Manatee sentries are one of them."

"Talking birds another?"

"Exactly."

"And the fact that you're a prince from a country you have yet to name?"

He did that cute, one-sided, kicked-back smile, probably to disarm her, but she wasn't going to let it.

"Valerie, my kingdom isn't… well, it isn't one you would have heard of."

"Oh, she's heard of it."

"Livingston, if you don't mind. There are ways to do this, in case you've forgotten?"

"Pardon."

Wow. Livingston had apologized. She hadn't known the bird long (and what was wrong with *that* statement?), but she had a feeling that wasn't a common occurrence.

"As I was saying, in my kingdom we try to keep to the old ways and not involve Hum—that is, outsiders."

"So, is it some insulated little world?"

"You could say that."

"What would *you* say?"

"Well, *I'd* say," Livingston grumbled, "that Valerie might want to keep her attention focused on the road." The bird flicked his beak toward the windshield. "Take a gander at that."

Dead ahead were four crows, flying in tandem like a Blue Angels squadron. Only these birds weren't doing tactical maneuvers. No, these four were flying in perfect timing with… a blanket hanging from their feet.

"Oh, for Zeus's sake." Rod exhaled and raked his fingers through his hair. "What do they hope to accomplish with that?"

"It'll stop us."

"Only until we remove it."

"He's getting desperate." Livingston tap-danced from foot to foot. "JR is running out of *avian* power. That's good for us."

"Yay, but we still have to dodge this very large bullet." Val fiddled with the gears again. Did one slow down for a blanket or speed up to outrun it?

"Pick up speed when they drop it, Valerie." Rod saved her from having to come up with the answer. "The draft you create should whip it over us."

The three of them peered forward, eyes glued to the eight scrawny, black legs that were zooming in fast.

Val checked the road. So far, so empty.

"Get ready…" Livingston rocked forward. "Get set…"

Then the skies opened.

The rainstorm hit so fast and so fierce that it was as if a tidal wave had been unleashed from the heavens.

The pounding rain knocked the crows off their trajectory. Then a huge gust of wind dragged the blanket—and the crows—into the field alongside the road.

"Go!" Livingston shouted with a laugh. He jumped onto the dash and held a webbed foot up toward Rod. "High four!"

High four?

Val glanced at the bird's foot. Four toes. Well, three in the webbing and one in the back. Bad enough the bird could speak, but now he had culturally appropriate anthropomorphic behavior?

She needed some explanations—and she needed them now.

A bolt of lightning zigzagged across the sky, followed by thunder so loud it rattled the car. While it was a little late to be tornado season, this storm had the makings of one.

Yeah, not her luckiest day.

The rain sluiced down her windshield, heavy drops splashing the runoff and everything merged with the spider-veined crack so she couldn't see. She turned the wipers back on, only to hear the *whir-whir* again. The damn thing was stuck under that wad of towels, which, with the rain, was only getting heavier.

"Let's get moving, Valerie!" Livingston settled himself in the middle of the backseat again, a grin from ear to, er, did seagulls have ears?

"I can't see anything." Val meant *visually* but *metaphorically* wasn't off the mark either. She rolled the window down, not particularly looking forward to getting soaked, but she did need to see.

She reached for the paper towels, missing them when the car hit some residual "shrapnel." The wheel jerked right, and the paper towel obstruction went sailing off the windshield, the wiper kicking into service with a frenzy.

Val grabbed the wheel, trying to regain control of the car and roll up her window while another bolt of lightning ripped through the air. Thunder reverberated around them like the percussion section of an orchestra. Rain slanted sideways, and Val struggled to keep the wheel heading straight. This was insane.

"We have to get off the road," she said, clinging to the wheel with both hands.

"What?" Rod yelled over the din.

"We need to get off the road!" But as she looked through the few seconds of clear vision the wipers created, she didn't see a single place to go. Acres of fields on either side.

"Keep driving!" Livingston ordered in her ear. He'd fluttered up to the headrest behind her. "Nothing is going to be able to keep track of us in this. It's a gods-send!"

A godsend? Maybe for him since he was a seabird—and sitting in the backseat—but driving in it was a nightmare.

Chapter 17

ANGEL TRITONE DIDN'T LIKE THE SILENCE SHE ENCOUNTERED in the High Councilman's domed, oval office. Dad and Charley usually weren't so quiet—especially with a bottle of champagne between them.

She set the slate tablets she carried onto the desk that'd been carved by the Human, Bernini, and nudged aside the sea anemone who'd taken a liking to the corner. Anemones did not belong on the furniture. The decorator had included perfectly good pedestals along the far corner for just such a reason.

"You are sure she's the one, aren't you, Dad?" Angel turned to her father, resting her amethyst tail against the desk and running her hands over the beveled edge.

Gods, what she wouldn't give for this desk to be hers. Humans had such interesting items. Since she collected whatever she could get her hands on, she knew what a find this was. But something like this, a cultural treasure on land, was guaranteed to be one off-land as well, something she'd never be allowed to own in the private sector. She'd had a tough choice between majors in college: museum curator or humanologist.

Humanologist won, but only because she harbored the hope to go on land one day and interact with Humans. And once Dad signed off on these land-study program slates, she could.

"It's her, Angel. Erica's law-enforcement friend handled the DNA analysis the gulls brought back," Charley answered while Dad set the champagne down on the sideboard among the marble busts of previous High Councilmen.

He and Mom had brought several bottles back from Reel and Erica's wedding. It was good, much better for catching a buzz than kelp wine, but the fact that Dad was drinking the hard stuff bothered her.

She glanced at the timepiece. It might be five o'clock somewhere, but not here. Dad wasn't usually a big drinker, and he'd had a good portion of that bottle.

"Did the Ones On High confirm it?" She didn't like that Dad hadn't answered her. Yes, Charley was her father's Olympian Advisor, but if this were on the up-and-up, why did Dad look so worried?

Which only worried her more.

She smoothed the Human tankini top Mariana had given her for her birthday, her fingers tangling in her necklace—dog tags, Erica said it was called, which made no sense. There were no dogs on it.

She untangled her fingers. "Rod's tail will come back, right? I know the mythology says so—and Reel's did, but Reel started off with legs. Earning a tail through heroics was all well and good for him, but what's heroic about Rod bringing a Human to our world?"

Nothing. That was the problem. What Rod was doing was simply a transport mission.

Dad turned around with a flick of his tail, the tip of one fluke dislodging a few arms from the basket starfish lounging against the table leg. "Yes, Angel. Rod will get his tail back." He took off his glasses and folded the ends together in the middle. He'd taken to wearing them only recently. About the same time she'd realized he was getting older. "You did give him the gods' oil when you dropped off the clothing?"

"Yes."

"Then everything's going according to plan," Charley answered, putting the stopper back in the bottle and resting the champagne in the wine rack. He nodded to a pair of sea ravens floating in alcoves beside the office door. The fish glided into place beside her, the yellow one puffing itself up to the size of the orange one. "Thank you for bringing the slates by, Angel. Your father will get to work on them right away."

She knew when she was being dismissed—and she wanted to know why.

She pushed off the desk and ditched her "escorts," swimming around Charley to put her hand on Dad's arm. "If everything's okay, Dad, what are you so worried about?"

Yes, he was the High Councilman, and, yes, people usually didn't question him once he made a proclamation, but at this moment, he was simply her father.

Finally, he looked at her, rubbing his fingers across his brow. "I'm not worried, urchin. Merely uncomfortable having him so far away on land." He glanced at Charley. "It'll be all right."

Who was he trying to convince?

A shoal of silversides burst from a narrow tunnel in the wall behind the desk, heralding the arrival of a Messenger lobster. Sometimes the little fish were *a bit* too self-important. As was the crustacean who scuttled out with a slate held tightly in his pincers. Gods, could Dad ever get a break?

"You should take a vacation when this is all over, Dad. Take Mom on that tour of the Seven Seas you've always talked about." Thank the gods Charley took the slate. Dad didn't need any bad news.

"What's it say, Charley?"

Of course, Dad couldn't let it go. It was his job and the reason the Mer world was lucky to have him on board.

"Just what Livingston suspected," Charley said, filing the slate in the middle of the ones she'd brought. "But they're on their way."

Dad's exhalation sent a herd of baby seahorses twirling through the seawater, up toward the mosaic-tiled ceiling.

"Livingston? What does the Chief of the ASA have to do with this? What's going on, Dad?"

Dad shook his head and reached for the champagne bottle again.

That frightened her. She'd never seen him drink like this before. Even when Reel had been "detained" by Ceto in her palace last year, Dad had been storming all over the place, tossing things port and starboard. But this, this was something else.

Charley zipped over, taking her by the arm and steering her toward the door. "Everything's fine, Angel."

Angel shook off Charley's grasp. "I wasn't born yesterday, Charley. What's going on? What are you two so worried about? Does Mom know?"

Dad looked up, his mouth a thin line. And a hundred new lines around his eyes. He really did need to retire.

"Yes, your mother knows. And everything's going to be okay now, urchin. Really."

"*Now?* Why now? What aren't you telling me?"

Dad glanced at Charley—a sure sign he was hiding something. She'd studied Human behavior enough to recognize it in Mers. And this was bad.

Charley sighed and removed his glasses. "There's been an attempt on your brother's life, Angel. But Livingston's with him, and The Council is going full-steam ahead with the investigation. We needed to get him out harm's way."

"An attempt on his life? And you didn't tell him?" She didn't know who she wanted to throttle more, her father, Charley, or the idiot who'd dared take a shot at her brother. Dad had kept a huge secret from Reel, which hadn't done either of them any favors—and now he was doing it again?

She'd thought he'd learned his lesson—which meant... "Dad, did the gods forbid you from telling Rod about this?"

Dad shook his head and straightened his shoulders. He swam over to his desk and rifled through the stack of slates. "Rod didn't need the added worry, Angel. There's nothing he can do here, and Lance's daughter has to be brought back. It's the perfect solution. We've got the top wrasse working on it. They'll find out who it was and round him up before Rod gets back."

"Dad, this trip is supposed to be two days at the most. Don't you think you're cutting it a bit close? And he's not going to be thrilled to find out you haven't told him the truth."

Dad pulled out a slate. She was betting it was the one Charley had just shoved in there on the pretext of everything being okay.

Right.

"Sometimes a High Councilman has to do things he doesn't want to, Angel." Dad squinted at the slate. "Rod will learn that. It goes with the job."

Which meant the gods had set down the decree and Dad had had to follow it to the letter.

"There's a lot to be said for Humans' independent thinking," she muttered, her hand on the doorknob. Nothing she could say would matter a hill of seashells when going up against the gods' decree.

"What was that?" Charley put a hand on the door to prevent her from opening it.

"Oh, it was nothing." No need to add treasonous talk to Dad's worries, but this was the reason she found Humans fascinating. Sure, they were ruining the planet with their greed and gluttony, but no one could tell them what to do and get away with it. They took tyrants down.

But how in Hades did one argue with a god?

Chapter 18

VAL PULLED INTO A ROADSIDE DINER AN HOUR LATER, OR maybe it was two—she'd lost track—arms aching, head pounding, stomach growling, and bladder screaming for a break.

"Valerie, what are you doing?" Livingston popped open one eye from his perch on the backseat.

"It's called answering the call of Nature, Livingston. Perhaps you've heard of it?" She grabbed her wallet from her bag then unclicked her seat belt while Rod did the same.

"Livingston," he said, "find the nearest airport. We need to get to the coast quickly. And see what you can find out about JR's plans. At the very least, I want to know if he's been by here. We'll wait for you."

The bird sighed, long and suffering. "Fine. But bring me a burger. All the fixin's. Oh, and fries. Cheese fries."

Val opened the door. The rain had slackened to a deluge, and the low, gray clouds didn't show signs of letting up. "You're not eating cheese fries in my car."

The bird rolled his eyes as he hopped back onto the dash for takeoff. "Fine. But throw on extra salt. You Humans never add enough salt."

They heard him cursing—at both Humans and the weather—as he flapped away.

The silver-sided diner was a throwback to the fifties, down to the clichéd, but atmospherically perfect, plastic red-and-white gingham tablecloth. A metal menu-holder with salt, pepper, and sugar—no artificial sweetener in sight—rested on every table beneath the windows, and the *de-rigueur* Elvis, Marilyn, and James Dean pictures shared wall space with vinyl LPs and vintage Coca-Cola paraphernalia.

Val headed toward the counter, but Rod put his hand on the small of her back and steered her to a booth.

"I thought we were in a hurry," she asked.

"We are, but it's going to take Livingston some time to find out what we want to know, and with this storm, he could miss us if we leave. Besides," he slid his hands to her shoulders and gave her a gentle massage, "you look like you could use a break."

She closed her eyes and enjoyed his touch on two levels: one being the fact that her aching muscles could use the relaxation, the other being purely feminine.

God that felt good. He felt good. And she should know; she'd replayed the moments he'd held her in his arms and kissed her for far longer than she should have last night.

She didn't normally kiss strange men right off the bat, but there was just something about Rod, and being in his arms, held against that chest, his hair falling forward, his eyes intense and focused on her... She'd seen his eyes dip down to her lips.

A shiver ran up her spine.

"Did I hurt you?" Rod stopped the massage and every nerve cell in her body started protesting.

A diner was not the optimum place to respond to protesting nerve cells, so she ignored them. Besides, if he'd kept that massage up, God only knew what would have come out of her mouth. A groan had already worked its way into her throat.

"No, I'm fine. Thank you. That felt good."

They slid into the booth, Rod's knees brushing hers. Each took a menu, but Val didn't look at hers. She knew what she wanted—and it wasn't on any menu.

Okay, not what she should be thinking about now.

She cleared her throat and looked out the window, focusing on the sheets of rain obliterating the view of the parking lot rather than watching his long, strong fingers turn the pages.

Except... the window acted like a mirror.

Oh, well. No one had to know that she watched those long fingers tap a fork on the tabletop, or that he sucked the side of his bottom lip between his teeth as he read the menu. No one should look as good as he did after being drenched.

While she looked like a bedraggled poodle, his profile was more chiseled than any of the movie stars she'd compared him to, and, even soaking wet, his hair was perfectly rumpled. The moisture made the waves shine, which brought out the green of his eyes even more beneath spiky black lashes. And then there was the drop of water that slid over his left cheekbone into the slash of dimple by the side of the mouth that had played way too big of a part in her dreams last night, with a few lucky drops making it onto his lips...

"What can I get you?" Their teenaged waitress's Goth makeup didn't go with the whole bobby sox and rolled jeans theme, and the look she gave Val let her know the window trick hadn't been quite as surreptitious as she'd hoped.

"I'll take a burger, no onions, and a Coke," Val said, knowing what she *really* wanted wasn't an appropriate answer—or feeling. She was here to get her inheritance, not run off with Rod. No more running anymore, remember? She'd made a decision and a promise to herself, and she was going to stick by it, hot guy or not.

"Oh, and another burger, no onions, with an order of fries to go," she added. They didn't need to ride with seagull-onion breath.

"Sure. And for you?" The girl's eyes widened when she turned toward Rod.

Ha. *Now* she'd understand about the window. Val felt vindicated.

Among other things.

"Is there no seafood?" Rod glanced at her, and Val wanted to smooth her hair but resisted. Really, it wouldn't do any good and why draw attention?

"Try the fish sandwich. It's fried, but the closest you'll get."

Turning a little green around the gills, Rod closed the menu. "I'll have that."

"Sure," said the waitress. "And to drink?"

"Ice water will be fine."

Val made use of the facilities, wringing a few ounces of rainwater from her shirt. She returned to find a straw bobbing in the ice-filled soda fizzing at her place at the table and Rod wiping something white and grainy from his hands into his glass.

"Rod, you can get another glass of water, you know." She slid his drink sideways.

"It's fine, Valerie." He grabbed her hand when she started to wave the girl back.

Okay, she could go for that.

"I knocked the salt over, that's all."

"Did you throw some over your shoulder?"

"What?"

"You know, when you spill salt, you have to throw some over your shoulder for good luck, or whatever that superstition is?"

Rod's eyes narrowed, then he smiled and tapped a finger against the back of her hand. "Exactly. That's what I did. We don't need any bad luck."

"I'll say." She took a sip of her soda. Ah, nice and cold. Perfect for sitting across from a hot guy—especially while still holding his hand. "So, about our bad luck today. Can you please explain what's going on? I've never heard of a government agency that has talking seagulls and mercenary albatrosses. Not to mention manatee spies."

Rod released her hand to reach for his water.

Damn.

He rolled the glass between his palms, the ice *clinking* against the sides. "The manatees aren't spies. They're informants."

"Isn't that the same thing?"

"Not in this instance. They don't purposely seek out situations, but rather, keep us informed of anything out of the ordinary in their territory. They're too passive for anything else."

Val took another sip of her soda, sliding her other hand beneath the table to pinch her leg.

Ouch.

Again.

She couldn't believe she was actually believing this, but then again, why wouldn't she? She'd talked with

Livingston. She'd dodged the falling fish. She'd seen the peregrines take aim at her car. And she wasn't dreaming. Which meant something weird was going on.

Hadn't she been trying to *escape* drama by coming home?

"Okay, so who's 'us'?" She fiddled with her straw.

"Us?"

"Yes. You said manatees keep 'us' informed. Who? Is there a king involved in all this?"

"Ah." Rod set the glass down and leaned back. His fingers thrummed the tablecloth. "Actually, Valerie, it's a lot more complicated than that, and I'd prefer to wait until I can fully explain it."

"Why not now? We've got time."

"But we don't have proof. Talking seagulls are just one of the many things you'll find strange in my kingdom. Would you have believed me if I'd told you about Livingston without seeing him for yourself?"

"Well, no, you're right. I mean, coherent birds just aren't possible."

He raised an eyebrow. "Unless he's right in front of you. Then it becomes possible. Trust me when I say there are other things you will need to see to believe."

What could be more unbelievable than the birds? As far as the general public knew, birds flew, ate, messed up your car after a good washing, and made little birds, but the not-so-general public, however, well... if this was one of those things he was talking about, he did have a good point about waiting for proof.

The waitress arrived, the tray of food perched on her hip, and she served Rod first.

That wasn't unbelievable. Val had felt the stares from half the women in the place. Okay, most of the women in the place. The window-reflection trick seemed to be a gender-wide phenomenon.

"Is there anything else I can get you?" the waitress asked, her hip, *sans* tray, still cocked Rod's way.

"Thank you. This is fine."

The girl lingered until Valerie coughed.

Rod lifted his sandwich, eyeing it as if he'd never seen one before. "You're certain this is fish?"

"Yep." Or whatever passed for fish with the FDA these days.

The look on his face when he bit into it was priceless. He grimaced and tried to swallow at the same time, with a little shudder for good measure.

"I think I'll order more fries."

She wasn't surprised to see him put it down. Besides having had the taste frozen out of it—and subsequently fried out of it—a prince, if he was that, probably never had reason to enjoy the delights of greasy diners.

"So. You're a prince?" She nudged Livingston's fries toward him.

Rod picked up a couple and studied them. "For your purposes, yes, you could say that I am."

"That has to be the vaguest answer I've ever heard. I mean, either you are a prince or you're not a prince. It's like being pregnant. You either are or you're not. You can't have a different definition for different circumstances."

He laughed at that, his eyes crinkling at the corners. "All right then. It's true that I'm the next ruler. We don't use the prince designation, but it is the closest reference for you. When my father retires, I will become the High Councilman of The Oceanic Council."

She took a bite of her burger. Greasy and good. What could she say? She wasn't royalty, and after years of making do with bologna, burgers could be considered gourmet.

"So where does my father fit in with all of this?"

"That, Valerie, will have to wait until we meet with the rest of The Council. They know more about him than I do." He reached for a fry.

"Lucky you."

"What?" The fry stopped halfway to his mouth.

"My father. The man who, for some reason, decided to leave me something after all these years. No loss that you don't know anything about him."

Rod set the fry down. "I don't understand. He was your father."

"Was he? Really? That would depend on how you define a parent." She took another bite of the burger. She wasn't going to let Lance Dumere ruin her meal when, God knew, he'd ruined enough of them already.

"Running out when the going got tough, or whatever the reason was that he left, doesn't qualify him in my eyes. My mom was my parent. She was there for me, took care of me, loved me, planned for my future, while he…" Val swallowed the lump in her throat and she couldn't say it was that bite of burger. "He ran off at the first opportunity."

"Valerie, that's not what happened. Your father didn't stop looking for you until the day he died. You must have misunderstood."

"I didn't misunderstand. I overheard my grandmother reminding my mom how he'd left her high and dry—in those exact words."

She'd stood behind the pantry door, reeling from the fact that Mom had spared her by telling her he'd died before she was born.

She would love to believe she'd misunderstood. Love to think what might have been if the reason she hadn't known him was because he *had* died. There would have been love stories and happy memories, but there hadn't been. Mom hadn't liked to talk about him, and Val finally knew why.

No, she hadn't misunderstood. What's more, she knew it was the truth, because she had those same running-away tendencies in her own genetic makeup.

That's why she was here. Mom deserved for one of her dreams to come true, and it was only fitting that Lance Dumere finally made it happen.

Valerie took another sip of her soda, her lips encasing the straw, and Rod tried to keep the tug in his gut from migrating to his brain… and other organs.

He'd tried not to remember what that kiss had been like last night, only to blow it when he remembered today's kiss. Sitting so close to her for hours in the small confines of her vehicle… They needed to end this journey for more reasons than just his inheriting the throne.

"Let's change the subject, okay, Rod? Something pleasant? Like what it was like growing up in a royal family with talking birds."

Gladly.

Rod drank more ice water, willing *that* to those other organs.

He should tell her about her father. The truth. That Lance Dumere had been the last of his line and wanted her as his heir from the moment he'd found out about her existence. That he'd searched for her for *selinos*, only giving up when all traces of her had disappeared.

But telling her that would involve revealing the sordid details of Lance's less-than-honorable weeklong fling with Therese Monet, and he wasn't going to hurt her more than Lance already had.

Instead, he chose a neutral topic. For her, at least. "My family. Okay, let's see. I have a brother and three sisters."

"Lucky you. I always wanted a sibling."

Rod smiled, remembering the chaos that had filled their house in those early *selinos*. "Lucky? Sometimes. At others it was exasperating, annoying, crowded, noisy..."

She rested her chin in the palm of her hand, a soft smile on her face, the anger and hurt replaced with wistfulness. "It sounds wonderful."

"It was." And it had been. Until that damn dare...

"I want a lot of kids someday."

He almost choked on an ice cube. Not because she wanted children, but because the minute she said it, an image flooded his mind like high tide in a storm. Her, beneath him, in his arms, as close as a man and a woman could be—

Except they weren't just any man and woman. He was The Heir. No High Councilman had ever married a Human and diluted the bloodline of the oldest hierarchy on Earth. Reel was the only member of the royal family to have done so in recent memory, and if there was one thing to be learned from that, from how he'd lost the Immortality he'd earned, it was that falling for a Human was dangerous. Life-threateningly so.

"So, tell me about your brother."

"Reel? Well, we're twins and look alike, but that's where the similarities end. He's—"

"Wait. Your name is Rod and his is Reel? Is your dad into fishing?" Valerie touched his arm, her smile growing beneath sparkling eyes.

He'd like to think her reaction had something to do with touching him...

No he wouldn't. Pure bloodlines, remember? Office of the High Councilman. Standards and protocols to be upheld.

Rod picked up his water glass again, resisting the urge to keep her touching him. "Something like that. Dad's name is Fisher, and my parents have a good sense of humor."

"Didn't you get teased?"

He arched an eyebrow at her. No one teased The Heir. Except his brother, of course.

"Oh. Right. Prince. Stupid question."

She took a sip of her soda again, her lips curving around that straw.

"So, did you guys pretend to be each other? I've heard twins do that."

Rod rubbed his hand over his jaw, thankful she'd asked another question. His shorts were becoming uncomfortable.

Then he realized the question she'd asked, and his heart became uncomfortable. *Be* each other? If only that had been possible. Reel had legs, and he'd had the tail—the fundamental difference between them that had started it all. "No. Everyone could always tell us apart."

Valerie, thank the gods, slid her glass away from her and picked up her sandwich. Surely there couldn't be anything arousing about her eating a sandwich?

"So what's he like, your brother?"

And even if there had been something arousing, her question squelched it again.

What was Reel like? Gods, where to start? "He's a good Mer—guy. A practical joker. A daredevil."

Both traits stemmed from their birth orders. Their physical differences were attributable to the gods; nothing could be done about that. The Heir had the tail, and any subsequent males born to the family got legs. But the daredevil part...

That could be attributed to him. Yes, the legs had been the instigation, but Rod knew where the blame lay for the daredevil part of Reel's personality.

Reel had hated that he didn't have a tail. He was a great swimmer, but legs couldn't keep up with tails, and Rod, in typical sibling torture, had taken advantage of that fact to no end. Always challenging him to a race, giving him a head start—which Reel had hated because it made him feel inferior—but, no matter what, Reel would take Rod on, trying his hardest to beat him.

And Rod would let him—until the last second. Then he'd pour on the power and Reel would be left leagues behind.

That always pissed Reel off—which Rod fully understood. That was why, when they'd seen Erica in the water by the jetty that day, he'd come up with a dare he knew Reel wouldn't be able to resist: touch her and escape without getting caught. The dare hadn't pitted them against each other; just Reel against a Human. Rod figured it was an easy win. In and out, a plus to add to Reel's tally.

Except that Reel had been fascinated by her. He'd hung around. He'd even brought the clamshell they'd found for their mother's birthday to the jetty in hopes of enticing Erica out further.

It had worked.

And Rod had panicked. He'd known what their father would say if he heard about it. He'd tried to stop Reel, but, typical Reel, he wouldn't quit.

Then Erica had seen him and screamed. And that was the beginning of the end of their carefree childhood.

If he'd only left his brother alone that day, if he hadn't dared him, or if he hadn't tried to "rescue" him, they wouldn't have been separated.

If he'd obeyed the rules of their world, Reel wouldn't have had to prove himself. He wouldn't have wound up married to Erica and living on land. For the duration of a mortal lifespan.

If only—Gods! He'd been through the "if onlys" for *selinos,* and it all came back to one thing. If he hadn't dared Reel, he wouldn't have to face saying good-bye to him one day.

"Rod? Are you okay?" Valerie waved a hand in front of his face. "You looked like you went on a little trip there."

He tried to smile, but the thought that it'd been his fault still ripped him in two. And once they bestowed the Immortality on him that came with the throne, he'd be able to revisit his guilt forever.

"Just remembering all the crazy things my brother did. One time he was hanging from the roof and dropped on top of his friend. Scared the guy so badly that he turned green." Literally. It was the first time Oryx had come home from school with Reel, and he'd been smitten with Mariana. Oryx had thought the wrath of the gods was falling on his head for daring to ask out the High Councilman's daughter.

"Off the roof? Wow, he really was a daredevil. Didn't he get hurt?"

Right. The roof. Gravity was more of an issue on land than underwater. He had to remember that or risk giving himself away. Another reason to get to the ocean as soon as possible—once he convinced her she wasn't allergic.

"No, Reel didn't get hurt. He had a lot of practice and knew how to do it."

"He must have been a handful for your parents."

"That's an understatement." Reel definitely had been. Rod? Not so much. Rod had learned that lesson then buckled down to learn the rest of them.

"What about you? What were you doing while your brother was off pulling his crazy stunts?"

Rod picked up a salty fry. He hadn't put enough of the mineral in his water to make it palatable and couldn't with Valerie watching him, so the fries would have to do. They weren't bad, actually, and provided what his body needed. "Not much. When you're in line for the throne, you have precedents and protocols shoved down your gullet. I spent most of my time in the library studying."

"Sounds like fun."

Right. He raised his eyebrows at her. "Fun wouldn't be my first choice to describe it, but it was necessary. I have a huge responsibility on my shoulders, and the only way to prepare for it was to study and observe."

"Well, at least you got to take this fun trip, right? Dodging fish bombs has to be more exciting than figuring out what kind of fish they were."

"Flying fish."

"I'm sorry?"

"They were flying fish. *Exocoetidae*. The easiest kind for JR to collect when he's going for quantity."

Val shook her head and laughed. "Rod, you need to lighten up. I was only joking about what kind of fish they were. The fact that they were fish—dead and bouncing off my car—is enough information for me. I guess you *were* stuck in that library too long."

True. It'd been a long time since he'd just laughed. Since everything hadn't been all about the throne.

Even this journey. He'd planned to bring her to the coast and immediately head into the water so she would gain her tail and he, the throne. His brother had suggested they take their time, introduce her to their world slowly, use his and Erica's home while they were visiting their parents, and enjoy a few days before all the responsibility and order took up his life. But Rod had said no. His assignment had been to bring her to The Council, nothing more. He'd been groomed for the job and was more than ready to take it.

But, he had to admit, sitting here, sharing the memories and her amusement, he was reconsidering. She was no longer something he had to "do," some abstract mission The Council had sent him on.

No, Valerie was far from "have to" material. "Want to" was more the idea.

Maybe taking a few days to ease her into their world wasn't such a bad idea after all.

Chapter 19

"WHAT'D YOU FIND OUT, LIVINGSTON?" ROD OPENED THE vehicle's door for Valerie, careful to keep from touching her. The rain, thankfully, had cooled his blood. He didn't need the added complication of an attraction to her. Obviously, spending time with her at Reel's was not only unsafe for everyone, but specifically his claim to the throne now that JR was involved.

"I managed to get a message to The Council." Livingston glided into the backseat. "That concern is now alleviated. But another one has cropped up. JR has all the airports in a hundred-mile radius surrounded. That's why he gave up after the crow-and-blanket fiasco. If we show up, they're going to ground the planes. I can imagine how, but not why these land avians are doing his bidding."

"Did you explain… things?" Rod took his seat and buckled in.

"Oh, I explained, Rod. But they kept their beaks zipped and their heads shaking. Whatever they've been promised or threatened with, they aren't budging, so we've got to come up with another plan."

"What other plan?" Valerie asked, starting the vehicle. "We drive or we fly. Flying appears to be out, and if we drive, he's going to be able to track us."

"True." Livingston shook himself, sending sprinkles of water all over the interior. "Sorry about that. Anyway, where we're going isn't a secret, so the tracking isn't the problem. It's what he plans to do while we're on the road that worries me." He worked his wings into place on his back and settled onto the middle of the seat again.

"Since every other avian out there is against us, I've put out a call for gull reinforcements, but this weather cell is staying put and stretches for miles in either direction. The guys back at the roost will have a tough time getting through, so we're on our own until the weather clears or we get far enough east where JR hasn't had a chance to do advance work. The guy knows his shit, that's for sure."

"That's because he trained at the same academy you did," Rod said, running scenarios through his head to quit replaying Valerie's comments from lunch and ignore the way her hair tumbled around her beautiful face—both of which were still making his shorts uncomfortable—and to find a way out of this mess. Simple recovery mission, his tail.

"Yeah, but our training methods have advanced since he left. I'd like to think I've got options he doesn't know about. Now if I can just figure out what those are." Livingston stuck his bill between the seats. "So, can I have my fries?"

The fries. Rod looked at Valerie.

"You ate them, didn't you? You ate my fries." The gull hrrrmphed and dropped his head over the edge of the seat. "The one thing I was so looking forward to—hot, fresh fries. By the time I get them, they're always soggy and cold." He shook his head when Rod passed back the sandwich bag. "I get no respect, I tell you. None at all."

No respect? Please. The bird was the highest-ranking security expert in their world. If they made it through this in one piece, Rod would make sure that Livingston had a french-fry line item added to his budget for the rest of his tenure. And then some.

The rain didn't let up. If anything, the sky grew darker. It was only afternoon, but it could just as easily have been night.

After hitting a couple of slick spots, Val reduced their speed, gripping the wheel tighter while laughing at the latest round of Tritone sibling escapades. Rod had told her about his sisters and, man, the whole large family thing sounded wonderful.

Most of the stories, however, were about Reel. Rod obviously loved his brother, and it came through with every word he spoke about him. She felt sorry that Reel had been the one getting toppled by waves and trying to surf on the backs of stingrays while Rod had stood on the sidelines during family vacations.

His father had put a lot of pressure on Rod to be the perfect ruler—the exact opposite from the way she'd been raised.

Mom had let her go. No boundaries, no rules—well, other than the societal ones, of course. But Mom had been all about experiencing life, going off the beaten path. And, yes, that might not have worked quite as well as Val would have liked, given her prior lack of focus and job history, but at least she didn't have what-ifs or coulda-beens.

And if the wistfulness she sensed beneath the surface of Rod's words was anything to go by, his by-the-book, structured life hadn't worked out any better for him.

Her cell phone interrupted a funny story about Reel and an overly amorous dolphin, and Val looked over her shoulder to Livingston. "Can you get that out of my bag, please?"

Livingston, doing wing lifts on the backseat (to keep in shape, he'd explained), stopped with wings at shoulder height and flipped them over.

"Valerie, I'm flattered that you think me so anthropomorphic, but one does need appropriate appendages to open a zipper and, sorry," he wiggled his feathers, "these aren't them."

The phone rang again. "I'll get it," said Rod, leaning behind her seat.

Hmm... She got her phone *and* Rod's shoulder brushing hers at the same time. A definite plus over having the bird get the phone.

The last ring before it went to voice mail made it to Val's ear. "Hello?"

"Hey, it's me," said Tricia. "What's going on?"

"You wouldn't believe me if I told you." Val glanced over at Rod as another round of lightning started. "What's up, Tricia?"

"First of all, where are you? The electrician came early, so I let him in, but I've been back and forth to the diner all day. Then Summer forgot her lunch, so I had to run to camp, but I'm keeping tabs on him."

"Oh, crud, I didn't call." Dive-bombing peregrines were a perfectly acceptable excuse, but not one she could give Tricia without sounding like she'd gone around the bend—and she didn't mean the one in the road. "I'm sorry. We had to leave early this morning."

"Leave?"

As another round of thunder boomed overhead, Val gave Tricia a highly watered-down—no pun intended— version of the morning's events, minus the talking seagull and fish-bombs, and tossed in the immediacy factor of the inheritance for tax purposes.

"So why aren't you on a plane?"

Good question and one whose answer wouldn't make a lick of sense out of context and without the experiences of the day. "We're heading to an airport now. There weren't any direct flights available on such short notice at the first airport, and Rod needs one. He's not much of a flier."

Okay, not the best excuse, but definitely more believable—even if Rod raised his eyebrows and Livingston fell to the floor laughing, his wings semi-wrapped around his stomach, orange-webbed feet running as if he were on an invisible treadmill.

"I guess I'll stick around then until all the new light fixtures check out."

"Thanks, Tricia. I really appreciate it."

"No problem. But, listen, I need an address for where you're going to be. I found something you'll want to see. It's a package. From your mom."

Between the thunder and the gull's laughter, Val was having a hard time hearing Tricia. She frowned at Rod and nodded her head toward Livingston. A click of Rod's fingers shut the bird up. "What did you say?"

"I said, I found the birthday present your mom bought for you. It was behind a bag of birdseed. I thought you'd want it as soon as possible."

Val's blood froze in her veins as memories and emotions hit her with as much force as the storm outside.

A package? From Mom? Months after her death?

Val didn't know if she could deal with this.

First the inheritance from her father, now a gift from her mother. At the place where they'd first met. The place she was deathly allergic to.

What was the universe planning?

Did she really want to find out?

Or...

Did she want to run away?

Again.

Chapter 20

THE SOON-TO-BE-OUT-OF-OFFICE-AND-LOOKING-FORWARD-to-it-with-each-passing-minute High Councilman, Fisher Tritone, signaled the Serving Nautilus to leave the tray of mussels with the spicy red and green peppers his Olympian Advisor liked. The Nautilus placed the platter on the anemone-covered table then fluttered from the living room with only a tiny *whoosh* from his gills. Two dozen cleaner shrimp clambered over Mariana's newest lava sculpture to trail after him, giving Fisher the privacy they'd need for this conversation.

He hated that they even had to have this conversation.

"Who's behind this, Charley?" Fisher reached for his wife's hand as she drifted in from the reef garden she'd retreated to after they'd received the communiqué confirming JR's involvement. She'd demanded answers, answers Fisher didn't have. He'd invited Charley to their home to include her in the discussion.

Kai allowed him to pull her closer, her jittery tail flukes belying the serenity on her face.

Zeus. He would never have expected this of JR.

Although...

He'd *known* that fishing-net accident would come back to haunt them, but there'd been nothing he could have done at the time. No Mer Rescue Teams had been dispatched to save JR's mate because Humans had been all over the deck of that ship.

Charley rested his flukes on the bristly, hedgehog-shaped Human artifact that Angel insisted on keeping by the sofa. He shoved his spectacles higher on the bridge of his nose. "We don't know who hired JR. Nigel swears he knows nothing, and the gods are mum on the subject."

"What about Drake?" Kai asked, her beautiful, seal-brown hair tied back at her neck, a sure sign she was worried. She'd barely eaten this morning and her knitting lay in a heap beside the sculpture in the entranceway instead of by her favorite seat.

"Drake?" Fisher and Charley replied together.

"Yes. Nigel's son. Why is that so surprising? He *is* next in line now." Kai's grip tightened on Fisher's, and her scales flashed between a roiling midnight blue and an angry jade green—yet another sign of her anxiety. His normally calm wife usually regulated her tail to match her environment, not her emotions.

"Drake couldn't swim his way out of half a clam shell, let alone plan something like this," Fisher answered—part of the reason, from a succession standpoint, that Rod had to return in one piece. The other part of that reason was so personal it hurt his heart. "The surveillance we've had on him says he hasn't gone anywhere."

"I'm so sorry, Kai." Charley had seen Fisher through many troubling times, but this... this was as bad as when they'd almost lost Reel.

"Sorry isn't going to save him, Charley." His wife's words were soft, revealing more fear than Fisher had ever seen her exhibit. When Reel had been sent to Ceto's lair, Kai had all but flayed the scales from his tail, her words carrying throughout Atlantis for hours on the rippling waters. That, he could deal with.

But this, this quiet, resigned worry. That wasn't his wife. And Fisher felt just as useless to her as he did to his firstborn.

He released Kai's clammy hand to massage the knot from the back of his neck—well, most of it. "Damn it, Charley. You promised me I wasn't sending him to his death. You said this quest was to keep him safe and to bring her home. That it'd be good for our world. How in Hades can having him land-bound with a limited supply of oil be good for anyone? And with a hired bird on his tail?" Fisher choked on that last word. "Wait. He doesn't *have* a tail, Charley."

"We weren't expecting the danger to follow him onto land, Fisher. The trap was in the ocean. Humans don't know about our existence, so there should have been no threat on land."

"Except someone obviously wants him out of the way and went to the lengths of hiring JR." Fisher shook his head. "How did we let this happen? I thought JR's retirement account was well funded. He should have no reason to take this assignment."

A pufferfish-shaped shadow passed over the octagonal holes ringing the top of the room, the flickering light highlighting Charley's grimace. "Who knows why JR does what he does? I know he was upset about his mate, but to go against the gods like this…" Charley took off his spectacles, wiping the lenses with a piece of seaweed, then perched them back on his nose. "We're looking into it, Fisher."

"And Rod?" Kai asked, taking a sip of champagne. Fisher hadn't been surprised to see her open it. It was better than kelp wine for numbing heartache. Well, that was the theory at least. It hadn't done anything for him back in his office.

Fisher wanted to enfold her in his arms and assure her everything would be all right. But she wouldn't believe it any more than he did. Son of a Mer, he never should have sent Rod on this quest.

He looked away, catching a glimpse of himself in the gilt-framed mirror by the front tunnel entrance. He was too old for this. He'd done his time. If the gods had wanted Valerie back so badly, they should have brought her back themselves. Interceded when Lance Dumere hadn't been able to. But they hadn't, and Fisher felt every bit the failure Valerie's father had.

He should have been up-front with his son. Should have told him about the rumor. Should have respected Rod's hard work and determination in preparing for his role as High Councilman instead of seeing him as a child he had to protect by sending him out of harm's way.

Puffer swam past the skylight again. The Council's messenger was always alert, always watching.

Always looking out for the good of Atlantis—as *he* should be.

Zeus! Rod was a man—a damn fine one—and Fisher had done the same thing with Rod that he'd done with Reel: blinded himself to that fact in the face of his fear of losing him.

Yes, Rod was his son, but he was also the next Mer ruler, and if Fisher didn't have enough respect for Rod to level with him, how could he expect anyone else to?

He thought he'd learned his lesson with Reel, but apparently not. And now he—and Kai—and especially Rod, were paying the price.

"The good news is that The Hybrid has been able to keep them alive," Charley said.

"How do we know?" Kai leaned forward, her slender fingers gripping Fisher's tail so tightly scales came loose beneath her nails.

"Livingston was in the vehicle with them when JR's bombs hit."

"They were hit?" Kai shot up so fast that she almost crashed into the pink marble ceiling, scattering Fisher's scales in the water around them and knocking a pod of prawns into the sixteenth-century galleon figurehead he'd given her for their anniversary.

"Nothing serious, Kai. A fish or two bounced off the vehicle. Valerie outmaneuvered them."

"Oh, thank the gods." She drifted back onto the giant clamshell sofa, the *Holothurians* adjusting to take her weight without complaint.

Fisher would increase the sea cucumbers' plankton rations first thing tomorrow.

"What about sending Reel to help him?" he suggested. Reel had acclimated himself to living among Humans; perhaps he could find a solution they couldn't.

Charley shook his head. "That was my first thought as well, but the gods nixed it. What if someone is looking to annihilate the entire ruling family, Fisher? We have to examine that possibility."

Kai inhaled enough water to the point of choking— and it took a *lot* of water to choke a Mer.

Fisher patted her on the back. "It's a good thing he and Erica came here after putting Rod on that plane."

Charley nodded. "The girls are being escorted back as well."

"But Angel… she's waited so long for her land study program…" Kai's linked hands twisted around each other, her knuckles white.

"She'll have to wait a little longer, Kai," Charley answered.

His Olympian Advisor was taking charge of the situation in a way Fisher had never seen. At Council meetings, Charley had let the other Council members work out issues among themselves, never offering more than a few words or ideas. But now…

Fisher's gut clenched. As an Olympian Advisor, Charley had lived longer than any of them. There were rumors he'd been around during the Flood of Atlantis. He had the ear of the gods, conversed with them in ways Fisher had never been able to.

If the gods were this concerned…

If JR was willing to go this far…

"She can do it later, honey." Fisher put his arm around Kai, ostensibly for her comfort, but, really, he needed her strength to buoy his spirits—because he'd just realized why JR was going after Rod.

When Fisher had sent Rod among the Humans, he'd done for his son what he hadn't done for JR's mate: flouted the rules to protect the one he loved.

And now JR was paying him back.

Chapter 21

DRAKE ZIPPED ACROSS HIS LIMESTONE FOYER WITH TWO TAIL flicks and grabbed the electric ray by the neck, shaking it until the thing went limp. "You worthless hunk of chum. Do I have to do everything myself?"

Oh, Hades, he'd just strangled his chief operative into unconsciousness.

As the barnacle colony on the lintel abruptly shut up, Drake flung Gonzo's inert body onto the pile of useless octopi outside his lair. Those damn suckers hadn't been able to tear the netting between the manatee enclosure and the outside sea so he'd had Gonzo zap them as incentive. In his self-importance, however, the brainless *torpere* had ramped up the juice, killing the cephalopods.

The ineptitude boggled the mind.

Sighing, he started to shut the door when an eye blinked at him from the sandy floor. *Oh, Hades.*

Drake flipped that stupid flounder over with the tip of his tail, the spotted body wiggling in a way it'd never been designed to. Tough. That's what it got for thinking the entrance to his lair was a smart place to set up shop. Incompetents. That's what he was surrounded with. Clownfish.

Yanking the door shut with enough force to dislodge the conch family living rent-free on the roofline, Drake shoveled a fin-full of sand over the pile of ineffectual invertebrates.

Why was it so hard to get manatees, those stupid sea cows, out of the way? All he'd wanted to do was set them free so they could scour the coastline for food and other floating sacks of blubber to their hearts' content, thereby keeping them out of his business.

A few inconspicuous rips here and there in the netting should have done the trick; he couldn't believe the damn octopi had failed. Hades, if they could pry apart mollusks, a group of them should have been able to make crabmeat out of simple Human netting. But no.

Morons.

Drake kicked his tail, swimming above the reef. Sea anemones fluttered their tentacles, little fish darted after their next meal, and a crab climbed to the highest peak and broke into song—until he got a look at Drake.

Drake flicked a sand dollar at the crab, missing it by inches—that, the damn crustacean, and the whole scene making a mockery of his anger.

At least JR was on his side. Despite the fact that Rod had made contact with The Hybrid, the albatross was the perfect hired hand. The bird would do anything for the right amount of money, or whatever cause he was championing that day, and wouldn't have a qualm about seeing the job through to the end.

Sure, he'd had to do a bit of clandestine sleuthing through his father's office and a lot of finagling to shift so many diamonds from the kimberlite vault to the albatross, but it'd been worth it to land one of the ASA's best operatives as his henchman. JR had better come through.

Drake flicked the hair out of his eyes and headed toward the sundial in his courtyard. Bad enough one part of his plan had failed; he didn't want to miss the next report.

His latest girlfriend, Tracy, was "sunning" herself in the crystal-clear water of the courtyard, her scales not a shade darker than pale salmon. She'd seen Humans doing it on the one trip he'd been foolish enough to take her on, and now she whiled away hours in the pursuit of the perfect tan. He wasn't about to tell her that she needed to be in the actual sun to do it and not resting on the bottom.

Drake shook his head. Females. It had to be innate to their gender.

"Going topside again?" She held on to her shell-filler cover as she flipped onto her stomach.

Drake's eyes immediately flew to the area just above her scales.

As if there'd be a royal trident birthmark there. He laughed at himself. Hades, he was so paranoid another Mer would appear out of nowhere and outrank him that he was looking for trouble all over the place.

"You're not coming with me." That was the last thing he needed. She wasn't smart enough to understand what he'd learn, but she was stupid enough to share it with her girlfriends. It was probably time to find a new lair-mate. Maybe he'd have Gonzo do to her what he'd done to the octopi.

"You never let me go along," she pouted, hiking herself onto her elbows and forgetting to secure the cover in place. Nice show. Well, there were *some* things to recommend she remain alive. Two, specifically.

"That's because it's business, Tracy. I wouldn't go if it weren't necessary. It's not a nice place."

"Rod must think so if he's willing to do that leg thing. And I've heard Reel likes it so much he and Erica won't be back for a few *selinos* once they return this time." She flopped back onto the chaise she'd bought from a Salvager, her fingers trailing in the white sand beneath her.

Drake's teeth ground together like shell shards on a lava beach. The Heir and his lucky S-O-M of a brother, Reel. The other white meat.

Too bad he hadn't been able to talk any of the sharks into snatching the royal brothers up in their youth, but the *Chondrichthyes* hadn't wanted to risk the gods' wrath.

Yellow-bellied tuna-shits. Oh, he was so going to clean house when he took over.

"Yeah, well, Reel gave up Immortality, so it's not like I put stock in what he thinks." Drake didn't get it. How Reel got so lucky to be offered Immortality, only to turn it down to adopt Humanity! Talk about a clownfish. Those Tritone brothers were whacked.

And he was going to see to it that the last Mer Tritone brother *did* get whacked.

The sundial, adjusted for depth and water speed, shimmered its line at ten minutes before the appointed meeting time. He took a last look at Tracy, who had her eyes closed and was humming to herself—completely off-key. A Mer who couldn't sing. Yeah, she was a winner.

Why could he surround himself only with incompetents?

Well, his luck was about to change once the albatross came through. When Rod was out of the picture, Drake would finally be the winner.

He exited the perimeter of his lair, keeping careful watch for travelers in the area. He'd set up his home base just past Ceto's waters in the Bermuda Triangle, enjoying the privacy having her as a neighbor afforded him. Not many Mers—none that he knew of, actually—would stop by to chat if it meant coming into her territory. No, most Mers steered clear of her on general principle, since, supposedly, The Council had a tight rein on her activities.

Or so they thought.

Drake took a leisurely trip to the surface amid a bloom of moon jellyfish, both to fool anyone who might be paying attention and to frighten inquisitive Humans away. He couldn't believe, after all the ships and planes that went missing in the Triangle, that the stupid Bipeds still ventured into this area. They were invasive on all fronts, and he planned to put the fear of the gods into them once he was running the show.

Clearing the surface, Drake shielded his eyes as he looked into the setting sun. He swore JR had told his minions to fly in that way just to keep him sunblind.

Ah, well, JR had earned his reputation, and if this was how he trained his team, far be it from Drake to challenge it. He just wanted results.

The soft fluttering of feathers joined the quiet ebb and flow of the sea's ripples as another petrel swooped in for a landing on the water's surface.

"Whatcha got?" Drake asked him.

The gray bird took his time dunking his head below the surface to splash water over his back, then settling his feathers into place. Drake fumed silently. Power plays were not something he enjoyed.

Unless, of course, they were played by him.

"Well? Did JR handle it?"

The petrel arched the feathers above one eye. "JR is handling it. He asked me to report in that all is going according to plan."

"According to plan? What does that mean? I want to know if Rod is dead on the side of the road somewhere in that gods-forsaken stretch of dirt. I want results."

The bird aimed its pointy beak at his eyes. "And you'll have them. Don't question JR. You hired him because he's the best. He'll get the job done."

"But he assured me he'd have Rod out of commission by today."

"Today isn't over." The bird stretched its wings, flapping them. "You'll get your results." Then he took off, quickly becoming a black dot in the waning daylight.

JR had failed.

Drake couldn't believe it. The one being he hadn't expected to fail, had. Rod was still alive and still heading to the ocean—where Drake wouldn't be able to touch him. Not now. Not when they were all on alert.

Desperation eclipsing his pride, Drake called the petrel back. If he wanted to have a prayer in ascending to the throne, Rod needed to die.

Soon.

Chapter 22

VAL PEERED THROUGH THE UNRELENTING WATER SLUICING down her windshield into the gray nothingness beyond. *Blah* road bled into black clouds, the deluge outside changing the cornstalks alongside the road into shadowy sentinels as fields stretched for mile after endless mile.

There hadn't been any more air assault incidents, unless one wanted to count Mother Nature's unrelenting torrent. No more painful phone calls—by unspoken agreement, Rod hadn't asked after supplying his brother's address, and she hadn't volunteered.

Instead, Rod had shared more stories of his childhood, about his sisters: Angel, the sociologist; Mariana, the sculptor; and Pearl, who was still in school.

Val had contributed as well, with stories from her offbeat jobs, keeping them as light and humorous as possible.

Rod had asked hundreds of questions about each one. What she'd liked, what she hadn't, why she'd chosen one over the other, why she'd left... It was as if he'd never heard of some of them.

And now, with Livingston outside somewhere doing more reconnaissance, they made a dash through a fast food drive-through. Rod actually liked this fish sandwich better, and they made sure to get a double order of fries before heading back down the road to somewhere, with Val rubbing eyes that were tired from all the driving, the emotions, and the now-possible impossibilities of the day, while Rod kept his eyes peeled for any sign of Livingston.

The seagull made it easy—by landing on the hood of the car with a *splat!* too reminiscent of JR's little "gifts" earlier not to scare the daylights out of her and bring her to full wakefulness.

"Crap!" Val swerved the Sentra, collecting a few honks from other drivers, all the while thanking God and Nissan she didn't hydroplane into anyone.

Rod rolled down his window and Livingston hopped in, wiping the water from his brow with his wing.

"Sorry about that. This weather's dicey." He ruffled some of the rain onto them and took the french-fry container from Rod's fingers as he hopped into the backseat.

"Okay, here's the plan," he said, with a fry hanging from the side of his mouth like a cigarette. "There's some sort of backup ahead, but that's not as important as the airport beyond it being all tricked out with self-important crows. The few blue jays and starlings in their ranks have been relegated to monitoring the parking lots, but the crows have commandeered the runways and turkey vultures have staked out the control tower. So that option's out. Luckily, though, I recruited a chickadee with a James Bond complex who's agreed to scout out the airport beyond that, which will keep me in the car and instill a false sense of security that we're continuing on our way."

"So we keep driving." Rod's voice, scratchy and hoarse after so much talking, slid over her like a blanket.

Especially that timbre, low and warm, as it'd been last night when he'd murmured something unintelligible in her ear. It had resonated through her bones and nerves and every cell in between while he'd kissed her senseless.

Well, maybe not too senseless since she remembered it well enough. Too well, actually.

"For as long as possible," Livingston continued, oblivious to the reawakening of her senses. "The farther east we get without incident, the better off for us. I'm concerned that if we stop, he'll have a chance to come up with more recruits and do major damage."

Val put her blinker on to go around the pickup in front of her. She hoped drivers behind her could see through this mess. God, she was tired. She'd driven at warp speed for hours this morning, then dodged raindrops all afternoon. She was sick to death of showers. The only one she wanted was hot and followed immediately by a pillow.

"Oh, and guess what I found out?" The gull went to work on the second pack of fries. "A pair of sparrows in the building next to Valerie's thwarted an attack on us."

"Sparrows?" With the way the guy in the SUV who passed her was driving, Val didn't dare risk turning around, so she angled the rearview mirror toward Livingston.

"Yeah. Apparently gossip can get through where military orders can't. Go figure." Livingston stood on the backseat, rifling his bill through his feathers. "Can you pass a napkin back, please?"

Rod handed him one. "What attack?"

"Thanks." Livingston swiped the napkin beneath a wing. "Anyway, those chicks conned two cowbirds out of a bag of industrial-strength carpet tacks. I'm assuming the cowbirds planned to sprinkle them on the road, but here's the best part. Not only did the sparrows replace the tacks with harmless objects, but they also convinced the cuckoos that the closest ocean is to the north. The north!"

Livingston's laugh was close to an annoying screech, but in this case, Val let it slide.

"What idiots," he went on, still laughing. "Thwarted by sparrows! Remind me to give those chicks a commendation when we get back. They earned it."

"Where'd they get the tacks?" Val asked, angling the mirror to keep the headlights behind her out of her eyes.

Livingston switched the napkin to the other wing. "Knowing how little effort cowbirds put into anything, namely raising their own offspring, I'd say they probably flew into a hardware store, but that would give them too much credit for figuring out how to do it and get out. JR probably had some industrious avian deliver them to the birdbrains."

"But how did the sparrows get the tacks away from them?" Even with the talking seagull and mercenary albatross, Val was having a hard time processing all of this. Well, maybe not as hard a time as she would have had, say, oh, last week, but still. It was as if there was a whole other world right under humans' noses that no one could see.

"That's the funniest part." Livingston slapped his feathers against the backseat. "The sparrows used the oldest trick in the book."

She didn't even want to contemplate what *that* meant.

"Flirting. Those boys must have been hard up. I mean, sparrows are cute and all, but so enchanting that you fail to do your job?" The seagull tsk-tsked. "Dodos. It's good to know JR's training methods aren't foolproof."

"Yes, it is good to know that," said Rod, "but only if we can counter it. We need to outwit him, Livingston. We need to find another airport, one that he won't expect us to go to."

"I know, Rod, and now's the perfect time. He's not expecting it, the weather is good cover, and there aren't enough birds left in the area to stop us. I was going to suggest getting off this road anyway to go around the backup that I'd bet my tail feathers he's had a feather in."

"There's only one problem, Livingston." Rod nodded at Valerie. "Valerie. We need to stop soon. She's tired."

"What? I'm not a problem. I've done my share of the work." More actually, since neither of them would be here if not for her. "Besides, this doesn't look to be a hot spot of motels."

"Valerie, you're exhausted. You can't keep going."

"I can if it means getting away from JR."

"Great!" Livingston stuck his beak between them. "Then it's settled. Take the next turnoff, and we'll try to outsmart the buzzard. Get in the right lane."

Val squinted through the windshield, trying to decide which of the six taillights in front of her were the real two and which four were reflections—and not enjoy the warm, fuzzy feeling of having Rod care for her comfort, while Livingston sat over her shoulder and directed her onto the off-ramp.

Rod kept staring out the window. At what, she couldn't imagine. It was black as pitch despite the car lights glowing on the rainy road.

Was he worried she'd see something in his suggestion that didn't exist? Was he worried that he'd kissed her and been kind to her—and she'd want more?

If the guy was a prince—and, seriously, with the seagulls and whatnot, the prince part of this whole equation was the least difficult to believe—he was probably used to women flinging themselves at him.

But she wouldn't.

She was going back to the store, and that wouldn't leave a lot of time for jaunts through his country in between his royal duties.

Still, it had been nice to lean on him, just for those few moments. For that short period of time, the loneliness had disappeared. She'd felt connected to someone else, something she hadn't felt or been since Mom died.

But this connection had been different. Oh, not the man-woman dynamic, though they definitely had that between them. No, this was human to human. Personal. For her, anyway—but she wasn't going to take it at anything more than face value.

He had a job to do and now, finally, after all her searching, all those years of looking for something, somewhere to belong, so did she. Still, she would miss him when this was all over.

"Have you heard a word I've said, Valerie?" Livingston tap-danced on her shoulder, the fried potato breath acting like smelling salts, banishing her fatigue in an instant.

"Hmm? What?"

"I said, the airport is—oh no! Watch out!" The bird dove for cover beneath Rod's seat.

"Watch what?" Val followed Livingston's backseat flight, then saw Rod stiffen.

Her eyes flew to the windshield, peering through the pouring rain.

A pair of round objects sat in the middle of the lane.

Val jumped on the brakes. The tires locked, jerking the car forward, the high-pitched, rubber-on-brake-pad squeal protesting such treatment.

But braking did nothing.

The objects loomed before them.

And the car kept sliding straight at them.

Chapter 23

VAL WRENCHED THE WHEEL. WHAT WERE THOSE THINGS? She couldn't hit them. Not now. Not at this speed. That would kill them all.

In slow motion, she watched her hands spin the wheel to the left, her left foot releasing the clutch as her right pumped the brake, each movement a conscious, singular action.

But nothing kept the car from careening toward the whatever-they-were.

Then suddenly, everything clicked in her mind and she was back at regular speed, the image of hay bales searing into her brain as the car broadsided one, Rod's side taking the hardest impact.

Tires squealed around them as the few cars behind them reacted. The jerk who'd passed her slammed on his brakes, bouncing off a minivan into the back end of her car with a nasty crunch and slamming them into the hay again.

Rod's head cracked against the doorframe, then he slumped onto her.

"Livingston!" She looked around, trying to peer through the rain to see if any other cars were headed toward them. She reached around Rod's face, feeling a sticky trickle of blood seep from his forehead. "Oh, my God. Rod's been hurt! We have to get out of here!" She jerked on the door handle, but they were penned in. She'd have to smash the windshield.

"Don't get out of the car. Just get it moving!" Livingston squawked from the back.

He was right. She had to get them out of there before other cars smashed into the pileup and something exploded.

She nudged Rod back into his seat and felt for the stick shift, her feet working the pedals. After a few grinding revs of the engine, the car jerked forward, a rattling sound coming from the tire well as the car screeched its way slowly from the jumble of vehicles.

"Go around," Livingston said by her ear, his wings fanning the back of her neck as he tried to grip the slope of her headrest.

"On what? The median?"

"Unless you want to wait for JR to come after us with more ammo, yes."

Good point. Plus, the car was damaged anyway; the median couldn't do much worse.

Besides, she had to get Rod to a hospital. Oh, God, the blood. What if he had a concussion? Internal injuries?

The car bounced over the lip of the road, the tires sinking into the wet grass. Hell. Watch them get stuck in the mud.

That wasn't going to happen. As she gunned the gas, the tires sped out, spewing grass and mud all around them, but with the passenger side tires still on the asphalt, the car crept forward.

The steering column protested as she turned the wheel to the right, trying to keep at least one tire on the road. After more squelching and tire spinning, the car gave a final whip around the hay bale and Val straightened them onto the road.

"We need to find a hospital. Can you look for one?"

"A hospital?" Livingston fluttered through the seats onto Rod's leg. "I don't think so. You need to get him to the first motel we find."

"Motel? Are you out of your mind? He's been injured. He's not responsive. We need a doctor."

"Valerie, listen to me." Livingston pointed at her with one black-tipped wing feather. "He cannot see one of your doctors. They'd do more damage than help. Right now, we need to get him someplace where we can tend to his injuries."

One of the wipers was bent at a seventy-degree angle and dragged across the windshield with a *thud, thud, thud*. "I'm not a doctor. Are you?"

"No. But I do have basic first-aid skills, and I know his people. More importantly, he's got what he needs right now in his pocket."

The steering had been knocked out of alignment, so Val had to turn the wheel off-center to the left to keep going straight. The damn rain made it that much tougher to see the lines.

"In his pocket?" She forgot to hold the wheel in position and almost ran off the road. She made the adjustment in time. "What are you talking about? All he has in his pocket is a wad of cash and a diamond. They aren't exactly first-aid material, Livingston, but hospitals can do wonders with both."

"Just look for a building, Valerie. We don't have time to argue. Every second counts."

"That's why we need a hospital."

Livingston sighed. "We don't want an international incident over this. Trust me. It's my job to protect him.

I know what I'm doing. Get us to a motel, and he'll be fine by morning."

Val didn't believe him, but then, things she would never have believed had happened today, and she didn't want to even consider that international incident thing. "You better be right."

"I am. I'll stake my life on it. And his."

Livingston poked at Rod's arms and legs, looking for breaks, while she tried to discern whether the blurry lights in the distance were from a tractor-trailer or a motel. Luckily, after a few miles, some of the lights turned out to be a motel.

Val turned in, slamming the car into park next to a dented maroon pickup, and rushed into the lobby in her half-soaked clothing. She threw the last of her cash at the kid on duty since she wasn't about to go rooting around in Rod's pockets for his stash. She didn't have much money since she hadn't exactly planned for this journey, so they were stuck with one room, and she'd have to make the best of it. Not that it'd matter, since the guy was *unconscious*.

Right. That.

She grabbed the key and an extra set of thin white towels before heading back to the car.

Rod groaned when she slammed the door.

"Is he awake?"

Livingston shook his head, his brow furrowed. "No. But he's been mumbling, so that's a good sign."

"Really? Mumbling is good?"

"Better than deathly silent."

True. She put the car in gear and squinted through the windshield, trying to find Room 5.

She pulled into the parking spot in front of the tarnished, brass room number and ran to the faded green door, the rain soaking the rest of her as she opened their room.

Musty, stale air greeted her, but at least the double beds were made. She tugged the chain beneath the beaded 1960s lampshade on the nightstand, pulled the sheets down on the bed closest to the door, the smell of bleach attesting to some semblance of hygiene, then ran back out to maneuver Rod from the car.

Livingston had somehow finagled the door open and was using his beak to undo Rod's seat belt by the time she returned.

Leaning against the headrest, Rod blocked the dim glow of the car light as she tried to figure out the best way to get him out of the car. God, he was so big. And so unconscious. How the hell was she going to do this?

She draped his arm over her shoulder. Blood matted his black hair to his forehead, a trickle drying along his jaw. She slid one of his legs to the pavement, gasping when she found blood there as well. "Livingston, his leg."

"I know. Let's get him inside. We'll tend to him there."

"But what if something's broken?"

"Trust me, Valerie. No one can heal him better than what he's got with him. Now, come on. I'll grab the back of his shorts once you've got him out. We'll get him inside together."

Right. A two-pound seagull and her measly one-twenty were going to move a six-foot-something guy.

The other option was to go ask the teenaged clerk at the registration desk. Yeah. He looked like he'd weigh all of a hundred pounds soaking wet.

She slid Rod's other leg to the pavement, lifting his other arm over her shoulder. "Livingston, give me a hand here. I'm going to turn around and hoist him onto my back. That's probably the only way this is going to work. Help me keep his hands around my neck."

With some ducking and spinning and holding of Rod's limp arms, Val managed to get herself into position, wincing when the broken window handle on the door sliced across her calf.

Oh, yay. They had matching injuries...

She bent over at the waist, pulling Rod's elbows over her shoulders. Rain poured down her face, a river channeling down her neck and between her breasts, following a straight line through her shorts, down her legs, and right into her shoes.

"You ready back there? Have enough clearance?"

"Don't worry about me." Livingston's words were garbled, which Val took to mean he had Rod's waistband in his bill.

Good thing Rod wasn't going to feel this when Livingston pulled upward.

"On three. Ready?" She double-checked her grip. "One... two... three!" She huffed, anchoring Rod's arms to her chest as she hefted him out of his seat and onto her back.

Livingston's wings flapped like a buzz saw behind her. Bent over, she took a tentative (squishy) step. Rod's weight shifted with her. So far, so good.

She took another step, and he moved with her. Then another. And another.

Slowly, they headed toward the door. She had to keep readjusting her grasp as the rain slicked her hold on his arms, but at last they made it into the room. Val slid Rod onto the bed, positioning his legs and arms as much onto it as she could, while Livingston made trips out to the car to grab their bags.

"I tried closing the doors, but I don't have the strength," the bird said as he dragged her duffel over the threshold, his chest heaving, wings drooping from his shoulders.

"I'll do it. Be right back." Adrenaline gave her the strength to sprint out to the car. She was going to collapse when it wore off.

She grabbed the spare towels from the dash, her keys from the ignition, and locked up. The car wasn't much, but there was no need to tempt Fate or teenagers into stealing it.

She returned to the room only to be greeted by a spray of water as Livingston ruffled the rain from his feathers.

"Sorry about that."

She shrugged, tossing the damp towels onto the maple veneer dresser. "It doesn't matter. I'm already wet." She locked the door behind her, the burst of energy waning. "Speaking of which," she crossed to the bed, "we need to get these clothes off him. He's already soaked the sheets. That can't be good."

The gash on Rod's temple didn't look good either, but at least it had stopped bleeding. The cut on his leg, however, was another matter. It looked as if his knee had snapped the window handle off.

"Get the bottle out of his pocket." Livingston hopped onto the bed.

It was one thing to talk about taking a guy's clothes off to keep him from catching pneumonia; it was another thing entirely to slip her fingers into his pocket to grab the lump that was right *there* next to something she didn't really want to be grabbing.

She tried to force her fingers onward, but her hand kept clamping shut as she got close.

"Come on, already, Valerie. I'd do it myself, but the beak's not equipped for grasping something that shape."

Val tried again, but there was just something so, well, personal, about slipping her fingers inside his clothes.

"Let me take them off, and then I'll get it." The shorts had to come off anyway, right?

She slid his shirt just above his navel and reached for the button above the fly.

He's commando beneath there, remember?

Yeah, it wasn't any easier to undo his clothes than it'd been to root around inside them.

She picked up one of the towels from the dresser and laid it on his flat, washboard, six-pack, totally sculpted, no-ounce-of-fat abdomen—not that she was thinking about anything other than his injury, really—took a deep breath, then did the lightest-touch, four-finger-button-opening that would've made any courtesan proud.

She draped the towel over his groin, then worked the shorts down his legs, focusing on his injured one so she wouldn't focus on what she really shouldn't be focusing on anyway. She removed his shoes and slid the shorts off, the lean hip-to-toe muscle she remembered from this morning right before her eyes.

She gulped.

"Come on!" Livingston stomped one of his webbed feet. "Stop ogling. He needs the shirt off."

"I'm not ogling." Liar. "I'm trying to assess the damage."

"Yeah, okay. Whatever. Just get his shirt off so we can get the oil on him."

"The oil?"

"The stuff inside the diamond bottle, remember?"

"I don't think we should put oil in a cut, Livingston. It can get infected."

"Not with this oil, it won't. I told you, you need to trust me. Now get his shirt off before he gets a chill. I don't know how rainwater will affect him—I mean, we don't want him to get pneumonia."

Val maneuvered the shirt up Rod's chest and worked it over his shoulder. The warmth of his skin tickled her nerve endings while the scent of rain-drenched masculinity tickled her senses.

Mind back on the problem, Dumere.

At least her exhaustion had abated, so that was a good thing.

Rod groaned as she slid his arm through. She lifted his head, gingerly working the shirt over it and trying not to jostle him. She ran to the other side of the bed and slid the shirt off his other arm, cleaning the blood off, no matter what Livingston said.

Rod shivered.

"You need to get him to the other bed where it's dry." Livingston ordered, oh-so-helpfully.

"And how do you expect me to do that?"

The bird cocked his head backward, then forward quickly, as if he were brushing something from the top. "Same way you got him in here."

"Really. And what, pray tell, are you going to grab to help?"

The two of them looked at the naked man.

Uh, oh. She really shouldn't have done that.

He was a fine, fine specimen of the species. A long, lanky, muscled vee from broad shoulders to tapered waist, the deep line by his hips highlighting his six-pack. Long, muscled thighs and well-defined calves... if not for the rainwater trickling down her cheek and onto her lips, the inside of her mouth would have gone dry.

As it was, her stomach was quivering with each inch she perused.

"Hello? Valerie? Do you want him to get sick?"

She closed her eyes and willed her tongue not to splat on the floor when she responded. "*I* was the one who wanted to get him to a hospital. It's your fault we're here."

"I'm not going to have this argument with you. Move him to the other bed so we can deal with his injuries. What? Have you never seen a naked man before?"

"Of course I have." Just not one like him, that's all.

"Then what's the problem?"

"The problem is that moving him is going to put his, er, naked parts against me."

"So? They were against you before if you recall, just with a layer of fabric between them. You still have your clothes on."

True. However, her clothes were plastered to her body and would be no help whatsoever in disguising said naked parts as they rubbed against her.

"What is it with you Humans and your hang-ups about nudity? You don't see avians and animals making a fuss about it."

"I don't have a hang-up about nudity."

"Then prove it by getting him onto that bed before he gets something the oil can't cure."

Right. Rod was unconscious. She wasn't a lecher for pete's sake. Move the guy to the bed. Don't think of it as moving the *naked* guy to the bed.

She pulled down the sheets on the dry bed, then went back to Rod and rolled him to the edge of the bed, some judicious towel maneuvers protecting everyone's modesty. Working him to a sitting position was a bit more challenging, but the towel pooled right where it was supposed to. Hiking him once more onto her back, she focused her thoughts on the three steps between the beds, then turned around, ready to ease him onto his back.

The towel mocked her from the floor. It must have slid off when she'd stood him up.

"Livingston? The towel."

The noise Livingston made might have been a snort, but at least he didn't say anything. He hopped over and grabbed it in his beak, fluttering to the bed behind her and Rod.

"Gotcha covered," Livingston said around the towel. "Or actually, I guess it's him I have to cover."

She lowered Rod to the bed, holding him upright until she felt the brush of Livingston's feathers against the back of her thigh. Then she turned and eased Rod backward.

The towel was at eye-level as she bent down to swing his legs onto the bed.

The huff she released had nothing to do with the image of what was beneath that towel and everything to do with lifting his long, toned legs onto the bed.

Really.

Moving the man as much as she had in the last fifteen minutes could only be called exertion. That's why her breath was coming in short, quick puffs. It had nothing to do with the manic butterflies in her tummy.

"Now for the oil."

Val amended her position on seagulls and, more specifically, talking ones: they were right handy to keep one's mind on the task at hand.

She picked the pockets in Rod's shorts, feeling like she was invading his private space as she removed the diamond bottle. It caught the lamplight, the facets sparkling with a prism of colors, the oil inside flowing with the consistency of melted honey.

She pulled the stopper, and the smell of coconuts and almonds and something tropical wafted from within. "There's not a lot here." She walked to the bed.

"You don't need a lot. A drop on each of his temples, and one on his leg. Put each drop on your finger and work it in." Livingston hopped onto the pillow by Rod's head. "Start here. We need him to be conscious."

Val took a deep breath and tipped a drop of golden liquid onto the pad of her finger. What kind of mumbo-jumbo was this? Honestly, if she weren't being directed to do this by a talking seagull, she'd think it was insane.

And that last sentence showed how close *she* was to being insane.

"So, do you think JR had anything to do with those hay bales?" Why *not* add to the insanity...

Livingston closed his eyes, a look of pain spreading across his face.

That she realized it was a look of pain worried her. Did insanity start with the ability to converse with seagulls or being able to read their expressions?

She pinched herself again, half-hoping she wouldn't feel it. Then she wouldn't be insane, just asleep.

Or maybe delusional.

Ouch.

"Think it? No. I *know* JR's behind this. And I'm pissed at myself for not outthinking him." Livingston stomped both feet. "Can you please get that oil on him already?"

"Oh. Right." Taking a deep breath, Val brought her finger next to the mess at Rod's temple. "Are you sure he shouldn't get stitches?"

"Valerie, just put the oil on it."

"Okay." She cleared her throat and transferred the oil to the middle of the gash.

She gasped as it was wicked in.

"What?" Livingston raised his head so that he looked like an egret, trying to see over Rod.

"Nothing. It's just that it… well, it almost looked like it got sucked into the cut."

"Good. That's supposed to happen. Now do his other temple."

Valerie repeated the process, amazed to see his skin absorb the oil as quickly on the uninjured side.

The bird tamped the bedcovers as he hopped to Rod's legs. "Now his leg."

Val was still trying to process the odd reaction to the oil as she looked at his leg. It definitely needed stitches. And that window lever was metal. He might end up with tetanus.

But Livingston said he knew what he was doing.

The fact that she was taking medical advice from a seagull should have had her running, screaming, for the hills. Sadly, there weren't any close by, so she had no option but to do as he said.

She tipped the bottle sideways and collected another drop. Then another. Two should be better than one, right? She shook her head. Was she actually starting to believe this might work? Or really, really hoping she wouldn't have to explain a comatose man with lockjaw tomorrow when he didn't wake up?

Taking another deep breath, Val steadied her hand as she slid it toward the injury, rolling her shoulders before making the initial contact.

Again, the oil was wicked off her finger as if it were a pod returning to the mother ship.

The argument for insanity was growing.

Livingston dropped onto the mattress. "Whew. That's done. Okay, now put about five drops in your palms and rub them on both of his legs. Thigh to toes."

"What?"

"You heard me. It'll help the oil work."

"But he only injured one leg." She put the stopper in the bottle.

"Valerie, just do it. Gods, woman, you need to learn to have a little faith."

In a talking bird. She was listening to a bird about treating an injured man, and he was talking about *her* having faith. What was wrong with this scenario?

She set the bottle down. "Livingston, I don't know what makes you think this is going to work, but he needs a doctor. God only knows what damage I did by putting oil into open wounds, but we have to get him to a hospital and—"

"How do you think your ankle healed so quickly?" Livingston said, irritated.

"My ankle? What does that have to do with anything?"

"Everything. Or have you forgotten that you sprained it? Have you ever heard of a sprain going away that quickly?"

"Maybe it wasn't a bad sprain."

"Or maybe it was the oil Rod rubbed on your ankle."

"Rod didn't—"

"Yes he did. I told him to. Remember that little ankle massage? You were cured. So finish the job already and put an end to the hospital argument. We aren't taking him to one."

Rod moaned, his legs sliding along the sheet, and guilt wicked down her spine every bit as quickly as the oil had been wicked into his cut.

What would it hurt if she did what Livingston wanted? She'd already come this far; what was one more oil application?

She unstopped the bottle and poured the oil into her palm, massaging it with the other one, then touched his injured leg. The edge of the towel rested in the crease of his thigh at his groin. Val tried to ignore it as she massaged the oil into the muscle there.

Sparks flicked up her fingers. Friction. That's what it was. The oil was a conductor.

She cleared her throat, aware Livingston was watching every move. No, she wasn't going to have her fingers slip beneath that towel to make sure the oil covered all of his leg. This was good enough.

"Don't forget underneath." Livingston closed one eye as she settled half her rear end on the edge of the bed.

"Underneath?"

"Yes, his entire leg. You might want to use that towel to move, uh, certain things so you can be sure the oil covers his whole leg."

Oh, God, she had to slide her hands between his legs.

She wasn't going to. That's all there was to it and Livingston couldn't make her.

"You *do* want this to work, right? You don't want him to die?"

Damn talking bird.

Val took a deep breath and tried to pretend she was a nurse. Right. She could do this. He was injured. Maybe dying. The only thing keeping him alive was her ministrations. Nothing sexual about it at all.

Then the backs of her fingers skimmed his sac.

Like hell there was nothing sexual about it.

Her nipples hardened. She could tell because they were poking through her bra, fully outlined by her shirt. Thank God the bird had his eyes closed.

Val worked the oil in, trying—really—not to catch a quick feel, but hey, his sac was *right there* and there wasn't enough room for her fingers and his naked parts to share the space and no way was she going to move *them*—with or without the towel.

Now why had she added that "without" part?

She tried to settle her breathing into the vicinity of normal and made quick work of that area.

Sliding her hands down the length of his thigh and over his injured knee didn't really do much to dampen her awareness of his skin beneath hers. She felt every muscle, its strength, its shape. She could only imagine how his muscles would feel when he was using them to hold himself above her, pressing himself inside her...

The bird coughed, bringing her back to the here and now. Good thing, too, because she was moments away from jumping on the guy—which was so not a good idea, since he was A) injured, B) royal, and C) leaving. Oh, and D) unconscious.

She finished with a quick massage of his foot, then worked her way up his other leg, trying to concentrate on Livingston and not the warm flesh she was touching more intimately than she'd ever touched anyone.

Finished finally, in more ways than one, Val covered Rod with the blanket and headed to the bathroom to wash the oil from her fingers.

"You might want to put some on that cut on your leg," Livingston said, his eyes still closed. "It'll heal it. Like your ankle."

Val stopped and looked at the blood dotting the slice on her leg. Looked at her ankle. Rotated it.

She slid a finger across the cut, a tingle following the path. Nothing burned, no searing pain, just a light buzz as if she'd poured hydrogen peroxide on it. Maybe there was something to the oil, but that didn't negate normal first-aid care. Fine for Rod if Livingston wanted to take responsibility for sepsis, but she wasn't willing to bet the farm—or her mom's shop—on it.

She returned to the bedroom to change out of her wet clothes. Rod would have to sleep as he was because exhaustion had come back with a vengeance and she wasn't up for wrangling him into any clothes. Since the other bed was soaked and she was going to share his, one naked person between the sheets was enough. Luckily, there was still another pillow his hair hadn't soaked, so she was going to take a page from a 1950s sitcom and put the pillow between them. Good for keeping wayward parts from straying where they shouldn't.

Val unzipped her duffel and reached in for a change of clothes. All she encountered was a soggy mess.

Oh, no. Livingston had *dragged* the bag in. It was cotton. Talk about wicking—the thing had soaked up puddles like a sponge.

Great. Two naked people in that bed.

Not gonna happen.

Val spread her clothes around the room, checked Rod's bag, and found the same messy scenario, and pretty soon she had the room resembling a Laundromat where the power had gone out. Well, it couldn't be helped. Now, as to what *could* be helped… her sleeping attire.

She returned to the bathroom, thankful to find two large towels for her concession to modesty. She wrapped one around her chest, securing it with a hair clip, and the other around her waist, tying the ends together. Better than shorts and a T-shirt, the impromptu outfit covered her from chest to toe.

"Valerie, can you open the door?" Livingston asked when she emerged, ready to hit the hay—oh, not a good cliché *vis-à-vis* their situation. "To pull that off, JR must have something big in the works, and I want to know what it is before we get moving in the morning. I'll see you then."

Which meant she and Rod had the room to themselves. Good thing one of them was unconscious.

Too bad it wasn't her.

She let Livingston out, arranged her pillows à la Rob and Laura Petrie, and tried to make herself as small on the bed as possible.

Hopefully she'd get some sleep.

Drake floated alongside the pipe Humans had extended into the sea. Another way for them to spew their filth into his world. Gods, he was so sick of Humans. Of having to pretend he didn't exist, of lurking around their beaches as if he were the intruder, when Mers had claimed those islands long before Humans had shown up. And now he was going to try to pass as one of them.

It would be laughable if it wasn't necessary. Damn JR and his failed plan. Drake hadn't stayed around to get the next report. Oh, he knew what that one would be—more of the same. As if JR were doing him some big flippin' favor, when it was the other way around. JR *owed* him.

Especially now that Drake had to become physically involved. Since the bird hadn't done the deed, he'd need to, and the only way to keep Rod on land permanently was to meet him there to ensure it. He couldn't let Rod get to the sea.

Drake looked at the slate chip in his hand, reading it by the light of the moon.

He knew *just* where to find Rod.

Chapter 24

CHARLEY FOLDED HIS SPECTACLES AND RESTED THEM AMONG the sea squirts occupying the ledge beneath the smallest and least inhabited island in the Azores. Where he was going, he wouldn't need glasses.

Nodding at the red-crested oarfish guarding the entrance to the Travel Chamber, Charley took his time swimming into the vortex at the center. The speed with which it zipped him to the top of the extinct volcano always gave him a headache.

He emerged in the crystalline lake, as usual. Despite the brilliant sunshine, white fluffy clouds hung low in the verdant crater—also, as usual.

Zeus, on a raft, reading a book, however, was not usual.

Charley hadn't expected Zeus. Usually Poseidon greeted him on the shore, more often than not with a piña colada in one hand and a nymph in the other. Charley didn't know how Amphitrite put up with it, but he'd never been one to question the gods before—nor their wives. At least, not about their personal lives.

When it came to Rod's and Valerie's, on the other fin...

Charley cleared his throat to announce himself. He'd had very few personal conversations with the head god and was wondering if questioning Zeus was as good an idea now as it'd sounded in Fisher's office after Angel's comment had set him to thinking.

Zeus looked up from his book. "Ah, Archangel Chayyiel. So glad you could stop by." Zeus dog-eared his page and tossed the book into the sky where it disappeared in a flash of miniature thunderbolts. He swung his legs over the side of the raft. "I understand you have questions for me."

Too late to back out now. Besides, Olympian Advisors had the right to address the gods—even if they rarely went straight to the top as Charley had.

He swallowed. He didn't like what this was doing to Fisher and Kai. He didn't like the possibility of failure for Rod. And poor Valerie, trapped unknowingly in this mess… "Yes, Sir. It's about what's going on with Rod."

"Oh?" Zeus arched an eyebrow.

Charley cleared his throat. "Yes. Um… JR is after him."

"You're right. He is."

"You know?"

Zeus sat straighter on the raft and crossed his arms, one side of his mouth quirking upward. "I *am* the top god, Chayyiel."

Right. Of course Zeus would know. "But I don't understand."

The grin spread to both sides of Zeus' face. "I know that, too."

This wasn't getting Charley anywhere. He kicked his tail and swam closer. "I'm wondering why, Sir. We sent him on land to remove him from harm's way, not put him in it."

"Who said he's in it?"

What? "But, Sir, the reports we've received—"

"Yes, the reports." Zeus flicked his wrist, and the raft disappeared. When he stood atop the water, a long, flowing gold robe hung from his shoulders. "Those reports are what's already happened. By the time you get them, they're obsolete. Disregard them."

Trying to make sense of a god's proclamation was like trying to figure out which came first, the chicken or the egg.

"You don't honestly expect me to answer that one, do you?"

The top god could read minds, too.

Zeus started pacing. "Look, Chayyiel, I like you. You've been one of the most loyal subjects in the last fifty millennia or so, and you've done your job well. So I'll let you in on a little secret."

Charley crossed his arms and rested them on top of the water, his tail flukes fluttering intermittently, keeping him upright.

"Rod is doing exactly what we need him to do. And so is JR. And... well, so is the one who hired him. There's a master plan—I *have* been at this for a few *selinos*, you know." He stopped pacing. "Which is why I'm the top god and you're an archangel."

An archangel the gods themselves had charged to ensure Mer safety, happiness, and lives.

Charley squared his shoulders, wishing he hadn't removed his glasses. He could swear his vision was getting a little blurry.

"I thought you hated wearing glasses." Zeus' robe fanned out over his arms when he slid his hands to his loincloth-clad hips.

"I do, but that's not important. I wouldn't presume to ask you to explain the plan to me—"

"Oh, come now, Chayyiel, we both know that's not true." Zeus tossed the gold fabric back over his shoulders. "You're dying to know what it is, and you'd love for me to tell it to you."

"Well, yes, Sir, that's true—"

"You're not 'yes-ing' me, are you, Chayyiel?" Zeus' eyes narrowed.

The good ol' Catch-22. Zeus was known for them. "No, Sir, I'm not."

"Good. Because we've had too many 'Yes-Mers' over the past few reigns. It was getting boring. Hence, this journey of Rod's and our change of venue." Zeus swept his hands over the lake.

"Sir?" Charley agreed that the island of Corvo beat out the top of Mount Olympus fins-down because, even with the gods' powers, the mountaintop had always been too cold. As to the "Yes-Mer" syndrome... he couldn't blame the previous rulers—it was a tough call to challenge a god.

Zeus sighed then whipped up a director's chair to sit in. The gold robe disappeared without any ceremony, to be replaced by a black T-shirt and cargo shorts. He sat in the chair, resting his Birkenstocks on the cross bar and his elbows on his knees. "Do you remember when we shifted the rule of the oceans from one hereditary line to another, generations ago? It didn't end up like we'd hoped. Decisions made on the fin, sirens luring Humans to their deaths, sea monsters claiming territories as their own, Mers playing along the surf line—it was one long period of hedonism."

"Yes." Oh, Charley definitely remembered the era before the Tritones had been restored to power, when Pontus's heirs had lived under the delusions of free love and flower power. Wine, women, and song. Togas and love beads had been all the rage, and the wine had flowed like lava down the side of a volcano—which had been a portent of things to come.

When the gods had finally put their collective foot down, those unlucky Humans near Vesuvius had felt the effects. And the Mers, the Mers had lost their autonomy.

Everything had become governed by decree. Laws set, statutes defined, protocol demanded. Thousands and thousands of slate tablets created, outlining the specifics of Mer life.

The Prophecy had come into being; The Council created, and governorship returned to Poseidon's most direct descendents, the Tritones—along with the proviso that they follow every dictate the gods prescribed.

"Don't look at me that way, Chayyiel." Zeus brushed a hand over his neatly trimmed white goatee. "We had our reasons."

Charley said nothing.

"Look. We realize our actions haven't served the Tritones as well as we'd hoped. Fisher's lost confidence in his judgment, and Rod is so careful not to repeat his past mistake that he's unwilling to take risks necessary for growth."

Zeus sat back, running a hand through his hair. "That's why we created The Prophecy, you know. Just in case it was needed."

"Valerie? How does she fit into this?"

Zeus' lips tightened. "No, not Valerie. She has nothing to do with The Prophecy. She's not the 'that which is lost' as you all assumed, but it certainly was convenient."

"I don't understand, Sir."

Zeus stood up, kicking the chair into non-existence, and pulled a thunderbolt out of thin air in one continuous movement. The thing crackled and zapped, singeing the air around them. "As well you shouldn't. If you did—if *they* did—none of this would come to pass. They'd be stuck where they are as a civilization for the rest of their time on the planet. Which wouldn't be long."

He hefted the bolt and pulled back his arm near his ear. "Do you know what happens to civilizations that stagnate? Ones that stifle creativity and independent thinking?"

Zeus threw the bolt toward the shore. It fell about ten feet short, hissing as it sank beneath the water.

He looked at Charley. "They die, Chayyiel. The entire population. Cro-Magnon, Neanderthal, Aztec, Mayan, Martian, Jamestown... Humans have already added Atlantis to that list. If Rod *doesn't* take risks, doesn't begin to think outside the box, listen to his gut, it will happen. There will be no more Atlantis. No more Council. No protection from Human discovery."

Zeus whipped up another bolt and prepared for launch. "It's all about Free Will, Chayyiel. A conscious decision on Rod's part to act because it's the best thing to do, not because circumstances—or you, or Fisher, or The Council, or the thousands of rules we've set down—dictate it."

He let the bolt fly. It scorched a twenty-foot stripe on the shoreline, ending with the point embedded in the base of a palm. The tree burst into flame, then exploded in a burst of golden ash.

Zeus brushed his hands together and hunkered down in front of Charley. "If Rod fails, Chayyiel, not only won't his tail return, but the Mer world, and all its inhabitants, will cease to exist. Humans will become the Chosen Race."

Chapter 25

ROD WAS HAVING THE BEST DREAM. WARM, SOFT FLESH pressed against him, pliant and feminine. He slid his hand up to find a full breast there for his touch. He fondled it, feeling a stirring in his *gono*. Gods, it'd been too long since he'd enjoyed a woman's body.

He released her breast, brushing the stirring nipple as he spread his fingers along her rib cage, pressing her back against him. Rounded, firm buttocks filled his lap, cushioning his rising flesh.

She smelled like rainwater, soft wisps of hair caressing his lips and tantalizing the skin of his throat.

She murmured something sleepy and unintelligible, then leaned back into him, pushing against his erection. Rod slid his hand down her belly, over the jut of her hipbone, along the smooth, sleek skin of her thigh...

Skin... Thigh...

Rod's eyes opened. This was no dream.

Darkness tinged with the faintest hint of dawn filtered in through the sand-colored window blinds, a scarred green door to the right admitting more gray light around its edges.

Valerie murmured again, flexing her legs, rubbing her heel against him, and Rod pulled her closer. He didn't know where they were, but at least they were both safe.

Her leg slid back between his.

Actually, he couldn't vouch for her safety at the moment.

His fingers trailed over her hip to the apex of her thighs. Soft curls invited him to slip lower. He did and her leg slid back farther.

She hummed, turning slightly in his arms, her curled arms trapping his other hand to her breasts.

A Mer could only take so much.

His fingers traveled lower, finding the swelling folds, the center of her that was reacting to his touch. He rubbed, almost groaning aloud when that sweet spot expanded for him.

He was at full mast himself and arched against her backside.

Valerie moaned and pressed back, the muscles there tightening against him. Her breasts swelled, and he moved his fingers slightly to find her nipples, caressing them. She moved against him again, this time opening her legs just enough for him to slip a finger inside.

But he resisted. He wanted her awake and welcoming him, not instinctively responding to stimuli.

"Valerie," he whispered in her ear, taking the opportunity to tug that soft lobe between his lips, savoring the sweet scent of her as his tongue flicked over it.

"Mmmm." She turned a little more, opening for him, and Rod groaned. A Mer could only take so much...

"Valerie, wake up." He trailed kisses down the column of her throat, his fingers fluttering the tips of her breasts while his other hand continued to cup and stroke her.

"Hmmm," she groaned, rolling in his arms until they were face to face. She slid her arms up his sides and over his chest, her fingernails scraping lightly over his nipples, her lips at the perfect angle for his kiss.

Her eyes still closed, she pursed her lips, tilting her head back in invitation.

Rod cupped her backside, filling his hands with the sleek muscles there, kneading her cheeks, his fingers sliding the full length between them, spreading her legs to place one over his as he nipped at her lips.

"Valerie," he said against them, more a litany than a request. He kissed her, savoring the sweet, sleep-plumpness of those lips, tracing their seam with his tongue. She'd better wake up soon. He didn't know how much longer he could take this and still retain his honor.

Valerie exhaled, her lips parting, her tongue slipping along her bottom lip, and he captured it.

Softly, he encouraged it out, stroking the tip gently with his own, tasting the essence of her.

She wound her arms around his neck, sliding her breasts up, pressing them against his chest with her core just above the tip of his *gono*.

Cock, he reminded himself. Humans called it a cock.

He was about to make love with a Human.

The thought should strike the fear of the gods in him, enough to curb this fast-rising fire in his veins, but... no.

Valerie wasn't just any Human. Hades, she wasn't even all Human, and all he could think, feel, see was how she fit into his arms, smell the way she wanted him, taste the sweet possession of her kiss as she deepened it, her tongue sliding between his lips, filling his mouth, flooding his senses with the essence of her. Pure woman.

He stroked that sweet, moist flesh between her legs, the swelling letting him know every bit as much as her moans did how much she wanted him.

But did she want *him*? Or merely the man in her arms?

Rod pulled back from the kiss. "Valerie. Open your eyes." He would not do this without her full awareness. He didn't want her hating him when all was said and done, and, even more, using it as an excuse to leave.

Gods, if she left now...

No. He would not fail. Not in this. The Council was expecting her back, and he would bring her. One failure in his life was enough.

Which was reason enough to end this, but, gods, he didn't want to.

He ran the backs of his fingertips over one smooth, sun-dotted cheek.

"Valerie."

Rod's voice sounded so close. So soft and deep and warm...

"Valerie, open your eyes."

Something nudged her nose, and she exhaled before blinking into wispy gray dawn.

Yes, very close. His eyes were right there, mossy green with the tiniest lines at the sides as they smiled at her. Hmmm, smiling eyes. So nice to wake up to.

"Rod? You're okay?"

"Okay? That depends on what you mean by okay." He slid his cheek against hers, and she shivered as his breath tickled the hollow beneath her ear. "How are you?"

"Hmmm?" Her eyes closed and she shifted in his arms, her fingertips feeling the smooth, hard warmth of his chest. "I'm..."

Wait a minute.

Her eyes flew open. "What—? Why are you—? What are we—?"

Oh, God, she was naked all over Rod.

Ohgodohgodohgodohgod... What was wrong with her? Where was her self-respect? Her pride? Her sense of self-preservation?

Her pajamas?

She scrambled off his thigh (oh, man, she had literally been *all* over him), clambering to get off the bed and cover herself and preserve some semblance of dignity.

One scooch and she landed on her backside on the thread-bare carpet, her legs still trapped on the edge of the bed.

So much for dignity.

"What did we do?" How utterly mortifying to have to ask that question. And why was she naked?

Slowly, the previous night came back to her. The accident, the "fun" of getting Rod into not one, but two beds... and her soaked duffel bag.

"Livingston!" She scrambled to get upright. Bad enough Rod was witness to her loss of self-control and nudity, but to have the bird...

"I don't think he's here." Rod's deep voice edged over the bed. "I don't see him, so you can come up. No need to be embarrassed."

Oh, right. Livingston had hopped out last night to check in with his spies or minions or whatever he called them. Gathering her legs under her, Val peeked over the top of the mattress.

Caressed by slivers of pale light, a gorgeous, sexy, *naked* man smiled at her. "Hi."

There was a naked man in her bed. The surprising thing was... that wasn't the surprising thing.

Now if only she could remember what she'd done with him and how she'd ended up naked...

"Uh… hi." She rested her forehead against the sheet. Big mistake. She could smell them from here. Yes, *them*. Rod and her. She knew exactly what that scent was and so did her hormones.

"We didn't…" She peeked up again. "We didn't, you know…"

Rod shook his head. "No. Almost. But I woke you up."

Phew. That was a relief.

Or… was it?

"Almost?" She pulled her knees under herself and knelt by the side of the bed, keeping all naked parts hidden. His, however, were not, leaving absolutely nothing to her imagination.

Blushing, she turned away, recognizing that some-where in her brain, she was remembering exactly how *that* had felt against her.

Rod sighed and she felt the bed move, heard the rustle of sheets.

"It's safe to turn around," he said with some amuse-ment in his voice.

Define "safe."

So, okay, he'd covered the Welcome Wagon, but the rest of him was there, plain as day, a scrumptious feast for the eyes, even in the dim, early morning light.

"Uh, so we didn't…"

"No. But I'm *up* for it if you are." A twinkle sparkled in his green eyes, a slash of dimple appearing in his cheek. His fingers slid along the bed toward her. "You seemed pretty up a few minutes ago."

Ohgodohgod…

"That was a few minutes ago." Really, she didn't sleep with strange men.

Not that he was strange—or a stranger.

Rod's sigh said so much with so little. "I figured you'd say that."

Val looked on the bed and saw one of her towels half under Rod. Fat lot of good it'd done her.

Change the subject, change the subject. "So you're okay? No headache? Leg's good?"

Rod's eyes narrowed. "I feel fine. Why shouldn't I?"

"You don't remember?"

Rod hefted himself onto his elbow. The sheet slid lower on his thigh, giving her a tantalizing glimpse of hipbone. "What should I remember?"

Val yanked the towel out from under him and wrapped it around herself, tucking the end securely beneath her arm, and recounted the accident and Livingston's medical advice.

"Son of a—!" Rod sat up, swinging his legs off the edge of the bed. The sheet, however, hadn't gotten the memo that it needed to keep up with his wayward body parts so she got another display of male perfection.

This morning peep-show was becoming a habit.

She glanced at the window where only the faintest glimmer of light trickled through the blinds. *Barely* morning peep-show, in every sense.

"Where did Livingston get to?" Rod stood up while she spun around, determined *not* to look at all that splendor. She was only human, after all, and had been wrapped around that magnificence not ten minutes ago. Her hormones were still clamoring for a return trip.

Livingston. Right. She remembered now. "He went to see what he could find out about the accident and work on some way to escape JR. He said to stay put until he came back."

She pulled his shorts off the chair by the radiator and handed them to him, eyes averted. "I think this is the best we're going to do, clothes-wise. Livingston hadn't realized our bags weren't waterproof. They went for a swim last night getting from the car to the room."

"Thanks." He took them from her and—yay!—she managed not to groan when his fingers touched hers.

Envisioning him stepping into those shorts as she'd watched him do yesterday, now with full disclosure of all parts involved, Val counted to fifteen—then added another ten just to be sure—before grabbing her clothes and turning around.

The shorts' low ride on his hips didn't help matters one bit.

"I'll, uh, just use the restroom, and..." She grabbed her wet duffel and inched toward the room at the back, sliding her butt along the dresser in an effort to keep from touching him.

"Valerie, I'm not going to jump on you. I think I just proved that, didn't I?"

Honestly, she should be a virgin for all the face-flaming she was doing. Talk about awkward. "I know. It's just that this is new for me."

"What? You've never slept with anyone before?"

"No. It's not that. I've never slept with someone I'd just met before."

Rod liked the sound of that.

And then wondered why he did.

It shouldn't matter to him whom she'd slept with because she obviously wouldn't be sleeping with him, since she was determined to return to her mother's store.

What that would mean for The Prophecy, he had no idea. Had the gods considered she might not want to embrace the Mer world?

The door to the restroom closed behind her. What would it mean for him?

Aside from the shot to the gut that thought elicited, he would not have the blame placed at his fins. The Council had said nothing about convincing her to accept Lance's legacy, only to bring her to the coast. He was doing that. It shouldn't affect his claim to the throne at all.

But what if they didn't make it to the coast?

Rod picked up the diamond decanter from the dresser. JR had almost succeeded last night.

That was what was so perplexing about this chase, this coup. The bird had nothing to gain by a coup. For all his seaworthiness, JR didn't live under the sea. He could never come to Atlantis, nor claim the throne.

And to have a personal vendetta against him? Rod couldn't see it. Admittedly, he'd earned JR's ire when he'd ditched the bodyguard during that school archipelago trip, but to have it in for him after so many *selinos* for a youthful indiscretion? That couldn't be the reason.

So who was he working for and, more importantly, why?

Rod sat on the edge of the bed and rolled the decanter between his palms. That's what was bothering him about this whole thing. What was he missing? Who was behind this? Who stood to gain the most?

Nigel was the obvious choice. Well, Drake would be, but that idiot couldn't manage to pass science class, let alone transport a bomb without blowing himself up. Nigel, on the other fin...

But the Mer had dedicated his life to The Council. He wouldn't jeopardize his station in life should the coup fail. He'd have to know all eyes would be on him, so it really made no sense.

It could be the shark contingent who'd been making noise throughout the oceans recently. Vincent saving Reel from Kraken last *selino* was enough to merit representation on The Council in the sharks' opinion—representation that hadn't yet happened. So when they'd planned a Swim-In, Rod had called them on the inadvisability of the demonstration. The arena wasn't large enough for the big guys to maneuver around and keep water flowing over their gills. He'd tried pointing out the logistical problems to the swim-bladderless beings, but good ol' Hammerhead Harry had shouted him down, claiming it was another example of Council discrimination.

Would that mark him for death? They couldn't hope to affect positive change on their collective image by playing into the very stereotype they were trying to overcome, but then, *Chondrichthyes* were known more for their brawn than their brain.

Of course, it could still be Ceto. She'd had a gripe against the gods ever since they'd forbidden her procreation abilities. She'd tried to kill Reel, and when that failed, she'd been put under Council arrest. She was still paying that debt to Mer society, so he doubted she'd be foolish enough to try something this big while all eyes were on her.

None of it made sense. The rumors of a coup made this more than just a recovery mission, but why would the gods risk Valerie's life?

He'd never find the answers sitting here. No, they needed to get to the coast as soon as possible.

Rod stood and stretched the kinks out of his back, then draped his damp T-shirt over his shoulders. He'd played by their rules, done what was required—as usual—so the gods had better follow up on their end of the bargain.

Valerie hadn't signed on for this, and she sure as Hades wasn't going to like it when it all played out, but it better have the chance to play out because, while he didn't mind what the gods threw at him, injuring Valerie was not part of the deal. And they'd damn well better make sure that didn't happen.

He waited for the usual rumbling.

Nothing.

Hmm… Either the gods weren't paying attention or maybe, just maybe, they recognized a valid argument when they overheard one.

Val turned off the shower and toweled herself dry. At least the toiletries in the zippered compartment of her bag had survived their swim—along with, in an ironic twist of fate, the condoms left over from one last night with an old boyfriend. And those were still usable.

Great. Did she really need the added temptation?

She put on her bra, thankful it was thin enough to have dried during the night. The shirt wasn't too bad, but her shorts were going to have her sitting in water all day. Ah, well, there wasn't anything she could do about it. She certainly wasn't going to go without shorts. Not after what she'd woken up to.

She blocked that thought. Thinking about Rod's naked body and hers sprawled all over it would do nothing but arouse her.

Yep. It did. Arouse her.

She sighed and ran her fingers through her hair. This trip was all about getting her inheritance, not starting a long-distance love affair.

And who said he even wanted one? Just because he'd been kissing her didn't mean he was thinking relationship. He *had* woken up to a naked woman in his arms. A naked woman who obviously returned the attraction.

At least he'd been gentleman enough not to take it too far before she'd woken up completely. Just like she hadn't taken advantage of him last night by not covering him with a towel—

Wait a minute…

He'd been injured last night. Badly. He shouldn't be up and walking around after what happened to him. She'd seen his leg. That gash at his temple. Yet, this morning when she'd run her hands through his hair, there hadn't even been a scar.

What the hell was in that oil?

She shoved all her personal effects into the duffel and yanked open the door, checking her own cut—now healed—on the way out. "Why don't you have any marks on you?"

Rod spun around, muscles rippling over his chest as he tossed a pillow onto the bed. "What?"

"Cuts. Gashes. Blood. You were really banged up last night and now you don't have a mark on you. And neither do I." She walked over to him and grabbed his chin, turning his face this way and that. Not even a blemish. "What's going on?"

Rod jerked his jaw from her grasp, and the shirt slid off his shoulder. "Nothing's going on, Valerie. That oil is a medication in my kingdom. That's why Livingston insisted you use it instead of taking me to one of your medical facilities."

"Where is this kingdom, Rod? Why won't you tell me?"

Rod scanned her from head to toe, and even though there was nothing sexual about that look, it turned her on.

Dammit! She didn't want to lose the thread of this conversation. "Rod, please. Tell me what's going on."

"I can't, Valerie. Not yet. You—"

"Don't use the 'won't believe it' excuse. I think I've seen enough that I'll at least consider whatever you toss my way. You owe me that much."

Rod raked his fingers through his hair. "You're right. I do owe you an explanation, but, unfortunately, that's not my call. The Council will tell you everything."

"Oh, for pete's sake. You're kidding me, right? You're not going to tell me because of some stupid rule that no one is even around to enforce?"

You know, she didn't have to do this. Those inheritance papers weren't in his duffel bag, which meant they were somewhere in her apartment. If she went home, she could find out for herself who to contact and she wouldn't have to go through this any more.

"Valerie, that rule was made for very valid reasons and, I'm sorry, but as the next ruler, I have to uphold it. So, no, I can't tell you." He turned away from her to grab his duffel and started shoving his clothing in it.

"Come on, Rod, you told me you've done everything your father asked of you your whole life. What's it going to hurt if, just this once, you don't do what he says? Live a little. Walk on the wild side. You certainly have enough stories of your brother doing that. You ought to take a page out of his book and give it a try. I mean, I may not have made the best choices in my life, but at least I wasn't so afraid of breaking the rules that I haven't lived."

Rod's hand paused halfway to the bag with the damp jeans. His shoulders stiffened when he inhaled. But he didn't turn around.

"I broke the rules once, Valerie. With the most disastrous results you can imagine. I haven't seen much of my brother since then and won't *get* to see him for much longer. Rules are created for reasons, as I learned to my eternal regret. I can't undo that one mistake, but I sure as Hades can prevent committing another one. So, no. I can't break this rule. Not even for you. You'll find out everything you need to know, all the answers to your questions, when we reach the coast. That's the best I can do." He shoved his jeans in the bag as if he were punching someone.

His voice was low and quiet. Different from when he'd been comforting her yesterday. Different from when he'd kissed her just now, when his body had let her know how much he'd wanted her.

It was a quiet that spoke of pain.

She never would have guessed; he hid it so well. Perhaps buried it so deep.

And she couldn't even begin to know how to respond to that.

Livingston's squawk outside their door saved her from having to. "Open up, folks. It's time to get moving."

Chapter 26

Rod opened the door, thankful for the interruption. Her comments had gotten to him. Walk on the wild side? Live a little?

First of all, he was done with this walking nightmare. It was time to get back to the ocean and swim. To use the Travel Chambers. Some way other than this ungodly long, cross-country journey.

Second, as instigator of that dare, he knew all about the wild side—*and* its ramifications, like "living a little." Hades, he'd live for a long time; Reel was the one who'd only get to live a little of life.

Livingston hopped into the room, a bagel around his beak. He slid it to the floor, stepped on it with one webbed foot, then took a bite.

"Livingston? Something you want to share?" Rod shut the door behind the ASA Chief.

The gull looked up, guilt in his eyes. "You want a bagel?"

Valerie snorted and sat on the bed. The bed Rod had woken in with her in his arms—"Your reconnaissance."

"Oh. Right." Livingston swallowed the bite. "Here's the good news. There's an airport about an hour south of here that's free and clear of JR's minions, as is this parking lot."

"And the bad news?"

"We have to leave now and the car doesn't look like it's in any shape to make it. If you buy the truck out there from the kid in the office, we can get out of here without JR noticing."

"Good idea." Rod drew the wad of soggy currency from the side pocket of his bag and peeled off a few of the larger bills. A pawnshop and a few sunken treasure artifacts had ensured that cash was the least of his worries. "Do you think this is enough, Valerie?"

Valerie stood up and shoved her fingers into the pockets of her shorts. The waistband dipped below her shirt, exposing the bottom half-moon of her navel. He'd traced that indentation earlier...

Rod stuck his hands in his own pockets, balling his fists so the fabric wouldn't reveal a *certain* part of him that also remembered her navel.

He dragged his eyes to her face.

Which didn't do any good when she ran her tongue over her bottom lip.

"Enough? Oh it'll be enough." She took the money. "You know, I really hope all this cloak-and-dagger stuff is worth it, guys, because so far I've had to take everything you've said on faith. Which has gotten me chased by birds, my car totaled, and now I'm going to beg the night clerk to let us borrow his truck so we can head to an ocean I'm allergic to, all without knowing who you are, what country you're from, and if all of this is even real.

"I deserve to know what's going on, Rod. If I can go with the flow of magic oil and suddenly appearing hay bales on an interstate, not to mention a wad of cash that would make a bank manager's day, I'm sure whatever you dish out won't be half as tough to believe as you think it will be."

She had a point. Most Humans wouldn't have taken everything as well as she had. "True."

"Good. Because I'm just about at the end of my rope, and heading home is looking better by the minute." She stuffed the currency into her pocket and went out the door. "I'll offer the clerk his jackpot, and we can talk on the way to the airport. Which plane I get on depends on you."

"You need to tell her something." Livingston tossed the rest of the bagel into the trash can with a perfect water-polo shot after she left. "She does have a point about having put up with everything else."

"What would you have me tell her, Livingston?" Rod sighed. "Tails are hard to believe without actually seeing them. Not to mention, The Council has forbidden it."

"Did they? Or did they say she can't know about Mers? You don't have to mention Mers at all."

Livingston might actually be onto something. "I'll think about it."

"Good. Because we need her on that plane."

"I know, Livingston. Trust me. I know *exactly* what's at stake here."

"At least one of you does."

Chapter 27

R OD USED THE SHOWER WHILE V ALERIE WAS GONE, needing to feel water sluicing over his flesh, even if it was fresh water. He hated to put clothing on when he finished.

He'd gotten the damn shorts in place just as Valerie returned triumphantly with a set of keys and Livingston swooped in from his lookout on the motel's sign.

"All clear," the gull said. "But let's hurry. Daybreak isn't too far off, and I want to get as far as possible in this thing before someone realizes we aren't still here."

The truck was roomier inside, although there was no backseat for Livingston, so the bird settled in between them.

"Do you want to drive, Rod?" Valerie held up the keys. "I know what guys and pickups are like."

Livingston snorted.

"You can, Valerie." Rod glared at the bird. "I have every confidence in you." And none in himself to operate this vehicle. There hadn't been the time to learn, and, frankly, he wasn't planning to have any reason ever to need to again.

"So, Livingston…" Valerie said, running her fingers through her damp hair, fluffing the curls around her face. For a second—just one—Rod allowed himself to remember how soft those curls had felt in his fingers. "What did you find out about the accident?"

Livingston's curse would have shamed a docklurker—and those barnacles had heard a lot of Human curses.

"It was no accident," Livingston said.

"But how? How could an albatross roll not one, but two bales of hay into the middle of a road? It's not possible. They're too heavy."

Rod almost laughed. Her argument wasn't that JR was a bird, and birds shouldn't even consider rolling bales of hay onto an interstate to intercept the people trying to outrun them, but that the bales were too heavy for him.

Perhaps learning she would inherit a tail wasn't going to be too hard for her to accept.

Livingston stood up and shook his head. "JR didn't do the manual labor. Deer did. He held some of their fawns hostage while their parents did his dirty work. Make no mistake, JR's not one to leave anything to chance."

"He did what?" Valerie fumbled with the stick shift, the truck jerking as it lost momentum.

"Hostages?" Rod caught Livingston before the gull hit the dash and set him on it instead. "He took young ones hostage?"

"Yeah, makes you sick, doesn't it? There's not much he won't do if he's doing that. I bet that's how he's controlling the avians." Livingston clacked his beak shut. "You're going to have to deal with him, Rod."

"There *is* no dealing with that. We don't negotiate with terrorists and we don't deal with kidnappers. JR will face a full accounting of The Council, be found guilty, and pay the penalty, just like any other criminal, his past be damned."

Okay, she could not process this. Fawns? Hostages?

"Rod." She reached out for his arm without thought. "Please tell me something that makes sense of all of this. I mean, I know it's happening because I'm living it, but I don't understand why it's happening. What country are you from where birds and deer and manatees are equal to humans?"

"Hey! I resent that," said Livingston, hopping onto his webbed feet. "Just because we don't have legs or hands doesn't make us inferior. Why, we can fly, something you Bipeds can do only with a lot of preparation and technology and gas — thereby fouling up the environment for the rest of us." Livingston got so worked up that he started moulting on the dashboard. "If anything, Humans are inferior to all those creatures you mentioned. At least we only take from the environment what we need, but you people... you damage it. You don't take care of it. You waste it. You wouldn't appreciate the beauty of Atlantis!"

The bird swooped his wings over his beak, but she heard the "oh shit" beneath them.

Atlantis?

Okay, Rod was right. She wouldn't believe this.

Explain the talking seagull, then.

She worked the truck back through its gears to get up to speed. She couldn't explain the talking seagull, and that one thing — or four if you tossed in the fish bombs, the air-assault peregrines, and the blanket-carrying crows — allowed her to consider there might be the tiniest smidgen of truth in his words. When Livingston had opened his beak and she'd seen for herself the bird could talk — and plan and reason — she had been willing to give Rod the benefit of the doubt, but...

She looked over at him, knowing her eyes were probably as big as saucers and unable to do anything about it. "Atlantis?"

Rod grimaced. "You've heard of it."

She wrapped her hands around the steering wheel so tightly that her knuckles turned white and looked out the windshield. They didn't need another accident. "Who hasn't? It practically has its own bookshelves in the sci-fi section of the library. Assuming, that is, that you're not talking about the resort in the Bahamas?"

Livingston made an odd choking noise but didn't say anything. Good. He'd said enough for today.

And if that statement didn't just add to the craziness of this moment...

"No. That Atlantis doesn't begin to compare. But this isn't science fiction, Valerie. It exists."

"I'm glad you believe that. The rest of the population? Well, we're just a tad skeptical. But then, we don't have talking seagulls or manatee spies or mercenary albatrosses to convince us."

"You think I'm making this up."

She sighed. "I wish I did." She really really did. "That's the crazy part. I don't, even though it'd be so much easier to accept that you're an escaped lunatic, but after Livingston and the fish and the peregrines? You don't need to hit me over the head." She chuckled, but not with amusement. "Actually, maybe you do. Getting hunted by peregrines is pretty convincing. But you're going to have to do some convincing of your own to prove to me that a civilization the rest of the planet thinks is imaginary exists. I mean, exactly where is this myth?"

Livingston choked again.

"In the Caribbean." Rod hated lying. Atlantis wasn't in the Caribbean, but Val would never believe that it was near Bermuda. There wasn't anything near Bermuda *but* Bermuda, and he couldn't very well tell her it was *under* Bermuda. Now, as long as Livingston kept his big trap shut, which he should have done in the first place, Rod might be able to pull this off.

"Okay. In the Caribbean. Where? Is it an invisible island? Floating one, maybe?"

"No, not floating, and not invisible."

Livingston wheezed as if he was having trouble breathing.

Good.

"Okay, well, that's good. So... any reason why the rest of the world doesn't know of its existence?"

"We don't advertise its location."

"Right. Lack of advertising. Pity. You might want to think about that. Could bring in all sorts of tourism dollars."

She hadn't looked at him yet.

But he hadn't taken his eyes off her. She was holding up surprisingly well. "We don't encourage tourists."

"Ah. Yes. Well, I guess if you have diamonds the size of that one in your pocket, you really wouldn't want to have tourists knocking on your door, now would you?"

"You certainly sound as if you think I'm crazy, Valerie."

She exhaled and finally did glance his way. "Actually, Rod, I'm wondering if *I* am. I've been following the directions of a seagull, of all things. Dodging fish falling from the sky. Now, Atlantis? It's the stuff of legends.

I'm half-waiting for you to tell me the Bimini road really does lead to it."

Rod glared at Livingston to keep his beak shut. The undersea road had fallen into disrepair since the gods had created the Travel Chambers, but he'd taken a high-school field trip there once. Ah, the memories of "getting lost" with Marquesa...

He *could* tell her all that, but she was already dealing with enough as it was.

Why hadn't her mother told her? This could have been so much easier if she had. The woman had seen Lance; she'd known what he was. But she hadn't told Valerie, and The Council had decreed *he* couldn't, since right now—technically—she was Human. Humans could not know about Mers, the primary law of his world—with which he was intimately acquainted.

"A lot of this you're going to have to take on faith, Valerie, until I can prove it to you."

"At the beach. Right. Providing I don't swell up like a puffer fish and end up flopping around on the dock like said fish out of water, you mean."

"I promise you that's not going to happen."

She turned back to look at the road. "That promise and your Atlantis story need five bucks to get me a cup of coffee."

"What?"

She shook her head and her shoulders fell. "Sorry for the sarcasm. I'm trying hard to believe you. Go ahead."

He wanted to tell her everything, but The Council was right. He couldn't risk her deciding he was crazy or thinking this was too much to take in and leaving. He had to get her to the ocean, now more than ever. Never

mind that he could fail and never gain Immortality. JR
and whoever had hired him now knew who she was and
where she lived. She'd never be safe. He couldn't leave
her to JR's mercy.

Rod brushed her shoulder with his fingertips. "I know
this is hard for you to believe, but I promise you I can
prove everything."

She looked more resigned than believing, but at least
she wasn't turning the truck around. "How, Rod? How
do you prove a legend?"

Rod withdrew his hand to run it through his hair,
taking the time to formulate his response.

Livingston, thank the gods, tucked his head beneath
his wing and stopped choking.

"Atlantis, the original Atlantis, the one you're
familiar with, was the center for commerce in its
day. Everyone flocked there, bringing their nations'
greatest exports. The country grew rich. So rich that
certain... dignitaries of the ancient world," the gods
forgive him for denigrating them to mortal *dignitaries*,
"decided it should be the center of the known world.
Others didn't agree.

"There was a war, but because Atlantis was so small
land-wise and most of its people were merchants, they lost.
To the victor go the spoils, and they carted off everything
of value, including the people. Legend says the downfall
had been written in the stars. Then a great flood covered
the island, taking anything left alive with it."

The legend of the flood, so pervasive in almost every
culture's myths and parables, had indeed caused massive
destruction for the residents of Atlantis. Only Poseidon's
Mers had survived.

"But, like the phoenix, Atlantis rose from the ocean bottom." Not that they'd risen all that far, and definitely not to the surface, but one thing at a time. "This time, they were determined to create a world where such greed and jealousy could not take hold. All ancient peoples were invited to send a delegation, to rule in harmony, and to protect Atlantis from the outside world. Their descendants continue that way of life today. That's why your kind, er, people don't know about it. That's why we allow the myths of Atlantis's demise to continue. We were once the center of the world, and it was our downfall. We don't wish to lose our heritage or our paradise again."

"So you live in a utopia." She glanced at him, the lift to her eyebrows more surprised than disbelieving. "You actually think you can create a world with no jealousy? You're making a good argument for being crazy, you know, Rod. That's just not human nature."

In that she was correct. *Human* nature was, at its most basic, greedy. Greedy to survive. Greedy to infiltrate and expand upon the earth until it covered every habitable place and destroyed the environment, just as Livingston had said.

Which was why it was imperative that he get her to Atlantis to fulfill The Prophecy and save the world.

Now if only JR didn't have any more tricks up his wing, they could do that.

Charley left Fisher's house with a heavier heart than the one he'd gone in with. He swam through the anemone park across the street, the beautiful colors there a balm to his spirits, as was the greeting he received from the starfish family he'd helped last week. Echinoderm limb regeneration was always a mood pick-me-up. He wished this last visit to Fisher's home had been, too.

At least he'd brought good news—unlike during the middle of the night, when he'd found out Rod had been injured and had to wake the family… That'd been bad.

Even worse was his inability to explain what was really going on.

The night had been spent on fins and needlefish—and restraining Fisher from using the Travel Chamber while they waited for Livingston's report.

He sighed and reached for a young sand dollar who'd moved onto the path, returning him to his pod. Just like a youngster, setting out to seek his fortune. Fisher had been that way once, but he was getting old. Worn out. This job took its toll. Delivering the news that Rod was fine hadn't brought the relief Charley had hoped for.

He'd listened to all of it—Fisher's despair, the frustration, yes even the anger at the gods for putting Rod and his family through this nightmare.

And all along, Charley couldn't say a word.

It'd been tough. Probably the toughest task he'd ever had to perform in all his *selinos* of Advisory. But it was for Fisher's own good. Rod's, too. And, of course, ultimately, the Mer race. So, his fins were tied.

A school of damselfish twirled in figure eights around him, showing off their latest stage show. He clapped when they were done, wishing he could set aside all his worry to truly lose himself in the beauty of that dancing rainbow. Sadly, he couldn't.

He knew how the gods like to toy with their creations, how they liked to taunt them, manipulate them, reward and punish them. There were no guarantees how this would all play out.

If only Zeus had told him the whole plan.

Chapter 28

THANK GOD, THE RIDE TO THE AIRPORT WAS UNEVENTFUL.

Although, honestly, Atlantis would be hard to top.

Atlantis. Of all things. What was next? The Loch Ness Monster?

Val wouldn't bet against it.

And now she was about to get on a plane to go to the coast to meet this Atlantian contingent who'd known her father. What had happened to her life?

"Okay, so you understand the plan?" Livingston waddled after them through the airport parking garage, trying to pass for just another seagull begging for food. The pigeons were looking at him funny.

The fact that she knew that showed just how far her reality had shifted.

"Livingston, I've flown before, if you recall." Rod slid the truck's key beneath the tire well.

Hey, even if no one stole it, the desk clerk was already ahead of the game. And if someone did, he'd have the insurance money and a thick wad of bills to get something nicer.

"Oh, yeah. That's right. Being a twin comes in handy. You do have the identification, right?"

"Yes."

"And the tickets. You have to buy the tickets." Livingston lunged as a pigeon hopped too close to a piece of flattened popcorn that, apparently, had Livingston's name written all over it.

Rod hoisted their bags onto his shoulder. "Livingston, relax. You're on runway detail. Nothing's going to happen."

Famous last words in her world. And with the way her world was going right now… "Rod? Maybe you should knock wood or something, you know? No sense tempting Fate."

"The Fates are not deterred by knocking wood, Valerie."

"No, for that you need a good bottle of ouzo," Livingston snickered as he grabbed a piece of bread crust before the pigeon could.

The pigeon said something in Pigeon that Val didn't need a translator for.

"I'll meet you at Reel's as soon as I can," Livingston said with the crust wobbling up and down. He needed to work on his manners. "Don't do anything st—er, rash before I get there."

Definitely so, if he was calling Rod stupid.

"And what do you consider rash?"

"Oh, I don't know. How about taking a running dive off a short pier before anyone's scouted the area?"

Rod laughed and wow, what it did to her insides. Or was that fluttery feeling the residual effect from the whole Atlantis discussion? It could be, but she wouldn't bet it. The man was more than gorgeous, and she'd been wrapped around him…

Okay, those kinds of thoughts were not getting her anywhere but hot and bothered, and the last thing she needed while digesting *Atlantis* was adding hormonal upheaval to the mix.

"Guys? We still have to get through security, so we'd better get going."

A few more last-minute instructions from Livingston, something about the chief of the Council Guards, and they headed into the terminal.

Security was light since it was early. Too early even for the coffee shop to open, so Val had to make do with a soda, which didn't have quite the caffeine kick she'd like, but after yesterday, then last night, then this morning, then the drive... letting her metabolism chill out was probably a good idea.

Waking up next to Rod hadn't exactly contributed to chilling out, but she wasn't going to think about that when she was facing a few hours shut up in close quarters with him. She was going home when all this was over, remember? Going back to Mom's store and, for once, sticking to the plan.

They boarded the plane, Val still trying to swallow the sticker shock at a last-minute, first-class ticket price—times two—that had barely made a dent in the wad of bills Rod still carried around. She'd been half-afraid they'd get stopped at security for the bulge in his pocket.

Okay, something else she didn't need to think about.

So, instead, she opted to think about Rod's father knowing hers. How, and what did it mean?

The flight attendant delivered her coffee, thank God, and yet another glass of water for Rod *sans* the salt. "Rod, if your council knows my father, does that make him Atlantian?"

Rod took his time swallowing the mouthful of water he'd taken. "Something like that."

"Something like that, how?"

Rod raised the glass, ready for another gulp. "Valerie, I'd really rather wait—"

She grabbed his arm, not caring that water sloshed over the edge. "And I'd really rather not. You can't just throw my father into a conversation about a mythical land—"

"Island."

"Whatever. You can't just include him with Atlantian-dwelling council members and leave it at that. I mean, he's not going to be waiting on the beach for me, is he?"

Rod set his glass down and picked up her hand, intertwining his fingers with hers. Val held her breath. *Would* Lance be waiting for her? Was this about to get more surreal than it already was?

"No, Valerie, your father won't be there. I'm sorry. But he really did leave you an inheritance, and yes, he was Atlantian. He was also royal."

"What?" She turned in her seat so quickly she wrenched the seat belt across her gut. That was what caused the pain there, nothing else.

"He was an heir to a throne of our kingdom."

"So I'm related to you?" Oh no no no no. That was just so wrong.

"No." A silky black wave of his hair fell across Rod's forehead as he shook his head. "Gods, no."

"Thank God," she said at the same time.

Rod smiled then, the dimple in his cheek winking at her. "I'll pass that along."

"So… if he was royal, that makes me… what?"

"A princess."

Please tell her it was turbulence that made her head swim and not the fact that he'd said something about her being a princess.

"You're an Atlantian princess, Valerie. That's why you need to meet with The Council." He reached up to tuck her hair behind her ear, his fingertips lingering on her cheek, then brushing softly over her lips. He tilted her chin up slightly. "Now do you see why I wanted to wait to tell you? I know how odd this is. Trust me. I do."

She was a princess. That made her sit back and shut up.

And if she was a princess, that made her father... what? A prince?

She couldn't stop the snort. Right. He was a prince, all right. A real *prince* of a guy. So princely, he'd left her.

Why?

Val looked out the window to the model-train-sized world beneath her. *That* was the question that had haunted her since she'd overheard her grandmother's comment. Why had Dad found it easy to leave?

Why hadn't he wanted her?

Wasn't she worth wanting?

She bit her lip and closed her eyes. She didn't want to do this, but stuck in a the middle of a metal tube thousands of feet above the earth with nothing but wind speed and a crying baby a few rows back to listen to—or the guy from Atlantis sitting next to her—nothing could stop her thoughts from going into overdrive. And in overdrive they were. Atlantis, royalty... and the man who'd left her.

That gut-wrenching, hole-in-her-stomach, wallop of pain didn't have a damn thing to do with the seat belt, unfortunately. She sucked in a breath, praying the engine sounds would hide it from Rod. She didn't want to have to explain it to him; hell, she didn't want to go there herself.

Of course, her subconscious went there anyway. It had years of practice, just as she had years of practice trying to put it aside. She'd done fairly well until Grandmom's little diatribe.

She'd never understood why she hadn't been happy at home. Why she'd always felt the need to go. Why there'd always been something missing in her life and if she just looked around the next bend or in the next town, maybe she'd find it. So she'd gone, every time, figuring it was just something inside of her.

Something defective, actually.

Then she'd overheard that conversation. Or rather, that argument. An apparent rehashing of the same old story and the same old parental disappointment on the part of her grandmother.

Aside from the shock of learning that she'd been abandoned by the man who was supposed to love her, Val had realized why she was the way she was.

She was like him.

And the thought had destroyed her.

Once she'd known the truth, she'd looked at the scenes of her childhood differently. Mom's quiet looks, the bitten lips, the quick-blinking eyes, they hadn't been from the sadness that he'd died too early. No, they'd been abandonment, hurt, lost love. Hopefully, anger.

And what had Mom done? Instead of bad-mouthing him, telling Val the truth, she'd created memories with the store of the beach where they'd met, and had allowed Val to grow up thinking she'd been short-changed by Fate instead of a fickle father.

How unselfish of her mother.

Val didn't think she could be.

No, she was worried that she'd end up just like him. What if she found someone—and, no, she wasn't thinking Rod, in particular—but what if she did, and married him. Had children. Raised them, then one day decided, *Wham! That's it. I've had enough.*

Would she do to her family what that man had done to his?

That was really why she was going back. Why she'd make a success of that store. To prove to herself that she *wasn't* like him. That she didn't take off when the going got tough. That she had what it took to stick it out.

That she wouldn't let Mom, someone she loved, down.

Rod looked at her profile, at the lashes that were blinking a little too fast. At the knuckle she held between her teeth, the shallow breaths she tried to hide. He knew what this must sound like to her. He knew how it had sounded to him when he'd found out, and he had the advantage of knowing all the history. Gods, the last thing he wanted to do was make this hard for her.

But to tell her the rest of it now would be cruel. Bad enough she was adjusting to Atlantis and her title; a tail would put her over the top.

Besides, it wouldn't be much longer.

He was proud of how she handled everything. She hadn't backed down from any of this. She'd outrun JR and his posse. She hadn't fallen apart. She hadn't turned into a quivering flounder who'd figuratively buried her head in the sand. Instead, she'd fought back. She'd outmaneuvered the birds, driven through the storm, and taken care of him in what must have been an unbeliev-able and frightening situation.

And she'd kissed him. Wanted him.

Dear gods, he'd wanted her, too. And sitting here next to her, seeing her huddled against the window trying to face the fact that she was suddenly something she'd never expected, he wanted her all over again.

The thing was... Rod rubbed his chest, just over his heart. The thing was, she'd behaved as a royal Mer should—so much so that it no longer mattered to him that she was only half-Mer. That she was an assignment The Council had sent him on. That she was the answer to The Prophecy.

Right here, right now, she was just Valerie.

And he wanted her.

He was amazed by that desire. She had Human blood—he shouldn't be attracted to her. He couldn't be. He was going to be the High Councilman. Hades, they were hours away from that event, and he wanted her.

Was this what Reel had felt? Was this why his brother had given up Immortality to stay with Erica?

But Reel loved Erica. This wasn't love; it couldn't be.

It couldn't be because it could have no future. His future was to marry a Mer and beget full-blooded Mer children. No matter that *he* didn't care that she was half-Human, diluting the bloodline was not an option for the High Councilman. The second son? Sure. But not the one through whom the dynastic line would continue.

He knew this because he'd checked every slate when Reel had declined Immortality, trying to find some way to convince his brother to remain in their world.

But there'd been nothing about second sons. Reel had
been free to make his choice and live happily ever after,
while Rod's ever-after was governed by the rules set
down by the gods.

So it was written; so it must be done.

And he was so screwed.

Chapter 29

BRINY AIR STREAMED IN THROUGH THE OPEN CAR WINDOWS. The smell of the ocean. Val recognized it at once. She didn't know how she recognized it, but she did. Crisp, sharp, so pungent she could all but taste it.

And in yet another shocker for the day, she felt as if the ocean *called* to her.

Almost without realizing, Val lowered her foot on the gas pedal as they crossed the last bridge over the bay that separated Peck Island from the mainland. She sped around the families lined up for the first bridge—so many bicycles and suitcases loaded onto the cars they no longer looked like cars—and headed down to the next one, not wanting to think about the last time she'd been here. The *only* time she'd been here.

Yet, the pull of the ocean made her feel as if she'd been here more than that one time. As if the waves were waiting for her. As if her senses were on alert for the first caress of a sea breeze, her skin thirsting for the warmth of the sun, her toes itching to dig into the sand.

The Atlantis thing wasn't bad enough? Now she had a weird compulsion to go running onto the beach and throw herself into the water, risking almost certain death?

What did it mean that the ocean called to her?

Rod leaned out his window and took a long, deep breath of the salt-laden air.

Val took a tentative one, rolling it around inside her mouth, letting it float down her throat, waiting for her air passages to react.

Nothing.

She took a deeper one, holding it in her lungs, waiting for that searing pain she remembered from her childhood.

Still nothing.

She could hear the waves beyond the dunes where the cross streets dead-ended at the beach, and her skin felt as if it was being tugged toward the sea—as if it were metal and the ocean a magnet, none of which made any sense to her.

Mom had told her she was allergic; she remembered the pain. So why did she feel compelled to go toward the water?

She chose, instead, to follow Rod's direction to his brother's home, though she still waited for that pain. But, if anything, the sea breeze relaxed her. It filled her lungs with deep cleansing breaths, and when she got her first glimpse of the ocean, it was as if the water flowed through her—a reaction so odd she considered, just for a second, that maybe Rod was right. Maybe she wasn't allergic.

But why would Mom lie?

The feeling of being pulled toward the water grew when she arrived at Reel's pale yellow Victorian house. The waves flowed onto the beach behind it, mesmerizing her.

They carried their bags up the half-dozen steps to the front porch beneath the blue-and-yellow-striped awnings and gingerbread trim, where pink impatiens overflowed whimsical planters and purple petunias cascaded over the wrought-iron railing.

Rod opened the front door into a homey living room, the furniture tan and peach and comfortable. Seashell floor lamps flanked a thick-cushioned sofa, the coffee table in front of it covered in boating magazines. The fireplace mantel held dozens of pictures beneath a large photograph of a smiling couple at their beach wedding.

"Your brother?" she asked. Not that she needed to. They did look alike. The same build, the same electric green eyes, the same black hair, only Reel's was curlier. Or maybe that was the way the breeze had tossed it that day.

Even the smile was the same, with the deep slash of dimple by the side of Reel's mouth, although she didn't know that she'd seen quite that look on Rod's face. Reel's look was one of happiness, genuine and carefree—and matched by his wife's smile.

He wouldn't leave his family. Not looking like that.

Rod's parents, too, had been married forever, according to Rod, and his sisters all lived near them. A close-knit family who stood by each other. Was that so much to ask for in life?

Apparently, in hers, it was.

Val shook off the thought. It only had been too much to ask for *before*. Now, things were going to be different. She would make them that way.

Rod opened the doors to the deck, sliding the screen door with a set-your-teeth-on-edge metallic screech. He braced himself in the doorframe and inhaled. Deeply. A few times.

Living on an island, he'd probably missed the scents, the breeze. She had to admit, after summertime Kansas, she could see the appeal.

Then he walked onto the deck and down the steps.

"Rod? What are you doing?"

He turned around, whipping his shirt over his head. "No time like the present, Valerie. Come on. Let's get this over with."

Get it over with? They'd just gotten here.

Oh. Right. She did want to get it over with. Collect her inheritance and that diamond, if she still needed it, and go home.

That *was* what she wanted... right?

He should wait for her, he knew, but gods! It'd been too long since he'd felt the sand against his skin, the breeze in his hair, the moist weight of the air filling his lungs.

Rod headed down the steps leading to the beach. He flung off that offensive piece of clothing and let the dry, wind-tossed grains of sand ping against his chest, wanting to shed his shorts, too. But he'd wait until he'd explained everything before diving into the water so his tail could shred them from his body.

He scratched the spot on his back just above his soon-to-return scale line where the royal trident tattoo would appear. He could feel it inside his skin, waiting for the first brush of salt water to bring it out.

He couldn't wait to get back into the ocean and bring her with him. To finally earn the throne and show Val her destiny.

And, maybe, to ask her to share it with him.

The thought stopped him six steps onto the beach.

His toes flexed in the sand.

Ask her to share it?

That sounded precariously close to love.

But he was smarter than that. Loving her would only bring heartache, and he didn't mean the unrequited kind. Oh, she wanted him, there was no denying that, but love?

Whether she did or not, whether she could or not, it didn't matter. A relationship between a Human and High Councilman was forbidden by the succession laws to ensure the line remained pure. He hadn't lived his entire life by those laws to break one now.

Rod shook it off. Physical. That's all it was. She was beautiful and she was brave and she'd held her own during this coup attempt and all the impossibilities he'd thrown at her. That's why he wanted her, but as soon as she was whisked off to wherever The Council and the gods needed her to go to fulfill The Prophecy, he'd be too busy, gods willing, taking over his birthright to think about her.

The sliding door slid closed with a soft *whump*, and Rod heard her footsteps on the deck. He turned, struck again by how beautiful she was with the sun dancing through her curls, her eyes as blue as the sea, and her smile so tremulous it made him want to comfort her.

He held out his hand. "Ready?"

"Is it safe?" She nibbled on her lip and looked at the sky.

"Don't worry. JR's not here. Even he can't fly as fast as an airplane. And while he might be a whiz at recruiting land birds into service, the birds here belong to The Council. As you can see, they've all been told to retreat. That's why there aren't any in the skies. Today, this is a no-fly zone."

She smiled then and came down the stairs. "A no-fly zone. A few days ago, that would have seemed so incredibly odd, but now?" She took his hand and he got a close-up glimpse of the sun-dots trickling across her nose. Mers didn't have sun-dots.

"Now I say, 'Thank God for no-fly zones.' I can only imagine what they could find here to drop on us."

He couldn't stop himself from tucking a few curls behind her ear before he took a deep breath, bracing himself. "What they could drop on you, Valerie, is nothing compared to what I'm about to. Are you ready for this?"

She nibbled her lip again. "I have no idea, but I can't imagine there's much left that will shock me. Do your worst, Rod."

Chapter 30

"I'm done, Drake." JR swooped over the waves, his massive wingspan inches above the tops of the crests as he circled around him.

"What do you mean, you're done? You're not done until I say you're done." Drake swished his tail at a jellyfish that unfurled a tentacle to see what it was sharing the water with. Stupid, brainless *Cnidaria*.

"Oh, give it up already, will you?" The albatross kept one eye on him as he completed another revolution. The spinning—and JR's words—were making Drake sick. "It's over. I'm off duty."

"What? You can't be! I paid you."

"Did you? Hmm."

The bird took more air under his wings and drifted upward—beyond arm's reach. Which, at this minute, was a good thing because Drake wanted to wring his slender, white neck.

"What, exactly, do you think an albatross is going to do with diamonds, Drake? It's not as if I've got any place to store them. Or use them. They're Mer currency. Avians don't use diamonds."

"What? Then why in Hades did you want them? Do you know what a pain in the tail it was to get them? How many near-misses I had trying to get the information from my father's desk for the combination to the Vault? How many times it almost didn't happen? I worked my tail off to get you those and you're damn well going to finish this." He pounded his fists against the ocean's surface, but all that did was splash water in his eyes.

JR circled ten feet higher. "Make me."

Drake wanted to kill him. *Make* him? The damn bird knew he couldn't reach him. "Come on, JR. We had a deal."

"A deal between criminals is unenforceable, Drake. Unless you can put every resource you've got into tracking me down, I'd say we're finished here." He circled higher.

"But you wanted to get back at The Council! Wanted to teach Fisher a lesson. You can't quit now. Rod's almost done for."

JR's grin was so big it was sinister. Drake had never heard of an albatross attacking a Mer, but he didn't want today to be the first time.

He ducked as the bird zoomed toward him, before veering off at the last second.

"You don't get it, Drake. I did do all of those. I have the diamonds from The Council. They now know they're not invincible. And Fisher has been sufficiently worried by the threat to his son."

"But we're so close. It won't take long to get Rod out of the way, then—"

"You're assuming I want you on the throne, Drake."

"I—what?"

JR coasted past him again, close enough that Drake felt the draft from his wings, but too far away to make a grab for him.

"You're assuming I was doing this so you could ascend the throne. I wasn't. I wanted them—Fisher especially—to know that being an anointed ruler doesn't make him an all-powerful being. I've done that. The Mer has finally realized his mistakes. It won't bring Margot back to me, but I can go to her with a clear conscience."

Drake flicked his tail to spin in a circle. "Go to her? You mean…"

"Of course, Drake. What else do I have to live for? Certainly not to help you. No, I've got a little trip planned to go see Zeus, and that'll be the end of that."

"Zeus will never go along with this, JR." Drake splashed the ocean again, frustrated at the bird's stupid reasoning. They were so close! "He certainly won't thank you. Fisher is one of his favorites. How do you think he's going to react when he learns—"

"Oh, Drake, you really are simple, you know that?" JR flew over him and tapped him on the head with his last wing feather. "All this talk about being ready to take on the leadership and you haven't figured it out yet."

"Figured what out?"

"The reason you got those diamonds so easily. The reason I even deigned to help you."

"I don't understand."

"I know. And that's the sad part." JR circled higher, his voice resigned. "You see, Drake, I've been helping you at Zeus' request."

"What?"

"You heard me. He let you set this up. I can't believe you've forgotten that the gods know everything. That they control everything. They let you get away with this to teach you—all of you—a lesson." JR flapped his wings once and turned east.

"Now, if we're done here, I've got a meeting with the head god I don't want to be late for."

Chapter 31

Rod held her hand and led her to within three feet of the water.

He'd asked if she was ready. Val honestly wasn't sure of the answer.

Then he smiled, the warmth in his eyes taking away her anxiety as the waves whispered behind him. She looked at the water, following its path up the beach.

"Beautiful, isn't it?" he asked, and he wasn't looking at the water.

But it was. Truly beautiful and grand and, humbling, really. "It is."

"How's your breathing?"

She looked at him then, a smile teasing her lips. "Fine. And you know it."

"True."

"So what is this big mystery you're going to share?"

He exhaled then linked their hands, his thumb rubbing the back of hers. "About Atlantis, Valerie. It really does exist. It's not something I believe to exist, but…" He looked down where their fingers were intertwined. "I did lie to you."

She held her breath. That, alone, was shocking.

"The thing is…" He squeezed her fingers before taking another deep breath. "Atlantis isn't in the Caribbean. It's near Bermuda."

He'd lied to her? Why would he do that? Caribbean Atlantis or Bermudian Atlantis... After everything else she'd had to believe, what was the difference where it was located?

Except...

"Exactly *where* near Bermuda is this island, Rod? Last I checked, there isn't much near Bermuda *except* Bermuda."

His smile was short and thin and didn't reach his eyes. "That's true. Atlantis is..." He cleared his throat. "It's under it."

Val blinked. "What?" She took a step back, but he didn't let go. "*Under* it? Under Bermuda? What do you mean?"

"Just what I said. Atlantis exists beneath the island of Bermuda."

"*Under* it?"

"Yes."

Okay, this made no sense. "How can anything exist under an island? It'd be under water."

He watched her.

And didn't say anything.

Another wave hissed onto the beach. "Wait a minute. You mean, it's under water? The whole island? You're not talking about a cave?"

"There are caves under Bermuda, but, no, we don't live in them."

"But under water? You live under water? That'd mean... that'd mean you can... that you're..."

"Mer."

Val had no idea what was going on here. *Mer*?

"As in mermaids?"

He arched an eyebrow. "Do I look like a Mer *maid* to you, Valerie?"

Well, no, obviously. That was silly. He wasn't a mermaid. So he'd have to be a…

"Mer*man*?"

That sexy, cockeyed smile kicked back one side of his mouth. "It's actually two words. 'Mer' and 'man,' though we don't use the gender tags. Humans added them."

"Humans?"

"You. Well, not you specifically, since you're a Hybrid, but the people you live around. They're Humans."

"Okay, I'm freaking out now." She needed to sit down because her knees just lost their ability to lock. "What do you mean 'hybrid'?"

"You, Valerie. Half Human and half Mer."

The knees gave out and she hit the sand, jarring her spine on the landing, her skin taking the bite of surf-crushed shells. "*Half* human?"

Rod hunkered down next to her and picked up her hand again, patting the top of it. "Stay with me, Valerie. You're doing good. You can handle this."

She shook her head. Handle it? She didn't even want to hear it. "What do you mean, half human, Rod?"

"Your mother, Valerie. She was Human."

"So that means my father was…?"

"Mer."

A few more waves stroked the beach while she digested that.

And it still made no sense.

"Rod, I'm sorry… but this…" She pulled her hands from his and wrapped her arms around her knees.

Amazing how cold that little ocean breeze could make her. "There's no such thing as merpeople."

"You're right, Valerie. There aren't."

She exhaled. Okay. That made her feel better. But what the hell was freaking her out like this all about?

And then he spoke again.

"We aren't called 'merpeople,' Valerie. It's just Mer." He stood up. "I'll prove it to you."

"How?"

"When I step into the water, my tail will appear. And when you follow, you'll get a tail as well."

"I'm not following you in there. I'm allergic to the ocean, remember?"

He smiled again. "No, you're not. A Mer can't be allergic to the ocean."

"Rod, please. Enough with the tail. The mermaids. Men. Whatever. Let's just go inside and forget this ever happened."

A *tail*. He actually thought he would have a tail. And that she would, too!

Ya know, she was sure she'd know if she had a tail or not, and for her entire twenty-nine years and three months, she'd had legs. She even had the baby pictures to prove it.

"We can't leave the beach, Valerie. This is too important. I'm a Mer and so are you. So was your father. And to claim your inheritance, you'll have to come in the ocean with me." He held out his hand to her.

She didn't let go of her knees. "Oh, no. That was never part of our bargain. You might believe what you're saying, but I remember, Rod. I remember the one time my mother put me in the ocean. There was pain. Burning, searing pain. That doesn't sound like something an aquatic creature should feel."

"Hey, no need to get insulting. I'm trying to help you."

"Insulting?"

"The 'aquatic creature' line. We're people, every bit as much as Humans. And you get to be both."

She didn't want to be both. She wanted to be her. Valerie Hope Dumere. And she wanted to be sitting at the desk in the back corner of Mom's shop, trying to figure out how she was going to save the store or if she should sell it to the developer, or, hell, if she should run away again, but she did not want to be sitting here on this beach, listening to him spout off fantasy as truth.

"I told you that you wouldn't believe me without proof. Now do you understand?"

No, she didn't. She didn't understand one damn thing. "But Rod, mermaids, men, whatever, are the stuff of myths and legend."

"Valerie." He knelt down next to her and cradled her cheek in his hand. "Think about it. About all of it. Talking seagulls, the albatross on our tail, the oil…" He brushed his thumb along her bottom lip. "None of that exists in the Human world. Oh, the birds do talk, but not around Humans. They know better. Your scientists dissect anything odd they come across, so the birds have learned to keep quiet."

He brushed his knuckles against her cheek. "As have we. Humans don't know about our world because they'd destroy it. Hades, they're doing that now. We've learned to keep ourselves hidden."

"So explain to me how my mother met my father and didn't notice something like a tail?" Now, see?

That argument made sense. In some weird, alternate-reality way.

She scrambled to her feet. "And you keep talking about a tail, Rod. Why? You've got legs." And pretty darn nice ones, especially in those shorts. Or sprawled out, as they'd been last night, with nothing but a towel over his groin—

Back to what's important, Dumere.

"I don't see a tail and haven't seen one on you—and we've spent the past two nights together." *One more* together *than the other, but again, mind on the moment...*

"That's why we had to be here before I could tell you this, Valerie. The ocean will turn my legs back into my tail. Your legs, as well."

"Rod, I... You're asking a lot."

"I know. But I swear to you, I'm not making this up. You saw what the oil can do, Valerie." He took a step toward the water. "Just watch."

Rod took a few more steps, and the water slid over his toes as he finally rejoined the ocean.

Valerie nibbled on her lip so much that he worried she'd make it bleed.

"Valerie, it will be all right." He took another step in, the water caressing his ankles. Gods, it felt so good to be going home. He wanted her to join him, but he could understand why she was nervous. Once she saw his tail, however, she'd believe.

She'd have to.

Another wave crashed over his shins.

But… he still had shins. Why?

He took another step into deeper water and looked down. The waves caught his knees.

He still had knees.

Something wasn't right.

He should have his tail by now. One drop of seawater started the change, and he had more than a drop trickling down his legs—yet he still had legs.

"Rod? You still have legs."

"I know." *Why* did he still have legs?

His chest tightened, and he sucked in huge gulps of… air.

He still breathed air.

Maybe he had to immerse himself. That had to be it. Perhaps staying out longer than the allotted time made it necessary to submerge all his cells in the healing water.

Decision made, Rod plunged beneath the surface, only to hear Valerie scream his name.

He kicked those stupid legs and let the water embrace him. It felt so good to once again be cradled in the sea, the weightlessness that accompanied it, the ability to twist and turn, up or down without effort…

Until he tried to breathe.

Then water went down his throat and his lungs seized. Instinct had him pushing off the bottom, propelling to the surface, gasping for air, coughing the seawater from his lungs, his arms working to keep him above water.

"Rod! What are you doing? This isn't funny!"

She sounded close to tears and Rod could relate.

He hauled himself through the surf toward the beach on the gods-forsaken bipedal appendages, stumbling up the incline. He didn't know if that was due to instability with the legs or the utterly blinding truth he'd just realized.

It didn't matter that JR hadn't followed them. It didn't matter that he'd brought Valerie to the beach. It didn't even matter that he'd religiously applied the oil to his legs since he'd arrived on land.

Because he'd obviously done the one thing the gods and his father had warned him no High Councilman should ever do. The very thing he'd studied and practiced and vowed never to do again.

The one thing he *could* never do again.

Somehow, somewhere, he'd failed.

Chapter 32

FISHER NUDGED THE DOOR TO HIS CHAMBERS CLOSED WITH HIS elbow, careful not to tip the tray. Nereida, his assistant, had volunteered to go for food, but Fisher had needed a break from their brainstorming so he'd gone, leaving his Olympian Advisor to review the intelligence data. Thank the gods, there was something he could *do*. Floating around at home had been torture with Kai and the girls looking to him for answers.

He hadn't had any. So he and Reel had decided to find some.

Armed with a full cadre of dolphin Guards, Reel had set out to trace the origins of those ignition wires they'd found in Rod's trench. Fisher had sent for Charley to meet him at the office to go over what they knew. He couldn't rely on the goodwill of the gods to ensure Rod came through this; *he* had to ensure it.

"Did you come up with anything, Charley?"

"I don't know." Charley slid his spectacles from the top of his head to the bridge of his nose and peered at the slate tablet before him. "But we did get another report from Livingston. Rod and the Hybrid got onto an airplane without complications."

Fisher set the tray down on the edge of the desk. "Thank the gods for that." Or maybe not. This was their doing. They were allowing it to happen, and he was pissed about it. "So now what? We still don't know who's behind this. I've half a mind to haul Ceto in for questioning. Drake, too."

"Ceto might not be a bad idea, Fisher, but Drake? Do you really think he's capable?"

Fisher swam over to the busts of his ancestors, great Mers who'd come before him. None of whom had lost *their* Heir.

"Who in Hades knows anymore, Charley? By rights, none of this should be happening. Diamonds, the bomb, now JR. Someone's had access to our information and that limits the possibilities. I know it wasn't you or me."

Charley set the tablet aside and reached under his glasses to rub his eyes, then swiped his forearm over his forehead. "So you're saying we need to investigate every member of The Council?"

"Do you have any other ideas? Because I'm ready to hear them." Fisher turned away from the marble statues, those unblinking stone eyes condemning him.

No more than he was.

He never should have sent Rod off unprepared. There were some things people had a right to know, no matter what the protocols decreed.

"Well, we could always—"

Charley's words were cut off by the clang of the ancient gong that heralded the arrival of vital intelligence.

Fisher beat Charley to the office door, flinging it open to find a midnight-blue parrotfish flapping his fins so fast they might detach.

"Chipper?" The kid had grown. Gotten braces.

"High Councilman." Chipper was sucking in water by the quart. "The Portal Sentries show a disturbance in the vortex of one of the top-secret Travel Chambers."

Fisher floated back to allow him to enter. "Where, Chipper? Which one?" Only a handful were top-secret, although the rest were off-limits to the general population without specific Council permission. The Council controlled every means of magical transportation, so he wanted to know who'd been able to breach their security.

Chipper gulped back another quart of water, the exhalation streaming from his gills in a current strong enough to whip a sea dragon out the door.

But Fisher didn't need to hear Chipper's answer to know which one was compromised.

Only one top-secret Chamber warranted this kind of urgency.

"NAL39," Chipper confirmed.

Even though he'd been expecting it, a knot twisted in Fisher's gut. North Atlantic, Latitude 39. The portal near Reel and Erica's home.

Where Rod and Valerie were headed.

Chapter 33

ROD LEANED AGAINST THE DECK RAILING, STARING OUT AT the ceaseless waves, each one striking the surf in its own unique rhythm. Each one reminding him he'd never feel it again.

Where had he gone wrong?

He kept replaying the last few days over and over. He hadn't told her about Mers before arriving here. He'd used the oil each night, including Livingston's quick thinking last night. He'd brought her to the ocean. What was he missing?

"Rod?" Valerie's voice, soft, just a whisper above the waves, came through the kitchen's screen door.

He didn't want to have to face her. Didn't know how he could. She must think he was crazy, and, frankly, he couldn't blame her.

"Are you okay?"

Such a generic phrase. He was so far from being okay, it was laughable. Unbearable.

What must she think of him? Dragged halfway across the country on a promise to collect an inheritance, only to find the guy she'd trusted had lied to her.

Not that he had, but how in Hades was he going to prove it to her?

And how was she going to fulfill The Prophecy if he couldn't?

Unless…

He turned around. "Valerie, you have to go into the ocean."

She scrubbed a towel through her curls, damp from the shower she'd taken immediately after the fiasco on the beach. "After what just happened to you? I don't think so. I can't, Rod."

He could understand why—he hadn't exactly put her fear of the ocean to rest. But she had to if he wanted a shot at regaining his tail and his throne.

"You have to, Valerie. I think that's why my tail didn't come back. My father said I had to bring you to the ocean. Not just the beach. Maybe you need to get your tail and fulfill The Prophecy before it'll happen."

She adjusted her T-shirt where it clung to her damp skin. "Rod, I'm telling you, I'm not going near the water. I mean, even if what you said is true—and, honestly, a tail? But even if it is, what's it going to do for me? It's not as if a tail is an appendage one needs in Kansas, and it'll certainly catch someone's eye, so there goes the 'humans can't know about merpeople' thing. Plus it'll definitely land me on some scientist's examination table, and you yourself said what a problem that will be." She shook her head as she hung by the door. "And the fact that this is my argument is just so utterly bizarre, I can't even believe—wait a minute. Prophecy? What prophecy?"

That had to be it. Rod took a step forward again but stopped when she took a matching one backward.

"There's a lot more I need to tell you, Valerie, about our world."

"It's not my world."

He'd convince her. He had to. "Not yet, Valerie, but it could be. It *should* be."

He walked toward the house, hating the fact that she shrank from him, and hoping it was only because of the ridiculous notion that she was allergic to the salt water coating his skin. But it didn't matter why. He wasn't about to give up.

"Listen, let me take a shower and wash the seawater off. Then we'll talk, okay? I promise you this will all work out." And it would. Somehow.

He wasn't about to fail.

Exactly how Rod thought this could work out was something she couldn't fathom. He'd also promised she would collect her inheritance and go back to the shop; now he was throwing some prophecy into the mix, which didn't sound as if he was planning for her to head home anytime soon.

Which was something they'd definitely need to discuss. She'd finally settled into her own world; she wasn't about to go traipsing off to his. Especially when his was full of fables and fairy tales.

Val opened the refrigerator after he left the kitchen. Right now, she needed something to do, and, with the hollow feeling in her stomach, eating sounded just right. She'd replace whatever she took later. Or send a check. After all, inheritance or not, Rod had promised her the diamond. The one filled with strange healing oil...

The showerhead in the hall bath kicked on with a screech.

Just like Livingston.

Right. Livingston. The talking seagull.

Val bit into a Granny Smith apple and leaned against the countertop, everything inside her telling her to make a run for the car and leave this insanity.

Seagulls didn't talk. Albatrosses didn't fly over Kansas. Peregrines didn't dive-bomb cars and oil didn't miraculously heal stitch-worthy lacerations overnight. Such was the natural order of things.

But now, having seen those things happen, her view on the natural order was skewed upside-down and sideways, so why *couldn't* Rod be telling the truth?

She took another bite of the apple, the tart juice washing over her taste buds in a reminder of what *was* normal in her world.

Mermen weren't.

Princes spouting tales of mythical islands and non-appearing tails weren't.

Walking into an ocean she was allergic to and getting a tail wasn't.

No, what *was* normal in her world was running away. Taking the first exit out of an uncomfortable situation and moving on to something else—just like she should do right now, diamond be damned. This was his nightmare; let him pick up the pieces. She had enough to deal with in saving the store and getting it operational; she didn't need this added insanity. She hadn't signed on for it; she didn't want it; she ought to leave.

Just like dear ol' Dad.

Val took another bite of the apple—right into a mushy bitter spot. She spit it into the trash can, tossing the rest of the apple after it, then headed to the sink to rinse the bad taste from her mouth.

She wasn't like her father.

She refused to be.

That's what sticking by the store was all about. To prove to herself that she wasn't like him. That *she* could make a commitment. That *she* could be counted on to handle responsibility and not balk at the first sign of trouble, no matter what her genetic pool said.

Yet, with all her protestations that she'd changed, that she wasn't like him, what had she done at the first sign of trouble with the store? Mention back taxes, and she'd taken off for the quick fix of a promised inheritance.

And what had happened? She found herself right back where she always found herself—with her hopes dashed and nothing resolved.

Val washed her hands of the sticky mess then dried them on a paper towel.

She was going back home. Today. No matter what. Diamond or not. She was not going to let Mom down.

But what about Rod?

That stopped her. What about him?

What did she owe him? He was the one who'd dragged her here, all for something he couldn't deliver—

Exactly. Something he hadn't delivered.

That made no sense. Why would he go through all of this if he knew he couldn't prove it? That was what she couldn't figure out.

Which had to mean that he honestly believed what he'd told her was true, and, with bird anomalies abounding— up to and including the fact that there was not one single bird anywhere in the sky (and when had *that* ever happened?)… maybe… maybe… it really was true.

She walked to the breakfast bar, finding the need to sit down once more.

Good thing, too, because he walked in just then, pulling on a black T-shirt, giving her yet another glimpse of those sculpted abs and the seductive line by his hip above low-slung camouflage shorts. Then he shook his head, the waves flinging off drops of water before he ran his fingers through them in a move so utterly masculine she let herself enjoy it, if only for a moment.

He walked to the sink, grabbed a glass from the cabinet, and filled it with water from the tap. All without a word.

Silence made her edgy. Especially when it was screaming with unasked questions.

"Rod, what are you going to do now?"

"That's a damn good question." He picked up the saltshaker, then cursed and set it back down. "Since I'm apparently out of a job and a home, I'll have to find others. I'm sure Reel can always use another deckhand at the marina."

"You said he lives here, yet, if you two are twins, that'd make him a merman also, right? How is that possible?"

Rod leaned a hip against the sink. "Reel left the sea. He was born with legs and the knowledge that he wouldn't inherit the throne, so when he fell in love with Erica, it wasn't a tough decision for him to give up Atlantis and live here with her."

"Wait. What do you mean he was born with legs? I thought you said merpeople had tails."

Rod rubbed the back of his neck. "I'm—was—The Heir. In our world, there can be only one Heir, and to prevent any challenges from subsequent males in the ruling family, they are born with legs. Makes it pretty obvious who inherits and who doesn't. There's never any question."

"So you were born with a tail?"

Something—pain, maybe—flashed across his face. "I was, yes."

Good thing she was sitting down. He'd been born with a tail, Reel with legs. Reel gave up the sea; Rod wanted to go back. A council, a talking seagull, the albatross...

"You really are a merman, aren't you?"

His cockeyed smile appeared and, while it was still sexy, she saw the sadness in it before he stared out the window. "I was. Now? I don't know what I am. Human, I guess." He set the glass down and looked out the window. "I never expected this. Never in a thousand *selinos*—Oh Hades." His shoulders hunched as he leaned onto his palms.

"Rod? What is it?"

He took a big breath and straightened up, turning around with a bleak look in his eyes that hit home with her. She knew that kind of pain. That alone kind of pain.

"A thousand *selinos*, Valerie. Do you know how often I've said that? A thousand *selinos*. Up until today, it'd been a number I threw out there in the most unspecific of terms, but now, I never *will* see a thousand. I'll be lucky to see a hundred."

"A hundred what? What's a *selino*?"

"Ah, yes, I forgot. 'Years' is what my sister-in-law told me Humans call them."

"A thousand years? You were expecting to see a thousand years?" That response knocked her for a loop, even while she was sitting down.

"Surprised?" His lips thinned as he nodded. "The High Councilman is Immortal, Valerie. I guess this serves me right for what I did to Reel."

"I'm lost." About a lot of things, but first things first. "What did you do to Reel and how does any of this relate to you not getting a tail?"

And why on earth had she just asked that question? It made no sense.

Not that any of this did in the first place.

He walked to the breakfast bar and sat next to her.

"That rule I broke? The one I told you about this morning at the motel?" He exhaled again before taking another gulp of his water. "I stripped Reel of his chance at Immortality."

He set the glass down behind him. "Reel and I were out swimming one day when we were kids and I dared him to approach Erica. She was a Human and we were forbidden from approaching them. We both knew it. Just as I also knew Reel would never pass up the chance to do something daring. In my defense, I knew he could pull it off. If anyone could, it was Reel. Trust me, his antics are legendary in Atlantis."

Trust him. That was the crux of this, wasn't it? There hadn't been many people in her life she could trust, and definitely no men.

"Reel would have pulled it off, too, if she hadn't heard us talking and looked underwater. According to Reel, when he saw her eyes, that was it for him. He fell head over fin in love with her all those *selinos* ago, and it's never changed."

Rod sat back and raked his hand through his hair again. "But it changed us. That's when Reel started getting sent out to train, though we didn't know that's what it was at the time. We thought he was being punished. That both of us were for risking the exposure of our world.

"What we didn't know was that he was being sent on challenges for the opportunity to earn the Immortality that didn't come with legs. I, meanwhile, got stuck studying the damp old texts of Mer doctrine and law. He rebelled while I... didn't. And he ended up leaving the sea, giving up Immortality, all because of something I'd done. I guess my guilt wasn't enough for The Council since they've finally made the punishment fit the crime."

Bitterness worse than the taste of that apple dripped from his words, but Val could tell it was aimed at himself. Which was just ridiculous.

And she said so. "Rod, you can't be held account-able for something you did when you were a kid. You *are* called kids when you're young, right?" Yes, it appeared that she actually *had* gone over to the dark—watery?—side.

Finally—some humor in that sideways smile of his. "Yes, Valerie, we're called kids. What? Were you expecting 'fish fry'?"

Okay, levity was good... Both for him, and for allowing her to realize that his story had stopped being so improbable.

"So where does that leave you? What about the throne?"

And what about her? If she believed him that there really was a world beneath Bermuda—okay, did she really just think that?—could she also believe him about her allergy? What if what he'd said was true? That she had to get her tail—and, yes, the room swam at that thought, and no, the pun was not intended—for him to be able to get his?

"I don't know what it means, Valerie. I honestly don't know."

He looked so forlorn, so lost. And that wasn't Rod. He was a guy used to being in charge. A guy destined for the throne, raised knowing he was going to inherit it and committed to the idea. To his people and his world.

That had to be the biggest irony of all. Here she was, Ms. Lacked-Staying-Power, a trait inherited from a father who had no idea what the word "commitment" meant, who'd never known who or where she was supposed to be, who'd never set down any roots anywhere and was finally ready to do so, only to find Rod—a guy so used to knowing where and who he was that when it was yanked out from under him, he floundered.

She couldn't be so selfish that she'd leave someone when he needed her, as her father had done.

She wasn't like her father, and, by God, she was going to prove it.

"Rod, I'll go in the ocean. For you, I'll do it."

His world just got rocked.

And this time, it wasn't by the gods, but by Valerie. She was setting aside her fear for him. She finally believed him.

And he loved her for it.

His world rocked again and, even though it was metaphorical, he grabbed the armrest on the barstool.

He did. He loved her.

He loved Valerie, and he didn't give a damn that she was a Hybrid.

Maybe, just maybe, there was a silver lining to this no-tail mess.

As High Councilman, he had to take into consideration that she was half-Human, but as the newly disinherited Heir, he no longer did. A High Councilman had rules and strictures and mandates and a whole pod of regulations to govern his life, but Rod-the-Tailless didn't.

He finally understood what Reel had known so long ago. That a life—even an Immortal one—without the woman you love is no life at all.

But to be able to choose to live that life with someone was the greatest gift any God or gods could bestow.

"Valerie." He took her hand. "Thank you. But no. I won't ask you to do this for me. Even though, as I've said, you aren't allergic, you don't want to be a part of that world. When you get your tail, you'll have no choice. Especially if The Council gets their hooks into you. No one has the right to tell you what to do with your life. No matter who you are, or what they think you're supposed to do with your life, no one—most certainly not The Council—should decide that for you. It's your life, and if you want to live it in Kansas, then that's where we'll go."

"We?"

He cupped her cheek with his palm, her curls reminding him how they'd felt against his chest as he'd held her this morning.

"Yes. *We.* If you'll have me."

"Rod, I… what are you saying? That you want to come to Kansas? Give up the ocean?"

He ran the backs of his fingers over her cheek, feeling a lightness in his soul he hadn't had in, well, forever. For the first time, he was in charge of his life. Where he'd go, what he'd do. "Yes. I do. I'd like to help you with your mother's store. Your store."

"But what about the prophecy and the coup and everything else? Your family? You're ready to give it all up? Why would you do that?"

He smiled, and it came from deep within him. "Because the one thing I've learned from the way I've lived my life is that living for the sake of existing isn't a life at all. Reel made his choice and I've never understood it until right this moment. I have no reason to feel guilty for ruining his life because I didn't.

"That day, the day he met Erica, was the beginning for him. As my brother, he had no chance of being anything more than what he was. Throne insurance. But with Erica, he could be his own man. Be more than the position he'd been born into. He knew that and chose to live with her. The Council has taken that decision from me, but you, Valerie, just now, you gave it back."

He lifted her hand, running his fingertips over her palm and along her fingers, the spark of electricity zipping along every place their skin met. He traced the back of her hand with his other one, enfolding it between his. "Don't you see, Valerie? If I ask you to go in the water and I get my tail because of yours, I'm right back within the rigid confines of a royal life, always having to follow the prescribed patterns. It won't be my life. It'll be the throne's. And it's one that doesn't allow for a relationship with a Human. Even one who's half-Human."

"Half-Human? Relationship?"

The words were out of her mouth before she considered the ramifications of what she was asking.

"Yes, Valerie. Half-Human." Rod brought their joined hands to his mouth and kissed the back side of her wrist with the softest brush of his lips, his eyes warm and mossy green above it. "You, Valerie. I'm in love with you."

And that, more than the tail, more than the birds, more than the story of Atlantis, was what threw her world into a tail... spin.

"You love me?" She looked at their joined hands, his large ones encompassing just one of hers. "How is that possible?"

"Fishing for compliments?" He tilted her chin up with one finger. "You're what I've always wanted to be, but couldn't. You've chosen your path in life. Every job you've taken, every decision you made were yours. Even threatening to leave me at the airport if I didn't give you what you wanted. The inner strength that takes, the ability to claim what you want... I like that in you, Valerie. I admire that in you and need that—you—in my life. Someone who can and does take what she wants."

She tugged her face from his grasp and slid from the barstool. He was giving her too much credit. Undeserved credit.

"That's not admirable, Rod." She walked to the sliding door and fumbled with the handle, trying to get away—as usual. "That was me, running from something I didn't want to deal with. Just like always."

He followed her and unlocked the latch, but he didn't open it. He stood a hair's breadth behind her. Close enough that she could feel the rise and fall of his chest against her shoulder blades.

She made no move to open the door.

"Except you didn't run, did you, Valerie? You stayed. Even when I told you one unbelievable thing after another, you stuck with me because of the bigger picture. Because of what you want out of life."

He made it sound so noble, but she'd just decided she was leaving before he'd shown up in the kitchen.

Except… she hadn't.

She'd had the chance to get out, yet she hadn't gone. She'd stuck around to eat that apple… and work this out.

She *wasn't* like her father.

Relief flooded her. Along with *something else* when Rod eliminated that last slip of air between them.

His hand brushed her curls before sliding along the slope of her neck, down her shoulder where he gripped her bicep, his touch slight, but by no means insignificant.

"Without my tail, without the throne, I finally have the same chance you've always had. I'd like to take that chance. To share my life. With you, Valerie."

This time when his voice dipped, it wasn't because he'd been disappointed. This time it was with hope.

And that *was* her middle name.

But she'd hoped before. And lost. Every time.

Would it be different with Rod? Did she want it to be? Could it be?

Her first instinct was to run—no surprise there. But she was done with that. And, scary though it might be, if she ran from Rod—from his declaration—she would always wonder. Would it have worked? Was he the one? Could she have had the life she'd always wanted?

Could she commit?

The answers were all right there, hers for the taking...

If she had the courage to try.

Chapter 34

"ROD, I…" VAL NIBBLED HER LIP, WANTING TO SAY YES. Wanting to give him the answer he wanted, wanting to make it all true, but still unsure. What if she was wrong?

He put a finger on her lips. "Sshh. I don't need an answer now. I know how hard all of this is to take in." He gave her that sideways grin he did so well. "I'm not going anywhere."

She smiled at that. He wasn't going anywhere because he *hadn't gotten a tail*. That big, life-altering, reality-shifting thing, yet she was worried about… what? Silly things like would he leave, could she trust him, what if she ended up getting hurt…

No guts, no glory. No pain, no gain. Pretty it up with clichés, it all came down to one thing: was her fear going to keep her from getting what she wanted out of life?

And was Rod what she wanted?

There was only one way to find out.

"Rod, kiss me."

"I—what?" The look on his face made her uncertainty worth it. He hadn't seen that one coming.

She hadn't either, really.

"Kiss me."

"You're sure?"

No. "Yes."

"Okay, but, Vale—"

Oh, hell. Any more talking and she'd lose her nerve. Val wound her arms around his neck and pulled his lips to hers.

It didn't take him long to wrest control of the kiss away from her.

She sighed when he nipped his way from her lips along her jawline to that spot he'd found beneath her ear.

God, he knew *just* the right spot...

Her head fell to the side as his tongue and lips did something magical to the cord in her neck and his hair brushed her lips, and every nerve cell in her body came alive.

Oh, she'd felt physical attraction before, but never anything like this. He liked her for her. For the person she was inside. Flaws and all.

No. That wasn't right. She was starting to get a little fuzzy on the details since he'd decided to swirl his tongue in the hollow of her collarbone, but she did remember that he didn't just *like* her. He *loved* her.

And that made all the difference.

He *loved* her. And she—

Val cupped his jaw in her hands and urged his lips to hers, wanting, no, needing to taste him, to be as active a participant in this as he was. She swept her tongue between his lips with all the urgency and inevitability of those waves out there on that beach, finding all the hidden nuances to his mouth, the taste and scent and feel of him oh-so-right beneath her lips and tongue and fingers.

Then he groaned and the want in his voice ricocheted through her. Her knees gave out and she splayed her fingers across the strong shoulders that rippled with muscle beneath her touch to keep herself vertical.

Vertical? That wasn't how she wanted to be with him.

Memories of how she'd awoken this morning, naked and sprawled all over him, skin to skin, her knee cradled between his thighs, flashed in her mind's eye and it was all she could do not to rip his clothes off.

Because she wanted, no *needed*, to connect with him as closely as two people could. To have him physically inside her because…

Because…

He already was.

Somewhere along the drive, or maybe during the flight, he'd slipped past her defenses and made her care. Made her *want* to care, to take that risk, to know that the risk was worth taking and that she wasn't setting herself up to be abandoned again.

He'd proved that when she'd volunteered to go in the water. He could have taken her up on the offer to get what he wanted, but he hadn't. He'd declined it. For her.

She slid her hands between them to cling to his shirt, the only thing beside his arms holding her upright, and Rod's lips skimmed over her cheek to her jaw. She tilted her head back, still clinging to him, not letting go.

Then his tongue danced along her throat, and her tummy fluttered with a million possibilities when he swept her into his arms.

"Tell me, Valerie," he whispered by her temple, his breath feathering across her skin. "Tell me what you want."

What was amazing was the uncertainty behind his demand. Rod was just as vulnerable as she'd always felt, and it made her believe, really believe, that he did love her.

"You, Rod." She scraped her teeth along his jaw, fumbling with his shirt, shoving it up his torso, seeking the tight flesh of his stomach as he hitched her higher in his arms. "You... and to share my life with you." She nipped his earlobe then slid her tongue into the shell of his ear and he shuddered against her.

"Hold that thought," he growled against her hair.

For a guy who hadn't been born with legs, he used them amazingly well as he carried her to the back-corner bedroom she'd changed in earlier. He rested one knee on the sunlight-streaked, pale-blue comforter and lowered her to the bed with tantalizing slowness.

A mixture of urgency and lethargy flowed through her limbs as she watched him watch her.

Then he inhaled, the muscles of his stomach contracting, and her lethargy disappeared. She sat up, running one fingertip along the line by his hip that so enchanted her and his groan covered the sound of the waves on the beach outside.

"Gods, Valerie... You see what I mean? You go for what you want, and I, for one, have no complaints."

She smiled up at him, nibbling on her bottom lip while she figured out what she wanted next.

Then she drew her lips along that line by his hip, glad she'd made that choice when Rod wavered beside her.

That was effective.

So was running her tongue across his nipple.

Rod groaned and leaned forward, forcing her back, bracing himself with his elbows by her head. But that didn't stop his lower body from letting her know exactly how effective that last maneuver had been.

"Still sure you like this about me?" She followed that with a nip to his jaw just before Rod shook his head.

"No?" She pulled back.

"No. I don't like it." He feathered his lips over her cheek. "I love it, Valerie. Don't stop." He did it again. "Ever."

Ever.

Ever meant permanence.

Stability.

Commitment.

And that was something she wanted more than anything else.

She turned her head so the next pass of his lips met hers.

She did want *ever* more than anything. Well, more than anything except Rod. And it looked like she could have both.

Rod needed this. He needed her. Something tangible to hold onto as this crazy, whirling eddy of a day finally flowed into a steady current, washing the guilt from him like an ebbing tide.

He couldn't believe how free he felt.

He *hadn't* failed Reel all those *selin*—years ago. No, he'd failed himself over the years, always accepting everything they'd told him as truth. That the throne came before all else.

But Valerie made him see things differently.

Rod found the hollow of her throat and inhaled. Her scent streamed through him like the Caribbean Current, warm, and full, filling every space inside him. He wanted to ride this wave for the rest of his life.

Her fingertips played with his nipples, sending shivers down his spine, straight to his balls, and he slid against her, feeling the soft muscles of her belly accept the thrust of his cock, and the tenor of the moment changed.

He framed her beautiful face between his palms. "I love you, Valerie." It was a truth so universal to him that he was surprised he hadn't realized it the moment he'd met her. But he'd been blind to the truth. Blinded by the dictates and statutes and strictures that had defined who he was.

Well, no more. *He* defined who he was.

He didn't need the throne, he didn't need Immortality, and he didn't need a tail.

All he needed was her and the chance to share her life. This beautiful, strong, independent woman looking up at him with eyes so direct and clear and full of wonder that he could see his future.

"I want you, Valerie." He kissed the corner of her mouth she so often nibbled. "Now and for the rest of my life."

Her breath caught and she nibbled that corner again. "For real?"

He couldn't resist. "No. For Rod."

Then she smiled and it was as brilliant as dawn over Antarctica, bright and vast and pure. "I... I love you, too, Rod."

He took her lips, tenderly at first, sipping at their sweetness, slicking his tongue over her soft lips, tasting something both tart and sweet at the same time, so very much like her.

She groaned into his mouth, and the sound vibrated down through his heart into the marrow of his bones and he needed to be inside her. As she was in him.

He pressed against her, his cock aching, and she moaned. Her legs shifted to accommodate him, cradling his hardness, her mound pressing against him, and Rod felt fire ignite at his core.

She slid her hands over his back, arching against him so that her breasts swelled beneath the soft fabric of her shirt, their hardening tips grazing his chest.

Rod shifted his weight so he could slide a hand down her side, into the indentation at her waist, curving around her hip, to palm the sleek flesh of her thigh.

She whimpered, or maybe that was a groan he muffled with his mouth as his tongue delved inside, when he slipped his fingers beneath the edge of her shorts, sleek muscle and soft, damp skin greeting him.

She turned her head just enough to break the gentle suction of their lips and inhaled, her moist breath skittering across his skin.

"Rod, are you sure—?"

"Sure?" He growled against her jaw. "Oh… yeah."

She smiled, her breath hitching with a soft laugh. "I meant about the water. I get that you're sure about *this*." She arched beneath him, sending a trail of fire from the tip of his cock to the base.

He slid his hand beneath her shorts, around to cup her backside. "I'm sure, Valerie. If it means I can't have you, then frankly, I don't give a damn."

She moaned when he clasped the firm muscle. "You forgot 'my dear,'" she panted.

"My dear what?" He traced the cleft there, down between her legs, wanting to tear the shorts from her body.

"My dear Scarlett."

He pressed against her mound with the heel of his hand and she arched again into him. "But your name is Valerie."

She shook her head and moaned. "Never mind. Just… oh… do that again."

Gladly.

But first, he tore himself off her, wanting the feel of her skin against his. She moaned, her eyes half-closed, her lips swollen and moist, skin flushed, curls jumbled around her head like a halo as she reached for him.

He ripped off his shirt, hearing the tear in the seams and not caring. The shorts were more difficult, zippers and buttons and all manner of fasteners to slow him down. He managed to get them off in one piece, kicking them aside as he reached for hers.

She'd caught on quickly, working the fasteners on her shorts the moment he'd left her, so Rod only had to reach out and slide them down her legs. He tugged, wanting them out of the way, then stopped himself.

He wanted to take this slow. Taste and see every inch of her. Experience all she was to him. Show her how he felt, so she'd never question how or why he loved her.

He spread his hands over her thighs, flexing his fingers against her firm muscles, and she wiggled, scooting back on the bed, trying to kick the shorts off her legs.

Rod pressed down. "Valerie."

She looked at him from beneath hooded eyes, the blue as pure and crystal clear as glacial waters, but so very different in temperature, and he felt his own temperature rise.

"I want you. Here. Now. Fast. Slow. All of you."

She nibbled her lip again as her chest hitched, breasts swelling beneath her T-shirt, nipples hard, begging to be released. She gripped the comforter, and her tongue flicked out to moisten her lips.

Rod sucked in a breath, putting a rein on the impulse to claim her. His balls tightened as he tugged the hem of her shorts and another inch of thigh was bared to him.

She writhed, trying to rid herself of the shorts, but Rod gripped her legs, imprisoning her. He tugged then, sliding the clothing to her knees—and her knees to the edge of the bed, the fabric beneath and around them, trapping her there for his pleasure.

And hers.

He slid one finger beneath her panties.

Her heat and her scent almost drove him over the edge.

He slid his finger closer to her core, already anticipating the wetness he'd find, the urge to slip inside her almost overcoming his desire to take it slow.

Next time, however…

And there *would* be a next time. And one after that, then another…

She flattened her thighs, straining against the confines of the band of clothing that prevented her from opening herself up fully and arched against him when his finger found her.

Wet. Hot. Swollen.

He touched her again, this time long and slow. Lightly.

She groaned, panting, her eyes shooting open. "Rod. Please." She shoved her panties down over his hand.

"I will." His own breath sounded heavy to his ears, his cock swelling at her plea and the blonde curls he found there.

He slid the fabric down to her knees, then found her again, lingering this time, slipping between the folds gently and she gasped, surging against his finger. Her backside lifted off the bed and Rod found himself engulfed in heat. In need so fierce he almost came with the force of it.

Fighting for breath and control, Rod slid her shirt up, needing to see all of her. "Take it off, Valerie," he said, his voice lower than he'd ever heard. Hades, he was lucky he could speak at all, with the breath barely able to reach his lungs.

She moved then, her abdomen contracting as she raised herself, her body sliding against and around his finger, and they both gasped.

"Take it off." The words fought for life in his dry throat.

Valerie nodded and removed it, pink lace beneath cupping her breasts. He had little time to enjoy that visual feast before she'd removed that piece of clothing as well and she was bare and beautiful before him.

He lifted her with his free arm, bracing one knee on the bed and took her breast in his mouth.

Ambrosia. He finally knew the meaning of the word and understood why it was the food of the gods.

He flicked his tongue over the pebbled nipple and she swelled beneath his tongue and under his finger. She moved then, working herself against him, and Rod groaned. He wanted to surge into her and make her his.

Slow. Long.

He kept her rhythm, suckling in time to the movement, wanting to feel her fall apart in his arms before he found his own fulfillment.

Valerie dropped her head back, arching even more fully into his mouth, pulling her feet onto the bed to open herself for his touch. Rod could smell her arousal and found himself breathing it in like the elixir of life.

She was his life. Anything else was extraneous, but this moment, this woman—not Mer, not Human, not Hybrid—this *woman* was where and how he'd spend eternity.

She whimpered when he slowed the pace, her hand finding his, working his fingers against her, pushing one inside. "Please," she panted.

Oh, he would.

He slid another finger inside, his thumb keeping pace against her swollen, tense flesh.

He traced a wet trail to her other breast, licking the tip as if it were the sweetest fruit. And, really, wasn't it? Sweet and luscious, there for the taking. His by the grace and generosity of Valerie.

She pressed his hand to her, moving against him, her breath heaving her breasts in short, quick movements, his tongue stroking her nipple in an ever-increasing tempo.

The bed jostled beneath them, her moans deep and primal. Then her knees fell wide, her hand slipping away to brace herself against the bed, and her body went rigid, his name a strangled cry from her lips, and Rod felt her gush of pleasure as she pulsed around his fingers in rhythm with his heart.

How could he have even thought about not experiencing this with her? Nothing was worth missing this, missing her. Immortality, the throne, Atlantis... If he lived forever without her, it'd be a long and hollow existence.

"Rod," she sighed softly when the world settled around them and Rod found his own pleasure in that.

He released her breast, placing a soft kiss over her heart, and laid her back against the bed. He lowered himself beside her, sliding his hands over her trembling tummy and rapidly beating heart, to curve around her neck, her pulse thumping strongly in time with his own.

He turned her to face him, smiling at the sleepy, sated look there.

Her eyelids fluttered open. "That was…" She smiled and licked her lips. Rod's cock jerked against her thigh. "…unbelievable."

"With everything else you've come to believe, it can't be, Valerie. Incredible, yes, but not unbelievable." He kissed her gently, needing to taste her.

She moaned against his mouth, into his mouth, thrusting her tongue inside, and wrapped an arm around him, crushing her breasts against him, nestling her moist curls against his leg.

"I… have… condoms. In my duffel," she whispered between the kisses, and Rod felt the heat flare between them again. "Make love to me, Rod."

Tearing through her bag, he found the package, then sheathed himself. He slid atop her, nudging her shorts off the bed after she'd freed herself, sighing when she wrapped those glorious legs around him.

Holding her face between his hands, his thumbs tracing her cheekbones, Rod slid inside her slick, tight heat, claiming her with his eyes and his body for eternity.

Immortal or not, they were joined forever.

It was utterly, perfectly right to have him inside her. To be here, like this, with him—mermen and tails and albatrosses be damned. Somehow they'd work it all out. They had to.

Because *this* was where she belonged.

As Rod started to move within her, Val realized that, at last, the restlessness in her soul had quieted. She'd found home. From the moment she'd met him, there'd been no sense of urgency, no "what's around the next corner," nothing. With Rod, this was where she was supposed to be and the *only* urgency was wanting him to move faster within her, to take her to greater heights, to share the moment and all the possibilities.

He trailed kisses across her face, stopping every so often to linger at her lips, and Val let herself be guided by his passion. Every touch, every kiss spoke to her.

His breath came heavy in her ear as he pumped between her legs, and Val reached around to hold on for every moment. Stroke after stroke of his hard, strong body gave new meaning to the word pleasure, new meaning to the word together. It was building again, the torrent of power and sensation only he could invoke in her, and she grasped the hard, sculpted muscles of his backside, urging him into her. Urging him to claim her, to make her as indispensable to him as he'd suddenly become to her.

When he called out her name, his release shuddering her into another world-tilting orgasm, Val knew that nothing had ever been as right with her world as it was in that moment.

And she was going to do whatever necessary to keep it that way.

Chapter 35

A VEHICLE DOOR SLAMMED BESIDE REEL'S HOME JUST AS the sun met the horizon. Even though Drake doubted anyone could see him in the twilight, he ducked beneath the dock, keeping his head low and his tail even lower. He didn't need any Humans getting curious about the big fish so close to shore.

Idiots. The few times he'd run into them on the open waters and they'd seen his tail, they'd thought they'd found the catch of a lifetime. He'd shaken his head at the fishhooks dropping into the water around him, amazed that fish were so gullible. What the stupid Bipeds thought to tempt him with were leavings of other fish so disgusting they made his mother's scallops look like the nectar of the gods.

No, the last thing he wanted to worry about was Humans. He'd bide his time in Reel's private hideaway until his tail dried out to legs.

With JR out of the picture, he'd had to take the drastic measure of showing up here in person. But it couldn't be helped. He wasn't about to give up when he was *this* close to his goal.

No one suspected him; no one even *considered* him. His father had written him off under Ceto's surveillance, expecting her to keep tabs on him. Just before he'd left, he'd gotten a *lovely* message from Ceto, backing out on him.

Well, screw her. See if he kept his end of the bargain when he took over. She deserved whatever she had coming to her.

And screw JR. Setting him up like some patsy.

JR had agreed to help him because of the gods? What in Hades did that mean? Were they allowing him to win? Did they want him to? Had the Tritones finally worn out their Olympian welcome?

He hoped so. He was tired of hearing about them. His sisters still couldn't say Rod's name without sighing, and the guy had tossed aside their interest like days-old chum.

Not that he could blame him, but still. It was the principle of the matter.

The vehicle started back up, a nasty rumbling that he was sure emitted noxious black smoke into the environment the way Humans were prone to do.

Drake submerged himself and headed for the secret bunker, hating that he had to hide from Humans again. When he claimed the throne and Immortality, he would have a long freakin' time to show those Humans they were second-rate planetary citizens. Third-rate, even. Nothing else on the planet did as much damage to it as they did.

That had to be why the gods were letting him win. The Tritones had done squat about punishing the Bipeds for the disasters they'd meted out on each other and the planet. Stupid, stupid creatures. They were intent on destroying the only place they could live.

Well, oceans covered far more of the planet than land. It was time for the Oceanic Community to swim up and be counted.

He was the one who would lead the way.

Rod's days were numbered... now down to O-N-E.

Chapter 36

Rod was having that dream again. Warm, soft woman next to him, the faint hint of sand and salt wending in and out of the gardenia scent clinging to her skin, the slightest brush of silken hair against his chest, a tiny sigh on the breeze...

And then she moved against him and Rod knew, again, it was no dream.

He'd made love to Valerie, and all the sirens' songs didn't do it justice. He'd felt as if a missing piece of himself, one he hadn't even known was missing, had slid into place.

He wrapped his arms around her, fitting her more tightly against him. She murmured something soft and feminine in her sleep, and Rod knew he needed that sound in his life for the rest of his years, however many he had left.

He finally understood what his brother had tried to explain.

Rod nuzzled the hollow beneath her hair, inhaling the luxurious scent of her skin and the tastes of the night. They'd awoken in the darkness and she hadn't pulled back from her desire, demanding things of him that had thrilled him, taking her pleasure and, in doing so, giving him so much more.

He'd fallen, sated, to the mattress beside her at some point, incapable of movement. Even breathing had been an effort, she'd so worn him out. Herself, too, falling asleep before he'd left the warm haven of her body.

He nipped the delicate cord in her neck when she murmured and moved, tilting her head ever so slightly. Her pulse fluttered there, a breast filling his palm as she drew in a breath.

"Good morning," he whispered against her ear.

She smiled, her eyes still closed. "Is it?" She captured his hands to her breasts, linking her fingers with his.

"I think it's a pretty good day to wake up to."

"Ah, but it could be so much better." She twisted suddenly, and Rod found himself flat on his back with Valerie over him.

He liked this already. "Oh, really? How so?"

Her grin was slow and sexy... just like she was as she crawled backwards down his body until she was between his legs, nudging them apart with her knees.

"I'll show you." She sank onto the mattress, her eyes never leaving his until his cock rose, turgid and long, between them.

She licked her lips.

Rod thought he'd come right then.

He closed his eyes and gave himself over to Valerie's care.

He was so big. She'd known that last night when she'd felt him inside her, but she hadn't realized until this very minute just how big and thick he was.

Her resolve wavered. She'd never actually done this before. Oh, other guys had hinted—okay, more than hinted, but it was too intimate an act for her to consider it.

But in accepting Rod, who he was, how he made her feel, she could do this. For him, yes.

Because Rod, with all his unbelievable tales and noble sacrifice, had done something no man had ever done before…

He'd made her feel wanted. Made her *believe* that she was.

She ran her tongue up the long length of him, circling the thick head, then taking him into her mouth.

He groaned and she slid her lips down a bit more.

He groaned again, this time whispering her name.

She smiled around him, liking that he was in her power, hers to command.

She took more of him into her mouth, working his velvety skin with her tongue. His legs trembled beside her and his breath came out in a harsh *whoosh*.

She settled her crossed arms more fully beneath her, raising herself higher, and angled her head to be able to take his full length in.

Rod gripped her head, threading his fingers through her hair with heart-rending urgency. "Dear gods, Valerie…" His head thrashed from side to side as he arched into her.

She released most of him then, only to take him back in as he sucked in a breath. He surged into her mouth, words in a strange language falling from his lips.

He'd whispered them in her ear last night, hot breath and huskiness combining with the foreign sounds to take her out of herself. Out of the moment and into a plane where only feelings existed. He'd transported her not just with his body, not just with his words, but with his heart, and Valerie, who'd always wondered whether she was worthy of love, no longer had any question.

She stroked his balls, loving the feel of them jerking in her hand as she sucked him. Loving the short pants he emitted with her name, over and over, intermingling with whatever else it was he was saying in his native tongue.

Her tongue spoke its own language. Up and over, around and around, she stroked him, working him hard then gentle, long, slow strokes from the base to the tip, frantic swirls around the head, dipping into that moist opening, tasting his arousal. The long vein pulsed in time with her heartbeat, and she created more suction around him, working the base with her fingertips, loving that she could give this to him, give back what he'd done for her.

Rod's heels hit the bed beside her, his hips jerking off the bed in time with her suction, and she slid her hands beneath his butt, her breaths coming heavy as his response turned her on. She hadn't known what this would do to her, hadn't realized that his pleasure would incite her own. That she'd connect with him on such a level as the one bringing him pleasure.

She could feel herself swelling and growing wet, pressing against the bed, searching for her own release. But not until he found his.

He groaned when she took him deep, went rigid when she scored his length lightly with her teeth, tracing his vein with her tongue. His muscles clenched in her hands, and she squeezed them, urging him deeper into her throat.

His cock jerked against her tongue and his hands flew to the bed, gripping the sheets, pulling on them until they popped free of the mattress. Her name emerged on one long, soulful moan as he speared himself into her, his legs shaking.

"Get… on… me…" The guttural words were half-command, half-plea.

She didn't want to; she wanted to do this for him. She licked her way to the tip of him to tell him so, but Rod moved faster than anyone should be able to in his state, pulling on a condom in record time and impaling her on top of him.

You gotta love a man of action. One who knew what he wanted and went after it.

And she did. Oh, how she did.

His fingers gripped her hips, his teeth bared as he pummeled her, harsh, jerky movements that lacked any finesse.

Not that she needed finesse, she realized in a split-second of lucidity. He hit that spot every single time, as if he knew her more intimately than she did. She could only reach back for his legs and ride the wave of intensity.

More strange words came from him as he jerked her up and down, the wave building. He changed the angle ever so slightly and Val forgot how to breathe. She couldn't. She was right there…

Rod slid a thumb over her, never breaking the rhythm of his hips, and stroked her. Hard, relentless and, all of a sudden… she shattered.

Stars exploded behind her eyelids while her body jerked against his. He was there with her, shuddering, pounding, exploding inside her, raising her up as his hips soared off the bed, his thighs bulging against her backside as he emptied himself inside her and she knew…

She'd never be alone again.

Chapter 37

"REST, VALERIE." HER SOFT, SATED SMILE FILLED ROD'S soul in a way he'd never imagined.

He would kill to protect this woman.

And he might yet have to.

Livingston should be here soon, bringing news of the coup, he hoped, and releasing the shore birds from their exile along this stretch of beach.

Rod slid from the bed, hoping, as well, for some word from his father. An explanation perhaps—not that it'd change his mind.

Because if he had to choose between Valerie and the throne, there was no choice to be made. Loving her was a state of being now, and the loss of the throne a mere change in his career path. He'd feel that way even if he had his tail.

Rod shook his head. Interesting how "failure" could have entirely different meanings depending on one's perspective.

Valerie sighed, shifting beneath the sheet he'd pulled over her in the early hours, one long slim leg slipping from beneath it. He'd discovered the polish on her toes before darkness had fallen, something he hadn't known about Humans.

From his perspective, life was fine, and this was far from failure.

Rod closed the bedroom door behind him and walked into the kitchen, banging the pantry door with his elbow.

He'd have to learn to make Human food now, but as Livingston had said, most of their food tasted good, even if those fish sandwiches left a lot to be desired.

He opened a can of pineapple, a treat rarely found in Atlantis. He could eat pineapple every day for the rest of his life now. See? Not a failure at all.

Something thumped against the front door. Rod emptied the pineapple pieces into a bowl then headed for the door. Opening it, he found a newspaper on the mat. Newspapers were so much easier to read and transport than the slate tablets that defined his world—in every sense.

He picked up the paper and, beneath it, found a box wrapped in brown paper addressed to Valerie, post-marked from Kansas.

Ah, the reason she'd given Tricia Reel's address. He vaguely recalled the sound of a vehicle last night, though at the time he'd thought the rumble was the effect of a particularly clever move Valerie had made...

Rod set the package on the dining table before heading for the deck with his breakfast, hoping whatever it was wouldn't prove bittersweet. She hadn't ventured the information in the car and, with the pall the conversation had settled over her, he hadn't asked.

But, no matter what the package contained, they'd handle it.

Together.

Grabbing the bowl of fruit, Rod slid the slider and screen open slowly. Reel needed to fix that screech. He crossed the beach to the pier behind the house and scanned the ocean beyond the entrance to the inlet for telltale dolphin fins breaching the green-blue waters. While the interlude with Valerie was both life-altering and where he wanted to be, the coup was a very real danger and not over yet.

If anything, he was more vulnerable than ever, should he enter the water.

He chewed a section of pineapple, grimacing at the metallic taste to it. Fresh was better. Could they get fresh pineapple in Kansas? He'd have to ask her.

He scanned the sky. Still no birds. What was keeping Livingston?

He would signal the Council Guards if he could find any. While the bottle-nosed dolphins were experts at stealth, able to hold their breath for a long time while practicing surreptitious breathing maneuvers and rotating formations to keep their numbers concealed, he wouldn't mind a little break in their discipline so he could be assured they were out there as Livingston had said they'd be.

Rod set the bowl down then put his hands on his hips, still searching for the dolphins. They should be here.

If he had his tail, he could find out. Shit. He was going to have to wait for Livingston to show up.

He didn't have long to wait—only it wasn't Livingston.

As Rod turned to leave the pier, a *whoosh* registered in his mind nanoseconds before a small harpoon plunged into his leg.

Then another one sheared off the bottom of his shorts before embedding into the dock behind him with a *thud*, and Rod didn't think. He dove off the pier, forgetting to gulp air before hitting the surface. The impact broke the short shaft attached to the harpoon, wrenching metal against bone. Son of a Mer, that hurt!

His vision impaired by the lack of Mer ability, Rod squinted in the murky water, his fingers finding the harpoon before his eyes could. Gritting his teeth as his air ran out, Rod yanked, tissue screaming as it came free.

Head swimming from pain and lack of oxygen, lungs protesting, Rod kicked toward the surface but allowed only his lips and nose to emerge above water. Whoever was out there would be waiting for him to show himself.

Taking a deep breath, he kicked back down. Blood flowed from the wound, carrying his scent out to The Guards, if they were even there. Not that it mattered because, with a land ambush, there was nothing they could do.

And with the birds out of the picture, Rod was on his own.

Chapter 38

VAL BLINKED AGAINST THE LIGHT STREAMING INTO HER EYES, the sun's angle high enough for its rays to shine through the downward-slanting blinds directly onto her. She couldn't remember when she'd slept so late.

A smile curved her lips. She couldn't remember when she'd slept so well.

She snuggled back and found only the soft give of a pillow, not the rock hard body that had claimed hers last night and again this morning.

Where was Rod?

She struggled out of the sheets, legs flailing as she fought to stand. He wouldn't have left her and gone back to the ocean, would he? What if he got his tail? Would he just swim off?

She caught herself just before she slid off the bed in an ungainly heap, reminiscent of yesterday morning.

What a difference a day made. In more ways than one.

She smiled and relaxed. No, he wouldn't have gone. She knew that. She trusted that. She trusted him.

He wouldn't leave her.

Val managed to get herself off the bed via her two feet and tossed the pillows decorating the floor until she located her clothes. Her shirt was a crumpled mess, but it was a good kind of crumpled. She pulled on her shorts and shoved her tangled hair out of her eyes. She should probably shower, but honestly? She wanted to see him. To remind herself that this wasn't a dream, that he really had said he loved her and was going to come back with her.

As for the "forever" part... well, no, she didn't necessarily need the extra reassurance, but it couldn't hurt.

Walking toward the door, she knocked his T-shirt off the arm of the wicker settee at the end of the bed with her knee. Hmm, maybe, reassurance wasn't the right word. Relive. Replay. She wanted to relive and replay that moment and those words and feelings all over again.

Putting a sexy sway into her walk once she was done in the bathroom, Val headed for the kitchen. She wouldn't mind reliving a bunch of things.

Then she rounded the corner, her shoulder knocking into the pantry door, and she had to amend that thought.

A package sat on the table.

From her mom.

Some things were just too painful to relive.

She sidestepped around it as if it were a living thing and took another apple from the refrigerator, fully intending to ignore the small, brown, white elephant sucking all the air out of the kitchen.

But she couldn't. She wasn't running away anymore. She would deal with situations and take ownership. Give it her best shot to work everything out—including dealing with the memories.

Taking a deep breath and setting the apple on the counter, Val straightened her shoulders and reached for the string encircling the box—

Only to have someone grab her from behind.

Chapter 39

Rod swam to a pylon, cautiously surfacing beneath the dock. No feet above him. So far, so good. But he had to get inside to protect Valerie.

Blood still flowed from his wound, and it hurt more than the time he'd gotten hooked with a Human fishing rod, part of the survival training all Mers were required to take. A harpoon was worse.

The screen door on the sliders slid open with its telltale screech. He didn't have time to mull over the pain. Tearing strips from where the second harpoon had ripped his shorts, Rod wrapped them around his leg as a tourniquet. It'd have to do.

Footsteps pounded down the steps from the deck. Good. At least Valerie was safe.

Rod hauled himself to his feet and headed up the beach. Time to end this once and for all.

And then he saw Valerie.

Rod slammed to a halt.

Her arms were secured behind her, tape over her mouth...

And Drake Cabot's arm wrapped around her shoulders, a harpoon at her throat.

Drake?

Son-of-a-Mer! The bastard had crossed the line. Drake had always been bitter about not inheriting the throne, but to actually attempt this? He'd never been the brightest anglerfish in the sea. Rod never thought he'd actually try something so heinous. *Treason.* No one had considered it, or Drake would never have gotten this far.

But the fright in Valerie's beautiful eyes and that weapon brought home how real it was.

"What's the matter, Rod? Catfish got your tongue?" Drake jerked Valerie toward the dock.

That got him walking again. Running actually, because if Drake got them to deep water, Rod would be useless without his tail. He intercepted them before they could get onto the dock.

"You want to explain how you expect to get away with this, Drake?"

Drake stopped, gauging the distance to the water. He'd have to get past Rod. With Valerie.

Rod wasn't about to let that happen.

"It doesn't look like I need to do anything, Rod." Drake nodded at Rod's leg. "That isn't healing, and, pardon me if I'm wrong, but didn't you just climb out of the ocean with legs? Looks like the gods have decided it for us." He took a step to the left.

Rod mirrored it. "Don't underestimate me, Drake."

"Right." Drake feinted right, dragging Valerie. That harpoon was too close. "You might have beat me when you had a tail, but I guarantee you'll be singing a different tune now. The throne is mine. And so is she."

"Not while I have breath left in my body." Rod crouched, ready to spring whichever way Drake moved next, wanting to reassure Valerie but knowing he couldn't risk taking his eyes off the slimy eel.

"Yeah, see, there's the sticking point." Drake jostled the harpoon at his stupid joke. But then he got serious. He yanked Valerie back against him, the harpoon at her jugular, and Rod found himself trying to *not* breathe for her.

"Give it up, Rod. You can't possibly hope to win this and we don't need any unnecessary bloodshed. You know how quickly the sharks can smell it in the water. All your Guards out there aren't going to be able to save her from Hammerhead Harry if I decide to let him have her."

"Let her go, Drake." Rod thrust his hands to his sides, fists clenched. It figured Drake would have Harry on his payroll. What didn't figure is why Harry would want to be. The shark was much smarter than Drake.

"And lose my bargaining shell? I don't think so. Now get out of my way."

"No."

"What? What do you mean 'no'? Do you see what I can do to her?" He slid the harpoon along Valerie's jaw, drawing a thin line of blood.

Rod saw red. "But you won't."

"Are you willing to bet on it?" He leaned down to Valerie's ear. "Pity he's ready to toss you to the sharks so easily."

Her eyes narrowed, a flash of anger in them. Ha. Drake was swimming up the wrong reef with that one. Rod would have grinned if not for the very real chance Drake would do exactly what he said.

"Get out of my way, Tritone. Your time in the sun is over." Drake plastered himself to Valerie's back.

Rod had to keep Drake talking until he figured something out or until Drake screwed up.

"You put the bomb in the trench."

"No kidding. It should have been a one-two punch, but your stupid father sent out a security team at the last minute." Drake shook his head. "Only you could get so lucky. But your luck's run out. Now get out of my way." The harpoon nicked the soft skin of Valerie's throat.

Rod held off lunging at them. There was no telling what Drake would do.

Rod had said he'd kill for her; no time like the present.

He glanced behind him. Thirty feet of dock stood between him and Valerie's safety.

"The Council will never appoint you High Councilman, Drake."

"The Council doesn't have a choice. I'm next in line. Nothing in that clause says anything about being squeaky clean, only who your ancestors are. I can't believe you and Reel never considered you might not be safe in your privileged little world. Besides, I have *her*. Now move, Tritone."

Drake's hand was shaking on the harpoon. Rod took a step back. "Why should we have been worried? There was never any threat."

Drake's face turned red. "Never? Are you really that clueless? What about the time your anglerfish died in the middle of the passageway on the cavern field trip, leaving you stranded in the dark? You think that was an accident? Or when you had to escape from that shark feeding frenzy during Spring Break? The electric ray 'trapped' in your bedchamber? Then there was the boat propeller incident."

Rod remembered those accidents. They'd started about twenty *selinos* ago and had seemed par for the course in the dangerous world of the sea.

Zeus. Drake had been planning this for a long time.

Reel's rejection of Merhood had only encouraged Drake's attempts at the throne. And now, it looked as if he'd succeeded.

Damn the gods for taking his tail! What he wouldn't give to get it back.

He took another step backward as Drake moved forward, closing the gap between them. He had to let Drake think he was getting his way, but he'd take a harpoon to the gut before he'd let Drake hurt Valerie.

"So what's the big plan now, Drake? Kill me? You really think that's going to swim with The Council? They'll petition the gods."

"Give it a break, will you, Rod? It won't matter. You'll be dead, and it'll be my word against hers. A Hybrid." Drake shrugged. "Actually, it won't even be against hers. Why in the sea would they put any stock in what a half-Human has to say? There must be something missing in your family's genes. First your brother hooks up with a Human, now you're bringing one back... Hades, the gods will be *thrilled* that I put our race out of that misery."

He shook his head then wrapped his arm around Valerie's neck, bringing her to a halt about ten feet from the end of the dock. "Now, we can make it painful and messy, or you can just stand there." He brandished the harpoon. "I promise to make it quick. I'll let her go after you're dead."

Drake never had been one of the smartest sardines in the can; the current situation proved it.

"If you think I'm going to let you run a harpoon through me, you're even more deluded than anyone ever thought you were. And trust me, that's saying something. A High Councilman doesn't give up the throne without a fight."

Drake jerked Valerie back against him, his face twisted in anger. He adjusted his grip on the harpoon as if testing its weight. His fingers closed around the shaft and his eyes narrowed. "You and your stupid chivalry, Rod. Whatever. Just shut up and die, already."

Thrusting Valerie aside, Drake lunged.

Oh no he didn't.

Val butted her head at the last second, knocking the harpoon out of whack enough so it glanced off Rod's arm.

Rod barreled into Drake, taking them both down onto the dock, the harpoon shaft clattering beneath them. Val jumped out of the way, trying to work her hands free from the duct tape. Damn, that stuff should be registered as a lethal weapon. It was cutting off her circulation and her air.

Drake whipped Rod onto his back then grabbed for the harpoon.

Val kicked it aside, cursing that she couldn't pick the damn thing up. Cursing that she couldn't curse.

Drake fell on top of Rod and began pummeling him. "You. Son. Of. A. Mer." Each word punctuated a punch.

Val winced. She had to find a way to help Rod.

Rod smacked his forehead against Drake's with a *crack!* She winced again. Okay, not going to try that.

Drake went limp long enough for Rod to buck him off—right on top of the shaft again.

Damn it. How the hell could she help Rod if she couldn't get her hands free? She had to get that harpoon.

And then she saw another harpoon embedded at the far end of the dock. She ran over to it while Rod proceeded to flay the skin from Drake.

"Don't you ever"—Rod let a punch fly—"go"—another punch—"after her"—and another—"again." Two more this time.

Drake growled and pounded his fist on the wound in Rod's thigh.

Rod roared.

Val kneeled on the dock, maneuvering her wrists next to that harpoon, then sawed like a madwoman.

Drake tossed Rod off him, scrambling to his feet and grabbing the harpoon. He aimed it at Rod.

Val tried to shout out a warning, screaming for all she was worth behind the duct tape. It wasn't enough.

Drake jabbed.

The tape on her wrists gave way.

Rod rolled to the side, right into the water.

Drake—and the harpoon—went in after him.

Val didn't hesitate. Taking off at a run, she ripped the tape from her mouth and dove off the dock.

Chapter 40

SO MANY THINGS HAPPENED AT ONCE THAT VAL WASN'T SURE what was what.

She lost sight of the men as hundreds of dolphins herded into the water around her, clicks, squeals, angry directives, and clipped orders filling the churning water, wayward tails and flippers spinning her upside down and sideways.

A searing, ripping pain slammed into her legs and she sucked in a gallon of water.

Dammit! So much for her noble act. She *was* allergic to the ocean and now she was going to go into shock and die, just when she'd finally found what she wanted in life. Someone to be with, have a family with, someone who made her stop running—and now this.

Another *thwack* of a tail sent her tumbling sideways. Where was Rod? Was he okay? Alive?

She shuddered when she thought how close that harpoon had come to him. If only Drake hadn't surprised her in the kitchen, Rod wouldn't be in this mess. *She* wouldn't be in this mess.

Christ. Even when she tried to be responsible and good, her life went to hell.

She should have left yesterday. Just grabbed the diamond and gotten on with her life where the only things oceanic would be the stuff in Mom's store and Flight 815 from her favorite television show—

Wait a minute.

Why wasn't she choking? Gasping for breath? Why had the pain in her legs stopped? Why was she able to see the dolphins more clearly? Hear their words? Swim easily...

Val looked down. Beneath the hem of her shirt was...

... *a tail.*

She blinked, then rubbed her eyes with her fists. She looked back down.

She had a tail.

Shimmery pale pink, the tips iridescent mother-of-pearl, the scales melded with her skin like a glittery belt beneath her waist. She flicked the fins, her torn shorts falling away with a powerful surge of muscle, and the silky caress of water flowed over it.

Holy mackerel!

Val looked around at the swirling gray bodies, her breath coming in short pants—but she wasn't breathing air. That was water coming out of her mouth... and water going in...

Then someone grabbed her from behind and her breathing—if that's what it was called—stopped altogether.

"Back off or the girl gets it." A bad line from a bad movie. With one bad-ass point stuck in her neck.

That answered the question of where Drake was, but what about Rod?

The dolphins formed a semi-circle around them while Drake dragged her this way and that, his arm binding hers to her sides while he backed away from those closest to them.

Something beige and finny flicked by her side. Drake had a tail, too.

"You can't hope to get away," one of the dolphins said—clear as day, which freaked her out enough to make her suck in another pint or two of water.

Which only freaked her out more.

"I don't have to hope, Lisa. I've got her." Drake shook Val around the middle, causing her head to jiggle and the harpoon to nick her neck.

Damn that hurt. Not to mention, it added blood to the water.

Oh, wonderful. What were these Mer people like around sharks? When Drake's arm tightened, she figured he probably had a great relationship with them.

So not comforting.

Oh my God. She was a mermaid! It was enough— almost—to make her forget that she had a crazy person with a lethal weapon half-wrapped around her.

Then the dolphin—Lisa, of all things—spoke, and Val remembered exactly where she was, who she was with… and who she wasn't with.

"It's Lieutenant Brackmann to you, Cabot. Now let her go. It's over."

Drake laughed, still dragging her backwards. She wondered where he was going, since she would've thought the open sea would afford him more avenues of escape, but he made no move to head deeper.

This was what she was contemplating while faced with *talking dolphins*? *Being kidnapped? A tail?*

"It's not over, *Lieutenant*. Not while Rod's still tail-less and I have her. The Council will pay any price to keep her alive."

They would? Oh… that princess thing. She'd forgotten about that on top of everything else. Or was it the prophecy?

She didn't know, didn't care, and just wanted to get out of here. She definitely didn't want anything to do with tails and councils and talking fish and *mermen*— especially if it didn't include Rod.

Rod crawled into the shallows, barely able or willing to salute The Guards who'd propelled him out of harm's way onto the beach, hating the fact that he'd turned tail and run.

Well, no. The Guards had taken the decision to fight from him, citing orders. And even if he'd wanted to turn tail and run, he couldn't because he didn't *have* a fucking tail.

How did the gods expect him to save her if he couldn't fight Drake in the water?

He flung the hair from his eyes, scanning the sea. The occasional dolphin breaching to refill his or her lungs was the only sign something was happening beneath the surface… something Rod had no control over, no say in.

It was as if all his rule-following, test-taking, law-studying hours—his atonement for the mess he'd made of Reel's life—were for nothing as he sat here, helpless. What had he done that was so gods-awful to merit stripping him of his tail? Where had it all gotten him?

Stranded on some beach, unable to save the woman he loved.

He stood up, frustrated that he *could*. Frustrated that he felt helpless. Frustrated that everything he'd worked for, all the time he'd put in, the effort, the energy, the guilt that had kept him striving toward the gods'—and his father's—idea of the perfect High Councilman, had been for nothing.

But Drake, the slippery fish, who would never live up to the High Councilman reputation, who was only out for himself, had dared to come after him. Rod couldn't believe the oily bottom-feeder had swum so far below the sonar no one had seen this coming.

So how did Drake hope to pull it off? He had to have known The Guards would move in the minute he hit the water. He couldn't hope to escape.

Unless…

Rod kicked the sand. Damn it! The Council had constructed a Travel Chamber portal here for Reel and Erica's wedding—a portal only Council members were supposed to know about.

Drake's father was on The Council.

Rod jammed his hands into the pockets of the stupid shorts he still wore. If Drake got Valerie to that portal, there was no telling where on the planet they'd end up. Rod would lose her for good and Drake would have the most powerful bargaining shell ever.

Nigel, with all his pomposity and hopes for the throne, had broken a cardinal rule by sharing portal information with his son, and The Council, with all their stipulations and protocol, hadn't been able to prevent it. They'd failed him.

He kicked a piece of driftwood with the gods-forsaken toes on his gods-forsaken foot. The gods had failed him too. He'd played by everyone's rules and look where it'd gotten him.

Talk about a failure of epic proportions.

Well no more. He'd paid for the dare; a dare that, apparently, had worked out well for all concerned except him. Even when he'd done all the gods and The Council had asked of him, it'd done nothing for him: Valerie's life was at risk.

Screw their rules and their orders. He was going to save her, fallout be damned.

He scanned Reel's shoreline and found the perfect solution. A Jet Ski. It was fast enough to take him out there, hopefully before Drake reached the portal. Rod took off toward the ski.

"Rod!" Livingston dropped out of the sky in a move worthy of an osprey, the rest of the newly arrived air cavalry remaining high above. "The Guards have him surrounded. It should be over soon."

Rod shook his head. "Don't count on it. Drake's a lot smarter than anyone gave him credit for and there's a portal out there. I've got to do something." He lunged around Livingston in a full-out run toward the Jet Ski.

Livingston wasn't the Chief of the ASA for nothing. The bird zipped in front of him, flapping his wingspan at shoulder height with enough strength to force Rod to a halt. "Are you crazy? What do you think you're going to do in your present condition? Five minutes underwater and you'll be a goner. My orders are to keep you beached. You're The Heir, for Apollo's sake. You can't risk your life."

"Am I The Heir, Livingston? How can I be without a damn tail? But it doesn't matter anyway because Valerie's with him. As far as I'm concerned, they've lost my loyalty by putting her in danger." He feinted left then took off to the right around the gull.

He and Livingston had trained under the same War Tactics instructors so he didn't get very far. "And who's going to save you, Rod, when you're drowning?"

"He can't hold two of us at once." Rod scrambled beneath Livingston.

The seagull flicked his wings and ended up back in front of Rod again, but at least Rod had gotten closer to the Jet Ski.

"Rod, you can't put yourself at risk. It's against every rule we have. As The Heir, you must be protected at all costs."

"Really? Where was that rule when we were dodging the fish and the peregrines?" Rod ran forward, but Livingston didn't budge. "I don't care what the gods want, Livingston. I don't care what The Council decrees. I will not let Drake have her and if they don't like it, they can keep the damn tail. I won't need it in Kansas anyway. Now get out of my way." He swung his hand beneath the bird, connecting squarely with his stomach, sending him tumbling through the air.

Rod ran the last few feet to the craft, tossed off the mooring line, then put his studies of Human mechanisms to work as he got the thing running on the first try. Thank the gods there were *some* benefits to all those hours locked in his father's study.

He nosed the Jet Ski toward The Guards just as Livingston returned.

"You're going to get yourself killed, Rod."

"Not if you help me, Livingston. Get them"—he waved skyward—"to show me where she is. I am *not* going to lose her."

He cranked the gear and churned water as he peeled away from the dock.

Chapter 41

THE HARPOON NICKED VAL'S NECK AGAIN AS LIEUTENANT Brackmann refused to retreat. Val was hoping the dolphin would, if only to get Drake to relax his hold, even for a second.

She'd been surreptitiously testing her tail movements as Drake had backed them away, trying to get the hang of it. It wasn't all that difficult, surprisingly. Simply kick her legs in unison like the butterfly swim stroke. All she needed to escape was a moment or two when the harpoon wasn't in the vicinity of her jugular.

This time, running was a good thing and the distraction of an approaching boat gave her the opportunity.

Drake looked toward the surface, his hold slackening enough for Val to whip her tail sideways and twist out of his grasp, her hands poised to grab the harpoon.

Surprise was on her side as she managed to get a few good tail whips in, throwing him off balance, and his one-handed grasp on the shaft wasn't enough to fend off her attack. Within seconds she held the weapon.

She had to hand it to Drake, however. He didn't let any seaweed grow under his tail. He took one look at the harpoon in her hands, a second look at the closing ranks of dolphins, and kicked so hard a wave of water sent her tumbling back into the lieutenant, giving Drake enough lead time to veer sideways toward a pile of debris.

Val didn't wait to see what other weapon he had hidden there. She swam out of the dolphins' way, hugging the harpoon to her like a lover, and let the dolphins move in for the capture.

Tail action churned the water around her, so it was a few moments before she realized the boat engine had stopped. Now what? Had the Coast Guard sent out a team? Would all the Mer secrecy be blown to high heaven?

Then she looked up and saw... Rod.

Swimming down to her—

With a tail.

And at that moment she didn't care that she was a mermaid and he was a merman and they were the stuff of myth and legend. She didn't care that whatever fantastical world he'd told her about truly did exist. All she cared about was that he was here.

And then he *was* there. In her arms.

Or she was in his?

Did it really matter?

No. All that really mattered was that he was kissing her and she was kissing him and she wasn't about to let him go.

Until he pulled back to cradle her face in his hands, the look in his eyes almost drowning her. She'd laugh about that pun later.

"Gods, I thought I'd lost you." He kissed her again.

"You didn't."

He brushed his lips over her cheeks. "I know."

"Rod?"

"Mmmm?" he murmured beneath her ear.

"Why do I have a tail? Why do you?"

"Hmm... I—what?" He thrust her back, still holding her at arm's length, and they both looked at the navy blue tail. "Holy Hades, it's back."

Throwing her disbelief to the wind, er, current, Val went with the flow and laughed. "I'll say it is. Pretty impressive, too. That's one whale of a tail you've got there, Rod."

"Actually"—Rod turned sideways, glancing behind him, still not letting her go—"this isn't my tail."

"Hate to break it to you, but it's definitely attached to your body." And she *knew* that body...

"I know. I mean, this isn't the tail I had before."

"Okay, that's making even less sense to me than this whole breathing-beneath-the-water/tail/fish thing we have going that I'm trying really hard not to overanalyze." Or she'd go crazy. "And why do you have a tail *now*? Why do I?"

He looked at her, still holding onto her arms, now stroking them with his thumbs, and Val didn't delude herself that the shivers rippling over her skin had anything to do with the water flowing around them as the dolphins searched the area.

"Valerie, I told you that you were half-Mer. That's why you have a tail. As to mine, I have no idea why it's back now. But this isn't my normal tail. This one's larger, and the color... it looks like my father's tail."

"Your father?" The High Councilman... the leader of The Council... the ruler of the oceans... the head of Atlantis... She was trying to piece together all the facts he'd thrown at her into one, coalescent body of knowledge and let it register that all of this was really true.

"Yes, just like my father's."

"So does he have yours?"

He raised an eyebrow at her. "That's crazy. Tails don't switch bodies."

She shrugged out of his hold and planted her hands on her hips... er, scales. "Well excuse me for not knowing proper tail etiquette. At least it came back. Besides, what difference does it make if it's bigger?"

He waggled his eyebrows. "Trust me, Valerie. Size matters."

She groaned and rolled her eyes. "Trust me, Rod. It's not the size of the... um... *ship*, but the motion in the ocean."

It was his turn to groan, but he reached for her anyway, pulling her against that hard, sculpted torso. "Bad, bad pun."

"But good, good plan, thankyouverymuch." She smiled up at him.

"Plan?"

"Yep. I was trying to get away from Drake and needed a distraction. Your arrival was perfect. Speaking of which"—she peered around him to see dolphins milling around, the frenzy of going after Drake having abated—"what happened to him?"

Rod followed her gaze and let out a whistle, followed by those tongue-clicks she'd been hearing. Lieutenant Brackmann swam over.

The fact that Val could tell which dolphin it was didn't surprise her—which should bother her, but didn't.

"Sir?"

"Lieutenant, what's the situation?" Rod asked.

The dolphin shook her head. "He's disappeared. We're not sure how. There are no known portals in the vicinity."

"Oh, there's a portal here, all right, only it's not common knowledge." Rod made an executive decision. He had the new and improved tail; he assumed that meant he was now The High Councilman. And if so, he could use the power that went along with it. To Hades with The Council's rules. If The Guard had been apprised about the portal, Drake might not have escaped.

He pointed to the pile of debris. "It's there, but where Drake exited is anyone's guess."

The dolphin bowed her head. "Then we lost him."

"For now, but it's not your fault, lieutenant. He had information you didn't. You should have been informed."

The dolphin's perpetual grin widened, and she nodded toward Rod's tail. "I can see things will be different under your reign, Sir. And if I may say so, thank you. It will make our jobs easier. I'll inform my pod and send contingents through the portal to all known exits. We'll get him."

As The Guards dispersed to continue the search for Drake, Rod was aware of Valerie's scrutiny. "What?"

"What you said earlier. About a High Councilman not giving up his throne without a fight... Did you mean it? Are you really going to fight for the throne? Now that you can?"

Rod pulled her back into his arms. "No. I promised you we'd go to Kansas and I'm not going back on my word. The Mer world has been around for millions of *selinos* without me. Not having me on the throne isn't going to bring it down."

"But Drake will inherit. You can't do that."

That gave him a chuckle. "Actually, he won't. That's one good thing to come out of all those hours I spent studying, which, obviously, Drake didn't do. There *is* a stipulation about murder—and attempted murder. It automatically negates the succession, so the minute he set out on this journey, he doomed himself. But I couldn't tell him that while he had you in his arms. No telling what he might have done."

"So if he's not next in line, who is?

That gave him another chuckle. And after the scare he'd had about losing her, he'd take them where he could get them. "Who? You really want to know?"

"Why wouldn't I?"

"Oh, I don't know. Maybe because it might alter your plans for the future."

"Rod, what are you talking about?"

"You, Valerie. Through your father, *you* are next in line for the throne."

If she weren't buoyed by water, he would've bet she'd have fallen down at that statement. As it was, she was fluttering water into her mouth, and he was afraid she'd hyperhydrate.

"Me? How can I be in line for the throne?"

He held out his hand. "Come on. Let's go somewhere private and talk."

Valerie took it. "Where? It's a pretty big ocean."

"Back at Reel's house."

"His house? Rod, in case you haven't noticed, we're bound to attract attention the minute we leave the water to go up the beach. I thought that was something to be avoided?"

Rod tucked her arm beneath his. "You'll see."

She cocked her head, her curls floating around her like a corkscrew halo... which was so appropriate for her. "All right, but I want to get the package Tricia sent me. After all this craziness, I could really use some normalcy."

Normalcy. Rod didn't know the meaning of the word any more. But he was going to.

And it'd be what *he* decided, not what The Council decreed. Tail or not.

Chapter 42

AFTER ROD SWAM TO THE SURFACE TO INSTRUCT LIVINGSTON to bring them the package, Val followed Rod beneath the dock to a hatch his brother had concealed in the depths. He led her through a long, upward-sloping tunnel until the water level gradually receded and they were below a ladder leading to a room—and air—above.

Rod pulled himself up the ladder, one strong tail-kick propelling him onto a platform. Seated there, his tail hanging over the edge, he reached down to help her up.

"Don't worry about breathing, Valerie. Your lungs will adjust. We utilize water and air as needed."

She wasn't worried. After all the upheavals in her life, at least this time she had someone to share it with. "What is this place?"

The room was outfitted with eight cots made of thick, braided rope, more knotted ropes hanging like bell-pulls from the ceiling, several fans and heating lamps on the walls, and thick, white towels piled on each makeshift bed.

One of the beds had half a dozen discarded towels strewn over it. Rod cursed and gathered them, tossing them into a clothes hamper.

"This is part of the hill beneath Reel's house. He built it so our family and The Council could attend their wedding. We use it now to visit. It's a secure place to quickly dry out our tails and go into the Human world without revealing ourselves." He pointed to another hatch in the ceiling. "That opens into Reel's basement. Obviously, Drake found out about it and used it to sneak into the house."

So Drake had been in here, drying out his tail, while they'd slept—among other things—upstairs. God, that was just creepy.

She rubbed her thighs to ward off the ick factor. No. Wait. Scratch that. She rubbed her *tail*—and the funny thing was, there was no ick factor to *that*.

Val propped her chin on her palm and stared at her new appendage. Shimmery and pink—she had *a tail*.

"I can get my legs back, right?" She stroked the smooth iridescent scales, amazed at so many things at once, she didn't know which to consider first—although not being allergic to the ocean was a biggie.

Why Mom had lied to her was another.

Rod linked his hand with hers. "Yes, you can. You can even keep them permanently if you want."

"Permanently?" She looked up. "As in, I'll be able to stay on land and won't ever have to have a tail again?"

He nodded.

"But what about the throne and the prophecy and the succession, and… last night? Or"—she pulled her hand from his as the thought struck her—"was that only because you thought you'd be stranded on land forever and should make the best of a bad situation?"

Her voice left her. Oh, God. Was that it? Was she really only good as a last resort when he couldn't leave?

She didn't know which was worse: her father choosing to leave or Rod choosing to stay because he *couldn't* leave.

"Valerie—"

"No!" She shook her head as she used one of the knotted ropes to pull herself onto a cot. She had to get out of here. She reached for one of the towels and began scrubbing at her tail, trying to soak up any water she could find. Now if she could just keep the salty tears from falling she might actually have a chance to do this with some dignity.

Not gonna happen.

When Rod joined her on the cot, her dignity went swimming off with the tide: one traitorous tear trickled out, no matter how hard she tried to stop it. She fought the tug of his fingers on her chin, but he wouldn't let go.

"Valerie," he whispered, his thumb doing amazing things to her bottom lip, "you don't believe that. How can you believe that after last night? I've never told another woman I love her. I love you, and if your life is in Kansas, so is mine."

"You're going to just walk away from your birthright?"

"Yes, I am. I'm going to *walk* away... and keep on walking. Down the aisle and into your life. For the rest of our days. I love you, Valerie, and I want to spend the rest of my life with you."

"But the council—"

"To Hades with The Council. I get one life, Valerie. One. With the tail, it'd be an Immortal one, but it's only one, and mortal or not, if I don't have you, that life is not worth living. So, no, I won't follow The Council's rules blindly as I have for years. I won't go along with their program simply because I was born The Heir. My father can keep running it. Or let them find someone else. What I want is a life with you. And if a man can't be true to himself first, how can he be to any people he's supposed to govern? My heart wouldn't be in it because it belongs to you. Where you go, I go, Valerie."

He gripped her shoulders and turned her so he could look in her eyes. "I've always done what I've been directed to, but in this, I can't. I won't. Choosing the throne over you would be the biggest failure of my life. I'm not going to make that mistake, so you're stuck with me."

He wasn't going to leave her.

She finally knew, deep down inside, that she didn't need to go searching for anything any longer. That she'd come home, only to find home wasn't a place after all. It wasn't a building on the main street of a little town in Kansas or the apartment above it. It wasn't the back corner of the storeroom, and it wasn't in any of the jobs or cities she'd gone to.

Home was in Rod's arms, and she never, ever wanted to leave it.

Livingston picked that moment to tap the small window at the top of their room.

"Pardon me," the gull said after Rod let him in. He set the package down on the cot next to him. "I can't believe this is finally over. All the months of looking for Valerie, bringing her back, getting you your tails, and, well"—he nodded at their joined hands—"happy endings all around."

Something stuck out about Livingston's comment. "Hey. Wait a minute," Val said. "What's that about finding me? How did you do that? You wouldn't happen to know anything about a flock of seagulls attacking me a few weeks ago, would you?"

"Attacking?" Rod sat up straighter, his jaw clacking shut so hard he might have broken a tooth.

Livingston coughed and shuffled his webbed feet, hopping from one rope to the next. "Oh, I wouldn't call it an attack, actually. More a fact-gathering mission."

Val reached for the package. "Baloney. You guys *took* my bologna, the rest of my lunch, and probably an inch of scalp when you yanked out my hair."

"What?" Rod grabbed for Livingston, but the Chief of the ASA was too quick. He flew to the top of a stack of towels on the far cot.

"We had to get her DNA, Rod."

"Her DNA?" Rod asked, but then his shoulders relaxed. "That's right. I forgot you couldn't identify her with the birthmark."

"What birthmark?" Val grabbed Rod's arm.

He put his hand over hers. "The birthmark on your back that identifies you as royalty, Valerie."

Ummm… "Rod? I don't have a birthmark."

Livingston coughed and hopped closer. "Actually, you do. Now." He nodded at Rod who leaned back and lifted the hem of her shirt. He traced a small design on the left side of her lower back. She wasn't sure if the shivers were from his finger or the fact that he actually found something there.

"It's a trident," Livingston continued. "The symbol of your father's hereditary line."

She twisted around, trying to see it, but if it was there, it was a damned awkward spot for a tattoo. "So how did I get it?"

"The birthmark appears only after you get your tail. All royal-born Mers have them." Livingston motioned for Rod to turn around.

There, in the same area he'd touched on her, was a small blue, three-pronged trident.

"You didn't have that last night." She traced it, unable to help herself.

"I didn't have a tail last night. It fades whenever we're out of the ocean so Humans can't identify us."

"Oh. So Mom never knew I had one?"

"It fades when we have legs, so, I doubt if she even saw your father's. She wouldn't have known what it was anyway."

"I guess it's a good thing it didn't show up, then."

"Good for you, bad for us," Livingston interjected. "Luckily, after years of searching the coasts, *someone*"—he coughed—"came up with the idea of searching inland for you. It didn't take us long to locate your mother once we sent word through the airwaves. The scouts thought you were the one, Valerie, but we needed DNA because we couldn't verify your identity without throwing seawater on you. For obvious reasons, having you transform in front of a bunch of Bipeds wasn't an option. Gods only know how we would have gotten you to the ocean. That's why we needed you here first."

Livingston bowed to her. "I'm sorry if we hurt you. I did try to be gentle when taking your hair, but you were dangerous with your arms flapping and whatnot. I had to get the job done. I did my best. I even stationed sentries around you to ensure your safety until Rod arrived."

"Sentries? As in birds?"

The look he gave her said, "Duh."

"Thanks for doing that, Livingston. It certainly explains a lot." Namely stalking sparrows. "But, it doesn't explain why my mom said I was allergic to the ocean."

"I'm sure she had a good reason. Telling your child she's a Mer would not be easy to do," Rod said.

"Especially living smack-dab in the middle of the landmass," Livingston added.

All good points, but Mom had lied. Not by omission, but she'd consciously fabricated a story for no apparent reason.

It was the "apparent" part that made her wonder.

Especially since the last time she'd been home, Mom had started to tell her something several different times. Val hadn't known what she was going to say and when she'd pressed, Mom had just looked at her with sadness in her eyes and a soft smile on her lips.

The appearance of this gift was probably just coincidence, but the last time something had been too coincidental to be a coincidence, the birds and Rod had shown up—and look how that had worked out.

Well, no more running for her. Val held out a section of the twine wrapped around the package. "If you'd do the honors, Livingston?"

Chapter 43

THE SHARP BIRD BEAK MADE QUICK WORK OF THE TWINE, THEN Val balled up the brown paper and shoved it beneath the stack of towels.

She peeled pretty floral wrapping paper from the fitted white lid, smiling when she saw the yellow tissue paper amid the packing bubbles inside. Mom always wrapped her birthday presents in yellow. Said it reminded her of what a beautiful day it had been the day she'd been born. The sun had been shining like a beacon from the heavens and Therese had felt hopeful that things would work out for them, hence her middle name.

Blinking away tears, Val folded back the tissue paper. Rod and Livingston hadn't moved but she could feel the curiosity rolling off them in, well, waves. She groaned at the bad pun.

Taking a deep breath, she nudged the last of the paper out of the way. Beneath it sat…

A bottle.

A crystal bottle.

No, not a crystal bottle.

A *diamond* bottle… just like Rod's.

She lifted it.

A diamond bottle *exactly* like Rod's, stopper and all. Only this one didn't have oil inside.

Livingston made some odd bird clicks. "So that's what happened to it."

"Happened to it?" She didn't take her eyes off the crystal—diamond—fracturing the thin stream of sunlight from the window into tiny rainbows.

"The Castor Diamond." Rod exhaled. "It makes sense."

Val shook her head and set the box aside, twirling the bottle between her palms. "Maybe to you, but I'm stumbling over why Mom had such a valuable jewel and still owes back taxes on the shop."

"The Council's going to want to know about this," Livingston said, hopping onto the window ledge.

"Go tell them." Rod took the bottle from her. "We'll discuss what's to be done with it later."

Val waited until Livingston left. "Nothing's going to be done with it, Rod. Mom gave this to me. She wanted me to have it."

Rod pulled the stopper out. "Actually, I think *this* is what she wanted you to have." He withdrew a roll of white paper from inside the bottle.

"What?" A letter. From Mom. Inside this crazy, unbelievable gift. That matched the one Rod had.

And she knew, somehow, that this had to do with her father. With her tail. What Mom hadn't been able to tell her the last time she'd been home.

With shaking fingers she took the note, glancing up to find Rod's eyes intent upon her.

"It'll be okay, Valerie."

Val took a fortifying breath and unrolled the note.

My darling daughter,

I've questioned myself over and over about sending you this gift in this way. Perhaps it would be better to wait for you to return home, as you invariably will. Oh, don't take offense, sweetheart, but, you see, it is inevitable. It always has been.

I've watched you come and go for years. Each time you leave me with such hope, and each time you return in despair. I know you're searching for something, something you can't define. What that something is, you don't know.

But I do.

And I must beg your forgiveness.

Val's heart lurched. Mom had known the reason all along.

Rod's fingers circled softly on her back near the birthmark, and she fought the surprise, the disbelief, inhaling raggedly as she continued reading.

What I'm going to tell you, Valerie, is unbelievable. I know that. But it's true.

Your father didn't die.

I know. I know you're feeling betrayed. Hurt that I would keep this from you.

I won't make excuses; I'll simply tell you my story, and you can draw your own conclusions as to whether or not I acted in your best interests.

I met Lance Dumere on a vacation at the beach, just like I've always told you. That's true. I fell madly in love, and we were inseparable. You were the result of that, Valerie, and I've never regretted it for a moment, although you know how your grandparents felt about my "shame." You were never a cause of shame to me, Valerie. You must believe that.

Your father told me he was a sailor, and as I

write this, I laugh at the irony. Oh, he most certainly
was a sailor of the seas; there is no disputing that.
So, when my vacation and his shore leave ended,
we promised to return every year to "our place,"
until he was finished with his commission.

How little I knew.

I wrote to him every day, more when I knew I
was pregnant. My letters were returned as undeliv-
erable, and I was frantic. I didn't know how to get
in touch with him. I called the Navy and the Coast
Guard, but they could find no record of him.

I didn't know what to do. The man I'd fallen in
love with couldn't have been a fantasy or a liar. I
refused to believe that.

So I made plans to return, but then you got
viral meningitis that first year and ended up in the
hospital. It wasn't until the next year that we could
make the trip.

I'm sure you can imagine how thrilled I was
when he was there. But I was cautious, too. The
government said he didn't exist, and I'd had only
his word to go on.

He was still charming, still wove that spell
around me as he'd done from the moment I'd met
him. But I'd grown. I'd become a single parent and
had gone through a frightening, life-threatening
illness with you. I'd learned to depend on myself
and raise you as I saw fit.

Suddenly, he was making plans for us. Or
so I'd thought at the time. What I realized later
was that those plans had been all about you. But
he still blinded me with his charm, his persona.

Make no mistake, I loved him. But I had questions. Questions that were answered that night you remember as your allergic reaction to the ocean.

Forgive me, Valerie, but I had to lie to you.

You aren't allergic.

Val blinked back the tears, knowing she would continue reading this but not so sure she wanted to. Mom had still been holding a torch for her father, and the bastard hadn't loved either of them enough to leave the ocean. Tail or not, that still stung.

You see, your father wasn't in the service. He wasn't even from this country. Perhaps not even our world.

Yes, sweetheart, I know how hard this is to believe, but every word of it is true. I saw the truth with my own eyes that night.

I'd brought you to a deserted beach on a cloud-covered night at his insistence. I'd thought he'd planned a midnight wedding ceremony. How wrong I was.

You looked so adorable in your pink dress, your toes curled in the sand, strands of seashells around your neck. I'd bought a beautiful white dress for the occasion and hadn't considered silly things like blood tests and marriage licenses.

I should have.

He looked magnificent in a cream button-down and cargo pants. Barefoot. It was the most romantic setting, and I fell in love all over again, knowing you and I would finally have the perfect family.

He lifted you in his arms, then kissed me, murmuring, "Thank you for my daughter," against my lips. I admit to standing there, swaying, listening to the soft lap of the waves on the beach, the muted cries of seabirds in the distance, my eyes closed in the magic of the moment.

But then nothing happened.

I opened them to see him carrying you toward the ocean, your pink dress whipping behind him as he almost ran to the water.

Something inside me said it was wrong. Something told me to go after you. Call it mother's instinct, woman's intuition, I don't know, but don't ever discount that feeling in your gut.

I ran after you, calling his name, calling yours. He looked back once, and the expression on his face was one I'd never seen before. Steeled determination.

He started to run, and I did, too. He was taller, his legs longer, he was closer to the waves. He made it there before me.

And then his legs started to change.

I know how this sounds, but I swear to you, it's true. His legs changed, Valerie. They changed... into a tail.

I screamed, and you turned in his arms just as he sank into the water. You reached out for me then, and I saw a look cross your face.

I'd seen that look before—when you were in the hospital and they'd put the IV in. It was pain.

I ran faster, screaming your name, begging him to stop. You were crying, but he didn't let you go.

And then I saw that your legs had begun to change, too.

Val glanced at her tail. Yes, she recognized that feeling. It explained her memories of that night.

You hear stories of women who lift cars off their children, of mothers who are infused with almost super-human strength to save their kids. It happened to me that night. I ran as I'd never run before, and from somewhere I found the strength to wrench you from his arms and pull you back onto the beach.

He couldn't follow, though he tried. To this very day I can see him pulling himself onto the beach, see his silvery tail tracking through the sand. I can hear his words imploring me to bring you back, that you were his heir. That he wanted to give you your birthright, but I couldn't let him, Valerie. You were mine.

You were my sweet baby, and he'd tried to take you from me. You were crying, and your legs, oh, God, your legs.

Your feet were covered in pink flippers, like a dolphin. I know this sounds crazy, but I swear to you, it happened. I ran to the room I'd rented, locking the door behind me, and watched as the skin around your ankles slowly turned the same pink. It started up your calves. You kept screaming. I didn't know what to do, except to put you in the tub and wash the seawater off you. The pink stopped spreading and you stopped screaming.

When I scrubbed your skin dry, the color receded and your feet returned.

I ran then. I packed everything, got in my car, and just drove. I wanted to be as far from the sea as possible. We ended up in Kansas—the center of the country, as far as I could go. I hoped he wouldn't be able to follow. I told you that you were allergic so you'd never go to the ocean where he could take you from me.

I don't know if I was wrong, but as you grew, I could sense something inside of you. A restlessness. You've been searching for something, Valerie, and I believe it's that missing part of you.

I tried to compensate by having the shop and filling it will all sorts of ocean items, but it hasn't helped. You're still searching.

I've done a lot of research while you've been gone, and I believe your father was a member of a race of Mer people. I know it sounds unbelievable, but the legends and myths explain everything I saw so clearly.

You aren't allergic to the ocean; I think you may actually be a part of it. And as I hung up the phone with you today, when you told me you were moving on again, I knew I had to tell you the truth.

This bottle is from your father. He threw it to me as I ran. It had been filled with oil that he said I was to give to you. I'm sorry, but I spilled it out. I didn't know what it would do; still don't. But I couldn't risk it.

It's a pretty bottle and something from him. I feel bad that this is all I can give you because he wanted you every bit as much as I did. Perhaps if you travel to the ocean, you'll find him. I've thought about it over the years, but I was too selfish. I didn't want to lose you.

But after last time, after seeing how unsettled your life is and how unhappy it makes you, I can't keep you trapped in the middle of the country any longer.

Go, Valerie, if only to find out who you are. I hope you choose to come home to me, but if not, I will understand.

I love you. I always have and I always will. No matter what you find or what you choose, you will always be the light of my life.

Love, Mom

Tears ran down Val's cheeks. Rod reached out to brush one away. "Do you want to talk about it?"

"It's all true. I'm a mermaid, or whatever you want to call it. My father—" Her voice hitched. "My father tried to take me from her. She hadn't known… what he was when she fell in love with him."

Her father had wanted her. Mom had wanted her, and neither one had tried to work out a reasonable compromise. Somewhere in the warmth of knowing they'd both wanted her was anger that they hadn't made it work.

But the tail thing would have freaked anyone out. Hell, it had her. Then there was Lance—Dad—not coming clean to Mom.

Val wasn't going to judge them. She didn't know the circumstances, and they made no difference now. Nothing couldn't change the past, and Mom had done what she had out of love.

And now Val knew why.

She also knew—now—that Dad had wanted her. He hadn't left her by choice.

Rod tilted her chin up. "Not 'what' your father was, Valerie. We're no different from Humans except for our ability to live under the sea. We've adapted to it, just as Humans who live in mountain regions are able to breathe thinner air, or people in the Arctic who have more insulation beneath their skin, or those at the equator whose darker skin is able to withstand the sun's impact. Yes, it's not something you're accustomed to, but we—you—aren't a 'what.' You're a 'who,' Valerie. You're the Mer I've been searching for."

She straightened her back, gently sliding her chin from his grasp. She was Mer, but she was also Human. Two parts of her that had finally gelled, giving her the peace she'd always sought. "I thought you called me a Hybrid."

"It doesn't matter. You're the woman I love, and that's good enough for me."

Okay, so *that* sealed the deal on the peace she'd wanted. She smiled at him. "And I love you, too. So, what do we do now?"

His eyes got serious, and he traced a finger over her tail. "We wait. By tomorrow morning, our legs will have returned and three days after that, as long as we stay out of the water, they'll stay permanently."

"But how did I get a tail now? Mom said she hadn't put any oil on my legs after that time my legs started to change."

"I think because you didn't get the full tail when you were a child. Mers, full-blooded ones, are born with tails because we're born in the water. You were born on land, so your legs didn't have a chance to become a tail. Then your mother stopped the transformation by pulling you out so quickly and washing away the seawater. Essentially, this is your first change."

"And you're saying I can undo it? Just stay out of the water for three days, and it'll all be over?"

"Technically, two sunsets are the catalyst, but essentially, three days."

She fingered the note from her mother, thinking of what she'd told her. Who she was.

Who Rod was.

"What if I want to try the Atlantis thing, Rod?"

"What? What are you saying?"

"I'm saying that my mother did what she thought was best by keeping me from the ocean, but she tried to give me that part of myself with the store. Don't you see? The store wasn't her dream, it was her gift to me. By writing me this letter," she held it up, "she set me free. I don't need to keep the store going to honor her memory. All she wanted was for me to be true to myself."

Val smiled, not quite believing what she was about to do, but knowing it was the right thing. She'd figure out something to do with Mom's shop later.

"I'm saying that I've tried running away to find happiness, and it doesn't work. There are things we have to do in life, things that define us, and the throne defines you. You won't be happy in the sweltering heat of a Kansas summer, in the dusty, dry conditions of a drought, or in the cramped apartment above the store, when you've only known the beauty of this world." She put her palm on his cheek. "I'm saying, Rod, that I'm willing to live with you here so you can be what you were born to be."

"And what about you, Valerie?"

"What about me? You're what I want, Rod. Where you are, I want to be."

It was the right decision. She knew because it settled around her with all the comfort of home.

She reached for his hand, entwining her fingers with his. "Since I met you, I've found peace. Sure, we've had the adrenaline rush of the chase and the accident, and fighting Drake, but not once have I thought of seeking out something more exciting, something different. Something *else*. Even with the birds and the tail and the craziness, I've felt a part of it. Here, in the water, with you, is where I'm supposed to be."

He tucked their hands beneath his chin, his lips brushing her knuckles first. "Valerie, I can't ask you to do this."

"You're not asking. I'm offering. Besides," she tapped his lips with a finger she freed from his grasp, "it's not every day a girl becomes a princess and gets to go to a legendary kingdom. *With* her Prince Charming on her arm."

"Prince Charming?" He arched an eyebrow, the corner of his mouth quirking up with it.

"Wait." She rolled her eyes. "Let me rephrase that. You don't need to get a big head. The tail's big enough."

"That's not the only thing that is." He ran his tongue across her palm.

"Oh, puh-lease." She laughed, pulling her hand away. Now was *not* the appropriate time nor place. "But I love you anyway."

"That's all I need, Valerie. Anything else is just foam on the waves."

"Foam on the waves? Don't you mean icing on the cake?"

He shrugged. "Icing, foam… does it matter?"

"No. It doesn't. What matters is that I've finally found what I've been searching for my whole life." She dropped onto the floor, angling for the opening to take her back to the sea. "Now let's go home so we can live happily ever after."

"Um… about that."

She stopped in mid-shuffle. "What?"

"The ever-after part? You do remember it's forever, right? Immortality comes with the throne. For my wife, as well."

"So I'll be stuck with you for the rest of Time?"

"If we decide to keep our tails, yes."

"And if we don't?"

He tapped the end of her nose. "Then we get a normal Human life span."

"Together."

"Unless you get tired of me."

Like that would happen. But, *forever*…

"You know what, Rod? I think I can handle forever as long as I've got you."

"Oh, you've got me, Valerie." He slipped over the lip of the platform. "Hook, line, and sinker."

Chapter 44

Nine days later

R OD WAS HAVING THAT DREAM AGAIN.

Only this time, he knew without opening his eyes that it was no dream.

As the sweet smell of the hibiscus blossoms filled the air, a smile worked its way from beneath his sleep to spread across his face, as warm as the sun that shone across his body through the window frame. The gentle ebb and flow of the waves outside the grass hut nudged him closer to wakefulness.

The warm body in his arms did the rest.

He awoke to find Valerie staring at him with eyes as blue as the tropical sky above their private island.

"About time you woke up, Your Highness. I've been up for hours." Valerie's eyes twinkled as brightly as the strand of diamonds at her throat, his wedding gift to her, and the only thing she'd worn in the five days since. Well, that and a coating of the oil from the enameled magnum-sized bottle the gods had given them for their honeymoon.

He wrapped his arms around her and pulled her even tighter against him, nudging one leg between hers. "Oh, I'm *up*, Valerie." He slid his hands down her back to cup the delicious curves he found there.

She sighed and laced her fingers through his hair, pulling his lips to hers. "You definitely are." She smiled as she pressed against him. "Now what are we going to do about it?"

"How about this?" He rolled onto his back and brought her on top of him.

"That works."

It certainly did. Especially when she stretched, rubbing her toes against his shins and her breasts against his chest.

But that was as much teasing as he could take. No matter how many times they'd made love since their night at Reel's home, the minute he touched her, he wanted her. Hades, the minute he *looked* at her, he wanted her.

Thank the gods they and The Council had rethought that stipulation about not diluting the bloodline.

Not that it mattered. He would have overruled them anyway, statutes be damned. Nothing was going to keep them apart.

Interestingly enough, Zeus had seemed more than willing to accept Rod's stipulations when he'd gone before the gods to make his claim and request answers as to why he hadn't gotten a tail when he'd first re-entered the water.

Typically, they'd spoken more in parables than cold, hard fact, but they did say that because he'd brought her back and fulfilled The Prophecy, he got to keep the throne, the tail and, most importantly, Valerie. They hadn't explained exactly how having Valerie back would save the world, but it was enough for him that she'd saved his.

Gripping her waist, Rod lifted Valerie above him, taking her sweet nipple into his mouth, whirling his tongue around it until it was a rigid peak, and tasted a hint of the pineapple he'd licked off it last night at dinner. And yesterday morning at breakfast—or had that been mango?

She gripped his hair and rocked forward with a groan. He didn't care which fruit it was; she tasted delicious even without it.

"Mmmm, that feels good." Her voice was rough.

He'd show her good. He'd be finesse personified.

He slid his tongue to her other nipple.

She moaned.

Success.

Doubly so when she slipped her legs to either side of his chest and her warm, wet core glided along his skin. Gods, he could smell her above the pineapple and mango and hibiscus, and his cock hardened almost unbearably.

To Hades with finesse. He grasped her backside, kneading her cheeks and spread her legs wider over him. Valerie tossed her head back, arching her neck, and Rod released her breast to flick his tongue over her fluttering pulse at the base of her throat, then up to the soft spot beneath her ear, sliding her down his body.

"Make love to me, Rod." Valerie took the words from him and thrust her tongue into his mouth as he thrust inside her.

He couldn't remember what life had been like before her.

And when Valerie teased him again with her tongue, he really couldn't remember. His body overrode his mind, banishing those—and any other—thoughts. All that mattered was here and now. Them. Together.

Rod lifted her off him so that their bodies barely touched. Barely... but still.

He circled his hips slowly. Achingly. The tip of his cock just brushing her swollen flesh.

Valerie whimpered into his mouth and pressed down, taking him inside her, and her slick wet heat drove him to the brink.

He arched beneath her, and she welcomed him in, smiling against his lips. Two weeks ago, he'd never known this could be, this all-encompassing feeling, and now... now he'd been willing to throw away a kingdom for her.

He still would.

Because without her, none of it mattered.

Rod slid out again, only to thrust back in, tangling one hand in her hair to angle her head just right, the other pressing her against him, into him. Him into her.

She'd insisted he couldn't give up the kingdom and had chosen, instead, to renounce her way of life.

But love and marriage were two-way streets, and Rod wasn't going to allow her to do that either. And he'd tell her that right after...

The tiny moans in the back of her throat got to him. He couldn't take the way she shifted against him, the way her fingernails raked his skin, the way her breath sent shivers down his spine, the fire her touch ignited in him, the tidal wave of longing and love sweeping over him; he had to do something.

So he did.

He flipped her over on the soft bed, white filmy sheets sliding against their skin with a caress that was almost as good as hers. He rose above her, staring into those blue eyes, now whirling like turbulent seas, and pressed a kiss on her heart.

"Rod—" Her eyes closed and she arched into him, and Rod could no more resist than he could stop breathing.

So he didn't.

Once more he claimed her body, claimed her heart, and gave over his own. Once more he took her with every ounce of feeling in him, showing her how important she was to him, how he needed her for the rest of their days, and how he'd bound himself to her forever.

How she was more important to him than any throne, any world, except the one they created for, by, and between themselves.

As the first tremors of orgasm raced through him, as he surged into her with that endless, pounding rhythm as old and as unrelenting as the waves upon the shores, Rod knew that only Immortality would grant him enough time to show her how much he loved her.

And because of her, because of her accepting him and his world, he—they—now had that time.

A light breeze whispered through the opening of the hut, drifting sand across the plank floor and rustling the edges of the light sheet Rod had pulled over them. Val's head rested in the crook of his arm, her hand swirling tiny circles on his chest. She could stay here for the rest of her life.

And she would, that was the amazing thing. Three days left before the tax deadline for saving the store, then there'd be nothing else to tie her to land.

Or to Mom...

Val sighed. Giving up the store *was* what she wanted, right? She didn't need it to remember Mom. She didn't need it financially, and she certainly didn't need it emotionally, so she could let it go.

Right?

"That was an awfully big sigh," Rod whispered against her temple. "Did I do something wrong?"

"Funny." As if he had any worries on that front.

"Then what is it?" He raised her chin with his finger. Gorgeous green eyes searched hers with a trace of worry. "You're not regretting this, are you?"

"No. I was just thinking about the store."

"Ah." Rod propped himself up on his elbow and brushed the curls away from her face. "About that. I have an idea."

Oh, she knew all about his idea. He'd practically tossed one of the diamond bottles to Livingston to deliver to Mr. Hill before Val had made him see reason.

"Rod, we've already decided that the Castor and Pollux Diamonds should remain here. They're treasures in your world—*our* world. Humans can't find them, or it'd raise more questions than saving the store is worth." She rested her bent arm beneath her head.

He smiled then, that sexy-as-hell, lopsided grin that deepened his dimple and turned her on. How was that even possible with what they'd just done? And before dawn? And in the middle of the night beneath the full moon...

"I wasn't talking about the diamonds, Valerie."

"Oh?"

"No." He leaned forward and kissed the tip of her nose. "I happen to have a storage room in my home that's full of useless junk Angel's been dying to get her hands on. I've been holding off for some reason, and it finally dawned on me what that reason is."

"Useless junk?" She propped herself up on her elbow as well. "How is that going to help?"

Rod adjusted the lay of the sheet over her: he slid it down to her hip. Well, where it *just* covered her hip. "Let me rephrase that. It's useless to Mers, but Humans, on the other fin…"

He hadn't removed his fingers, and it was getting harder to concentrate on what he was saying. "Um… yes?"

He moved closer, and his hand slipped around to just above her butt, sending delicious tingles all over her as he, unerringly, found where he knew her birthmark to be, even though it was no longer visible, and traced the pattern on her skin. With his fingers this time. Last night, it'd been his tongue.

She really did try to focus on what he was saying. Really.

"Let's just say there's a reason your people haven't found Blackbeard's treasure." His lips were so close…

Wait a minute. What? She pulled back to avoid the temptation those lips presented. "Blackbeard? You're kidding."

"No, I'm not."

"But…" Okay, this boggled the mind. And cooled the hormones. "But… *treasure*? Pirate treasure? Gold doubloons and jewels and—"

"Silver drinking vessels and vases and an assortment of other items… Yes, Valerie. I have all of it. And you're welcome to it."

"But… but…"

He laughed. "You sound like one of those motorboats when the engine doesn't turn over." He slid his hand back to her hip and readjusted the sheet. *Not* that he pulled it any higher. "Anyhow, the treasure is yours to do with what you want."

She'd rather he be hers to do with whatever she wanted... oh, that's right. He was. And she could. But later. Right now she wanted to concentrate on this conversation, so she scooched back a bit so *certain* parts weren't quite so close.

"Rod, I can't take that treasure. If I show up with some long-lost pirate booty, every treasure-hunter in the world is going to be after me to tell them where I found it. Then the government will get involved... it would end up being more trouble than it's worth."

Rod sighed and dropped his hand. "True... *unless* Reel and Erica just happen to 'find' it on one of their fishing charters. Then they can funnel the proceeds to the store, as well as some of the actual treasure, too, if you want. It would bring people in."

Which would ensure that Mom would never be forgotten.

The idea was looking better by the minute.

"I *could* always hire Tricia permanently. She was a little miffed when I told her we were running off to get married in Mexico, then heading to your home. This could placate her—let her be her own boss. Working for her in-laws outgrew the honeymoon stage long ago."

"And we'll visit whenever you'd like."

"We will?"

"Sure. The gods have given us enough oil."

Not if they kept going at this rate...

"But what if the tails don't return? That's already happened once, remember."

Rod tucked her closer to him. "The gods have assured me that it will not happen again. They, of course, won't tell me why, but said we are fine to travel on land."

It could work. And she'd end up with the best of both worlds. "Okay, Rod, I'm in. But can I do all of this in three days? Do I have time?"

Rod lifted her chin and brushed his lips against hers. "*We* can do all of this, Valerie. *We* have time."

She shook her head, trying to keep the smile hidden. She hadn't realized it at the time, but he really *did* hate flying. "Rod, you don't have to come with me. Since JR's with Zeus, Drake's locked up, and Nigel's exonerated, there's nothing to worry about."

Especially since Drake hadn't been able to touch one particle of the treasure he'd headed to after she'd gotten away from him. His greed had made him easy to track. It hadn't taken Lieutenant Brackmann long to figure out where he'd gone and dispatch a contingent after him. King Solomon's treasure was still as safe as could be, and Val was still trying to wrap her brain around the fact that that legend was as real as Atlantis.

"What was it you said to me when I gave you a choice, Valerie? 'Where you are is where I want to be'?" He pulled her against him, all alpha-male bossy. "It's not even a decision I have to make. Now that I've found you, I'm not letting you out of my sight."

Which definitely had its advantages. "Okay, but as long as you're sure you don't mind giving up the treasure."

"You did hear the 'useless to Mers' part, right? As the High Councilman, I have access to palaces, diamond mines, and an unlimited expense account. The treasure is pocket change."

"You don't have pockets."

That devastating smile slid slow and sexy across his lips, and his fingers trailed slow and sexy down her body. "Neither do you, my darling wife."

When he wrapped those big, strong arms around her, Val realized she did know which part she liked more. Sure, saving Therese's Treasure Trove and honoring Mom's memory were good things, but this—being here, with him, on this island paradise, their own Garden of Eden—this was what she'd always wanted.

After all the running she'd done throughout her life, all the searching and instability, there truly was no place like home, be it Kansas or Atlantis, as long as she was in Rod's arms.

Epilogue

"ADELE, HAVE YOU GOTTEN ANY SLEEP?" MAYBELLE OPENED one eye to see Adele pacing the ledge exactly as she'd been doing last night before Maybelle closed her eyes. As she'd done for the past week.

"It's not right, Maybelle. It's just not right."

"What's not right?"

"Those cowbirds. How can they hope for a better life if they're abandoned by their parents and raised by others who don't love them? It's no wonder the albatross could recruit them to his side. No wonder at all."

"Adele, what are you chirping about?"

Adele stopped pacing and pointed her wing across the alley. "I feel awful, Maybelle. Just awful. We shouldn't have tricked those boys. Goodness, they start out life being tricked. Their parents—and I use that term loosely, because being able to donate genetic material does not make one a parent—but those parents drop their eggs in someone else's nest to be raised.

"They start out life thinking they're with their family, then, lo and behold, they squash their siblings or push them out of the nest. Why? Not because they're evil, but because they're so much bigger than the foster home into which they've been dropped unceremoniously by two parents who don't have the good sense not to procreate. It can't be good for their self-esteem, and I feel just awful for contributing to it."

"Adele, that's what cowbirds do. What are you getting yourself all in a dither for? We did help The Heir and Valerie."

"That doesn't make it right, Maybelle. It's just not right. Of course those boys couldn't help themselves. It's all they know. If they'd been raised in a loving home, where the truth was explained to them, if they were shown the proper way to treat others, I just know they wouldn't have gone to the dark side."

"So, what, Adele? Are you going to go out and save all the cowbirds?" Maybelle sniffed.

"Sniff all you want, Maybelle Merriweather, but maybe I am." Adele slicked the feathers back from her crown. "Yes, maybe that's what I'll do. Someone has to look out for those poor things, and maybe I'm just the avian to do it."

This Maybelle had to see. Adele would save the cowbirds. Sure. And while that was happening, Maybelle would join the ASA and round up all the bad guys. Teach that seagull a thing or two about surveillance, and keep the land safe for two-legged Mers.

Hey. Wait a minute. *There* was an idea...

~Fin~

Author's Note

During the gas crunch of '79, my family set off on Day 1 of gas rationing to drive across the country for an unforgettable twenty-eight-day trip. From only being allowed to buy two dollars worth of gas (until we got out of Pennsylvania; apparently other states didn't have to follow those rules—or chose not to) to the Gateway to the West, the Grand Canyon, Devil's Tower, Mount Rushmore, Vegas at 2 a.m., the Pacific Ocean, and all the things in between and back, it was an amazing journey.

I've made that trip; I know the route—and I've always wanted to claim literary license. So I will for any driving discrepancies in this story—as I also will regarding our family's annual vacation spot: Ocean City, New Jersey, which, prior to November 1879, was known as Peck's Beach. Some locations have been altered for the telling of Valerie and Rod's "tale," and if you can find a bunker similar to the one Reel constructed, please point me to it.

Acknowledgments

Since one of the Tritone brothers got his happily-ever-after in *In Over Her Head*, I'd hoped the other one would get his shot as well. Thanks to everyone who made this possible:

My editor, Deb Werksman for making this story as strong as it can be; my publisher, Dominique Raccah, for giving Rod the opportunity; my agent, Jennifer Schober, for helping make my career dreams come true; Susie Benton and Sarah Ryan for making sure all parts of the happily-ever-after are included; and Sue Grimshaw, again, because I just *have* to!

The Writin' Wombats for all their encouragement and vast knowledge on so many subjects, especially: Beth Hill for the deadline-driven reads and honest critique; Pat and Ed Shaw for making a picnic excursion to the motels for research; Jamie Chapman for taking a drive to fill in what the internet couldn't; Mike Stromer and Suzette Vaughn for the *avian* help; Sia McKye for the marketing assistance; Jill Anderson for such creativity; and Lisa Brackmann for coming up with the title—I hope you enjoy "your" sojourn beneath the sea.

Adele Dubois, for spending her cross-country drive time describing the landmarks and scenery for me and picking up all those brochures; and Stephanie Julian for the friendship and for the truth—no matter how much work it means I still have to do.

The wonderful authors who took time from their schedules to read this story.

Kristina and Bob Doliszny of the Atlantis Inn, and Colin Rayner and Raleigh Hill of the Hibiscus House, for coming on board with the Romantic Getaway contest on my website with their beautiful Bed & Breakfasts.

My grandmother, for always believing in me. My parents, who took us on a cross-country drive to show us this great country, creating so many lasting memories. I don't know how you managed not to strangle us, but thanks for not doing so. My children, who, amid my deadlines and their schedules, are making more lasting memories; and, of course, my husband, who got me hooked on *It's a Mad, Mad, Mad, Mad World*—complete with an actor named *Merman*.

What could be more perfect for this story?

About the Author

Judi Fennell is an award-winning author whose romance novels have been finalists in Gather.com's First Chapters and First Chapters Romance contests, as well as the third American Title contest. She lives in suburban Philadelphia, Pennsylvania, and spends family vacations at the Jersey Shore, the setting for some of her paranormal romance series.

Judi has enjoyed the reader feedback she's received and would love to hear what you think about her Mer series. Check out her website at www.JudiFennell.com for excerpts, reviews, fun pictures from reader and writer conferences, and the chance to "dive in" to her stories.

For more of Judi Fennell's unique Mer trilogy,
read on for a sneak peek of

CATCH
OF A
LIFETIME

Coming in February 2010 from
Sourcebooks Casablanca

Chapter 1

THERE WAS A NAKED WOMAN ON HIS BOAT.

Logan Hardington shook his head and rubbed his eyes, but the picture didn't change. Lady Godiva was sprawled over a pillow on his deck, a navy blue blanket draped over the bottom half of the curviest ass he'd seen in a long while.

Long, blonde—almost yellow—loose curls tumbled over creamy shoulders all the way down to that blanket, the ends pooling in the dimples above her ass, some strands twirling along the visible portion of her cleft near the light blue markings of a faded bruise.

Shapely legs, one slightly bent, only a shade or two darker than the fiberglass boat deck, trailed from beneath the blanket, one small foot flexing in the soft morning breeze. A hint of upturned nose peeked from beneath the blonde jumble, pink lips pursed in sleep, slender fingers disappearing beneath her cheek. He wondered what color her eyes were.

And why she was naked.

On his boat.

Hungry gulls cawed overhead, but she didn't stir. The wake from McKye's charter jostled the *Mir-a-Mar* as the day's fishing tour set out, but that didn't rouse her either.

Oh hell. She was probably a drunk co-ed who'd followed some "sailor" home. He'd seen that walk of

shame many mornings. Didn't these people think of
the repercussions?

Logan looked back down the pier where his son,
Michael, chatted with Tony as the wizened old salt
chopped chum, and Logan smiled. Ah, the things he
would have loved to have seen as a boy. The things he
should have been able to show Michael from day one—

And would have if his ex-girlfriend had only
mentioned a little thing like a pregnancy...

Logan tamped down the anger at Christine—who,
according to his son, now went by *Rainbow* for
God-only-knew-what reasons—and focused instead on
the next female to make him wonder what men ever saw
in women.

Then Lady Godiva moved and the blanket slipped
to the side and Logan knew *exactly* what men saw
in women.

But *not* what he wanted his son to see. No matter how
much Logan wanted to savor the image.

"Hey, um... Miss." Logan hunkered down and shook
one of those shapely legs.

She mumbled something and flipped her head the other
way, a tangle of hair tickling his arm. Logan pulled his
hand back and captured the curls as they slid across his
palm. Silky. Soft. The way a woman's hair should be.

He blinked. What the hell was he doing thinking
about her hair? She was naked, for God's sake, and
his six-year-old was going to get one hell of a birthday
present if she didn't wake up and cover herself.

"Miss, wake up." Logan shook her shoulder, glancing
back to Michael. Thank God Tony had a ton of fish tales
to keep the boy occupied.

The woman sighed, and her shoulder slid beneath his fingertips. Her skin was just as soft and silky as her hair.

He should not be noticing.

"Lady, you really need to get up." Not that getting up was a problem he seemed to be having. Christ. How long *had* it been if he was getting hard over the naked back of a lush?

Then she rolled over.

One lone curl encircled a taut, pink nipple.

Oh, boy…

No problem getting up now.

A naked woman… Right there in front of him. A naked goddess, more like. A gift from the gods just for him.

Except, of course, there was Michael…

Logan shook his head and reached for the blanket that had slithered to the deck atop some crushed shells and dried seaweed. Fighting with himself the entire time, he tossed it over her.

"What in the sea?" The blonde bombshell awoke as if she'd been tossed overboard, sputtering and spitting the blanket away from those perfect lips, the most incredible eyes widening above that mouth. The color of the sea… aquamarine. He'd never seen anything like them.

"Um, hi?" The corners of her eyes turned up along with her mouth. A dimple winked high on her left cheek.

"Oh." Logan cleared his throat. She didn't sound drunk. "Hi. I'm Logan Hardington." He rocked back on his heels. "Who are you?"

"I'm, ah… Angel. Tritone."

She was an angel all right. Straight from Heaven, via

the bowels of Hell. A temptress. Flushed with the haze of sleep, innocence and sensuality stared at him from those ocean eyes, and she had the most delectable lips he'd ever seen. Slender arms clutched the blanket to breasts that spilled from the sides, leaving barely anything to the imagination. Not that he needed to imagine since he remembered every splendid inch of those heavenly delights. If this woman wasn't walking temptation, he didn't know what was.

"So, Angel Tritone, did you have one too many last night?" *Remember that, Hardington. No matter what kind of influence she'd be on you, she'd be a bad one on your son.*

Having to kick her off his boat definitely sucked. But he was a father now. A responsible, practical father who didn't fool around with sexy, naked women on his boat.

A horny, recently celibate father who'd *love* to fool around with this sexy, naked woman on his boat.

But who wouldn't.

Damn. This responsibility thing wasn't all it was cracked up to be.

Angel cocked her head to the side, curls spilling over her shoulders in perfect centerfold-fantasy mode, and he had to work really hard to keep his groan from escaping.

"One too many what?" Her tongue flicked over her lips again in an unselfconscious and utterly sexy way.

He had to get her off his boat. For sanity's sake. Propriety's, too. Not to mention an impressionable six-year-old's. Logan stood up and held out his hand. "Never mind. Let's get you up and at 'em."

"At who?" She reached for his hand.

Logan forgot the question the minute her fingers touched his. Hell, he almost forgot his own name, and the six-year-old down the pier was fast becoming a distant memory.

Everything was becoming a distant memory, fuzzy and out of focus, because the moment her skin met his, everything else faded to black. Fire, hot and long and needy, sped through his fingers to every extremity, zipping along his nerve endings like a match to gunpowder, the heavy *thud* of his heart blocking out the call of the birds and the sounds of the marina.

Then she tugged on his hand to stand, and he had to steady himself so he wouldn't fall on top of her—but man, did he want to. Especially when the blanket slid down her body to pool at her feet.

"You're naked," slipped out. Since making that comment was better than falling on top of her, he wasn't too upset.

"I'm what?" Five-foot-nothing dipped her blonde head forward, the curls now caressing his wrist, one encircling his forearm, and Logan had to focus on his breathing. He'd never had such an intense reaction to a woman. Then again, he'd never seen a woman like this before in his life.

Pink stained her cheeks when she glanced back at him and, dog that he was, he compared the color to the tips of her breasts. Only for a second, but it was enough—her cheeks were lighter pink.

But the curls between her legs perfectly matched those brushing her hips.

"*Why* are you naked?" Oh hell. What kind of a question was that? "I mean, what are you doing here?"

"Sleeping?" She moistened her lips quickly, with just a hint of pink tongue—which was more than enough to get him thinking about that tongue…

"I gathered that. The question is why?"

"Oh." She ran her fingers through her hair, lifting it off her neck, and glanced toward the ocean. "Well, I was swimming, and… and there was a shark. Yes. A shark. And he was coming after me. So I climbed aboard your boat, and, well," she shrugged her shoulders and a few strands of hair fell across her breasts, one curling again on her nipple, "here I am."

Logan peeled his eyes off her breasts to meet her gaze. "Here you are."

"Yes."

A moment of silence followed. Well, silence between them. The gulls were making a hell of a ruckus. Logan cleared his throat, then picked up the blanket and handed it to her. "So, is there any particular reason you're naked? Where are your clothes?"

She gathered the blanket against her chest. Not that Logan needed help with that image or anything… "My clothes. Yes. Um. Well, I was swimming—"

Right. Skinny-dipping. "Alone?"

He was asking solely so he could get her off his boat and back where she belonged; that was it. No other reason.

"Not alone. There was the shark."

"But what happened to your things?"

"Oh. They're gone."

"Gone? Everything? Money, clothes, whatever? Somebody take them while you were swimming?"

She looked away again toward the ocean, her eyes blinking rapidly. "Yes. Everything's gone."

So he had a naked, destitute woman on his boat. And a six-year-old who'd be here any minute.

Logan reached into his back pocket and pulled out his wallet. "Look, I can give you some money. Get you a ticket back where you came from—where are you from?"

She licked her lips again and turned those stunning eyes on him. "Have you ever been to Kansas?"

"Me? No."

"Oh. Well, I'm from Kansas."

"You do realize you're a bit of a ways away from Kansas, right?"

She shifted her feet to balance on the rocking deck as another charter left the dock. "Yes. About four-hundred-and-thirty leagues or so."

Leagues? Only if she was swimming, and *that* he'd like to see from the middle of the country.

"So what are you doing here if you're from Kansas?"

"Studying."

"You're a student?" He'd figured her for a little older than college. Maybe she was a grad student.

And he cared, why?

She looked back at the ocean. "I'm... doing a field study for the summer."

Ah, yes. Older. "What field?"

"Biology. Maritime biology."

"Don't you mean marine biology?"

"Yes," she said, licking her lips again. He should probably get her a drink. "Of course. That's what I meant. Marine biology."

The boat rocked again and the blanket slid to the side, showing off her shapely leg in all its perfection, toes to thigh.

He should probably get himself a drink. Preferably a stiff one—

Not going there.

"So… where are you staying? I'll call you a cab." Anything to get her off this boat.

"Actually, I just arrived. I don't have a place to stay."

Logan was about to suggest a local apartment complex when he heard Michael yell, "Thanks, Tony!" and decided he'd worry about where she was going to stay later. Right now he had a six-year-old he didn't want to have to explain the birds and the bees—or naked women—to, so he yanked his T-shirt over his head and skimmed it over Angel's. Yes, it hung on her like a tent, but at least she was covered.

Not that it diminished the image burned into his brain, nor the incredibly hot vision of her in his clothing and nothing else, with her hair askew and that blush on her cheeks.

With his faded green T-shirt bringing out the green swirl in her eyes, the woman could be a mermaid come to life.

"Logan! Look what Tony gave me!" Michael ran down the dock holding up the perfectly filleted carcass of one of Tony's recent catches in one hand and keeping his baseball cap on his head with the other hand. From Michael's abrupt halt and the way his mouth dropped open, Logan knew the moment his son saw Angel.

Great. How was he going to explain this?

"Hey, Michael. Why don't you come say hi to Angel?"

What else was he going to say? *Come meet the naked student*? The kid would be signing up for college tomorrow.

"But… how? What…?" The fish skeleton hit the dock and fell apart, but Michael didn't seem to notice. His eyes were glued to Angel.

"Hi… Michael? I'm Angel." Even her voice was beautiful—like a song dancing along the crests of the waves.

Oh, hell. Where had that fanciful thought come from? Logan never spouted poetry to beautiful women, preferring to keep every relationship real and out of the realm of fairy tale, though more than one woman had called him her Prince Charming. Usually right before he broke up with her.

"Ang… Angel?" Poor tongue-tied Michael. Logan could totally empathize.

"She's… um… a friend." One he'd just met, who didn't wear clothes and showed up out of nowhere, but the kid was six. It should fly.

"Your friend?" Okay, perhaps the incredulity in his son's voice indicated a need for more proof.

"Um… yeah." He focused on Michael. "She's new in town and was using the boat because she doesn't have a place to stay."

Michael's face perked up and he jumped aboard, adjusting his baseball hat. "Cool! Then she can stay with us, right?" He went right over to her and shook her hand. "Nice to meet you, Angel. You can be my friend, too."

That wasn't exactly what Logan had in mind.

"I'd like that, Michael."

There was that melodic voice again. Maybe she was a singer. She certainly had the face to be a celebrity, and enough of them flocked to these beaches every year.

Meanwhile, his son was literally jumping all over the place. "So, can she, Logan?"

Can she what? There were a lot of things he wanted her to do—

"Can she stay with us? She can sleep in my room."

Logan tried not to laugh. Sleep in Michael's room? Logan didn't think so. If she was going to be sleeping in anyone's room—

"Michael, I think the guesthouse would be a better idea."

Angel smiled and Michael started bouncing again. "Cool!"

Shit. What had he just agreed to?

IN OVER HER HEAD

by Judi Fennell

"Holy mackerel! *In Over Her Head* is a
fantastically fun romantic catch!"

—Michelle Rowen, author of *Bitten & Smitten*

○ ○ ○ ○ ○ ○ **HE LIVES UNDER THE SEA** ○ ○ ○ ○ ○ ○

Reel Tritone is the rebellious royal second son of the ruler
of a vast undersea kingdom. A Merman, born with legs
instead of a tail, he's always been fascinated by humans,
especially one young woman he once saw swimming near
his family's reef...

○ ○ ○ ○ ○ **SHE'S TERRIFIED OF THE OCEAN** ○ ○ ○ ○ ○

Ever since the day she swam out too far and heard voices
in the water, marina owner Erica Peck won't go swimming
for anything—until she's forced into the water by a shady
ex-boyfriend searching for stolen diamonds, and is nearly
eaten by a shark...luckily Reel is nearby to save her, and
discovers she's the woman he's been searching for...

978-1-4022-2001-2 • $6.99 U.S. / $7.99 CAN